NOBODY'S
HEROES

NOBODY'S HEROES

by Lt. Dan Marcou

Thunder Bay Press

Holt, Michigan

Published by
Thunder Bay Press
Holt, Michigan 48842

First printing July 2009

12   11   10   09   5   4   3   2   1

ISBN: 978-1-933272-21-4

This book is a work of fiction

Cover photography by Victoria Marcou.
Book and cover design by Julie Taylor.

Printed in the United States of America
by McNaughton & Gunn, Inc.

This book is dedicated to the
honorable men and women
of law enforcement.

CONTENTS

ACKNOWLEDGMENTS

A special thanks for inspiration and encouragement to Sergeant Marcus Young, Officer Gary Clements, Sheriff Randy Stammen, Sergeant Brad Burke, Captain Gordon Rieber, Assistant Chief Tom Jacobs, Master Larry Klahn, Katie Conway, Officer Grant O'Neil of the Western Australian Police, Victoria Marcou, Nathan Marcou, Paul and Christa Modderman.

I would also like to give special thanks to the men and women of the La Crosse Police Department, whose courage and perseverance have inspired me to become a teller of stories.

PROLOGUE

William Ripp would always love watching the terror of his chosen victims when they realized they were standing at death's threshold. There was the futile struggle to live, the screams, the cries, and the pitiful whimpers for mercy from someone whose heart held none. Then there was that end-of-life moment which would be eternally the last or last eternally: sweet irrevocable death. William Ripp had been drawn to the death of others, enthralled by it, seduced by it, and infinitely entertained by it, all of his life.

This would be William Ripp's first human life-taking. He would, in the future, replay this first kill over and over in his mind, and it would bring him great satisfaction. To live out his life's wildest fantasies gave him a thrill beyond description. As a child he had tormented and killed small creatures in a variety of ways. The young William Ripp knew even then that his unique extracurricular activity had to be kept secret. Early on he learned to share his secret obsession with no one except his best and most trusted friend, himself.

Fantasy was about to become reality. He had picked up the young runaway at a truck stop just off I-90 west of Madison, Wisconsin. The boy's name was Isaac, a good biblical name. Ripp thought it appropriate that the biblical Isaac's life had been saved by the hand of an angel. This Isaac's life, however, would be taken by the hand of a devil. William Ripp was not literally the devil, but if he was to be placed under an ecumenical microscope he would most certainly be deemed to be in league with that notorious entity.

Poor Isaac was dealt a bad hand in life up to his chance meeting with William Ripp. This last losing hand would lead to an even more terrible death. Isaac sensed no danger in the gentle eyes of William Ripp. Like so many predators, Ripp hid his intentions well.

1

The evil he planned was camouflaged with humor, empathy, a good meal, some good wine, and even some LSD. Although William Ripp did not consider himself a homosexual, he used a loving touch to bring his victim in closer. This was the first time Isaac had been with a man. Ripp was kind, gentle, and gave him $100 to just lie back and "enjoy." Ripp would find sex the most fitting lure for this and many of his future victims — male or female. Ripp learned with Isaac that the sexual experience immersed each victim into a near total sense of complacency. Then Ripp would strike.

Isaac had just lain back, and suddenly his head began to reel. The LSD allowed him to smell colors, taste music, and hear the growing of the grass around him. He remained conscious but felt that the world around him was being sucked into a spinning vortex of pleasure. The pleasure came first and then came the pain, the horrible tearing and sudden mind-numbing pain. The kindly face of his new friend had become distorted like a face in a house of mirrors. Isaac saw the face, felt the pain, vainly and only momentarily thrashed at the knife, but then he succumbed, becoming Ripp's first victim.

William Ripp took his time with Isaac. He savored the kill. When he finished with Isaac, he bagged Isaac's clothes and his dismembered his remains like the turkey carcass after thanksgiving dinner. He threw the bagged remnants of young Isaac unceremoniously in the back seat of his Honda Civic and hopped into his car. He left Madison heading west on I-90 en route somewhere, anywhere. When he reached Highway 39, he turned north. He did not know quite what to do; this was his first. To lose Isaac to the world, he would need to be disposed of in a place which was impossible to find.

Isaac was no longer Isaac. He was a loose collection of parts that once belonged to the body of Isaac. Ripp planned on the disappearance of Isaac to remain a puzzle with too many missing pieces to ever be assembled. That would require that Isaac's remains be hidden well. This was the first body that Ripp had to dispose of, and he realized that if he was to continue killing he would have to develop an expertise at disposal.

As the Honda Civic droned on heading farther and farther north, he sharply rebuked his now long-dead passenger, "Dude, you stink." He rolled the window down and sped up, hoping to create a venting effect. Then, "Oh shit!" There were headlights behind him. Ripp watched them gaining on him rapidly. "That has to be a cop," he said to himself. He checked his speedometer and saw he was speeding. "Damn. You are an idiot!" Focusing, Ripp calmed himself and made a plan. "He's just stopping you for speeding. Just be cool."

Ripp reached under the seat and pulled out his Colt Detective Special he had bought from an old neighbor. The man planned on moving into a high-rise and was selling everything he owned. Ripp had gone to his neighbor to purchase the gun, but like he was shopping for his first pack of condoms, Ripp had bought a lamp, a painting, a fishing pole, and then in an uncaring air he added, "Oh yeah, can I buy your revolver?" The old man sold it to him for forty-five dollars.

Ripp slid the small-framed revolver under his right leg. He decided that if he was stopped he would try to charm the cop, and if that did not work he would harm the cop with the most extreme prejudice. Ripp watched in his rearview mirror as the headlights grew nearer and nearer, and then the cop lit up his overheads and burped the siren. William immediately pulled to the side of the road.

He watched as the officer cautiously made his approach. The cop reached the window and asked, "Sir. Let me see your hands. Please place them palms up on the steering wheel." It was the kind of caution that would cause some citizens to snap and complain sharply from the midst of their mundane and relatively danger-free existence, "What do you think I am, some sort of criminal or something!"

Not William Ripp. Ripp smiled and slowly placed his hands palms up on the steering wheel, keeping the pistol concealed under his leg. "I'm sorry, Officer. I was speeding, wasn't I? I was just listening to the song 'Magic Carpet Ride,' and that always makes me speed up."

"Yes sir, you were indeed speeding. You were going 78 miles per hour. This is a 65 miles per hour zone. May I please see your driver's license?" asked the blue-shirted village cop, who looked relieved to see the friendly smile on Ripp's face. He had been trolling for action on the one mile of his jurisdiction that had the interstate running through it. He was killing two birds with one stone. He was fighting boredom and crime all at the same time since his entire village had closed up for the night.

Then William Ripp reached with his right hand and paused slowly next to the weapon and asked, "Is it all right if I get my wallet?" Ripp's hand hovered inches from the Colt waiting for the officer's reaction.

"Sure. Sorry I am being so hyper-cautious, but not everyone I stop is as nice and cooperative as you," said the village cop.

William Ripp smiled largely, trying to hide the relief and by-passed the pistol. He took out his wallet and handed his license to the young super trooper, staring into the smiling eyes of the most dangerous criminal that he would ever meet. The village cop did not, nor would not ever know how close he came to death that night.

The cop took the license and tripped easily back to his squad car, showing no signs of alarm or even an ounce of concern. He had relaxed. Ripp could see it. He would get a ticket or a warning, which did not concern him, and Ripp would be sent on his way. One more smile, that's all it would take and he was home free.

The cop returned and handed Ripp his ticket. "Mr. Ripp, I reduced the actual speed you were traveling, to 75 miles per hour and that saves you some money. There is your court date and all you have to do is mail in the amount that is in the upper right hand corner to the address on the bottom of the ticket. You do not even have to appear in court. I see you have a clear record so this ticket will not put your license in jeopardy. Do you have any questions while I am still here?"

"No...," Ripp tried not to look hurried or nervous. He feigned reading the ticket over carefully and then said, "No, I don't think so. I think I will just mail it in. I was speeding. It's that song

'Magic Carpet Ride.' It always has that effect on me," said Ripp as he folded up the ticket and slipped it neatly into his wallet and then slid his license back behind the plastic window. "I am not making an excuse; that is just the reason. Sorry, Officer."

"Cruise control will take care of that," said the village cop with a smile. Then his expression changed as sniffed in the window like a pet rabbit picking up the scent of the lettuce crisper being opened. He shined his flashlight for the first time on the bulky trash bags tossed about the back of the car on the floor and the seat. "What's that smell? Whooeeee!" said the village cop. He was young and as of yet had not experienced the unique odor of a decomposing body.

"You're telling me," Ripp said with a chuckle. He was ready for this question and he had prepared for it. "I missed garbage day two weeks in a row and this stuff was stinking up my back porch. I decided to drive it to a dumpster by my dad's cottage and get rid of it. I'm afraid I am not going to get this stench out of my car though. It's not the smartest thing I have ever done in my life," said Ripp with his hand sliding undetected to the side of his leg. He slipped his right hand, unnoticed, under his leg while he motioned wildly with his left as a distraction. He established a grip on the butt of the revolver ready to take a shot if he had to, "Hold," thought Ripp.

"Well good luck with that! Good night and drive safely," said the young village cop as he turned and walked back to his squad. He climbed in, turned off his lights, and pulled out. He waved as he drove by the still idling Civic.

William Ripp sat quietly for a moment in disbelief. His heart was pounding and his right hand was still tightly gripping the butt of the revolver. He suddenly became giddy. He laughed uncontrollably and shouted, "Isaac! Dude! Did you see that? I told you, dude, you stink! I can't believe it. He just drove off." Ripp then realized his first killing was far from the perfect crime. He was lucky. He would never be so ill-prepared again. He was determined to kill again but just as determined to get better at it. He would perfect this, his new obsession.

Ripp's luck would not end after the village cop drove away. He had met a young police officer whose duties had not introduced him to the uniquely sickening odor of a decomposing body. If he would have stayed in law enforcement long enough, he would eventually be called to a long-dead body, and that smell would flash him back to the friendly man with the Honda Civic filled with "two-week-old garbage." Nothing in the world smells like long passed decomposing flesh.

The young village cop would never be called to the scene of a decomposing body, however. His career in law enforcement would come to a bitter end. He would be fired by a village board who did not want their police making traffic stops. He would be fired before he ever discovered that he had smelled reeking decaying human flesh on that night. His memory of the meeting with this butcher of humans would decay to dust like the body of Isaac in its lonely unmarked grave.

William Ripp would find a barren spot deep in the northern woods of Wisconsin. He would bury the dismantled Isaac deep, much too deep to be uncovered by erosion, coyotes, or any other scavengers. Isaac would be reported missing and missing he would remain. Isaac was a complete nobody and a perfect choice for elimination according to Ripp. He would be forgotten by most and only a special memory to one. William Ripp would always remember Isaac. In William Ripp's mind he had greatly honored Isaac by making him his first.

CHAPTER ONE

"WELCOME TO DEADWOOD"

Sergeant David Compton led the woman out of the front door of the Wal-Mart in handcuffs. She was a small blonde bearing the moniker Britney. Some would call her petite, except it appeared that it was a meth-enhanced petiteness made lurid by the telltale scabs of the chronic user. The woman's wrists were so small Compton was worried that she would slip her handcuffs.

"Why did you have to handcuff me? I'm not a criminal. Do you think I'm going to beat you up?" the woman asked. She had attempted to shoplift seventeen DVDs from Wal-Mart and was caught by an alert loss-prevention clerk. He noticed that her coat was excessively bulky for the weather. When he stopped Britney, he found the DVDs hidden in aftermarket pockets that had been sewn into the lining of her coat.

Sergeant Dave Compton had heard the question over a thousand times in his long, illustrious career. Compton was in his fifties and was still a sergeant working the night shift. Some would consider this fact an indication of a failed career, but it was quite the opposite. Compton had succeeded in everything he had ever done. He worked night shift because he preferred it. It suited him perfectly. He could have retired years earlier but chose to stay. He could have been on day shift years earlier but still had not tired of the way his officers charged into the action with the unadulterated enthusiasm of youth.

Compton had decided he had the best job in the world. He was a first class, first line supervisor. He was a police sergeant and he was doing police work in the best place to do it — on the night shift.

This night had been a crazy-busy night. Every officer in the city of La Claire was tied up handling calls all over. La Claire was a city of 60,000 nestled between bluffs and the Mississippi halfway between La Crosse and Eau Claire, Wisconsin. It was a busy place for a policeman to work but was still a nice city in which to raise a family. Compton would say, "La Claire is a perfect place to be a cop. It is big enough to have enough action to keep it interesting and yet small enough to allow the cops to keep on top of everything."

Tonight was unique. Sergeant Dave Compton had been saddled with an Explorer Scout ride-along by La Claire's Chief of Police, Chief Hale. Hale had cautioned Compton to "keep the little guy out of trouble."

Compton then asked what he thought to be a reasonable question, "Respectfully, sir, if you want to keep him out of trouble, why are we putting the young man into a police car? I am a police officer and I am supposed to look for trouble. When I can't find any, the dispatcher usually will rustle up some for me." He had made this observation with a tone as serious as an Irish Tenor's while singing "Danny Boy."

"Knock off the sarcasm, Compton," was Hale's terse response.

The young explorer tripped behind Compton, swinging the meth-head's purse, trying to be helpful. At this point in the explorer's life, he was oblivious to the possibility that riding along with a police officer was anything but a wonderful adventure. Compton reached his squad car and scanned the lot, seeing that they appeared to be alone. He unlocked the squad and eased Britney into the back seat. Compton belted her in and shut the door.

"Opie, could you please set the purse in the trunk," said Compton as he reached into the front of the squad, located the trunk release button and popped the trunk.

"Yes sir," replied the explorer with a laugh. Opie was not his name, but Compton had taken to calling the youth "Opie" because his red hair, freckles, and easy smile conjured up thoughts of the character from Mayberry RFD. The young scout liked the name. He liked the fact that a legend on the La Claire Police Department would give him a nickname. For a youth who dreamed to be a police officer some day, it was more than he could have hoped for to be noticed by a legend.

Bryce Packwood had carefully concealed himself behind a white panel van which belonged to the night cleaning crew at Wal-Mart. He watched as his girlfriend, Britney, was being tucked into the squad car. Packwood sized up the sergeant who had Britney in tow. He looked formidable for his age. The senior sergeant looked like superman with salt and pepper hair and no cape. Bryce decided the only way to take this man was to ambush him. Packwood slipped the 38 caliber Smith and Wesson five shot revolver out of his waistband and gripped then re-gripped the weapon as he felt his heart pounding a jungle rhythm in his chest.

Bryce moved quickly and silently around the van. He closed the distance between himself and Compton. He moved closer because did not want to miss this cop. Packwood had made his decision to kill the cop. He also planned to kill the goofy looking kid. With this accomplished there would be no witnesses. He would kill them both and rescue Britney. The plan was flawed but so was the meth-addled brain that devised it.

Britney saw Bryce coming and was shocked by what he was about to do. The shock registered on her face, giving Compton a reason to wonder "why is her mouth hanging open?" Britney's visible but silent terror was the only warning the sergeant would receive. Compton spun as Bryce began firing. The first slug ripped through Compton's cheek. Sergeant Compton reacted instantaneously, moving laterally to avoid being hit again. The rounds kept coming. The next four slugs hit the scrambling sergeant in the chest and his right arm. The vest stopped two rounds right over his heart. He saw Bryce, a tall lanky man with scabs that matched Britney's. The assailant was wild-eyed. In the world of meth-users, Bryce Packwood was "tweaking," and that was not a good thing. It was a time meth-users showed erratic, unusual, and unreasonable behavior. Since Packwood's girlfriend was being arrested for shoplifting, shooting at this police officer fit the category of unusual for everyone except tweaking meth-addicts. If an armed ambush was not frightening enough, Bryce had tattooed the horns of the devil into his forehead, which in Packwood's view, enhanced his ambience.

Bryce, firing wildly on the run, managed to have incredible accuracy hitting Compton with all five shots. One round broke Compton's right radial bone and another lodged in Compton's shoulder tearing through his rotator-cup. The round that hit Compton in the cheek looked more devastating than it was. The bullet managed to pass into his momentarily startled open mouth, miss his teeth and exit through his cheek. The two rounds which hit Compton in the chest were stopped by his vest.

Dave Compton pictured himself drawing and firing his weapon in his mind's eye; instead, Compton realized that his right arm was dead weight, hanging useless at his side. Dave should have been devastated, but adrenaline, the old warrior's best friend, had kicked in. He was feeling no pain and he found himself once again in that mudroom between life and death and knew he would have to fight his way back to the light.

Bryce was almost on the cop when he noticed he was clicking the hammer on a used up cylinder. He was out of ammunition. He was aghast that the cop was still standing. As he reached Compton he yelled, "Die, you mother fucker! Die!" He threw his revolver at the sergeant and it went over Dave's shoulder. Packwood then drew a buck knife from his pocket and flicked it out. Packwood threw himself at Compton once again. Compton blocked the knife, taking a cut to his left hand, pivoted, hooking his left arm around the waist of Packwood, and threw his hip into his attacker executing a perfect hip throw. Packwood hit the pavement hard and rolled, somehow cutting himself with his own knife as he landed. "What the fuck?" he shouted in pain as he hit the pavement and rolled away. Now Bryce Packwood was afraid.

Compton realized his disadvantage with only his left arm operational and his left hand bleeding badly. He needed his firearm but could not get to it. His right arm was out of the fight, and he needed time. He needed distance. Rolling over the back of his squad car, he ran to a fire hydrant and keyed his mic with his bleeding left hand, "10-78! 10-78! Officer needs assistance. Shots fired at Wal-Mart!"

With that transmission, all the cops in La Claire dropped what they were doing and were instantly heading his way.

Compton would need to buy some time. Packwood looked at his bloodied buck knife and decided that the knife would not bring down this cop. This cop had taken everything he had and still tossed him to the pavement like he was a small child. Britney lay forgotten across the back seat screaming like a teenage girl in a haunted house on Halloween. The front squad car door was standing open. There was an M-4 Benelli Shotgun in the rack. Packwood reached in and began tugging at the shotgun. It was locked into the rack. He climbed into the squad and started pushing buttons still tugging frantically at the shotgun, determined to free it and bring it to bear to kill this cop once and for all.

Compton began reaching around his back trying to remove his 40 caliber Glock from his security holster, but now the pain was setting in. The pain coupled with the disability of the injury was making it impossible to get his weapon from its holster. Then there he was, like a guardian angel standing behind him and looking over his shoulder. A red haired, freckle faced angel carrying... a purse. "Opie, would you like to help?" said Compton so matter-of-factly it startled the young scout.

"Y-Y-Y-Yes S-S-Sir. How?" replied the future cop.

"Take my Glock out of my holster. Keep your finger out of the trigger guard and place it in my left hand. There's a good fellow," said Compton in a mock British accent trying to calm the boy while calming himself.

Opie intently worked the Glock out of Compton's holster, ran around Compton and carefully placed the black final arbiter of justice in the bloodied but operational left hand of this seemingly un-phased warrior. After Opie had fearlessly performed this possible last request, he took three steps back and stood up to watch how the drama would play out. Opie should have run, but he couldn't. Heroes can't run. The fear was there. There was fear enough for an entire Explorer Scout Troop, but fear makes some people run, some people freeze, and some people act with even greater intensity. Besides, Opie was on a ride-along, and like it or not this was *his* ride-along.

Opie watched as Compton sat with his legs extended on either side of the fire plug. His right arm dangled bloody and useless at his side. Compton used the fire plug as a bench rest for his left hand. The hand looked horribly cut, but it was functioning enough to make the Glock go bang, and that was all David Compton needed. Compton calmly took careful aim as if he was sighting his weapon on the range.

Packwood was tugging at the shotgun and appeared to be about to wrest it out of the rack. Compton decided to fire twice. He would fire one round to break the window and a second to fly straight, in the event that the first round was deflected by the glass. Opie watched. Everything was so slow, so deliberate, so dream-like, but this was no dream. The fear was swept from the young scout. He felt the confidence of this modern Sir Galahad who would not be defeated. Compton would not die at the hands of a horned meth-addict in the parking lot of a Wal-Mart while sitting in a puddle of a spilled Slushy. He would not let anything happen to this courageous young scout who he had miserably failed in his lackluster effort to "keep him out of trouble."

The front night sights on his Glock rested clear in the center of Packwood's forehead and, "Bam! Bam!" Packwood disappeared in the flash and the shattering of the safety glass in the side window. Then once again Compton fired two more, "Bam! Bam!" at the spot on the door where he thought the suspect would have to be lying if he had just ducked for cover. Compton fought through the pain and fatigue and covered the window, but he knew the round had found its mark. Packwood sprawled across the seat with the gaping stare of a blind man locked on his face. How appropriate it was to have such a look permanently to carry him into eternity, for he never saw it coming. He shared the fate of so many criminals who foolishly choose a victim who would never stand by while there was an ounce of fight left in them.

The sounds of the night returned slowly to Opie and Compton simultaneously as if they were joined psychically, for they were, as are all those who share a fox hole, survive a fire fight together.

Britney's incessant screams were the first noise that made them realize they had survived. "You killed him! You fucking bastard, you killed him!" Then the distant approaching sirens came on louder and louder as the first back-up was arriving at speeds that would only be attempted by cops rushing to aid another officer.

Compton held cover on the shattered window of the squad. The pain told him to drop his weapon and lie back down and surrender to blissful unconsciousness, but the Marine in him would not allow this. Like all Marines before him he would not surrender, he would not retreat, and he would hold until relieved.

Opie would be a La Claire cop some day years later. He would always be Opie. He would be one more police officer sent on the quest down the difficult path to be like Compton. He would always cherish the memory of watching Sergeant David Compton in his element. Compton's element was to be standing in the midst of chaos, calmly and sometimes violently bringing peace back to his little corner of the world.

As McCarthy slid into the lot, he saw the squad car first with the passenger door standing open. The long lifeless legs stretched out of the open door. There was something about death. Police see so much there are times one can sense death even from across a parking lot. Checking for vital signs at that point is a mere formality.

Then McCarthy saw his sergeant. "Thank God. Compton's alive," Dan said to himself as he saw Dave Compton straddling the fire hydrant and holding cover on the squad with his Glock in his bloody left hand. Sergeant David Compton had been McCarthy's mentor, commander, and role model since McCarthy was a child. When Dan heard the transmission, he knew Compton was in a fight, but he always thought him to be indestructible.

McCarthy pulled his squad in at an angle, drew his weapon, and exited. "I think he's down, but I'm not sure," called Compton forcing each word through the pain as if he was talking while bench pressing 300 pounds.

McCarthy approached with his weapon out, covering the limp legs until he could see inside the squad. Britney screamed, "Let me out of here! You fuckers! I'll kill you mother fuckers!" as she rocked back and forth slamming her head against the squad car's window. McCarthy shined his flashlight on the lifeless shell that once carried the dark soul of a would-be cop killer. The rounds had hit Packwood in the forehead right between the horns. The small pieces of safety glass from the window shimmered on Bryce Packwood like Jack Frost had marked his passing on the dead man with an early Wisconsin frost.

The Benelli was still in the rack, but the rack had been torn from its mount with a rage and fury that was quickly ignited and suddenly extinguished by Sergeant David Compton. McCarthy discovered Compton may not be indestructible but he most certainly was not to be destroyed on this night.

After seeing Packwood was no longer a threat and Britney was dissatisfied with her current residence but still secured, McCarthy ran to Compton. "The man is dead. The woman is secured and unharmed. Are there any more threats?"

Compton's left arm, still holding the Glock, slid limply off the fire hydrant and lowered slowly to his side as if his muscles had received the order from on high, "At ease."

"No. If the male is down it is over," said Compton in a labored whisper that was slurred as if he had sat down at the fire hydrant and drank "ti martoonis" too many. His cheek, where the bullet penetrated was swelling inside and out, putting pressure on his tongue, making proper diction impossible.

McCarthy pulled his supply of four by four bandages out of his aid kit, which he carried in his side pocket along with his cling and applied a bandage to Compton's cheek, shoulder and another to his forearm to slow the bleeding. "Shot's fired officer down. Send an ambulance to Wal-Mart 10-33 (emergency)," said McCarthy as calmly as he could. Dispatch copied the transmission but could determine the injuries must be severe due to McCarthy's tone, which was on the edge of frantic.

McCarthy had not noticed his arrival, but there was Stanley Brockman on the other side of Compton. Stanley was the La Claire Police Department's poster boy for cynicism, but of late you could always count on him in a pinch. McCarthy rolled up his jacket and he and Brockman slowly lowered Compton down on to his side. This caused Compton to wince. "Sorry," said McCarthy. He had no desire to add to this good man's pain.

"Don't worry guys. Nothing but death or morphine is going to relieve the pain now," said Compton. "Get me to the morphine. I am pretty sure they have a supply at the La Claire General ER."

"Do you know who that guy is?" asked Brockman motioning with his head back toward Packwood.

"No. He didn't introduce himself before he asked me to dance," said Compton trying to ward off the pain with a forced smile.

"That's Bryce Packwood. I recognize those horns anywhere. There is a felony apprehension request out for him. He is a bad dude. He'll have to change his name though... to Deadwood." There was a twinge of concern in Brockman's voice as he tried to keep Compton with them with some light "cop dead guy humor."

While Brockman kept talking to Compton, McCarthy could see the holes in Compton's shirt and opened it, checking for any other wounds.

"Deadwood, you're priceless, Stanley," said Compton, who now turned his attention to McCarthy's concerns. "The ones in the chest are all vest hits," said Compton, incredibly lucid. "They hurt like hell, but the vest stopped them. I think it's just the arm and shoulder and the new dimple I have in my cheek." He looked at the wounds in his arm and said, "Useless... Useless. Hey, Opie, you saved my life." Compton then looked around frantically, "Opie, are you all right? Opie, where are you?"

The young scout came over and knelt beside Compton, "I'm right here."

"Kid, you saved us, man. Thanks. I owe you my life."

"I-I-I you're welcome, sir," replied the young scout. He did not see it that way, but he would not argue with Sergeant David Compton.

Compton then relaxed back on the pavement as if the cement was a cushion-top mattress and the rolled up coat was a down-filled pillow and said, "Damn I'm tired... I think I'll just take a nap." Compton let out a long slow exhalation which caused a moment of intense fear in McCarthy. There was what seemed like a long silence. McCarthy's and Brockman's hearts stopped.

Britney slammed her head against the window again and screamed, "Die you pig mother fucker! Die!"

Then it came. That beautiful sound that told them it was all right for them to breathe again. Compton inhaled and slept. This warrior's body having survived the battle had already begun to heal.

Brockman and McCarthy looked at each other and they both exhaled. Compton would not die. He would not let a tweaking ambushing devil-worshipping meth-head stop his noble heart. Compton would live. Bryce Packwood was not the first person to try to kill Sergeant David Compton in peace or in war. Packwood appropriately would discover if there were literally fires in hell. He had the horns tattooed permanently in his forehead so he was dressed for the party Hell was eternally throwing if that was to be his next stop. He would discover that there was hell for the likes of him, but he would not be welcomed to hell as Bryce Packwood. Hell had prepared a warm *welcome to Deadwood.*

CHAPTER TWO

AN OASIS OF SERENITY

When a wounded police officer is rolled into an emergency room, it injects a visible energy into the doctors, nurses, and technicians. There is a buzz that can be seen, heard, and felt throughout the ER. It may have come from the seriousness of the situation, but as McCarthy watched the swirl of activity around him, he sensed that part of the up-tick of activity came from the fact that this was Sergeant David Compton, who was a man the emergency room staff knew well and loved.

Dan stood by in the doorway of the treatment room as Compton was rolled into it. He watched as Compton slipped in and out of different levels of consciousness and awareness. The green clad medical miracle workers were trying first to save Compton's life and second to save his arm. They were desperately attempting to stabilize him before they rolled him up to surgery.

The doctors and nurses working on Compton were his friends. If they'd seen Compton come to their aid once, they'd seen him come a thousand times. Now they were trying to save the life of a buddy. The urgency of their mission was written in their faces and visible in the movements. There was no fumbling, cursing, or looks of confusion. They handled themselves as if someone else's crisis was their routine.

McCarthy then heard the automatic door at the end of the hall swish open and he saw Captain Jackson, who was commander of the Field Service Division, leading Alice Compton down the hall toward McCarthy. Alice had been married to David Compton for two years. Three years ago she had fallen in love with David Compton, the man, after her life had been saved by David Compton, the cop.

Judge Alice was lying in her hospital room after the rescue, devastated by the event and David Compton came to visit. During the visit a strong emotional bond formed. One year later they were married. She now was not only a judge but she was also the wife of a cop.

Judge Alice had been awakened in the middle of the night by the dreaded doorbell, the sound that every cop's family hopes will never come, followed by the words, "Dave has been shot."

Alice pulled out of the gentle caring grasp of Captain Jackson and ran to McCarthy. "Where is he, Dan? Tell me he is going to be all right." Her voice was so far removed in tone and inflection from the measured, confident voice McCarthy had heard so many times from the bench. Right now she was not a judge, she was a woman and the love of her life was "shot."

"Your Honor, you know Dave. He's indomitable," said Dan.

"Dan, tonight I am Alice, please," pled Alice Compton.

"Alice, trust me, he's going to be all right." She took a long look at the blood on McCarthy's uniform and then looked deep into his eyes to see if he believed what he was saying. She saw McCarthy spoke the truth. Her husband would make it.

Alice then threw herself into McCarthy's arms and cried quietly sobbing, "Thank God. Thank God. Thank God. I was so afraid I was going to lose him."

McCarthy then saw Josie, a third shift emergency nurse who had been nursing in the ER as long as McCarthy had been policing. "Josie, this is Mrs. Compton. May she see Dave?"

Josie gently laid both her hands on the shoulders of Alice and said quietly with a calming smile, "Certainly. He is conscious. He will be going into surgery soon and he has been asking for you. You are Alice, right? I hope you are Alice or I will be very embarrassed."

Alice smiled, appreciating the effort to cheer her with humor. "Thank you."

Alice then entered the room cautiously leaning her head around the door frame unsure of what she might find. The moment her head appeared in the doorway Sergeant David Compton was looking at the door. He had heard Alice's voice in the hallway and prepared himself for her. He had a smile on the side of his face that was not covered in bandages and he winked at her, causing Compton considerable pain. "How are you doing, beautiful? Come to take me home? It's looking like they might have to keep me overnight for observation. You know, just as a precaution," Compton said, managing with great effort to form his words from inside his swollen face.

McCarthy watched her light up and move to him in a cautious rush. Dan did not know how Compton did it, but he always managed to say the right thing... the best thing... the thing that needed to be said. Compton had a talent, a gift, to be able to make people feel better with words at times when others could not find the words.

"Come here, beautiful, and give me a kiss," said Compton. "Right here," and he touched his left index finger, which was the only part of his left hand that was not bandaged, to his lips. He then slowly set his left arm back down so as not to disturb the myriad of tubes attached to it. His right arm was immobilized, wrapped, elevated and looked three times its size.

Alice hurried to Compton's left side and then stopped two feet short of the bed and inched slowly to the railing as if she was walking across April ice on a Wisconsin lake. She leaned to the spot Compton had tapped with his left index finger and her loving kiss lightly touched down on his lips. The kiss was as long as a first kiss, as long as a last kiss, and as loving as both combined but somehow twice as gentle.

When the kiss ended, she stayed close and all she could say was, "Oh David," nothing else. She had said it all.

"Don't worry, honey. I'll be OK. It could have been worse. You should see the other guy," said Compton with a barely perceptible laugh.

"I'll vouch for that," agreed McCarthy.

Compton then slowly put his left arm around Alice ever so gingerly and patted her with the only part of his body that did not hurt until he arrived at the hospital and it became the pin cushion for blood samples, IVs, and leads of all kinds and descriptions. "I am going to be able to take some time off until I heal. I will still have one arm to hold you with." He patted her and said, "I think I am going to sleep for a while. They gave me some pretty good stuff. It doesn't hurt a bit," the normally truthful Compton lied.

"I love you, David Compton," Alice said in a whisper to her husband.

"I love you, Alice Compton, always will," replied the sergeant, his eyes closing. David Compton had been shot less than two hours earlier, but McCarthy could not help but notice he had a smile that made it appear that with one kiss from his wife, he had been blissfully transported away from a place of pain to *an oasis of serenity*.

CHAPTER THREE

DOES IT MAKE SOUND

"Hi! You look like you could use a ride," called out the Ripp with a warm, friendly, but practiced smile.

The young man with long curly brown hair stopped his jog along the highway and looked at the interior of the late model Chevy. He had a dirty knapsack slung over his shoulder. It had seen more mileage than William Ripp's rented Chevy. The driver looked normal and friendly. He was dressed in khaki Dockers, a brown sweater, and loafers. He had wire-rimmed glasses, and he looked safe. "Sure. Thanks!" The young man then threw his knapsack in the back seat of the Chevy and slid into the front seat.

"Where are you headed?" asked Ripp.

"West," answered the young man, flopping himself down onto the front seat.

"Bingo!" thought Ripp, "It's time to continue the interview." William Ripp at times interviewed his potential targets like some might interview a potential new employee for a job opening. Ripp would not destroy and discard just anyone.

"I took a ride from a guy who drove me to the Tomah split and then dropped me there at the spot where I-90 and I-94 separate. There was no exit ramp to stand on so it left me a couple of miles to walk before the next ramp. I appreciate you picking me up. I can get arrested for walking on the interstate. You saved me quite a hike and possibly a ticket," the winded young man chattered as he shut the door and fastened the seat belt.

Twenty years had passed since Ripp had killed young Isaac. He had killed many more since then. He had avoided capture by becoming very good at what had become his passion. Ripp meticulously chose his victims. They were sometimes male, sometimes female. What would be called "the tie that binds" in his case, Ripp chose victims who were cast-offs from society. They were runaways, drug users, prostitutes, drifters, and homeless, who were susceptible to an engaging smile, the offer of a ride, a warm meal, a kind word, or a $100 bill. They were victims that would not be readily missed. In Ripp's mind he chose "social misfits." To William Ripp each one was a definitive nobody.

Ripp not only had never been caught, but his serial killing spree had not yet been detected by law enforcement anywhere in the country. His policies of "spread the wealth" and "variety is the spice of death" had served him well. He would kill on the road. He would hide the graves well and bury them deep. He was passionate about his killing but patient, savoring in the selection, planning, execution, and even expert disposal of his victims.

"Why are you heading west?" asked Ripp.

"I am just seeing the country. After high school I took off a year to travel. I hitched across Europe, and now I am just traveling around America seeing the country before I have to act like an adult," said the young man.

"What's your name?" asked Ripp.

"Noah."

"Noah built the ark. Are you destined for a career in boat building? If you are you have the right name for it."

"As a matter of fact, I am. My parents own ARK International. Have you heard of it?" queried Noah.

"ARK? Of course I have! They are in the fortune 500. They build everything from kayaks to super tankers, right?" said the Ripp. "Why are you hitch-hiking?"

"I don't usually tell people my background, but you look really safe. I want to make this trip on my own. I know I will be sucked into the family business. It is inevitable, but I thought it would be neat to see well... how the other half live," explained Noah.

"You mean how the other 99.8% live, don't you? Your family is richer than the Rockefellers," said the Ripp. "I don't know if I would tell too many strangers who you are though. It could get you badly hurt or even... well, killed on the road," cautioned the Ripp.

"Yeah, I know. Like I said, you looked safe... like I can trust you," confided Noah.

"You know, people tell me that all the time," said the Ripp turning away from the road and looking at Noah with a toothy grin.

Noah's instincts were wrong but golden. Ripp was not someone who could be trusted. He was as vile and venomous a snake that ever slithered through the grass after an unsuspecting victim. By sharing with William Ripp his family background, Noah had saved his own life. William Ripp knew a rich father would be relentless in a quest for a missing heir and would have the resources to mount a search on his own. A rich man would have the power and influence to lead the media to report it nationally. Police would scour the Earth to find a rich man's son. William Ripp did not wish to expose himself to that much scrutiny. Ripp had determined long ago that if there was no one with a pedigree on his list of victims there would be a strong likelihood that there would never be a compilation of his list of victims.

William Ripp and Noah chatted for about 90 minutes until Ripp reached the Rochester, Minnesota exit. "I am heading to the Twin Cities. I have to turn north here on Highway 52. It was nice to meet you," said the Ripp.

"Same here, thanks for the lift," said Noah as he reached across the seat and shook hands with the friendly looking killer of 22 innocent human beings.

As Ripp shook the hand of the young heir he whined, "Gee, I am kind of sorry that I have to be in Minneapolis tonight or we could stop some place off the highway and I could buy a rich man's son dinner."

"Yeah, that's too bad. Well, maybe some other time. Thanks again," said Noah.

"Damn! Rich guy's son," said the Ripp to himself. "Not worth the risk. Damn!"

Noah had saved his life by being someone who had powerful people who would search for him and care about his sudden disappearance. One of William Ripp's many witticisms that he called his "Rippisms" was, "Pick the fruit that has fallen far from the family tree. If a body falls in the woods and no one cares, *does it make a sound?*"

CHAPTER FOUR

DARNELL'S TAB

McCarthy sat down at lineup and popped the tab on his Mountain Dew, "Ftssssshew!" McCarthy enjoyed this moment every night. It was the first Dew of the night shift. "The elixir of life," declared McCarthy.

"McCarthy you must have that stuff flowing through your veins," observed Stanley Brockman. Stanley was the shift's most seasoned and most cynical veteran.

"No, it is still mostly red when I get the opportunity to see it. Unfortunately, this job affords the opportunity to see your own blood occasionally and whenever that happens I always do a quality-control check, because I share your concern, Stanley. It has not turned Mountain Dew green yet," replied McCarthy. McCarthy then held his pinky out and sipped it genteelly, swished the Dew in his cheeks, and gingerly swallowed, "Effervescent, robust, a good year; this is a fine Bor-DEW. I'm a connoisseur you know." said McCarthy mimicking a wine taster he had once seen in the movie *Sideways*.

"Aren't you supposed to spit it out when you're tasting wine?" asked Carpenter.

"Nah," chimed in Stanley. "Sandy took me to a wine tasting once. I wore a tie and expected a classy crowd, which they were, at the beginning. There was no spitting at the wine tasting. There was a lot of tasting going on, all right, but I did not see one single, hawker, loogie, or even a small dentist chair swish-spit. They were tasting and drinking and tasting and drinking. They started out talking about art, politics, and literature with refined accents, and they ended the night slurring their R's and telling limericks like a bunch of drunken sailors."

"Boy, Stanley Brockman at a wine tasting event. I'm impressed," said Carpenter as he dropped his gear on the table and sat down.

"Yeah, that was Sandy's idea." Sandy was an office worker at the La Claire Police Department that had created a real change in Brockman. Everyone thought she was too nice and absolutely too gorgeous for Stanley Brockman. It was one of those couple combinations that created many a furrow in many a forehead when they were discussed. The most repeated comment about Stanley and Sandy was, "now those two sure don't go together."

If asked, Stanley would agree when this was brought to his attention. He would say, "We are the original odd couple. The only thing we have in common is our first names both begin with S, and I have seen her S and her S is a lot nicer to look at than mine." No matter how many times Stanley used that line it would crack him up. Sandy was beautiful and refined while Stanley was... Stanley.

"How's Compton doing?" asked Gary.

"He's doing well. He is sore as hell, and it's going to be a long road back if he comes back at all. He's not going to lose his arm," answered McCarthy.

"I saw Joe Darnell in a uniform upstairs. Is he taking Compton's place?" asked Hartley.

Officer Maddy Brown, an attractive blonde female officer who people said was a dead ringer for exercise guru Denise Austin, set her gear down at one of the tables and quietly listened to catch up on the conversation already in progress when she entered.

"Yeah, he was sergeant already so they can save a lot of money on the lobotomy if they just transfer one to nights and not make a new one," said Brockman sardonically.

"They can't make a new one until Compton retires, so as long as he is on the fence they will have to temporarily fill his position," said Carpenter.

"What's Darnell going to be like as a sergeant?" asked Shep, the youngest officer, as he set his gear down on a table in front of him. He sat down and opened a bottle of water and took a drink.

"He's always treated me and every patrolman like something he had to scrape off the bottom of his shoe," replied Stanley.

"Jeez, Stanley, since when did you stop saying shit? It would have been easier to say, he treats us like shit," said Carpenter.

"Sandy has been working her magic on Stanley. She says she doesn't like him utilizing, get this," said McCarthy sitting up straight in his chair and turning to face everyone in the room excitedly, "such vulgar prose."

"Vulgar Prose!?" said Dooley, Carpenter, and Shep in unison, followed by a hearty group laugh.

"Aw you guys can all go F-F-F-F-Forget about it," said Stanley sitting back in his chair and crossing his arms and legs in disgust as the laugh continued.

"What he said was forget about it, but I will translate for those who are not bi-lingual and only speak vulgar prose. Stanley wants you all to go fuck yourselves," said Maddy extending the laugh.

Sergeant Joe Darnell walked slowly into the lineup room as enthusiastically as if he was walking into his own execution. He crossed the room ignoring the jocularity of the officers waiting for his lineup. His gloomy entrance did not diminish the laughter. The laughter naturally played out and the conversation stopped to accommodate Darnell's lineup. Darnell dropped the general information book down on the table in front of the room and sat down. As he did he let out a long sigh and began, "I am going to be your sergeant until Compton decides to shit or get off the pot."

McCarthy leaned over to Carpenter and whispered, "Now that's vulgar prose," and Carpenter laughed.

This exchange caught Darnell's attention. He glared at the two in a manner that showed his disdain for patrol, his disgust for his assignment, and his desire to make everyone on the third shift as unhappy as he was. "I'm glad you thought that was funny. I for one do not plan on laughing or smiling until I get off this cursed shift. I will be honest. I do not want to be here. I have been promised, no matter who denies it, the next lieutenant's position in the Detective Division if I put up with this shift and you people and all of the assholes out there for a few months. So... you guys better not fuck it up! If it looks like any of you are going to fuck up this opportunity I will burn you down!" Then there was silence. It was not out of fear but instant loathing.

No one loathed the man more than Stanley Brockman. The others had never lived and breathed and worked on a daily basis next to a small-minded, vindictive, obnoxious supervisor before, except Stanley Brockman. Compton had always been these officers' sergeant. He was the wise father figure who made good decisions. Compton was someone who would say, "I am not here to be your buddy; I'm here to make you better, but if I can be your buddy and make you better, all the better." They were used to having a supervisor who helped them succeed and made coming to work fun.

Darnell would be nothing like Compton. Darnell had been a cop for twenty years. He had spent fourteen of those years in the Detective Division, first as an investigator and then as a Detective Sergeant. The sergeant position was not a supervisory position but a pay grade raise recognizing achievement. Darnell was a good detective but had developed a disdain for patrol. He looked at patrol officers as a subspecies in law enforcement. He was notorious for putting the finishing touches on a case that was handed to him through the fine work of a patrol officer and then taking full credit for the end result.

McCarthy liked just about everyone he worked with, even Stanley Brockman. He did not like Darnell. There was a meanness about him that seemed unjustified no matter how you cut it. Darnell had treated McCarthy badly in every contact he had ever had with him. When McCarthy was new, Darnell had smeared the term "Rookie" in his face at every juncture. When McCarthy, Stammos, Brockman, and Dooley shot it out with a bank robber named "Mad Mattix," it became necessary to shoot the suspect many times. The shooting was justifiable, but Joe Darnell had interviewed McCarthy and treated him like he was the criminal. Such treatment during that difficult time was something no officer would ever forget and some never forgive. Not even McCarthy had forgiven Darnell yet. McCarthy, Dooley, Carpenter, and Maddy Brown all silently came to the same conclusion. In the language of those fluent in vulgar prose, "Sergeant Joe Darnell is an asshole. Working with him will suck the big blue weenie."

Stanley Brockman had the same thought. Sandy may have managed to control the vulgar prose that exuded from the pie-hole in Brockman's face, but he still owned his thoughts. Stanley then began to think hard to conjure up another description that he could use that would be acceptable to Sandy but instead he thought, "If it looks like an asshole and farts like an asshole then it's an asshole. Joe Darnell is an asshole. There is no other word for him." Brockman smiled to himself. There was a joy in thinking "what an asshole." There was also a reward for not saying it. Sandy had promised this. The thought of the reward made him smile.

"Brockman! What the fuck are you smiling at? Wipe that smile off your face and hit the street!" barked Darnell.

Stanley, shaken back into the real world began piling up his gear and joined the group as they shuffled out toward their squad cars to begin their shifts.

"McCarthy, see me before you leave!" exclaimed Darnell with anger in his tone.

"Yes, sir!" said McCarthy using the term "sir" deliberately. It was a term of respect to most, but tonight the term sir had the meaning that one of his instructors had given it. "When you want to call someone an asshole, don't. It will get you fired. Call them sir. Sir stands for sincerity isn't required, but it can mean asshole."

McCarthy had used this technique effectively many times on the street. He could see he would be calling Darnell "sir" a lot.

After McCarthy finished his squad check, he came into the command room and Darnell was paging through a three-year-old Sports Illustrated Swimsuit Edition that looked as if it had been read by about 100 people before it reached Darnell. He was chewing on the sloppy wet end of an unlit Swisher Sweet cigar. McCarthy interrupted, "Sir."

"Yeah, what?" said Darnell without looking up.

"You said to stop in after I checked my squad in. What do you need?" asked McCarthy.

"Oh yeah, I want you to stop over to the nearest Kwik Trip and fill this up with French Vanilla Cappuccino and bring me a couple of hot ham sandwiches. Tell them to put it on Darnell's tab," said Darnell.

"You can get a tab at the Kwik Trip?" asked McCarthy.

Darnell looked up from the sand covered, nearly unclad beauty with a look of disbelief, "Aren't you fuckin' precious? Still the rookie I remember, McCarthy. Go get my coffee and stop askin' stupid questions. Tell them to put it on Darnell's tab." Darnell then turned the page of his magazine showing a long lean blonde wearing only a triangle-shaped piece of blue fabric. The spray of a waterfall managed to discreetly hide her areolas from view, but this caused Darnell to look closer into the magazine to be certain that he could not see them. As McCarthy began to walk away, Darnell shouted to him, "Oh yeah and that reminds me, two apple fritters."

McCarthy left Darnell gawking at the magazine and slobbering his Swisher Sweet. McCarthy was certain that more of the slobber on the end of the cigar was inspired by the model than by the cigar. As he reached the exit, Darnell yelled, "Remember, tell them to put it on *Darnell's tab!*"

CHAPTER FIVE

SMILEY

McCarthy pulled cautiously into the Kwik Trip lot as he always did. He loved the Kwik Trips. They always had friendly service, and merchandising experts had placed each store exactly where they needed to be. They supplied just about anything you could imagine that you would need in a hurry inside each store.

The Kwik Trips had begun in La Crosse, Wisconsin, which was just to the south of La Claire. They had spread out and McCarthy imagined and hoped that they would soon be in every state of the union because they were catching on. Since they were open 24 hours a day, they were targets of robberies. McCarthy also knew that they were a place at night everyone went to. He would often spot people wanted on warrants and intoxicated drivers. McCarthy routinely scanned the lot and the business before he rushed in. "Nothing," McCarthy said to out loud to no one in a disappointed tone.

McCarthy drove slowly past the window, and the clerk Smiley spotted him. Even though he was already smiling, he smiled larger and waved. It was their secret signal that everything was all right. If something bad was happening inside Smiley would look at McCarthy and not smile and not wave. Smiley's face without a smile on it would be as unnatural as the statue of liberty with her hands in her pockets. The signal had worked many times before, and McCarthy had caught everything from shoplifters to felons.

Since all appeared well, McCarthy entered the Kwik Trip and said, "Hey, Smiley."

"Hey, Dyno," said Smiley in return, beaming. Smiley was a portly and outwardly joyful human being. He was working full-time nights at the Kwik Trip and going to college full-time days. He was from a poor background, but his parents, who were Polish immigrants, had instilled in him the American Dream that anything is possible in America if you work hard. Smiley worked hard.

Smiley was working the long line. It was shift change for many workers, and they were stopping to get gas, frozen pizza, and beer—trying to beat the midnight cutoff when the coolers containing beer would be locked and chained shut.

McCarthy sauntered over to the French Vanilla Cappuccino machine and took Darnell's thermos, filling it with the hot frothy caffeine-laden delight. Dan screwed on the cap taking the time to take a whiff, and it smelled like something he might like. McCarthy then turned around and right behind him were the sandwiches. He found a couple of foil-wrapped ham and cheese and tossed two of them in a bag and then approached the counter. Smiley was just asking a customer, "Hey Joe, would you like a big cookie or some banana bread," which were laid out conveniently on the counter. Smiley then patted his own stomach and smiled an even bigger smile, "Trust me, they are both good."

"Yeah, Smiley, they look good. I could use a treat. I had a rough day," said the man dressed in a gray uniform shirt with a blue patch above the right pocket that said in white letters "Joe." He paid and grabbed his cookie and banana bread and walked out the door pocketing the big cookie and peeling the cellophane off the banana bread.

"I hope you are getting into sales, Smiley," said McCarthy, "I've never seen anyone that works here sell as many big cookies and banana bread as you."

"Everybody sells something, don't you think?" said Smiley.

"I guess you're right. This goes on Darnell's tab," said McCarthy pushing the bag forward. "Two hot ham and cheese sandwiches and this thermos is full of French Vanilla Cappuccino."

"You mean free," laughed Smiley.

"What? He said he had a tab, and I should put it on his tab," said McCarthy a little embarrassed.

"No. I've worked days before when Darnell comes in and says, 'Put it on my tab,' and then he walks out without paying." Smiley was still smiling but no longer laughing. He could see McCarthy, who always insisted on paying, was embarrassed as other customers were lining up behind him.

"Well, I am paying for it," said McCarthy.

Smiley leaned over the counter and stopped smiling as he whispered, "Darnell's going to be pissed."

"I'm paying," whispered McCarthy.

Smiley's fingers quickly traveled across the cash register and he said, "Well, Dyno, that will be $5.02."

"Smiley, I forgot two apple fritters," said McCarthy slapping his forehead.

"That's no problem." He tapped the register a couple more times and then said, "OK then, that will be $6.00 on the head, and I hope that will be all because I would hate to see you hit yourself on the head again. You will have one heck of a headache before the end of the night," Smiley chortled.

McCarthy laid a five and a one on the counter. "That leaves me with $1.00 for lunch if Darnell stiffs me."

"If you want, Dyno, we can start a tab for you," said Smiley, his ever present grin getting bigger once again.

"No thanks, Smiley, I'll stick with pay as you go. I probably won't have time for lunch anyway."

Then the smile returned as big as ever. With his red Kwik Trip employee shirt, his portly persona, and his bright red cheeks, Smiley looked like a young Kris Kringle. Then with a devilish twinkle in his eyes Smiley asked, "Are you sure you wouldn't like some banana bread and a big cookie with those fritters?"

"No thanks, Smiley. No sale," said McCarthy as he slid the five and the one across the counter. McCarthy laughed and repeated as he headed for the door, "Banana bread and big cookie with those fritters..." Shaking his head, McCarthy looked back at Smiley whose smile once again had somehow gotten even bigger. He had a customer waiting to pay, but he was waiting for what he knew McCarthy would give him, one more laugh. McCarthy did not disappoint him; he laughed again, "Banana bread and big cookie with those fritters." McCarthy shook his head again and said the name that always brought a smile to his own face, *"Smiley."*

CHAPTER SIX

VULGAR PROSE

William Ripp sat toward the back of the room, almost conspicuous in his attempt to be inconspicuous. He was driven toward his prey by the hunger of a jungle predator whose last meal squirmed out of its grasp.

After dropping off Noah at the Rochester exit on I-90, Ripp headed north and then cut over to 61 and headed south along the Mississippi until he reached the bridge crossing over into La Claire. William Ripp had been consistently treating himself with a kill once a year, but this year he had already snuffed out two lives. He raped, strangled, and disposed of a woman of the night somewhere north of Reno.

He had shot a hobo, ending the seedy existence of the "gandy" who had been riding the rails to see the country for years. He disposed of that body south of Tucson, Arizona. Ripp felt his appetite becoming voracious of late. He hoped that it had not become insatiable because that would lead to his becoming sloppy. Sloppiness would inevitably lead to his capture. It was his goal to become the serial killer that never was. He hoped to enjoy his unique pastime without ever becoming famous. He did not want to be a "Green River Killer" or "The Boston Strangler" or the "Son of Sam." His glory would to be the "No-Name Killer." No name would be his fame. The fact that he would not be famous would make him infamous. The bones of his victims would be spread all over the United States left to be discovered 2000 years in the future by some archeologist who would wonder what kind of culture would do this to their own. He wanted to retire some day undefeated like Rocky Marciano.

The thought made him smile as he watched the dancer spin around the pole. He had walked into this place drawn by its name,

The RUMPelstiltskin, with the word "RUMP" in capital letters on the sign. "My kind of place," he thought.

There were twenty potential victims. Eight of them sat around the circular stage watching the woman dance. Ripp could not help but notice that the dancer actually could dance. She had large natural breasts and a proportional ass that excited him so much it caught him off guard. She had what appeared to be a blonde "Britney Wig" and was spinning about in her naked beauty to Britney Spears' throaty rendition of the song, "Womanizer." The eight were giving up their Abe Lincolns readily to get within touching distance of her womanhood.

He was momentarily transfixed by the beauty and grace of this stripper whose professional name was "Darla Darling." It most certainly was not her real name. He finally managed to look away, thinking, "Back to business." Ripp looked about the room. The rest of the patrons were spread across the room seated alone at tables. Three of their heads were subtly spinning, following Darla's performance.

William Ripp's radar zeroed in on one of the patrons whose head was also subtly spinning. The spinning was owed to the large quantity of Jack Daniels he had drunk before coming to the RUMP. Alcohol induced vulnerability was one of Ripp's favorite prerequisites. Ripp got up and left, his next victim chosen.

Bill "Good Buddy" Blakely was a simple man. He worked five days a week at a Fast-Lube changing oil, filters, and every once in a while he would talk some sap into an unnecessary "full fluid flush for $99.95." When Bill would have a night off, he would drink until he could drink no more. He would drink until he could think no more. Then he would get into his car and turn on the automatic pilot and somehow navigate home… sometimes.

Other times he would be arrested before he reached home. He had met Dan McCarthy on four such occasions, and on the last meeting he had spit out the ultimate chastisement Bill "Good Buddy" Blakely ever used. He said to his arresting officer, "McCarthy, you're no good buddy of 'Good Buddy' no more." The sincerity of this rebuke made McCarthy unable to resist chuckling at the comment.

"That's pretty harsh, Bill, but you know a man's got to do what a man's got to do," said McCarthy with a mock hurt in his voice that Bill Good Buddy Blakely took as real.

"Well, arresting me four fucking times is pretty harsh, so there. Fuckyaaaaaa!"

As Blakely staggered out of the RUMP, he had no idea he was being followed. He could not have noticed even if he was only a little drunk. He would not have noticed if he was sober and expecting to be attacked. William Ripp was good at what he did.

Blakely's car was parked on the street in front of the RUMP. He pulled out, and to Ripp's surprise he drove remarkably well for a man whose blood alcohol content nearly matched the first two digits of his zip code.

Blakely pulled into the Kwik Trip lot and parked. He opened his door, dropped one foot to the ground and stopped. It was as if the Big Guy upstairs had a remote control and pushed the pause button on Bill. Blakely just sat there with his hand on the door, one foot on the ground, and the other inside on the floor board of the car. The only movement visible was a slight subtle swirling of his head as if he was following a conjured up picture of Darla Darling spinning around the bar.

Ripp saw an opportunity. This one was already "medicated." He parked his car up the street from the Kwik Trip and walked up to the car. Ripp was hungry and suffering from tunnel vision. He did not see the officer inside the Kwik Trip. He did not notice the squad parked on the opposite side of the Kwik Trip.

Ripp walked up to the unsuspecting Blakely and in his most concerned voice asked, "Sir, can I get you home? I would be happy to drive you home."

McCarthy held the door for a pretty college-aged girl wearing a T-shirt that said, "Drink until you want to take me home." McCarthy thought she was much too pretty for the shirt that he had seen before on women whose faces would make a pit bull jump off a meat truck. Then Dan noticed a familiar face that stopped him in his tracks. His former good buddy Bill "Good Buddy" Blakely was leaning out of his car. He had one foot on the ground and the other still in the car. The car was still running and Bill was obviously too drunk to drive, too drunk to walk, and quite possibly too drunk to even crawl. He was, however, clearly sober enough to drool, the long silvery thread shimmering from the corner of his mouth down to his lap.

McCarthy apparently was not the only person that was concerned about Blakely. Dan noticed a tall thin man walk up to Bill and say something to him. McCarthy could not hear what was said, but the man clearly looked concerned. McCarthy thought, "That's unusual. I guess there still are a few civic minded people left in the world."

McCarthy keyed his mic, "255, I'll be out at the Kwik Trip on Bluff Street. There is a William Blakely sitting behind the wheel of a running vehicle, and he appears very 10-55 (Driving while intoxicated). I believe his driver's license is also revoked."

At that moment Blakely looked up and made eye contact with McCarthy. Blakely's head stopped spinning. He was not so numbed by the alcohol to prevent fear from sending a shock through his body. As intoxicated as he was, Blakely knew that a fifth offense charge of driving while incredibly drunk would be a felony. Bill had been warned at length by his attorney, by the district attorney, and by Judge Alice Compton who heard his case. The fear woke him up and called him to action.

McCarthy saw and said, "No, Bill! Don't Move! Don't do it!"

It was the first time Ripp had noticed the policeman. He heard the command and looked up. The fear was immobilizing. All Ripp could do was ask himself, "How did this cop know my name? How did he know what I was about to do?" Then he realized that the officer was yelling to the drunk in the car.

Blakely exclaimed, "Fuckin' McCarthy!" and he pulled his foot quickly inside the car. As the foot disappeared, the door slammed and Blakely put the car into gear. He looked over his shoulder to the rear and accelerated. The tires squealed in response but Bill "Good Buddy" Blakely had put the car into drive instead of reverse.

The tires squealed loudly and then it lurched forward, roughly jumping the curb for the sidewalk between the building and the lot. The car crossed the narrow divide and slammed into the quaint red brick wall, which managed to do what it was not designed to do; it held. The car was kept from crashing through the wall, over the cappuccino makers, and into the last few apple fritters.

McCarthy ran up to Blakely's car and swung the door open. Bill was wiggling the gear shift in an effort to flee the scene, but McCarthy reached around Blakely's head and slipped in next to him cheek to cheek as he put a wrist lock on Blakely's left wrist. McCarthy then slid his right arm around the back of Blakely's head and his right index finger into Blakely's mouth and secured his cheek. After securing his cheek and head McCarthy corkscrewed Blakely out of the car and face down to the ground without a whine or a whisper. McCarthy then turned the wrist lock into a rear compliance hold. As drunk as he was, the painful hold instantaneously made Bill "Good Buddy" Blakely want to be a better man.

McCarthy snarled, "Blakely, stop resisting and give me your other hand. Do it now!"

Blakely lay on the ground contemplating what just had happened. One second he was making good his escape. In the next moment he found himself on the ground face down. He understood this turn of events. He had experienced them all before.

"Fuckin' McCarthy," he snarled back and then he gave up his other arm instinctively. He knew this to be the only remedy for the pain. "F-F-F-F-Fuck me dry, McCarthy," stammered Blakely.

Then McCarthy thought to himself, "F-F-F-F-Fuck me dry... *Vulgar prose.*"

CHAPTER SEVEN

PURE SATISFACTION

When McCarthy finished at the Kwik Trip, he looked one last time for the man he thought looked like a college professor who had tried to keep Blakely from driving, but he was nowhere to be found. He had disappeared like the morning ground fog hanging suspended over the floor of a coulee.

McCarthy took Blakely to the hospital for a check up and to have blood drawn. As he waited, Carpenter stopped in to make sure Blakely had calmed down. Blakely had indeed calmed down. He had fallen asleep in a blood draw chair, which looked like a desk in a high school classroom with an extra long and wide arm rest.

"Is sleeping beauty going to wake up cranky?" asked Carpenter.

"Once Good Buddy has submerged himself in the arrest process, he usually becomes cooperative, but you never know," answered McCarthy as he watched a bubble expand and deflate from Blakely's right nostril.

"He drove into a wall and didn't get a scratch?"

"That's the way it goes. If it would have happened to a sober person they would have been killed," reasoned Dan.

"Ain't it the truth. I've seen it a hundred times," said Carpenter.

"I am guessing it is because they are so numb from alcohol they become like Gumby in the crash and you can't hurt them," theorized Dan.

"Have they ever studied the phenomenon?" asked Carpenter.

"No. They have no trouble getting volunteers to get drunk in a study, but I guess they continually balk at the idea of driving at high speeds into immovable objects without a seat belt on," said McCarthy who then laughed at the development of one extraordinarily large snot bubble that rose to perfection and then popped, spoiling the show. "Did you see that one?"

"Kind of like pop goes the sneezle," quipped Carpenter.

McCarthy observed, "Letterman-worthy. He could go on stupid human tricks."

"Anyway, if they ever do a study it will cost a million bucks and I will swear that they'll find drunks survive more ergs of energy on impact than sober people," declared McCarthy.

"Ergs?" asked Carpenter.

"That's what they're called. It's a measurement of energy, I think," said McCarthy.

"I'll take your word for it. Before they do these studies they should ask us first. For cops every shift is a study, man," said Carpenter with a sage-like wisdom in his tone. "I would give them the information for half a million, no half a half a million."

The lab technician entered the room carrying her rack of vials and she went about her business. Bill "Good Buddy" Blakely woke up looking at a pretty face and he smiled. The Good Buddy nickname suited him. Except when he was being arrested, he could be anyone's good buddy. If he didn't have such a drinking problem he could have sold hog futures to Porky the Pig. Bill gave the blood without a fight and then McCarthy put him to bed for the night at the place Blakely called, "The Crowbar Hotel."

McCarthy walked into the station three hours after he had left to pick up Darnell's cappuccino and ham sandwiches. McCarthy set the cold and flat French Vanilla Cappuccino in front of Darnell. Next to it he placed the bag containing the even colder and slightly deformed hot ham sandwiches. McCarthy then said, "Oh, I almost forgot here is your dessert, sir," and with that said he set down the apple fritters.

Then, in Darnell's world, McCarthy added an unfathomable insult to this injury by adding, "That will be $6.00, Sergeant Darnell. Here is the receipt."

"What the fuck you talking about, McCarthy? Get the fuck out of here. $6.00, my ass! Didn't you tell them to put it on the tab?" asked Darnell, his face turning red.

"Yes, sir, I did. They said that means it is free and I don't take anything on duty for free. Our shift all agreed that none of us would take anything for free years ago. I paid $6.00, and I respectfully request $6.00 in return," answered McCarthy.

Compton had always cautioned McCarthy and all members of his shift, when having a disagreement with someone of a higher rank use the words sir and respectfully copiously. When McCarthy asked what "copiously" meant, Compton answered, "Look it up and you'll remember!" McCarthy did. It meant that he should use sir and respectfully a lot.

"Respectfully, sir that is my last $6.00, please give me the money?" McCarthy held his hand out while he held his wallet open showing the one lonely dollar bill occupying its deep recesses.

Darnell looked up with a mask of puzzled, angry wonderment on his craggy face. After a long silence, Darnell began frantically tugging at his rear pants pocket for his wallet as if he was a hospital patient having a seizure who was suddenly asked to pre-pay for his treatment. Darnell yanked the wallet out and threw down the six dollars. He growled, "Last time I send you for food!" He then opened a sandwich and threw it down on the desk complaining, "How am I supposed to eat this shit. It's cold and-and-and- what the fuck did you do, sit on it? Get the fuck out of here, McCarthy."

"Yes, sir, but I have a report to write. Do you want me to do it first and then get out?" asked McCarthy with an attempt to not appear contrite in the midst of his contriteness. McCarthy waited for Darnell's command.

"You're not going to suck up any overtime because of this. Get your damned report done and then get the fuck out of here!" Darnell had taken a bite of a sandwich and as he said "fuck," he launched a piece of ham out that landed on the sipping hole in the lid of the cappuccino thermos.

"Yes sir," said McCarthy as he turned and walked out of the command room. It was nothing he had done deliberately. It was nothing he planned. In fact he could not have planned it so perfectly if he had planned it, but all in all he was more satisfied than if he would have planned it. As McCarthy walked back to the report room, a small smile formed on his face. It was the kind of smile that forms when witnessing a natural thing of beauty, such as the birth of a young colt, a hummingbird flitting from flower to flower, or a sunset. He had just witnessed natural justice. It was a smile of *pure satisfaction*.

CHAPTER EIGHT

SERIAL KILLER

As Ripp drove East on I-90 in the sparse late night traffic toward his home in Madison, he was lost in his thoughts. He had been thwarted by a cop. That had not happened before. He had come dangerously close to arrest and found it exciting. All he could think was, "What a rush!"

The cop stepped between Ripp and his intended victim and swept the man out of the car with an expertise that he had never seen before. Ripp had seen the Rodney King beating and that was all he knew of cops arresting "motorists." He thought, "This was smooth and almost… artistic, and I was right there, invisible."

William Ripp thought, "The real beauty of the act was the drunken man would probably hate the cop for arresting him. The cop saved the drunk's life and neither of them knew it. Hah!"

Ripp then began to speak to himself out loud, "Noah. A missed opportunity. I was being cautious. *Cautious!*" Ripp drove on turning southeast toward Madison where Interstate 90 meets with 94. It was the spot where he had seen Noah walking on the highway. "Cautious. I know now why moths fly ever closer to the flame. Being that close to destruction is thrilling, exciting, exhilarating."

William Ripp's thoughts drifted to the dancer he had seen at the RUMP while he was reconnoitering his next victim. He had never seen such beauty in a dump like that. She had the grace of a prima ballerina, the elegance of a diva, and the sexuality of a porn star.

"I must have her. That's it," he said out loud, "and I will meet this cop. I will fly closer to the flame," his eyes on fire, lit up by a passing semi, and stoked by his unearthly passions. William Ripp turned off on the next exit and headed back to La Claire. He knew it was dangerous, but William Ripp had not been endowed with vast reserves of self control.

As McCarthy worked on the diagram of the crash scene, Darnell came in, cleared his throat, and announced, "McCarthy, there is a guy at the front desk asking to see the officer who arrested the driver from the crash at the Kwik Trip earlier. He said he was a witness," said Darnell

"A witness?" puzzled McCarthy.

"That's what I said," Darnell stated with his usual impatience. "You gonna make me say it twice?"

"I'll talk with him," said McCarthy, setting down his template and picking up his note book.

McCarthy recognized the man at the front desk immediately. It was the professor. "Good evening, sir. Thanks for coming in," began McCarthy. "I remember you from the Kwik Trip. I wondered where you went."

"The thing happened so suddenly that my instincts were, well, you know, I better get out of here, and then I thought I better come back because you might need a witness," said Ripp, ever the actor now playing a role far outside of his character, a good citizen.

McCarthy extended his hand and said, "I am Officer Dan McCarthy. I really appreciate you coming in tonight."

When William Ripp returned the handshake McCarthy noticed the handshake was warm, friendly, but firm, the handshake of a confident man. "I'm glad to help," answered Ripp.

"Can I get some information from you?" asked Dan.

"Certainly, that is exactly why I came in here," said Ripp.

"What is your name, sir?" said McCarthy, opening his notebook to a clear page.

"William Robert Ripp," said the friendly killer.

"That's a unique name," said McCarthy.

"Not really. In fact, you startled me when you yelled to the driver. His name must be William, too, because you said, 'No, Bill. Don't move,'" answered Ripp.

"Yes. His name is William. We'd met before so I knew his name was Bill," said McCarthy with a puzzled smile as he continued, "I meant your name Ripp is a unique name."

"Oh yes," said Ripp, shaking his head, while he removed his glasses. He slipped a folded handkerchief from his pocket and wiped the lenses slowly and then replaced them on the bridge of his nose, refolded the handkerchief carefully and returned it to his pocket.

"Of course you meant Ripp. Sorry, what was I thinking? It really is more common than you might think," said Ripp, a little embarrassed.

"Where do you live?" asked McCarthy, obtaining his address in Madison, which was on Mifflin Street. "Isn't that in the college area?" asked McCarthy. "Don't they have riots there?"

"Yes. The house has been in the family for generations. The neighborhood has deteriorated, but I keep the house up. The young people coming and going are something I enjoy. Mifflin was the hotbed of anti-war activity in the 60s and 70s," said Ripp. "Recently they have even had a few riots at an annual Mifflin Street bash. Like I said, I stay out of trouble, but I do like the excitement."

"I would like to get a written statement from you," said McCarthy handing Ripp a statement form and a pen. "How did you happen to land at the Kwik Trip in La Claire?"

"I was on my way home from a business trip and it got kind of late, so I was going to get some gas and maybe a hotel room and get off the road. I saw this man you called Bill sitting in his car, and he was clearly, as they would say, three sheets to the wind. I stopped to see if I could convince him not to drive any farther. That's when he saw you and tried to take a short cut home through the Kwik Trip. Clearly not a very sound idea," said Ripp.

"What kind of business are you in?" asked McCarthy.

"I am a Computer Database Consultant," said Ripp, removing his glasses and his handkerchief and cleaning them again more fervently this time.

"Sounds important. Do you work for a company?" asked McCarthy.

"No, ah, actually to be perfectly correct, well yes, but I am the company. I am self employed. I am a freelance database consultant.

It requires that I travel quite a bit," said Ripp folding the handkerchief and once again carefully returning it to his pocket.

"Boy that sounds kind of heady. What does a freelance database consultant do?" asked McCarthy out of pure curiosity.

"Since you ask, I specialize in optimizing system performance and architecture. Customers contact me when they are looking for improving performance of their databases queries, refactoring and optimizing their stored procedures, and tuning table design for optimum business intelligence analysis," said Ripp with a wry smile. McCarthy looked dumbfounded for a moment and Ripp laughed, "Well, you asked."

"I asked. I hope you are not going to give me a quiz on that later," said McCarthy.

"No, you're safe. I always give that answer when someone asks and I usually get the same response. If someone actually knows what I am talking about I immediately don't like them because they are probably my competition," said Ripp looking over the statement form.

"Well if you could complete this statement describing the condition you saw Mr. Blakely in and then why you were intervening and, of course, what you saw after I arrived and then sign the sheet right here," said McCarthy as he stepped up and pointed out the line where Ripp's signature was required.

"Blakely, William Blakely. I take it that's the driver's name?" asked Ripp.

"Yes, that is his name," said McCarthy as he motioned to a chair and desk in the front lobby. "Is this OK for you right here? For now it looks like you have the lobby to yourself."

"This looks comfortable. It's my first statement," said Ripp, smiling as he sat down placing the statement in front of him on the desk. Ripp then wiggled uncomfortably and reached into a back pocket and pulled out his car keys. He shook his head, still smiling and set them down on the table in front of him.

Ripp said it with a prideful tone that McCarthy thought oddly to be almost gloating. He then asked "You've never once made a statement before?"

"Never."

"Not as a witness?"

"Nope."

"Never once as a um, no I shouldn't ask; you've been so helpful," said McCarthy awkwardly.

"Go ahead, ask," encouraged Ripp with a smile that would have put Smiley to shame.

"You have never been cited for anything?"

"Not so much as a parking ticket," gleamed William Ripp. His smile waned slightly as he remembered the speeding ticket he had received on his way to dispose of Isaac many years ago. Ripp kept that thought to himself and smiled on less enthusiastically.

"You should be proud," declared McCarthy. Even though the man seated before him appeared to be a paragon of virtue, McCarthy felt the hair on the back of his neck stand up. Dan's intestinal indicators became aggressively active. These indicators in McCarthy were very much like some human turbine that started turning in his stomach when something was truly wrong. Sometimes McCarthy could easily identify what was setting off his intestinal indicators in a matter of moments by surveying his surroundings, but the only one here was Ripp. All he was doing was smiling and making a statement. He was a good citizen. This truly puzzled Dan.

"I am. Very proud!" said Ripp as he looked down at the statement for a moment and then began to write.

McCarthy hesitated. He felt like there was something to say, something to ask, but no words came. He looked at the man before him. This man was a "freelance computer database consultant," whatever that was. It all seemed to fit. He stopped to convince an intoxicated person not to drive, even though he was a stranger from out of town. That was very unique, but not unheard of and certainly not criminal. Then without being asked he came back to leave a statement, and that was certainly not unheard of. It was even laudable.

McCarthy looked Ripp over. His face was red, flushed, as if he had just run a mile in record time. Ripp was even smiling as he wrote. McCarthy could not put his finger on it, but something was wrong.

McCarthy went behind the front desk and contacted dispatch. He ran a full check on Ripp. He found that Ripp had a valid Wisconsin Driver's License with his home address on Mifflin Street in Madison. William Ripp had a clear driving record and had never been arrested before. The stop twenty years earlier had long ago been expunged from his record administratively by the Wisconsin State Department of Transportation.

Ripp had no unpaid taxes, no unpaid parking tickets, and if McCarthy would have pushed further on he would have discovered that Ripp gave regularly to the United Way. If they were asked, Ripp's clients and all of his neighbors would vouch for his many fine admirable qualities. Something was wrong with this guy, and McCarthy was not going to figure out what.

Maddy Brown came upon McCarthy in pensive and deep thought and asked, "What's up McCarthy? You have a look on your face that I have seen before — just before all hell breaks loose."

"Just puzzled," said McCarthy. "My intestinal indicators are going off like crazy over this guy out front, and I don't have a clue as to why."

"Did you check him for warrants?" asked Maddy.

"Yeah, he has no wants," said McCarthy.

"Is he valid to drive?" Maddy asked.

"Yeah, clear record," said McCarthy with a sigh.

"Is he on probation?" Maddy chanced.

"No," checked McCarthy.

"Parole?" Maddy checked.

"Clear criminal record," checkmated McCarthy.

"Unrepentant terrorist with a bomb strapped to his chest?" stabbed Maddy.

"Nope, he's a witness that came in to leave a statement," parried McCarthy.

"Then if he's none of those I would say you need your intestinal indicators recalibrated," said Madison Brown, "except..." There was a long pause as Maddy tucked into position some of her beautiful blonde hair that she kept hidden in tight braid she put it in for duty. A few strands had come loose and fallen out. Maddy then continued "Except I have never known your intestinal indicators to be wrong, Dyno. There is another possibility. It happened to my father later in his career," said Maddy, whose father was a retired Los Angeles Police Officer.

"What's that?" asked McCarthy, his interest piqued.

"IBS," answered Maddy matter-of-factly.

"10-9 (repeat)?" said McCarthy, unfamiliar with this police term.

"Irritable Bowel Syndrome," Maddy explained.

"I don't think so," laughed McCarthy, totally caught off guard by his own more somber concerns.

"Well there is one other possibility, Dyno. You just may have a serial killer on your hands, my friend," declared Maddy with an air of certainty. "There is no denying that you're intestinal indicators have foretold the future more accurately, more instantaneously, and more often than Nostradamus' Quatrains."

"Wouldn't that be something," said McCarthy proud of the comparison to Nostradamus. "Should I go ahead and lock him up before he kills again?" asked McCarthy.

"Lock him up if you must, except you're lacking that one small thing," said Maddy putting her thumb and index finger together in a pinch.

"What's that?" asked McCarthy.

"Probable Cause," answered Maddy with a certain tone of finality.

"He would be my first serial killer, and here I am with no probable cause. In fact I have no probable cause, reasonable suspicion, indicators of deception, no bodies, not one ounce of evidence, a hunch, or even a wild-ass guess," said McCarthy as he ticked each point off on the fingers of both hands.

"I can't do everything for you," said Maddy with a laugh. "He's a serial killer; now go out and make your case." Maddy then turned and threw both of her hands up in the air as if frustrated by his incompetence, "McCarthy, I'm telling you, you have an uncanny gut. If you are sensing something big, I trust your gut. He's a serial killer, a burglar, an armed robber, or child molester. If your gut is acting up, he must be something. Just go find out what and make your case." Maddy walked down the hall and turned, smiling, and said, "I can't do everything for you, McCarthy, besides I'm not the one they call Dyno." She turned and walked off leaving McCarthy puzzled without knowing why or what to do about it.

Dan returned to William Ripp, who was still smiling, still red faced, and apparently proofreading his statement.

"How does it look?" Dan asked.

"I think between the two of us we have him convicted," said Ripp who appeared to be about to bubble over in his chair.

McCarthy thought, "This guy's enthusiasm for what is happening is beyond unusual. He looks like he is building toward an orgasm. Maybe I am just reading too much into all of this. He's just making a statement."

After reading the statement, which was well written, thorough, and even complimentary toward McCarthy, Dan shook Ripp's hand. "Thank you, Mr. Ripp. Are you going to be leaving La Claire and heading out to Madison tonight?"

"No, I am going to spend the night here. Heck, maybe even a couple nights here; it's a nice town. I've never been here before. Are there any hotels that you can recommend?" asked Ripp.

"We are not supposed to recommend, but I can tell you how to get to the Radisson, the Marriott, or the Comfort Suites."

"Which is the closest?" asked Ripp.

"They are all about the same, so pick one," repeated McCarthy.

"I will be staying at the Radisson then," said Ripp. "If you need me, I'll be there."

"You mean if we find out you are a serial killer instead of a freelance computer database consultant, we can catch you there." It was not something McCarthy planned on saying, and he did not know why he said it, but as the words "serial killer" came out of his mouth, he immediately saw the smile disappear. The color drained from his face and his hazel eyes changed from green to brown to black in moments. William Ripp took his glasses off and removed the handkerchief once again from his pocket and cleaned them frantically. He looked down then away as he placed the glasses back on the bridge of his nose. He folded the handkerchief into the perfect square from whence it came and then shoved it back into his pocket, ripping the corner of the pocket slightly.

"You will find nothing as exciting as that on my record. I live the mundane life of a computer geek, but if you have any questions you know where to find me," Ripp then turned suddenly away, seemingly incapable of even feigning a smile and he walked toward the exit without even saying goodbye.

Just as Ripp reached the door McCarthy called, "Stop, Mr. Ripp!"

Ripp froze and appeared in a state of near panic, and McCarthy walked over to the desk Ripp had been at and picked up his keys. He walked slowly over to William Ripp, handed the keys to Ripp, and shook his hand one more time saying, "Thanks for coming in, Mr. Ripp. You were a great help." McCarthy could see the sweat forming, beading, and then running down the forehead of Ripp as if he were a boxer seated in the corner chair of the ring, between rounds ten and eleven of a title fight.

Ripp took the keys and would not look McCarthy in the eyes. Something about this cop scared him. Ripp thought, "He knows! I don't know how, but he knows. I should not have come here tonight." Inside his head, Ripp was screaming, but outside his silence was as cold as an abandoned mine shaft and just as dark and mysterious to McCarthy.

McCarthy, upon taking Ripp's hand, felt the sudden unmistakable cold, wet, clamminess of it. The temperature of Ripp's hand had dropped like the temperature at sunset on a day of Wisconsin Indian Summer. The grip had none of its prior confidence and Ripp did not smile nor would he engage McCarthy in eye contact as if his eyes held his heart's most terrible secrets. The cold sweating palm of William Ripp slid flaccidly out of McCarthy's as if it needed desperately to escape. Without another word, Ripp was out the door.

"I'll walk you out," said McCarthy.

"Not necessary," said Ripp, flustered with his eyes scanning the ground away from McCarthy.

"I insist," said McCarthy his tone still friendly. "You have been so helpful." Now McCarthy was the actor.

McCarthy walked Ripp to his car and then watched and waved as William Ripp drove away. He wrote the license, make, model, and year of his car down. McCarthy had never seen two words change the demeanor of a man as quickly as he had seen tonight. As the taillights of Ripp's car disappeared into the night, McCarthy said out loud to himself in disbelief, "What if? No, it couldn't be. Wouldn't that be something though, if William Ripp was a... *serial killer?*"

CHAPTER NINE

DRESSED TO KILL

When Ripp knew that he was out of sight of McCarthy, he exploded, "Fuck! Fuck! Fuck! Fuck! Fuck! Fuck!" He screamed as he pounded his hand down hard onto the steering wheel of his rented car. "You dumb son of a bitch. What the fuck were you thinking?" he asked himself. "You're so fucking stupid!"

He had never felt such rage. His killings were never out of rage. They were out of some unnatural passion. He looked at his killing up to this point as his gift. Painters paint, poets write poetry, musicians make music, and his gift was to kill undetected, until now.

Ripp calmed himself as he drove. "Think! McCarthy knows something. I don't know how. I don't know why. I don't even know what, but he knows something. I could see it in his eyes. Those damn eyes, I'd like to cut them out. Fuck! Fuck! Fuck! Fuck!" He shouted slamming his hands down on the steering wheel again, this time causing his car to sharply swerve into the opposite lane. Once again, there was no one else on the road to see his transgression.

Before he knew it, Ripp found himself in front of the Radisson Hotel. "I must sleep. Tomorrow it will all be clearer."

Ripp woke up with knock at the door of his hotel room, "House keeping," said the timid female's voice. He rubbed the sleep from his eyes and looked at the clock. It was 4:00 PM. He looked at the door and saw that he had not hung the "Do Not Disturb" placard on the outside of the door. He always did that. "What is wrong with me? Shit! I am getting sloppy."

He forced himself up to his elbow and then to a sitting position and finally he was out of bed and standing. He walked to the door, opened it slightly and saw a portly maid, smiling sheepishly at him just outside the door. "House keeping," she said now almost in an apologetic whisper.

"No thanks. Not today. I am staying one more night," answered Ripp barely finishing the word night before he yawned heartily in the face of the cleaning lady and he then shut the door and secured the bolt. "Damn! I didn't secure the bolt. What's up with that?" he asked himself out loud. "No good can come of that. I cannot afford sloppiness."

Ripp rubbed the sleep from his eyes, yawned, stretched and looked at himself in the full length mirror. He scratched himself in a manly manner and then shook his head at the scruffy looking figure that he awoke to every morning. "You look like shit," he declared as he yawned one more time. The late night hours always seemed to age him ten years in one night. "You can't shine unless you shower," he observed.

Ripp climbed into the shower and washed the years away and stepped out refreshed. He stepped into his gray slacks and slipped on a gray shirt and sweater.

The night's sleep had given him perspective and made his next target clear. Officer Dan McCarthy's statement was off the cuff and just dumb luck. There was no way he could possibly know that Ripp was a killer.

Ripp's usual confidence was restored. He would do what he had set out to do. He would claim a victim in La Claire, the beautiful dancer, Darla Darling. She was a stripper and a nobody that would soon be forgotten after she disappeared. She would make for a memorable night for him, quite possibly his best yet.

Ripp strapped on his shoulder holster. He checked his stainless steel Smith and Wesson revolver, dropping open the cylinder and then slapping it shut. He tucked the revolver into the holster and then slipped his gray jacket over the rig. He folded up an impressive wad of cash and slipped it into the pocket on the gun side of the jacket and then stood in front of the mirror. He smiled at his image and practiced pulling the money out and then replacing it after which he quickly drew his weapon. He practiced this about ten times. He did not need the practice since it was a distraction he had practiced and used many times before. After a few repetitions, Ripp added the proper facial expressions showing a smile as he pulled out the money and then transforming his friendly expression to the look of a killer as he pulled out his revolver. The smile was fake, but the look of the killer came naturally. It was the real face of William Ripp.

Once he was satisfied that the abduction would be smoothly accomplished, he stepped into his loafers and looked at himself one more time in the mirror. He combed his hair into place and admired what he saw. He smiled, winked, and declared himself *dressed to kill.*

CHAPTER TEN

A PRAYER FOR DAVID COMPTON

McCarthy sat at the front table in the lineup room with one foot up on the chair next to him. He had shaken from his thoughts the incredibly strange reaction of William Ripp to two little words, "serial killer." The thought that a serial killer would come in to the front desk of a police department to make an unsolicited statement against an intoxicated driver was laughable. He had reasoned that Madison Brown's second possibility was probably true. Maddy Brown had declared that if Ripp was not a serial killer, "I would say you need your intestinal indicators recalibrated."

It made sense to Dan that there comes a time in a cop's career when they become suspicious of everyone if they are not cautious. He had done everything he could to find the reason for his internal alarms to be sounding so loudly in the presence of a man who was a witness and who had absolutely no prior criminal record or police contact in his life. He concluded, "McCarthy, you have been working the night shift for too long. Everybody is not a bad guy!" That being decided, he tucked the memory of William Ripp on the top shelf in the back row of his long term memory bank.

McCarthy had arrived early at lineup and was reading a book he had ordered written by the Sun Tzu of police tactics, Chuck Remsberg. He had Remsberg's entire *Street Survival* series and now was just finishing the first chapter in Remsberg's fourth book, *Blood Lessons.* In the very first chapter an officer from Sheboygan, Wisconsin was searching a garage and discovered a man who had hung his wife by the wrists from the rafters. The husband was in the process of torturing and killing her. The man began stabbing his wife, and the officer arrived just in time to shoot the fiend and save the wife. It happened just across the state from

La Claire. Sheboygan was smaller than La Claire. He thought, "Everything happens everywhere."

Carpenter came in as McCarthy was closing the book on the first chapter. "Wassup, Dyno," said Carpenter.

"Did you ever hear about a shooting in Sheboygan, where the guy was torturing his wife while she hung from some God-awful rafters in a garage, and a Sheboygan copper arrived in the nick of time and gunned down the guy righteously while he was stabbing her?" asked McCarthy.

"No. Sounds like a movie I saw once. I didn't hear about anything like that happening in Sheboygan though," answered Carpenter.

"What happened in Sheboygan?" asked Maddy Brown, as she entered the room taking a sip out of her Big Gulp.

"Some Sheboygan copper shot a husband who was stabbing his wife," said Carpenter, "McCarthy's reading books again. I'm waiting for the movie."

"Hey Carp, if they write a book about you, will you read the book?" asked Maddy.

"Nah, I'll probably wait for the movie then too. I'll take you, Maddy, but you might have to bring your ID, because it will have to be a **Hard R** to catch my essence," declared Carpenter.

"Yeah, I caught your essence when I came in the room. Carp, I would suggest you upgrade from the Old Spice, my friend. It makes the station smell like a nursing home, no offense," said Maddy.

"None taken, but you can't argue with success. Ladies of all ages find my musk irresistible. It breaks their heart that I am spoken for. Since I am married, I should either dial down the mojo, or cheese it with the Old Spice. They make a deadly combination," said Carp, running his comb through his hair.

"Anyway, getting back to the book, what are you reading there, Dyno?" asked Maddy.

"*Blood Lessons*," said McCarthy, holding up the book. "It's written by Chuck Remsberg and it's filled with true police stories. My question is how come this thing happens in Sheboygan,

Wisconsin, not two hundred miles from here in our own state, and we don't hear a thing about it. Something like that should be national news."

"Nah. It would only be national news if the cop would have missed the bad guy and shot the wife or the next door neighbor's Shih Tzu," reasoned Carpenter.

"Who's got shit on their shoe?" asked Stanley Brockman as he entered the lineup room.

"Not shit on their shoe, Shih Tzu. It's a dog," said Carpenter. "Fuckin' A, Stanley," added Carpenter shaking his head as he opened the sports section of the La Claire Leader.

"Well, it seems to me that if everybody knows Rodney King's name they should know the name of this cop that saved the lady. A cop makes a mistake or even appears to have made a mistake and it makes national news. A cop does something heroic and no one ever hears about it," said McCarthy slipping the book into his 10-4 official police duty bag.

"McCarthy, if you said that with a little more feeling and used the term fucking assholes, you would sound like me," said Stanley Brockman proudly. "I guess I've trained you well, grasshopper."

"Well, I don't always agree with you, Stanley, my friend, but I never said you were always wrong," declared McCarthy.

"Well, I'm not. In fact sometimes I'm fucking brilliant!" said Stanley with a brilliant un-Stanley-like smile.

"Stanley, did you get laid or something?" asked Maddy Brown.

Stanley turned red and began pulling his notebook out of his duty bag. He opened it and took out his pen, preparing to take diligent notes. Stanley never took diligent notes so everyone turned their attention to Stanley.

"Fuckin' A," proclaimed Carpenter, "Stanley got laid!"

Then Stanley tossed down the pen and stopped the charade, "Fucking way better than laid."

"Stanley, you're using vulgar prose," said McCarthy.

"That's part of it. Sandy says that if I get grief from you guys in my effort to improve my vocabulary to tell her about it and that she would…" he looked down, turned even redder, and shook his head.

"Come on, Stanley, give it up," laughed Madison.

"Yeah, Stanley, we're your bros. You can tell us anything," prodded Carpenter.

"OK. Here's the deal. McCarthy, you know how Victoria makes you that unbelievable lasagna on your birthday?" asked Brockman.

"Yeah," answered McCarthy.

"Well, Sandy gives me a little something special every birthday and anniversary, and it ain't lasagna if you know what I mean," said Brockman curving one eye brow halfway up his forehead.

"Birthday and anniversary?" said McCarthy. "I only get the lasagna once a year."

"That's what I'm saying," said Brockman. "My birthday comes ten maybe twenty times a year if I fucking play it right and you assholes give me grief once in a fucking while," answered Brockman.

"Fucking assholes? Stanley, it sounds like you have had a major relapse. At this rate you aren't going to be celebrating your birthday even once a year," said Dooley, who had quietly entered the room listening with delight and felt the time was right for his learn-ed input.

"No, that's what I'm saying. It has to be a struggle. Even if I was good every day, I wouldn't get my birthday present every day. I have to falter and continue to maintain a maximum effort. If she sees it is a struggle for me, then the rewards will continue. I can maybe play this card for years. I can have 10, no 20 birthdays a year, and no man gets tired of," he paused, looked at Madison Brown, cleared his throat and said, "lasagna."

"Lasagna?" said McCarthy, "Stanley Brockman, you are a work of art."

"I am a regular moaning fuckin' Lisa," said Brockman putting his feet up on the empty chair next to him.

Everyone laughed. Darnell entered the room to give lineup.

McCarthy looked around the room. Darnell did not say a word, but somehow he sucked the cheer right out of the entire shift. "God, please bring Sergeant Dave Compton back to us soon," thought McCarthy. The thought was almost so fervent it may have been mistaken in heaven for a prayer, *a prayer for David Compton.*

CHAPTER ELEVEN

I Must Have Her Tonight

Ripp hunkered in the shadows of the RUMP as Darla spun round and round from the shiny silver pole at center stage. She was wearing nothing but a light layer of body oil that made her shimmer like the Hope Diamond under a crystal chandelier. She was dancing, twirling, and gliding nude across the stage as Lionel Ritchie sang "Lady."

Ripp could not believe such a beauty as this would waste her talents on a seedy stage surrounded by men such as these. Whenever Ripp's sub-human nature led him into a crowd of people who he thought were below his dignity, he never looked at himself as a resident of the subculture he was occupying. He thought of them as being graced by his presence. Ripp never looked at his killing nature as sub-human. He viewed it as a being god-like—not the loving God most people pray to each night but the kind of gods ancient peoples worshiped like Thor, Odin, Neptune, or Zeus. He looked at himself as if he was a vengeful, life giving and like taking god. He gave Noah the gift of life and Noah did not even know it. He took Isaac's life and he felt the power of the "God Ripp."

Now he was drawn to Darla, who seemed to be dancing for him, just him. He had become god-like to her, and she was totally unaware of his presence. He was the master of her destiny, and she did not know his name. He felt incredible power in that thought.

Her long brown hair floated through the air in the breeze created by her own movement. Her arms and legs were sinewy from the years of dancing. Her limbs were long, light, and lithe like those of a gazelle. Her breasts were large with prominent brown nipples that were taut from the excitement of 100 eyes caressing them. In a time when it was in vogue to shave, she had her pubic mound trimmed neatly in the shape of a heart. She was indeed a natural brunette. She appeared to be the perfect visual aid for the song "Lady." Every bit of her was a woman, and her entire body appeared to be in an erotic state of arousal.

"My God, this woman is so alluring. I must have her," thought Ripp. The thought came so clear to him, he looked about, worried he might have said it out loud. No one near or far in the room looked at anyone, nor anything other than Darla. The bartender was even transfixed by this beauty. She had seemingly been torn from the pages of some ancient text, such as *The Arabian Knights* or, quite possibly, *The Kama Sutra*. She was the essence of sexuality put to music.

One set a night, Darla would not cater to the patrons trying to draw her to them with ones, fives, tens, twenties, and occasionally more. She would just dance. Ironically, at the end of the dance there would be more bills on stage than any other set because bill after bill, bribe after bribe were thrown to the stage urgently bidding her to invade their personal space with her personal spaces.

As the song ended, she gracefully lowered herself to the floor of the stage, and the bartender pushed a button. Rose petals floated and fluttered down upon her from above. "Rose petals? Darla would make the rose wither in shame if one tried to match her beauty. I must have her!" whispered Ripp, almost overcome in his passion. It was a passion that he rarely could control. He stood up, bumping his table, and clapped causing everyone in the room to stand up and clap. If ever a stripper deserved a standing ovation, Darla did. It was not the norm in strip clubs, but this performance was truly remarkable to behold. Darla was moved by the sentiment to stand and curtsy, as if she was acknowledging the applause at a command performance to the queen. She waved, blew kisses to all parts of the room, waved one more time, and retired to her dressing room.

Ripp sat down slowly and sat quietly for less than a minute. He then stood up and walked out of the RUMP with one booming thought, feeling, emotion, and desire clouding his consciousness. *"I must have her tonight!"*

CHAPTER TWELVE

ALL THREE

McCarthy and Carpenter had just cleared from the station after releasing an intoxicated driver to his wife. The man and wife reminded McCarthy of Fred and Ethel from *I Love Lucy*. He was a gruff grouchy old grizzly bear all during the arrest process, but when his wife, "Ethel," showed up with her icy glare and her hair in curlers he melted into a teddy bear. "I'm shorry shweetheart. It won't happen again. How 'bout some kishes shweetheart. Don't be mad… please."

Her answer was, "You're darn right it won't happen again. I am tired of your Shenanigans. Kishes? Get out to the car, before I give you the kishes you deserve right here in the police station. You want kishes after these shenanigans. I think not!"

McCarthy laughed. No one used the word shenanigans any more. He found the word added to the unmistakable charm of this couple.

As they were hitting the streets again McCarthy asked Carpenter, "Who did those two remind you of from TV?"

"The Mertzs, you know, Fred and Ethel from *I Love Lucy*," said Carpenter certain of his answer.

"You are so right. I almost laughed at one of those times where it could be explained but would have been so wrong to laugh that our Mertzs would have made a complaint," observed McCarthy.

"All units, is anyone close to Division Street?"

"255, we are at Fourth and Division," reported McCarthy.

"There are three males in a black Tahoe that just left the Marriott Hotel. Security contacted us because the three of them had kicked the taillights out of a vehicle that was parked too close to them. When the security guard tried to get them to stay, the driver beat him up and they drove off. They should be coming right at you."

Just then headlights turned off Second Street onto Division, coming from the area of the Marriott Hotel and came right toward the squad. As the black Tahoe passed, it was apparent that the driver had drunk his share, his passengers' share, and quite possibly two or three strangers' share that night. McCarthy hit the lights as the vehicle passed and the car pulled over right at the intersection of Fifth and Division.

As McCarthy walked up and made contact with the driver, the driver turned dully toward McCarthy and said, "I can walk home from here if you want me to." The driver looked puzzled, confused, and just plain drunk. It became apparent why the driver drove when McCarthy saw the passengers. As intoxicated as the driver was, he was probably the closest to sober as anyone in the vehicle. The radio in the Tahoe was blasting Ted Nugent's "Cat Scratch Fever" while the man in the middle was on air drum and the man on the passenger side was playing air bass.

McCarthy said to the driver, "Sir, could you turn the vehicle off and hand me your keys please?"

The driver did not hesitate. He turned off the Tahoe, removed the keys from the ignition with a couple extra tugs, and then handed McCarthy the keys. McCarthy could see that the driver's knuckles were bloodied, and Dan thought, "Probable Cause." There was no doubt that these were the guys who had been described by the security guard. He radioed dispatch, "255. We have the vehicle stopped at Fifth and Division. Send a back up since we will most likely be arresting *all three*."

CHAPTER THIRTEEN

BLACK HOLE

As Darla walked to her car, she was talking and giggling with two other exotic dancers who had been working the RUMPelstiltskin for two weeks. They were road girls who toured the country as a dance team called Sugar and Spice.

The two ladies were a very popular draw at the RUMP. They were a mathematical phenomenon. If the amount a man loved watching one beautiful woman dancing naked on a stage could be quantified and then compared to the measurement of how that same man loved watching two beautiful nude women dancing together on a stage, the number would be much higher than twice the original calculation.

"This is nice of you to give us a ride to the hotel," said Sugar.

"It's really nice. Usually we have to take a cab," added Spice.

"I know what it's like to be on the road, living out of a suitcase with your whole show packed in a trunk. I've been there," said Darla, digging in her purse for her keys. "Here they are. I have to clean this purse," Darla said showing her keys to make her point.

"How long have you had this gig?" Sugar asked.

"I've been dancing here for about three and a half years."

"Three and a half years dancing in one place. Wow! That has to be some kind of record. Sounds like heaven," said Spice in amazement.

"Do you have any boyfriends? Usually in the long term gigs the dancers I have known are sleeping with the boss, no offense," observed Spice as she slid into the back seat of Darla's Subaru Legacy and buckled the seat belt.

"No, I'm not sleeping with the boss and I have no boyfriend. I tried that once, you know, finding a boyfriend in the club, and it didn't play out well," explained Darla.

"If you don't mind my asking, what happened?" asked Spice, "Mind if I smoke?" she added, pulling out a pack of Marlboros.

"No, I don't mind you asking, but I'd rather you didn't smoke. Thanks," said Darla.

Spice shrugged and put the cigarettes back in her purse.

"The guy seemed like a great guy. He was always in the money, good looking, and treated me like a queen. We had incredible sex and said he loved me," shared Darla.

"Sounds perfect," said Spice.

"Too perfect," agreed Sugar.

"Yeah, it was. He is sitting in prison right now. It was all an illusion. After that, I swore off dating the customers. The money is good and I am saving quite a bit. I plan on working two more years and then moving somewhere out of here and opening a dance studio. That's what I plan on doing. I love dance and I think I could teach some day. I picture myself in a large room with mirrored walls and hardwood floors filled with little girls in their tutus wobbling about on the tippy-toes," Darla said with a smile. "I hope it's not just a pipe dream."

"I don't think it's a pipe dream. You're a professional dancer. When you get paid to do something that makes you a pro," said Sugar, picking up the hint of uncertainty in Darla's voice. "A girl's got to have her dreams."

"I would say so. Anyone who can hold an audience's attention in one place for three and a half years, who's not fucking the boss, has to be a dancer," said Spice.

As Darla pulled out of the parking lot to the rear of the RUMP, she scanned the area as she always did. Darla was acutely aware of the fact that being a fixture in the exotic dance business here in La Claire meant she had attracted some fans who had grown to love her too much in a less than healthy way. She had been receiving some unsigned notes, flowers, and some graphic art work.

Attracting a kook-following was one of the less sought after perks of "the business." Sometimes they would shower a dancer with cash during the performance and that was OK. Sometimes they would send gifts and that was OK. There were some that became outwardly enthusiastic in their affection. Some were just zealots in their adoration, but there had been some who gradually crossed over into the category of "stalker." She always scanned the area when she left each night. Darla loved taking the traveling talent to their hotel because then she did not have to leave the place alone after bar time.

Tonight her antenna went up as always, and her heart raced as she saw a dark sedan parked at the far end of the alley. Its driver pulled out as she did and began following her. At first the driver had his lights out, but after turning onto River Street the driver hit his lights.

"Girls, we are being followed," Darla said.

"Are you sure?" asked Sugar and Spice snapping their heads around.

"I am sure. That black car behind us had its lights out and left when we did. I am going to make some turns to see if he follows," said Darla making a sudden right turn.

The driver of the black car turned right. Darla then turned left into the next alley and the driver of the black car followed and accelerated, aggressively gaining ground.

Darla reached the end of the alley and stopped, but the driver did not. The driver continued and deliberately hit her car. Darla's passengers screamed. It was apparent that this collision was no accident. Darla hit the gas. "We're getting out of here. I am going to try to make it to the police station. It is about one mile from here."

Darla turned out of the alley left and the driver of the black car cut the corner sharper and hit her again on the left front corner of the Subaru, blocking her exit. Darla could see the face of the leering driver. She recognized it as one of the men in the front row who had tried so hard tonight to bring her in closer during her performance. The face of this man looked lustful, maniacal — the face of a killer. Darla could no longer hear the screaming of Sugar and Spice. The only thing that Darla could think of was her own survival.

She rammed the stick into reverse and did an incredible straight line backing maneuver as if she had been stunt driving all her life. She reached the next intersection and spun the car north. The suddenness of the maneuver caught the driver of the black car unaware. The flustered pursuer had to orchestrate an awkward Y-turn and he lost ground but did not loose the desire to have these women tonight.

Darla was heading away from the police department now, but she sensed that if she could make it to Division Street and turn she could lose this guy. She watched the rear view mirror after she managed to hold her little Legacy through the turn and saw that the driver was still in pursuit. Then she saw the lights. "Look!" Darla shouted enthusiastically. "They always say there is never a cop around when you need them, well look, cops!"

The two out-of-towners became ecstatic and turned toward their persistent pursuer and began to sing, "Bad boy, bad boy, what you going to do, what you going to do when they come for you?"

Carpenter was entertaining the two passengers of the Tahoe while McCarthy was walking the staggering driver to the sidewalk with the intent of running him through some field tests when they both heard the incredible squeal of tires. All five of them could not help but look in awe at the Subaru, seemingly on two wheels, coming around the corner on Division about seven blocks up. It was followed by another car making the corner in an identical manner as if they were playing a very dangerous game of "follow the leader" with cars.

Then it was a straight-on race, apparently to beat each other to the cops. Darla was the only driver whose finish line was the police car. The man in the black car could only see the object of his affection: the contents of the Subaru. He did not see the squad car until Darla skidded to a stop in front of it. Darla jumped out and yelled to Carpenter and McCarthy, "He's trying to kill us!"

The driver of the black vehicle slid to a stop and was shocked. "What the fuck? Where the fuck did the cops come from?" He then backed up and turned north on Fifth Street and fled.

McCarthy yelled to the females and the driver of the Tahoe, "Stay here!"

McCarthy and Carpenter immediately hopped into their squad car and were instantly pursuing the driver of the black car. "255." McCarthy said into the mic.

"255, go ahead," said dispatch expecting a check for wants and warrants on the occupants of the Tahoe.

"255, we have a 10-80 (high speed pursuit) with a black sedan northbound on Fifth. It is unrelated to our stop. Have the unit that was going to back us up continue to Fifth and Division. Have them stand by with the Tahoe if it is still there. There now is a Subaru with three ladies in it. They are the complainants in reference to this pursuit. They state that driver we are pursuing tried to kill them," said McCarthy, handing the mic to Carpenter, suddenly remembering he had a partner.

The driver of the black sedan turned east then north and, again, east then north cutting a stair-step pattern through the city. Suddenly the brake lights came on hard and the driver skidded to a stop. The door swung open wildly and the driver was running.

"255, we are in foot pursuit east bound in the 700 block of Evers Street, cutting through yards, mid-block."

McCarthy and Carpenter were both running at a dead sprint. Carpenter was in the lead as the driver ducked between houses and through yards. When McCarthy saw he was heading for the alley, he decided to guess on the direction. Most people choose to cut right so McCarthy headed the opposite way around the garage to the right, while Carpenter stayed in direct pursuit. McCarthy thought, "I'll cut him off. He will run right into me."

As McCarthy rounded the garage cutting into the alley, he could hear the thud and long scraping sound of Carpenter impacting on the suspect and the suspect's body scraping into the gravel alley. He would not need to cut off the driver. McCarthy saw the bodies sliding to a stop in the cloud of dust and he quickly scrambled to the opposite side of Carpenter and within seconds the squirming, frantic suspect was handcuffed.

"You hurt?" asked Carpenter of the suspect.

"Fuck you. I want to see my attorney," snapped the man, whose face was covered with a white powdery dust. The alley had just been graveled, and it was covered with the clean, white rocky layer that precedes the laying of the asphalt. Carpenter and the suspect had a pale white layer of dust covering them that made them look as if they had just spent a week wandering about the Mohave Desert.

As Dan and Gary pulled their squad back to Fifth and Division, they were pleasantly shocked to see that not only were the three attractive dancers still there but also still hanging about were the three Marriott Maulers, who stuck around to be arrested. As it turned out, it became clear in their dulled state they had forgotten the possible impending arrest and could only see three strippers that seemed perfectly happy not to be driven away by their immature drunken boorishness.

McCarthy remembered one other obstacle to their escape, "I still have their keys," he said out loud.

Dan did not waste anytime. He went to his SWAT duty bag and found as many pre-prepared flex-cuffs as he could shove into the side pockets of his tactical pants. He had all three men sit on the curb and place their hands behind their back. Carpenter stood by as the cover officer while McCarthy handcuffed each one.

Carpenter called in, "255, we have four to transport now 10-95 (in custody). Send us two more squads, please," requested Carpenter.

"10-4. I am trying to get someone to you, but most everyone is tied up. I am trying to keep your situation straight; can you itemize what you have there." Melissa the dispatcher shook her head after that transmission and said out loud to herself, "Itemize? There's a word I don't use very often."

As Carpenter was about to explain, there suddenly arose a squealing of tires from the alley in the 400 block of Division and then a continuous crashing and clanging, corresponding with an engine racing after the metallic sounding impacts. It was the sound that usually follows the statement, "Gentleman start your engines," at the start of the Indy 500.

"Standby," said Carpenter, "They're still coming."

Suddenly the alley spit out a gray Ford Taurus like a good old southern boy would spit out a watermelon seed in a down-home seed-spitting contest, and the car instantly crossed the street, jumped a curb, and smashed to an abrupt stop against a large tree adjacent to the alley. Two heads inside the car snapped forward, then back, then forward again as McCarthy ran toward the vehicle, instinctively. Carpenter stayed and covered the one under arrest in their squad and the three under arrest seated on the curb.

Dooley was just turning the corner off Fourth onto Division and saw the alley spit out the Taurus. He immediately hit his lights and pulled into position behind the Taurus. Dooley radioed dispatch, "I'm 10-23 (on the scene), and a gray Taurus just smashed into a tree in mid-block on Division Street. I will be assisting 255."

"10-4?" Melissa answered in a puzzled voice. "What the...?" she asked no one.

As McCarthy reached the passenger's side of the Taurus, he noticed both the driver and the passenger were laughing hysterically. Amazed, McCarthy thought once again, "Only a drunk could walk away from a crash like that without a scratch, a couple of Gumbys." As his light flashed the interior of the car, he saw the revolver lying on the floor between the feet of the passenger, a drunken spiked-hair Gothic, with more piercing then a Nez Perce War Chief.

The driver was identically attired. They looked like Gothic twins, disowned by their mother after an incredibly painful delivery. McCarthy shouted, "Gun! Let me see your hands." Both drivers stopped laughing and first realized that they were flanked by cops and the car they were sitting in had been stolen and smashed by them. They sheepishly put up their hands and then each slid out of the car to their bellies where McCarthy slipped another set of flex-cuffs on the passenger. The driver had no firearms, but Dooley pulled a set of "numchucks" out of the Gothic's back pocket and showed them to McCarthy, who nodded. The Gothic said, "I know how to use them. Take these handcuffs off and I will show you."

"Maybe some other time," said Dooley in his usual amiable manner.

By the time the Gothic twins were handcuffed, Maddy Brown, Jim Hartley, Stanley Brockman, and Michael Shepherd arrived on the scene, and the normally quiet neighborhood was lit up like Macy's the day after Thanksgiving.

"Hey, Dyno, are you having a blue light special again?" asked Dooley. "You know we get enough business as it is without you advertising."

"You know, we have never had to spend a cent on advertising. Our business is 100% word of mouth," said McCarthy.

After each prisoner was tucked away in the cars of Dooley, Brown, Brockman, Hartley, Shepherd and one was stored upright in McCarthy's car, the entire night shift of La Claire had a parley in the middle of Division Street. "We need some help on this one guys," said McCarthy

"Fuckin' A," agreed Carpenter with a big nod in agreement.

"I'd say you bagged your limit tonight," observed Dooley. "Who takes what?"

"Carpenter has the guy in the chase. He will take that one. It's a possible attempted homicide."

"Yeah, I have to get statements from the ladies. They are heading to the station, and I'll sort out what happened there. We have plenty to hold him. He fled, he's wanted on an outstanding stalking warrant, and his license is revoked. It sounds like we will have other charges after talking to the ladies. His car is filled with a variety of porn magazines and a plethora of wadded tissues that I'm going to need a volunteer to un-wad and check for

DNA," said Carpenter with a smile. "Are there any volunteers? Come on, anybody?"

"Listen!" asserted Stanley Brockman, "I don't think un-wad is a word, dick-wad, and even if it is, plethora is a word that should be neither uttered nor muttered by cops. It's not a cop word," explained Brockman. "How about you, Shep? The guy is chasing strippers so that means chances are he likes girls. That means he isn't one of those Mississippi muddy-wadders," Stanley laughed hard at his own joke.

"No thanks," said Shep shaking his head not having a clue as to what Brockman was laughing at.

After Stanley recovered from his own wit he asked, "What did the Goth in my car do?'

"He was the passenger in the car that smashed against the tree. It is stolen, so he should be jailed for being a party to a crime to auto theft, and he had a fully loaded Ruger revolver between his legs, so he should be jailed for carrying a concealed weapon. If you can lock him up and get a statement from him, I can write the report," said McCarthy.

"Check," said Stanley. "I get an arrest and no report, the perfect crime. I'll be leaving you ladies and gentleman to figure out the rest. I believe my plate is full." Stanley then got away while the getting was good.

"I'll take the Goth I got in my car, "explained Dooley. He is intoxicated. I will handle the DWI and write up the stolen, because I saw him driving too. How's that sound?"

"Great," answered Dyno.

"Fuckin' A. Two thumbs up with me. Spread the wealth, I always say," answered Gary.

"Shep has the original guy from the hotel that battered the security guard. I'll take him on the battery, and he is also intoxicated so I will handle the DWI," said McCarthy.

"Maddy and Jim, you each have one of his two passengers in your cars. Can you lock them for criminal damage to property and disorderly conduct for kicking out the taillights of the car at the Marriott?" asked McCarthy.

"Can do," said Hartley.

Maddy added, "I'll get a statement from the security guard."

"I think this could be considered the proverbial cluster fuck," said McCarthy.

"It was, but I would have to say we just un-fucked it," said Maddy Brown. "I don't think even Compton could have handled it better," beamed Maddy showing her dimples that always seemed out of place at the scene of carnage and confusion, but even so they were always a welcome sight.

"That's a reach," said McCarthy incredulously.

"OK, better than Darnell," laughed Maddy.

"Handled better than Darnell? I'll give you that," answered McCarthy.

As the last squad and the last wrecker pulled away from the scene, a lone figure sat quietly less than one block away peering through his small set of opera glasses watching. He sighed. "That was absolutely amazing. What a rush! If I would have tried to take Darla tonight, I would be either dead or on my way to jail. This town is like a black hole for criminals. I have never seen anything like it. These guys are like some sort of crime magnets," thought Ripp seated comfortably in his Lexus. For the second time in his life and for the second time in two nights, he was once again a witness. For the second time in two nights he was once again an unfulfilled killer. He felt disappointed but exhilarated.

"What a rush, though. Being this close to the victim and this close to being a victim is such an incredible turn on." He set down his binoculars. He undid his pants, tight from the pressure. He closed his eyes and pictured all the sights he had seen tonight without being apprehended. He had seen it all and gone un-noticed. In his mind's eye he pictured Darla dancing before him, twirling about the stage, a naked private dancer. He pictured what might have been with Darla and her two friends, a splendid Trifecta. He pictured the careening cars, the guns, the lights, the chaos, and he pleasured himself to a crescendo and then release. He was caught unprepared.

As William Ripp reached into his glove compartment and found some napkins to clean himself, he thought, "That's two close calls in this town. It is an omen. I shouldn't be here. It's too dangerous. I'm getting out of here now! La Claire looks like some sort of bizarre trap for criminals. I have never seen so many arrests in my whole life as I have since I came to this town. This cannot be a simple coincidence. I am going to get out of here before I get sucked into their strange vortex... their *black hole.*"

CHAPTER FOURTEEN

THE BEST THERE EVER WAS

It had been nearly seven months since Sergeant David Compton's gun fight with Bryce Packwood in the parking lot of Wal-Mart. He had undergone a series of operations big and small since he had been shot and slashed by Bryce Packwood. It had been the longest and slowest seven months of his life. Some days the sun seemed to go backwards as the waves of pain came and went. Other days were filled with relentless boredom sitting in his sun room listening to the loud tick, followed each time by the distinct tock, of the grandfather clock he had made himself. In another time in his life, he committed the sin of pride whenever he mentioned that he had made the clock. Now he wished he could justify taking a sledge hammer to it.

The countless surgeries were performed by orthopedic surgeons, neurosurgeons, and plastic surgeons to repair, replace, and reconnect. Initially, when Compton asked, "When will I be able to return to duty?" one doctor answered coldly, "First, you are lucky to be alive. Second, you are lucky to still have your right arm at all, and third, you will be lucky to achieve about 75 percent back in that arm with extensive rehabilitation. I would consider retirement if I were you since you are old enough."

Compton's response was, "We'll see about that." Compton set his GPS on a recovery and steered a course toward the goal, which was barely visible on the far horizon. He showed grit before, during, and after each surgery and gutted out an incredibly painful rehabilitation regimen. He told his physical therapist, "I may retire, but I am going back to work first. There will be no discussion about that."

Dave Compton sat in his all weather room with a book open but face down on his lap. Compton had his feet up with his recliner leaning back, and he was watching the water drip from a large icicle hanging from a birch tree in the back yard.

Carpenter and McCarthy entered the room. They had not even knocked because Compton had told them to just let themselves in months ago as they began their weekly visits. Dave Compton's expression lit up as they entered. "Can I get you guys something?" Compton asked. "Would you like a beer or some soda?"

"A Pepsi or Mountain Dew," asked McCarthy, "if it's not too much trouble?"

"No trouble," replied Dave, opening a small refrigerator he had next to his chair containing enough beer, soda, sandwiches, and venison sausage to keep a Marine alive for a year. Compton snatched a cold Mountain Dew and with his left hand tossed it to McCarthy.

"Thanks, Sergeant," answered McCarthy.

"Same here, just soda," said Carpenter. "We have to work tonight."

Compton reached into the small refrigerator door and pulled another Dew and threw it to Carpenter.

They each opened their Dew, preparing for the overflow caused by the flight across the room. The fizz was anticipated and sucked up by each of them with a laugh.

"How are things on shift? Are you guys missing me?"""

"You wouldn't believe it. Where do I start? First the answer is yes, we are missing you. Your replacement, Sergeant Darnell is... well Joe Darnell hates working on the night shift. It's a trickle down kind of hate, so in turn he hates us. He hates police work, and it is miserable to work for a guy who is supposed to instill enthusiasm in you and he hates what we do," said Carpenter starting slowly, but finishing with a flourish.

"Granted, he has had big shoes to fill. We always say, 'He is no Dave Compton.' Everybody wonders when you are coming back. Everyone on shift hopes that it will be soon. We don't want to rush your recovery, but we all miss you. It's not the same without you."

"Well I can tell you the doctor has been encouraged by my progress. Initially they were ready to write me off. They were saying, 'You're old enough, just retire.' Now they are looking at letting me come back to light duty soon." Compton was as cheered by the words as Carpenter and McCarthy. "I cannot tell you when, but I believe soon."

"I hope you don't think we came over to pump you about your retirement plans," said McCarthy.

"To tell you the truth, Alice and I were talking about me pulling the pin before, before... well, you know, and then it happened, but I don't want the likes of Bryce Packwood to put me out of my career. Fuck him! That's not going to happen."

"So we're going to get you back?" asked McCarthy with a hopeful tenor to his voice.

"If it is up to me, yes, but I have to get the OK from the doctor. I'm telling you, I know how Brett Favre felt when he faced the decision," said Dave Compton. "When you are used to action and then you find yourself thrust into a position where you are watching soap operas and game shows... well I am not ready for that, boys."

"Don't get us started on Brett Favre's retirement," said McCarthy. "That's one of the three things that can get you in a fight in Wisconsin: politics, religion, and Brett Favre's retirement."

"Don't forget Harleys versus Hondas," added Carpenter.

"Oh yeah, four things," agreed Dan, holding up four fingers to emphasize the point.

"Ain't that the truth," said Compton, tearing open a pack of beer sausages and offering them to Carpenter and McCarthy, who each eagerly took one.

"If I were to retire, I'm curious, how are you two sitting on the sergeant's list?" asked Compton. "They just had a test and interview, and a little bird told me you two are sitting in a pretty good position," said Compton.

"Yeah, we didn't do so badly at all. McCarthy is number one on the list, I am number two, and Dooley is number three. Brockman took the test, too, and he is number four," said Carpenter.

"Who is number five?" asked Compton. "The chief has to select from the top five on the list."

"Seth Johnson," said Carpenter, "retired Chief Ray Johnson's boy. He spent his field training period on patrol and was then moved into DARE (Drug Abuse Resistance Education). He writes a good test, gives a good interview, but he has almost no street experience," said Carpenter.

"Common sense would tell you he doesn't have a chance at a third shift sergeant's position," reasoned McCarthy.

"Common sense is a misnomer. It is not that common, Dyno," said Compton. "Seth Johnson also has a master's degree. The brass loves a degree. It pulls more weight than street time every time. You have prepared for your promotion, but I am going to tell you both, prepare yourselves to not be promoted. If it doesn't happen this time or the next or even after that, stay positive in your attitude. Stay consistent in your efforts on the street, and stay persistent in the process," cautioned Compton. "I hate to jinks you, but there is one more thing I should tell you."

"What's that?" asked Carpenter.

"Like I said, I don't want to jinks you," cautioned Compton.

"I don't believe in that shit," said Carpenter.

"I don't know if I believe in it or not, but you have to tell us now," urged Dan.

"OK, but don't say I didn't warn you. You two need to avoid any aw shits."

"Aw shits?" asked Carpenter.

"Yeah aw shits, wrong moves, dumb calls, major run scoring errors, fumbles on the goal line, missed pucks in overtime, and generally avoid any unfortunate calamities befalling you. You know… aw shits. One aw shit wipes out 1000 atta-boys. Dat's a Fact Jack!"

"Got it! Avoid the accumulation of even one aw-shit," declared Gary.

"One more thing. Only one person can get promoted. Don't let a promotion ruin a friendship," Compton stressed, gesturing emphatically with his half eaten beer sausage.

"Never!" they both responded.

"Sergeant Compton, we don't want you to retire. We want you back. If you do decide to retire though, I don't think I would get any argument from anyone on the department that as far as sergeants go, hell as far as cops go, you are the best there ever was," said Dan McCarthy quietly to stress the point.

Compton looked down and away and brought his hand up and rubbed something from his eye.

Carpenter quietly agreed, "Fuckin' A."

McCarthy repeated the sentiment one more time in almost a whisper, "... *the best there ever was.*"

CHAPTER FIFTEEN
Aw Shit

It was late March in Wisconsin. Morning had broken with the warm sun rising to a winter scene. Trees were barren stick figures starting to show the nubbins of the spring buds to come. The ground was still covered with a heavy blanket of the season's snow. By day's end the unseasonable warmth had done its worse to the trappings of winter. The white shroud had given ground to winter's casualty, the brown grass. The grass was sprinkled with the dingy brown, yellow, and orange wilted leaves that had been blown into their final resting place by the winds of fall. The warmth in the air was the promise of spring about to replace the fallen leaves and revive the dormant grass for another season of picnics, baseball, and mowing.

McCarthy had stowed his leather jacket in the trunk of the squad and was patrolling in long sleeves for the first time since November. It had been a cold heartless winter. He personally worked one hanging and two shotgun suicides, which some attribute to what is often called cabin fever. Cabin fever is the informal name given to a state of morose and emotional distress attributed to long months of short cold days, long cold nights, and minimal exposure to the warmth of sunshine. McCarthy believed in the deadly legacy of cabin fever having personally witnessed its sometimes staggering body count.

Tonight, McCarthy and Carpenter were scheduled together in a trouble car. They would handle anything that required two cops for an initial response. They were also responsible to go out and find trouble before it started. It felt like a spring night, and the two partners were patrolling the city with their windows open. Both were thoroughly enjoying the change of weather. "What's that?" asked Carpenter rhetorically.

"That is a sure sign of spring," McCarthy answered.

"As sure as a robin, by God," Carpenter said.

"A crotch rocket with a license-applied-for plate and a driver wearing sunglasses at night for eye protection—he is saying with every fiber of his being, 'Stop me I'm not valid to drive.' Shall we?" asked McCarthy.

"Fuckin' A," said Carpenter as he the hit the lights. When the lights went on, the young inexperienced driver wobbled to the side of the road. "Yeah, he's a newbie for sure. He's having trouble controlling all that power between his legs."

"Yeah, and the motorcycle too," quipped Dan.

They pulled over the sixteen-year-old driver. The permit he held only authorized him to operate in the daytime. The youngster parked his motorcycle and was given a ticket and a ride home. The driver using sunglasses for eye protection at night was the perennial dead give away mistake that crotch rocket rookies made.

After dropping the newbie-biker at home, Carpenter and McCarthy turned onto Washington Avenue and saw a commotion ahead at the intersection of Washington and Miller. Traffic was stopped and people were running frantically in and about the intersection. Carpenter grabbed the mic, "255."

"255 go ahead," replied the dispatcher.

"We will be out at Washington and Miller. It appears that there is a possible accident there. Traffic is at a stand still and there are people out on foot in the intersection. We are going to be working our way up there to see what the problem is," reported Carpenter.

"10-4, 255, we are sending rescue in that direction. We are receiving reports of a very serious multiple pedestrian accident at that location. The striking vehicle involved has left the scene."

"10-4, we are 10-23 (at scene)," replied Carpenter.

The scene was beyond chaotic when the two officers arrived. Traffic was at a stand-still. There was a drunken idiot yelling, "I'm a paramedic! I'm a paramedic! I'm a paramedic!" as he staggered about flapping his arms as if the combination of the yelling and flapping could in itself save lives and possibly fly him to hell out of there, where he was useless to everyone anyway.

As Carpenter and McCarthy arrived at the scene of the tragedy in the middle of the intersection, they could not help but notice that there were two things spread all over the intersection. The first thing they noticed were dozens of fresh donuts. There were donuts with sprinkles, chocolate donuts, coconut donuts, strawberry donuts, and frosted donuts.

Lying in the midst of the abandoned baked goods were three college-aged victims, struggling to hold onto their lives. McCarthy and Carpenter did a quick triage on the three. The first one McCarthy checked was hit so hard that she was clearly gone and no one was going to bring her back. She looked like a little girl's pretty new doll that had been twisted and broken by a very cruel big brother.

The second was unconscious but still breathing, and McCarthy assessed that she would make it to the hospital. The third young lady was not breathing, but Carpenter was able to open her airway with a jaw thrust technique. With a gasp she began breathing. "Two are breathing and one is not," said McCarthy.

They moved over to the young girl that was not breathing, and Carpenter immediately began mouth to mouth. McCarthy called dispatch, "We have three victims. Two are critical and need transport 10-33 (emergency). One is not breathing. We need a Technical Accident Investigator at the scene and two Cadets for Traffic Control."

Carpenter was calmly delivering breaths for the young victim, and Dan handed him a rescue mask while Carpenter continued without missing a breath after he sealed the mask on the girl.

At the same moment Dan handed Gary the mask, Dooley appeared, slid in beside them and began chest compressions on the female. McCarthy checked back with the other victims and saw they were holding their own, but both were still unconscious. He checked each one for signs of consciousness but found none. He felt a strong pulse and steady respirations on each and under the circumstances was satisfied with that.

All three girls were dressed prematurely in summer clothes, taking advantage of the warm day. The temperature had dropped about 20 degrees in the last hour and McCarthy put blankets on both victims that were not being worked on to minimize the possibility of shock. As he unfolded the second blanket and laid it over one of the sadly crumpled young women, Emergency Medical Services arrived on the scene and took over care of the victims. McCarthy marked their locations with chalk just before EMS began their calm but frantic efforts to save the ladies.

Dan looked about and saw one distressed young man in the crowd whose eyes seemed to be saying, "I wish I would not have seen what I have seen."

Dan walked to him and asked the obvious question, "Can you tell me what happened here?" This question apparently served to press the play button on this bystander.

"They are friends of mine. We were together. We had just gotten donuts at Donut-Land on that corner," as this was said he pointed emphatically at the corner of the intersection, where Donut-Land sat. Donut-Land was open 24 hours and did a brisk business every night when the college students were on their way home to campus after leaving the bars downtown.

"We were eating our donuts and waiting for the light to change. Heather, Kris, and Mary Ann were cold and in a hurry, so when the light changed for us they started across. They were in the crosswalk and cars had stopped. They almost made it across, but then I saw a big black car with no lights on heading northbound. I could see no fucking way was the car going to be able to stop at the red light and I screamed to the girls *Look Out!*" He screamed it again reliving the moment. His eyes were wide seeing the inevitability of the impact once again and his face reflected the sheer horror of the moment.

"The car hit them, and the driver never touched the brakes before or after she hit them. She hit all three of them so hard. Oh God, I can't believe they are still alive she hit them so hard. They flew into the air like-like-like... caps at graduation." The young friend then looked at Carpenter and Dooley working to bring back the young girl who had been hit the hardest and who had flown the farthest.

As the young man spoke, the EMS personnel in the second ambulance arrived and quickly replaced Dooley and Carpenter in the desperate rescue attempt.

Dooley stood up and watched his replacement for a moment. Carpenter stood up and wiped his face with his sleeve and then crossed himself silently, almost imperceptibly, after saying a quiet prayer for all three girls. Carpenter then quickly covered the distance between McCarthy and himself.

When Carpenter reached Dan, the witness was still pouring out information, proving that he was not only the girls' good friend but a great witness. "The car was a black, late model, full sized sedan with lights all the way across the back. It might have been a Lexus. I'm not sure. There was a young woman driving it, and there were no lights on it. The woman had long brown hair and she was going about 45-50 when she hit the girls. God, she hit them so hard. She hit them and just kept going north. I couldn't read the plate number. I'm sorry, but I tried. I can say it was a Wisconsin plate," said the witness.

The young man had his eyes on Carpenter when he walked up to McCarthy and after he finished he asked, "Are they going to be all right? Is Mary Ann going to be all right?" he asked bringing his hands together as if he was praying.

"They are doing everything they can do for her," answered Carpenter.

McCarthy radioed the description of the car to all units. The Cadets were in place and had prepared a detour for the traffic. EMS had loaded Mary Ann into an ambulance and headed for the hospital. The other two were being carefully secured to back boards and removed more cautiously since they were both breathing. EMS was trying to not make a bad situation worse.

"This is my beat. I'll take care of working the scene," said Dooley.

"Do you need us to help with anything?" Carpenter asked.

"Nah," said Dooley. "I have a Reserve with me tonight. He can hold the dumb end of the tape measure for me. The Cadets are taking care of traffic. Just write up the information you got from that witness and go find the black car that did this," said Dooley, who was the best team player on the shift. Dooley always knew his responsibility and did it. Dooley was as solid as a rock and just as tough. He was a tall muscular cop. His father was the sheriff and Dooley could have gotten a job with the Sheriff's Department, but he made his own way on the La Claire Police Department. People on his beat knew and loved Dooley about as much as a beat cop could be loved. They looked upon Dooley as if he was a neighbor with a gun and badge.

"You bet, Dooley. We'll find it," said Carpenter with determination in his voice. Try as he might, he could not bring Mary Ann back. No one would. No one could. Carpenter was determined to find the driver for Mary Ann.

One of the worst things a police officer has to do is spend the last moments of a person's life with them. The hardest of these moments are those spent with children and young people. They have their whole happy lives ahead of them, but then they are propelled into eternity too often by acts of stupidity and cruelty. When this happens, there is always a cop there left to fathom the avoidable loss of the young lives.

It seems to cops present at the passing of a soul that the time should be spent with a father, a mother, a sister, a brother, a priest, or a rabbi. All of these people would be more appropriate witnesses to the last breath exhaled, the last tear shed, the last word said. Instead, the person fighting to keep them in this world is a police officer. Carpenter and McCarthy always took opportunity to say a little prayer for the victim on their passing while simultaneously trying with all their might to hold them in this world.

There are some groups, small in number, who would chastise a policeman for saying a prayer over a citizen. They would scream, "That is a violation of Separation of Church and State!"

Any cop would tell them, "You folks can go to hell. If I cannot keep them in this world, I will try with all my might to properly send them on their way to the next." The only more deeply sincere prayer a cop may pray is the one that is said over his sleeping children at night after one of these many bad shifts.

After doing all that could be done at the scene, Carpenter turned to McCarthy and said, "Dyno, let's find this car."

McCarthy and Carpenter headed north. They worked their way by and through the parking lots of malls, taverns, hotels, side streets, and alleys. They scoured the city slowly, meticulously, randomly, specifically, in a pattern and in no pattern. They searched relentlessly for a Lexus or a black car that could be mistaken for a Lexus. They looked for green cars and midnight blue cars that might look black at night under the lighting at the intersection of Washington and Miller.

As McCarthy and Carpenter drove by an apartment complex with eight units, they checked the line of cars in the assigned parking spots. Then, just as they passed the driveway, Carpenter said, "Whoa," and in response McCarthy hit the brakes. Dan had almost driven right by it. It was parked between a large hedge and a dumpster for the complex. It was tonight's "holy grail," a black Lexus. No one would park a Lexus between a hedge and a dumpster unless they were trying to hide it.

McCarthy cut the lights and parked on the street. They circled the apartment complex on foot keeping to darker shades of night to see and yet remain unseen. They could not tell if the suspect was hidden within.

Given time, hit and run drivers routinely develop a fairy tale to tell police as to why they could not have been driving their own vehicle when it smashed into a car, a person, a fence, a tree, or whatever they hit. The most common tale to tell is the ever-popular "My car was stolen."

Some hit and run drivers will kill, cripple, and maim then flee while their victim's life bleeds out into a gutter, just to hide long enough to sober up. It is selfishness and a style of death that is oft repeated. One driver drove home with a seriously injured victim lodged in his windshield. The driver parked the car in his garage, and the victim, who could have been saved with proper medical care, was denied any treatment, comfort, liquid, or even nourishment. The victim bled to death lying in a bed of broken glass.

McCarthy and Carpenter were determined to bring justice to the person who rolled over three young women, who were gaily gossiping and enjoying such a harmless pleasure as eating freshly made donuts, and then left them lying broken and helpless on the asphalt in the middle of a busy intersection to possibly be run over again like a trio of road-kill raccoon.

Dan and Gary silently worked their way around both sides of the car and lit up the interior brighter than day with their surefire flashlights. The car was unoccupied and clean inside except for a mixed drink with melting ice still visible setting in the cup holder next to the driver's seat. To these modern day trackers, this was synonymous to the scout in the old western movies feeling the warmth of an extinguished camp fire and saying, "We are less than half hour behind them." The drink looked like a brandy old fashion sweet, if McCarthy was to guess, but he did not have to.

Both officers' flashlights scanned the hood of the large black harbinger of death. They knew instantly it was the object of their search because of the fabric impressions visible on the hood. Something or somebody had been dragged across the dust in the hood leaving it incredibly disturbed like a demented child attempted to finger paint in the light patina covering the surface of the car. Something or someone had rolled over the hood of this car. McCarthy and Carpenter both squatted in the front of the vehicle to check for further confirmation that they were looking at the black car which was their white whale. They blipped their flashlights on the grill and froze in place, temporarily aghast.

Stuck firmly in the grill was evidence nowhere near as fragile as the fabric impressions in the dust on the hood of the car but compelling evidence nonetheless that the object of their quest was sitting before them. There they were, the strawberry ones, chocolate, coconut, frosted and even one with sprinkles. Donuts!

Carpenter looked at McCarthy and the smile became the only feature visible on his face. In an incredible impression of Jacques Clouseau of "Pink Panther" fame he stated to McCarthy, "A Cleeuuuue."

McCarthy radioed dispatch and said, "255, we have located the 10-57 (hit and run) vehicle," and then he ran a check on the plate. After a brief delay, the dispatcher asked McCarthy to switch over to channel four, which was the secure channel. The secure channel was used for more sensitive transmissions. Information and calls that might be compromised if overheard by the people in "scanner land" like suspects, the terminally nosey, and the media. Under these circumstances, it was not unusual because the suspect was still at large.

McCarthy turned his radio to channel four and he keyed his collar mic and said, "255, go ahead. I'm on secure." The secure channel made everyone sound like they were in a big marble box. The technology somehow muffled and echoed the voice.

"Are you 10-61? (Is the person within earshot of you?)" asked the dispatcher.

"Negative, go ahead," said McCarthy.

"That vehicle is registered to… Chief Hale."

McCarthy left his hand on his collar mic, but did not depress the key. His mouth dropped open and he turned to Carpenter and Carpenter looked like his mirror image. They were both stunned. At the same moment they moaned, *"Aw shit!"*

CHAPTER SIXTEEN

ACCIDENTAL FELON

McCarthy and Carpenter stood in the darkness in front of the car and behind the dumpster for several minutes. Then Carpenter said, "Let's just sit on it for a while and see if someone comes out. This is not the chief's house, and the chief was definitely not driving. Someone is going to come back... I can feel it."

They backed into the bushes and made themselves as comfortable as they could. After only a few minutes they realized they were now under-dressed for the weather. It had suddenly gotten considerably colder and they had both left their coats stowed in the trunk of the squad.

Just as Carpenter and McCarthy began to shiver, two figures approached on foot. Carpenter whispered, "Shhhh, here comes somebody," and they both got smaller and quieter.

Two drop-dead gorgeous college girls, dressed identically, shuffled, jogged, and skipped toward the dumpster. They were whispering and giggling as they slowed to a walk and at last a definable stagger as they hunkered up next to the dumpster, oblivious to the well-concealed cops. They looked about and one said, "No one is around. Do it!"

McCarthy thought they might be talking about driving the Lexus, but they paid no attention to the big car at all other than to use it as a shield. Both of the beauty queens dropped their identical jeans revealing their identically pear shaped bums. After a slight delay they both "tinkled." The beauties were not prepared for the splattering that is caused by high pressure water flow hitting a flat hard surface, and they danced around in place and giggled, trying to avoid the splash back. Both ladies started and finished at the same time, leading McCarthy and Carpenter to deduce that they must have shared identical bladders with an identical capacity. After finishing both blondes slipped up their identical jeans and buckled them and the first giggled, "Identical twins in every way."

The second laughed, "I thought you were going to keep a look out first."

The first laughed and said, "No, I thought you were going to watch first and then once I squatted it was too late to stop."

The second agreed, "Way too late; you can't stop in mid stream."

The first then said, "We're sooooo lucky there aren't any cops around."

The second added, "I wish we would have gotten caught. I am so in the mood to make a sweet deal with a cute cop."

The first retorted, "You are sooooo terrible. That would be OK if he had a cute partner that was going to arrest me too. That would make an awesome story."

The second agreed, "Totally. That would be a story no one at the sorority could top."

The girls then walked back through the parking lot and out to the sidewalk, not noticing the identical splatter marks they had on the back of their identically tight jeans.

Carpenter slowly stood up and whispered to McCarthy, "Dyno, if we weren't sooooo scrupulous, we could have given them a night to remember."

McCarthy stood up, stretching his legs and said, "Twins. I don't think we dare go there. I think once you go down the path that twins are on there is no turning back."

"Yeah, you're right. I think that's the second 'aw shit' tonight," said Carpenter.

"You know it. That was a double aw shit. It was an aw shit if we did and aw shit because we didn't."

"Hey, McCarthy, you're teaching ethics in the academy. Would that be bribery to an officer if they would have offered a bounce on the bed for us not to cite them for pissing in public?" asked Carpenter. "I'm serious here," he emphasized.

"Well by statute, the elements of the crime are to offer something of value to us to convince us to do something we shouldn't do or to not do something we should do," explained McCarthy.

"They would have to offer us something of value? Bed bouncing with twins? Priceless!" whispered Carpenter emphatically. "Is priceless something of value or without value because you can't put a price on it?"

"Carp, you're giving me a headache," whispered McCarthy, rubbing his forehead.

Carpenter laughed, "Mission accomplished." Then his face turned abruptly serious, "Twins," whispered Carpenter.

"Twins," whispered McCarthy.

"At least I forgot I was cold for a few minutes," said Carpenter smiling while he rubbed his hands quickly on his arms for warmth.

"Someone's coming," said McCarthy as the door to apartment two in the complex opened. An attractive young brunette in her early twenties closed the door and put a black coach purse with a long strap over her shoulder as she clipped down the steps. At the bottom she stopped and tentatively peered cautiously left, then right, and repeated the motion again as if she was crossing a busy intersection before she headed through the parking lot. Her balance was as unsteady as her gait as if she had been drinking for most of the night. At first she looked like she had been punched in the face, causing both eyes to blacken. As she grew closer, it was obvious that she had been and still was sobbing. The steady flow of tears caused her makeup to smear drastically.

Other than looking as if she was made up by Alice Cooper, the young lady was a very pretty girl. She was about 5'2" and had long flowing brown hair worthy of being chosen for a model in a Lady Clairol commercial.

As she approached, she looked pathetic. She was heading straight for the Lexus, and as McCarthy listened to the mournful sobs emanating from her makeup smeared, tear-stained face, he suddenly felt sorry for this gentle looking creature. She had just run down three ladies, killing one and leaving the other two clinging to life, and she had kept going. Now she was walking unwittingly toward an unexpected arrest and the just punishment she undoubtedly deserved. McCarthy had a knot of sympathy in his gut the size of a regulation football. "Damn! Knock that off!" thought McCarthy. "She killed somebody."

As she reached the Lexus, McCarthy moved around one side of the car and Carpenter moved around the other, "Don't move ma'am. We will need to see some kind of identification."

She gasped and threw both of her hands up to cover her mouth and finally she dropped her hands and crossed them in front of her as she sighed heavily. "I'm the one you are looking for. I am Amanda Hale," she paused to sob loudly, seemingly disgusted by the words. "I was driving. I hit those poor girls. Are they going to be all right? I was just going to turn myself in." She dropped her purse on the ground and covered her eyes with both hands and cried, "Oh God, I'm so sorry. I'm so sorry."

McCarthy walked up to her left, and Carpenter walked up to her right side and then with one hand they patted her shoulder in shared sympathy and the other they each took one of her arms and pivoted it behind her back. McCarthy handcuffed her and said from memory, "You have the right to remain silent...."

Carpenter stayed with the vehicle. It was rich in physical evidence, and it would have to be carefully moved to an enclosed area to be thoroughly processed by a criminal evidence technician. Photographs would have to be taken of the fabric impressions. The impressions would be able to be matched with the clothing on the victims if they were properly photographed. There would be DNA in hair samples, blood samples, and tissue samples. There would be paint samples, fabric samples to be taken from the vehicle, and last but not least the donut samples. It was a CSI's mother-lode.

It was obvious that this vehicle was involved in the tragedy, but this was still a homicide investigation. One young person was dead and another was dying. Compton would often say, "People are worried about gang bangers and terrorists, but what is most likely to kill you before your time in La Claire is either a drunk driver or a husband." As usual, Compton was right.

Dan walked Amanda over to the squad car and found nothing on her, but when Carpenter searched Amanda's purse he found a "key" piece of evidence in the purse, the keys to the Lexus.

"I am transporting the driver to La Claire General for a blood sample," radioed McCarthy.

Before McCarthy reached the hospital, he received a transmission that made no sense, "10-25 (report to) the station and personally administer a breath test on that subject at the station."

"I will need to go to the hospital for blood. This is in reference to the felony hit and run," McCarthy reported to the dispatcher, certain that there was some sort of mistake.

"Negative. You will come in to the station and personally administer a breath test. That is an order straight from the sergeant," relayed the dispatcher with a "you better do it now or you are so fucked" tone in her voice. There was also a hint of "stop asking me questions about this or I will be really pissed" tone blended in.

"10-4," said McCarthy.

Dan was puzzled but thought there must be a good reason for this deviation from policy. As he passed the glass enclosure surrounding the command room, he looked to Darnell for some signal that would clear it all up for McCarthy. When McCarthy walked his prisoner past the command room, Darnell gave the only signal that Dan needed. With a deeply furrowed brow, which told of absolute displeasure, Darnell mouthed the words, "Breath," and then "do it!" McCarthy did not need to be a lip reader to understand what was said. He did not need a body language specialist to tell him there would be no atta-boy for McCarthy and Carpenter on this particular homicide arrest.

McCarthy reached the Breath Testing Room, which held the Intoximeter. Dan carefully removed the handcuffs from the waif-like wrists of Amanda. The tears continued to flow, but now the sobbing had diminished to an occasional sniff.

Amanda agreed to take the Intoximeter tests. When asked she said, "I will take any tests you want. I am so sorry." Just then

Chief Hale, Daddy, entered the room and the sniffs turned once again to sobs. "Oh Daddy, I am so sorry. I am so sorry."

"That's all right, baby-girl. We'll get through this. You'll be all right," comforted Chief Hale, patting his little girl's back and looking at McCarthy.

"Sir, respectfully, maybe you should wait outside," suggested McCarthy to his commander-in-chief.

With a barely suppressed rage, Hale responded, "I may be a father, but I am still your chief! You need to know that I am going to stay right here and that's not negotiable, Officer McCarthy. Do you understand?"

Chief Hale and McCarthy had history. None of this history was good. Hale was Joe Darnell with more rank. He had risen to chief treating his superiors like kings and his inferiors like so many peasants that he could step on. The thing McCarthy had going for him was Hale did not like anyone in patrol. So until tonight he had no special reason to dislike McCarthy any more than anyone else. Tonight McCarthy thought, "The worm is going to turn. He now has a reason to specifically dislike me."

After Amanda sat back down, Chief Hale took a chair behind McCarthy, which made him feel very uncomfortable. Hale was the chief of police, but he was also the father of this attractive young homicide suspect who was sitting in the chair next to him. This seemed to violate every standard of safety, common sense, and procedure. McCarthy thought of a phrase that Compton would use right now. He would tell Dan, "McCarthy, the man has the authority to be wrong. The man cannot make you do anything against the law, but he has the authority to be wrong."

"This man has the authority to be wrong and he is wrong," thought McCarthy.

As McCarthy readied the machine, Chief Hale asked, "McCarthy... Dan, I was going over the sergeant's list just yesterday, and well, I could not help but notice there was your name right on top of the list. Congratulations! You did very well, son."

"Why, thank you, sir?" McCarthy half asked and half answered, puzzled by the sudden turn in the conversation to his own future.

"Yes, I think you have a very bright future with this department if you continue to show the kind of departmental loyalty that you have shown in the past," said Hale.

"Yes, sir. Thank you, sir," said McCarthy as he busied himself with the air blank tests and internal calibration on the machine.

"I know I can count on you to do the right thing, McCarthy," said Hale.

"Yes, sir," said McCarthy, answering the chief and attempting to concentrate on the task at hand. This was not just a breath test, tonight. He was gathering evidence in a very important homicide investigation. He was so focused on the task at hand that he failed to read anything into Chief Hale's conversation that could be construed as improper. It would not have mattered anyway. If McCarthy had ever been a prize-fighter, he would never have taken a dive for anyone. It was against his nature.

The machine was ready, so Dan turned to the sobbing felony hit and run driver and said, "Miss Hale, could you please step over here, seal your lips around this mouthpiece, and blow into this. Take one steady long breath until you cannot blow any more." McCarthy held out the mouthpiece and she blew until she ran out of breath. McCarthy was jealous of the Intoximeter's insensitivity. The heartless machine did not have to feel sorry for the sobbing young lady who had just made a series of terrible mistakes that she would have to live with. The machine did not have a memory of the crumpled gasping young women, looking like old, discarded rag dolls in the middle of the street. The machine did not have a chief seated behind it who was about to hate it forever for doing its job. The machine cared not one bit about any of this. The machine just mindlessly beeped and accepted the sample.

After another cycle of machine calibrations and air blank tests, the machine, as always, asked for another sample. By this time Miss Hale had stopped crying. Having something else to concentrate on helped take her mind off what she had done. She blew again and the machine beeped and accepted the second sample.

After completing the test, the Intoximeter ignored the sobs, paid no attention to the presence of power, and gave McCarthy exactly what he had asked for. McCarthy in turn handed Amanda a pink copy of the form the impersonal machine had printed out. The machine did not lie or even editorialize about the results. "Miss Hale, the results indicate that your blood alcohol content right now is slightly over .13. You are over the legal limit."

".13?" asked Hale.

"Yes sir, .13 milligrams of alcohol in every 100 milliliters of blood. Evidence of intoxication in Wisconsin is .08, sir," answered McCarthy as respectfully as possible.

Hale got up and stormed out of the room, only needing a door to slam for a full effect. "I know, McCarthy. I don't need the legal update. Thanks a lot, McCarthy!"

"I'm so sorry," said Amanda, sobbing again "I cannot believe I have done this. I am so sorry. I hope those girls and God forgive me for what I have done."

Later in the evening as McCarthy was taking the handcuffs off Amanda at the county jail, she turned to him and said, "Will you forgive me?"

"I have to do this, but you have done nothing that I am able to forgive. You have been one of the most cooperative people I have ever arrested and I appreciate that."

"Please. Will you forgive me?" she began to sob again.

"I can see how sincere you are," said McCarthy, "and although it is not for me to say, I sense how sorry you really are. I will indicate how sorry you are in my report."

"I cannot believe I have done this. Oh my God, I killed someone. I can't believe this is not a dream," and the sobbing continued even worse than before. McCarthy helped her to a seat. The female jailer came around the booking counter and sat down comforting her.

"Do you need me for anything else?" asked McCarthy.

The jailer shook her head no, looking more like a big sister than a jailer.

"She has not made any statements to that effect, but you might put a…" and McCarthy pointed at his eyes trying to indicate "suicide watch." He did not want to say the words, afraid he might plant the thought in the young, mournful girl's mind.

The female jailer nodded understanding and waved goodbye to McCarthy.

McCarthy returned to the station and walked past Darnell, Captain Jackson, and Chief Hale in the command room, and all turned and looked at McCarthy. They said nothing. They did not have to. The looks said it all. Captain Jackson's look said in any language, "I am glad I'm not you."

Sergeant Darnell's look clearly stated, "Just wait. If you think I didn't like you before now, here comes some real hate bombs." Chief Hale's look was a wistful look. It did not tell the world what he was thinking. What does a father think at times like this, even fathers who are chiefs of police?

McCarthy did not notice any of the looks, and even if he did he would be loath to try to analyze them. He had a vehicular homicide arrest to write up. This homicide had been unintentionally committed by one of the nicest people he had ever arrested in his life, and there was neither joy nor satisfaction in this night's work.

Four young women had started the night thrilled by the promise of spring. One was dead. One would die before the week was out. A third would be facing months of recovery wondering why she had lived and her friends had not. There would never be an answer for her in this life.

A fourth woman would have to live knowing she had been responsible for all of it. She started the night the daughter of a chief who had never given her father an ounce of trouble. She would end the night with one arrest on her record. It would be the only arrest she would ever have on her record. That arrest would ultimately lead to a guilty plea and an impassioned apology for a terrible mistake she could "never undo."

Some would forgive, most would forget. Amanda would move on but could never forget nor forgive herself. Forgetting might allow it to happen again. She could be considered a success story of the criminal justice system. She would not be a repeat offender. There would not be so much as a parking ticket in her future. She was rehabilitated from the moment she realized what she had done. The knowledge of the pain she had inflicted on others would be carried all her life. Such is the burden of the *accidental felon*.

CHAPTER SEVENTEEN

Shots Fired

It had been over a month since the arrest of Amanda Hale. Carpenter and McCarthy had been scheduled on foot patrol every night since then by Sergeant Darnell. Darnell had meant it as a punishment, but he did not know Dan McCarthy. He did not know Gary Carpenter. He did not know the shift he was working on. Walking downtown was a preferred assignment for working cops. Every cop that worked for David Compton was a working cop. As long as David Compton was still their sergeant they were still his shift. Darnell had made no attempt to be their sergeant. Therefore he was merely a sergeant, not their sergeant.

Walking the bar area was filled with action for cops and inter-action with the creatures of the night. The term "walk-man" had been coined in the 1800s when La Claire was a rowdy bawdy river town. Walk-men had always generated most of their own calls.

In the old days they had no radios. When the walk-men made an arrest, the brawler would come peacefully or painfully. Each walk-man was equipped with a "Bat-on." The first three letters pro-nounced like bat and ball. If they needed help, the walk-men would rap the baton on the curb to summon it. Until help came, they would rap it on the brawler until he decided that he had enough.

As time passed the walk-man would only have to drag a brawler to one of the call boxes to summon help. The process to summon aid was the officer would have to unlock the call box by inserting his call box key into the box and then phone the station. In those days the walk-man was also issued "the claw." It was a metallic claw which would be applied and tightened painfully onto the brawler's wrist until he became cooperative. The walk-men were always a friendly but hearty lot who went looking for trouble and generally found it. Some loved the work, some hated it, and some even feared it.

Darnell thought since he hated and feared the job, it would be the perfect way to unofficially punish McCarthy and Carpenter for something that he could never officially punish them for. Darnell's vindictiveness fell short of its mark and Darnell did not even know it.

In the month they had been walking downtown, McCarthy and Carpenter had broken up more fights than they could count, walked up on drug transactions, domestics, indecent exposures, and even a few decent ones. They even broke up one rape in progress. The fact that this assignment was a punishment was totally lost on McCarthy and Carpenter. They liked walking downtown, and they liked working with each other. They would have thought Darnell actually liked them if they did not know better.

As the two friends walked the beat on this evening, they noticed a 21 year old with a high and tight hair cut wearing a "Be all that you can be" T-shirt. He stepped out of the door of the Red Lion Tavern and headed around the corner. "101st Airborne, is in town. They have been at Fort McCoy all week pretending they are in Europe again," said Carpenter.

"Yeah, they haven't been at McCoy for years," said McCarthy.

"They have been busy kicking Al Qaeda's ass all over Iraq and Afghanistan. Now Russia's flexing its muscle's again. McCoy area looks a lot like the Ukraine. I guess someone decided the 101st should be preparing to jump into trees again instead of sand," added Carpenter.

They both started toward the private because he clearly was about to empty his bladder in the alley next to the Red Lion. The private was reaching for his privates and he wasn't even in the alley yet.

"Let me handle this one," said Carpenter.

"OK, Gary. He's all yours," said McCarthy. "Like I would stop you if I could."

"Never hurts to ask I always say," said Carpenter. Carpenter was a former drill sergeant. He had been a military policeman in a war zone, and he had a way with the enlisted men who came to La Claire to have a good time. Carpenter had a way with everyone he talked to. You could not find Carpenter's communications approach in any book or manual. It was unique to Carpenter and he was a master at it. There was only one Gary Carpenter.

As the two police officers rounded the corner of the alley they found exactly what they expected. The private was now emptying his privates in public. Carpenter became a drill instructor, "Ten-hut!"

The GI instinctively snapped to attention, his fingers properly curled along the seam of his pant legs. He held both eyes straight forward with his "pants puppy" still spraying against the brick wall until it dribbled to a stop.

"Soldier, stow that gun and batten that hatch!" barked Carpenter in a tone that had an "areehup" sound to it.

The soldier instantly put the puppy in the kennel and zipped. Then he quickly returned to attention yelling, "Sir! Yes Sir!"

"Do you see butter bars on my collar, Private?" asked Carpenter now inches from the young warrior.

"Sir! No Sir!"

"Then do not call me sir. You will answer 'Yes Officer.' Do you understand?!"

"Yes Officer!"

"Do you see this brick, soldier?" asked Carpenter pointing at a brick in the wall of the building directly in front of the soldier's eyes.

"Yes Officer!" said the soldier.

"There are many bricks in this city, but this brick is special for this brick is my brick, do you understand private?!"

"Yes Officer!" barked the soldier with his eyes now fixed on the brick as if it was razor wire on the perimeter at 2:00 AM in a war zone after he heard a suspicious noise.

"You are to watch that brick until I return. Protect that brick at all costs and if you are here when I return and my precious brick is here when I return I will not write you a ticket for urinating in the presence of my precious brick. Do you understand?" asked Carpenter.

"Yes Officer," yodeled the private, glancing momentarily at Carpenter.

"Do not eyeball me, Private!" barked Carpenter.

The private looked back at the brick and shouted, "Sorry Officer. I won't, Officer."

"Hold until relieved, Private!" said Carpenter walking away.

As Carpenter then walked away, McCarthy stood for a moment in awe and then left, looking back occasionally to see the private standing motionless looking at the brick... guarding the brick.

Carpenter never looked back.

"That never ceases to amaze me," said McCarthy.

"It's the training. He has been trained to hold at all cost. He knows that I am not some guy pretending. He knows I have done it before. He would guard a mountain pass with his life, a scrubbed filled desert with his life, a Bosnian village with his life, that brick with his life. That private will hold that brick until he is relieved," after a short pause Carpenter added, "Oh yeah, and he is smart enough and sober enough to know that he does not want a ticket."

As the partners approached the opposite end of the same alley, they saw two familiar figures leave the back door of Your Uncle's Place Tavern and head over to a dumpster. McCarthy and Carpenter stepped into a shadow less than 50 feet from them as they backed up to the dumpster, looked both ways, giggled and wiggled down their identical tight jeans and squatted their identical pear shaped bums side by side, nearly touching, followed by the unmistakable sound of liquid splattering on asphalt.

"The twins!" whispered McCarthy.

The two officers walked up to the twins as they were putting themselves back together. Both officers could not help but notice that the twins were not French for they clearly had a daily ritual of shaving. "I'll handle this one," said McCarthy.

"Sure you will," said Carpenter with a twinkle in his eye.

"Good evening, ladies, I am Officer McCarthy of the La Claire Police Department. You cannot do that in public. May I see some kind of identification?" asked McCarthy and both quickly slipped their identification out of their pockets as if they were used to being asked.

"You are," McCarthy said looking at the twin on the right who answered "Mindy."

"and you are?" He then glanced at the twin on the left, who answered "Cindy."

"You are both going to receive a citation for unlawful deposit of a refuse. Please be patient and stand right here," said McCarthy.

"Is there any way we can, well…" started Mindy.

"No, Cindy, there is not. Just stand there and wait for your citation," said McCarthy a little flustered anticipating the question before it was completely asked.

"I'm Mindy. You called me Cindy," said Mindy.

"I'm Cindy, you called her Cindy," said Cindy.

McCarthy then looked at them confused and said, "Just wait here both of you."

After citing the twins, the two walk-men turned and headed back to the soldier, who was still guarding Carpenter's brick.

"I'll tell you what's really something," said Carpenter.

"What?" Dan said.

"I have seen you as cool as a snow cone in December during chases, shootouts, bar fights, and every other damn horrific thing you can imagine, but I wouldn't have missed this for the world. All it takes is a couple of good looking blondes to shake up the unshakable Dyno Dan," laughed Carpenter.

"They weren't just blondes. They were twins, and they weren't just twins, they were shaved twins. Shaved twins!" explained McCarthy tucking his ticket book into his right rear pocket. "I didn't notice that the first time we saw them."

"Touché, point, match, game, McCarthy. They were indeed shaved twins," reasoned Carpenter. "This truly was a good excuse, but certainly not a good reason for an urban warrior to be shaken."

"I am telling you, Carp, urban warriors are especially shaken by shaved twins," reasoned McCarthy.

"Why didn't you let Mindy finish her sentence and see what she had to offer in return for leniency," Carpenter said with a mischievous twinkle in his eyes.

"I didn't want her to finish. I didn't want to know. You know what the prayer says?" asked McCarthy.

"How's that?" asked Carpenter.

"Lead us not into temptation," reasoned McCarthy.

"Fuckin' AAAAAAmen," said Carpenter.

As they reached the soldier, Carpenter stepped into his drill instructor role again, "At ease, soldier. You did a truly admirable job defending and protecting my beloved brick. Carry on soldier," said Carpenter in a forgiving tone.

"Yes Officer," said the soldier turning to run off.

"Soldier!" barked Carpenter.

"Yes Officer?" answered the soldier, stopping dead in his tracks.

"Your orders are, while bivouacking in this city, to neither fight nor take part in any other disorderly behavior. You will only void your bladder inside a room clearly marked 'MEN,' in one of the porcelain receptacles provided for that activity. I just saved you $100 dollars. Are we clear, private?"

"Yes Officer." The soldier then looked at Carpenter's name tag, "It was Sergeant Carpenter once, wasn't it?"

"Yes it was."

"What was your unit?"

"I was in the 101st Airborne," Carpenter answered with a smile.

"Hooah!" barked the private.

"Hooah!" answered Carpenter.

"Thanks bro!" said the GI with a handshake to Carpenter.

"We have to stop meeting like this, OK?" said McCarthy also accepting the soldier's hand-shake.

"The last time you'll see me fucking up in your town," called the GI as he ran off to rejoin the party. He was telling the truth. In less than a month he would be exchanging small arms fire with Al Qaeda at the Khyber Pass in Afghanistan. There he would also faithfully hold until relieved. His actions would earn him a silver star and the eternal gratitude of a grateful nation.

This warrior would rarely tell the story of his own bravery at the Khyber Pass, but he would often fondly relate the story of the D.I. named Carpenter who made him stand at attention and guard his beloved brick rather than issue a ticket to a fellow Airborne Ranger. He would laugh until it brought tears to his eyes.

McCarthy and Carpenter continued on their sweep of the downtown. "Best job in the world, walking downtown," said McCarthy.

"Fuckin' A. This is where the rubber meets the road," answered Carpenter.

"I'm wondering if Darnell is starting to like us. He has been assigning us to walk every night."

"I can't tell. He seems to still hate us pretty much. You don't think he believes he is punishing us do you?" asked Carpenter.

"He might be, but don't let on that we like it until, say, next October," said Dyno.

"Can't stand the cold? Are you getting soft?" asked Carpenter giving Dan a good natured elbow.

"No, this just seems more like work when it's cold. How about you, Carp? Would you like to walk all the way through the fall into the winter?" asked Dyno.

"No. Walking all night makes me sleep like a baby when I get done. So when I walk and stay up and go deer hunting in the morning, I keep falling asleep and falling out of my deer stand," explained Carpenter, rubbing his head.

The two friends talked, chatted, debated, and just plain bullshitted as they continued on their circuit, walking through taverns, into alleys, saying a thousand hellos and shaking 500 hands.

As the bar-time crowd cleared out, McCarthy and Carpenter were about ready to split the beat and start pulling doors. It was one of the must-dos of being a walk-man. Just as they were about to split, McCarthy commented, "You know it was a quiet night tonight. Did you notice that the downtown is much better behaved when there are walk-men down here every single night?"

"I'd like to say two things, Dyno. Maddy Brown insists that we call this foot-patrol. She wants you to stop using the term walk-men," said Carpenter.

"OK, I will use the term foot-patrol, only because Maddy asked, because the term is about 150 years old in La Claire. I wouldn't do that for just anyone," agreed McCarthy. "What's the other thing?"

"I wish you wouldn't have said that. Whenever you mention how fucking-la-di-da-wonderful the world is, something bad happens. I have told you before to keep it to yourself while we are working, OK?" pleaded Carpenter in an honestly worried tone.

"255 and 256," crackled the radio.

"Son of a suds-sucking sailor, see what I mean, Dyno," said Carpenter, genuinely certain McCarthy had brought this calamity on and just as certain it would be a calamity.

"Sorry, Gary," said McCarthy. "255-256 go ahead," answered McCarthy.

"Respond to a 10-10 (fight in progress) inside of River Street Pool. No weapons reported," droned the dispatcher.

"10-4," answered McCarthy. "No weapons, just a room filled with pool cues and drunken combatants, that's all," said McCarthy. "Hey, Carp, front or back?"

"I'll hit the front and you hit the back," said Carpenter. River Street Pool was a 24 hour business that had a bar, a large pool playing area, and a restaurant. The restaurant and pool area were open 24 hours. There were two entrances, so the fight could be in the front or back, inside or outside. The general response for walk-men going to a call at River Street Pool was to hit it from both ends at once to prevent escape.

Carpenter called when he arrived at the front, "Nothing going on outside."

McCarthy replied, "Stand-by. I am going in the back and will advise what I see."

As McCarthy entered the back door, he could see that nearly every table was in use, but the pool players had moved their pool cues to port arms to watch the action that seemed to be occurring toward the front. McCarthy could see a mass of people near the front door who were being pushed out the door by the bouncer. The eye of the storm was a large man who appeared to be backing out the door as fast as he could under his own power, trying to get away from the flailing arms of a much smaller man. McCarthy got on the radio, "Carp, the fight is at the front door and it is about to be pushed out the door right at you," radioed McCarthy.

Dan reached the crowd and cut his way through it, but by the time he had made it to the front door the two men and some of the onlookers had poured out onto the sidewalk. McCarthy yelled, "Police Officer coming through. Step aside and let me through."

Carpenter was on the sidewalk just to the right of the glass door as it burst open. The large man had both hands open and crossed in front of his face, which wore a mask of terror and pain. His hands were cut and bleeding badly. Then came the small man spitting vile expletives in a mixture of Spanish and English at the large man as he slashed left, right, up and down, trying to carve him up with a large Rambo-like knife.

Carpenter drew his weapon as the large man took a slash across the bridge of his nose and forehead giving him a brand new bright red crooked eyebrow. The large man squealed and in two distinct movements dropped to his knees and then slumped to his elbows onto the sidewalk. He instinctively covered his head with both arms trying to ward off what most certainly would be the impending death blows. He appeared out of options and resigned to his fate.

The small man yelled, "Te voy a matar, puta!" as he spun the knife in his hand as if he had been practicing the movement since birth. The man paused, ready to drive the knife "psycho-style" into the back of his victim.

Carpenter understood two words that the Hispanic man yelled as he spun the knife in his hand like an expert. They were the Spanish word for "kill" and "bitch." Gary did not need to understand any Spanish to comprehend that death of the large man was imminent.

To witnesses, Carpenter's movements were a blur; he reacted so quickly. To Carpenter, he would later say he wondered why he did not move faster even though it could be argued that it could not have been done faster. Carpenter saw the impending homicide and decided to shoot. He aimed his weapon as he yelled one last hopeful warning, "Drop the weap__," but the small man gave him no time to finish the sentence. "Bam! Bam!" Both bullets spiraled surely into the only target presented to Carpenter that would endanger only the small man. The bullets tore into and through the attacker's back and right kidney just as he was preparing to drive his knife deep into the large, helpless, bleeding, quivering mass of human flesh on the sidewalk, just below the serrated edge of his blade.

The small man instantly dropped the knife and slowly slid off the large man like a glob of butter off a stack of hot cakes.

Dooley had appeared out of nowhere and had also drawn his weapon, but the gun versus knife fight was over before any pressure could be brought to bear by Dooley on the trigger of his own Glock.

The small man lay still on the sidewalk as the large man crawled out of his reach and propped his large frame against the wall of River City Pool, astounded that he was still alive. The crowd gathered around, suddenly silent, wondering if what they had seen was real or some elaborate street theater acted out for their excitement.

Carpenter covered the suspect as he moved in on him. Gary slid the knife out of the man's reach as he radioed, "256, shots fired, suspect's down. We need two ambulances for two subjects. They need to be transported separately if possible. One knife wound and the other a gunshot wound. Send a commander to the scene. This was an officer-involved shooting," said Carpenter in one breathless transmission that said it all.

McCarthy tended to the wounded victim, applying a four-by-four bandage to the gaping wound on his forehead and securing it with a cling bandage. McCarthy asked one simple question as he bandaged the wound, "What happened here?" which opened the flood gates on a torrent of words, stuttered and sputtered through the blood covering the man's face.

"Man, I was playing pool with that guy and he lost, man. He wouldn't pay me and he said I hustled him. W-W-W-Well I m-m-m-made him pay. Then he left and was screaming at m-m-me in S-S-S-S-S-Spanish. Ten minutes later I am playing pool and he punches me out of nowhere. I start f-f-f-fighting b-b-b-back and the b-b-b-ouncer yells, 't-t-t-take it outside,' so I start heading for the d-d-d-d-door, and all of a sudden he's got this huge f-f-fucking kn-n-nife and he f-f-fucking tries t-t-to k-k-k-k-kill m-m-m-me. That c-c-c-cop s-s-s-saved m-m-my ass. I haven't s-s-s-s-stuttered s-s-s-since I w-w-w-as n-n-n-nine years old."

McCarthy did not ask the man any more questions. It seemed that the man's effort to talk looked as painful as his wounds. His first statement was incredibly cohesive under the circumstances.

Carpenter found the suspect conscious and lying unnaturally still. He moved his eyes to watch Carpenter, but nothing else moved. He felt the burning path of the bullet entering parts of his body he knew to be vital to life. He sensed moving would make his condition more painful and more dire than it was now. He stayed perfectly still and dead-calm quiet.

Carpenter slipped on his gloves and applied pressure to the two small wounds over the right kidney. If you had to be shot in a vital organ, the kidney would be a good choice because there were two. He could find no exit wounds. As Carpenter's hand placed pressure on the wound, the small man's eyes squinted in pain. "You're going to make it, Slim. Just breathe in and out slowly. I can hear the ambulance coming. They'll be here in less than a minute," said Gary trying to put the wounded man's mind at ease.

The suspect, who was a Cuban immigrant, turned his eyes over as far as he could, and even though he had only been in America for six months, he showed an appreciation for the rights and freedoms the United States lavishes on its citizens. He proclaimed, "Ramon remain silent. Ramon want attorney," then he turned and looked at Carpenter with disdain and said, "Puta," and he spat.

Carpenter stepped away as the Emergency Medical Technicians swarmed the scene. As Carpenter glanced around he was amazed to see how many people had gathered. He wondered how many had been there when he shot Ramon and how if they had been there he had not seen them… he had not heard them. He had only been able to see Ramon, the knife, and the large man's impending death as clear as a mountain brook.

Carpenter then noticed a young disciple gang member admiring the bloodied Rambo knife. Carpenter walked over to the knife and stood by it. "That's all I need is to have that knife disappear," he thought. Carpenter made eye contact with the gang banger. That was all the communication needed. The gang banger started to drift into the crowd and then turned and said to Carpenter, "Nice shootin' Holmes." The gang banger then turned his fingers of both hands into handguns and fired each one, "Bang, Bang," and blew the imaginary smoke from the pretend muzzles and holstered them and flashed Carpenter a gang sign out of respect.

"Do me a favor and stay to make a statement," called Carpenter.

"A'yite. I be at my crib," answered the banger and he was gone. He would eventually leave a truthful and insightful statement to the events leading up to the shooting, one month later after Carpenter picked him up on the outstanding warrant. He hustled away from the scene on the night of the shooting because he knew there was an outstanding warrant for his arrest. This night, however, was not a convenient night for him to be arrested. He had a lady to pleasure, 3 grams of rock left to sell, which was crotched, and if that wasn't reason enough to not be a good citizen, he was strapped. He had a stolen Beretta 9 mm shoved into his belt in the small of his back. Tonight Carpenter would have to forgive him and color him gone.

Carpenter stood by the knife. It was an important job. Right now it was a job he could handle. He had been shot before, but he had never fired his weapon at another human being before tonight. "Shot's fired!" He had heard those words called out when he had been shot in the wrist and the chest with a 20 gauge slug as he, McCarthy, and Dooley were attempting to enter an apartment to rescue a hostage.

He had heard those words called out when he tried to deliver a throw phone to a barricaded bank robber called "Mad Mattix" and witnessed McCarthy, Brockman, Dooley, and Stammos, all fellow members of the SWAT team, fire fifty rounds into that suspect while Carpenter held the throw phone. Tonight he fired two rounds from his Glock 40 into a man trying to cut the spine out of another helpless human being and heard himself say those words one more time. "Shots fired!"

Carpenter stood in the midst of organized chaos, quietly guarding the evidence of the assault, the large ugly killing knife. One human being shooting another human being could be considered attempted murder. For a police officer on the street there is a fine line between a crime and a justifiable use of force. The line between the two is drawn by a convincing argument that there was justification. Carpenter looked at the bloodied blade of the knife. If the blade would have been a few inches longer it could be considered a short sword.

Carpenter guarded the knife with his life, because the quality of his life would depend on this knife being produced. Many cops who have saved lives using their weapons have had their lives ruined by some wise cracking street thug stealing the downed suspect's weapon that lay unattended in the chaos of a scene. Not this time. Not this scene. Carpenter would guard the knife like his life depended on it. He knew he could not depend on witnesses to tell the truth. He could not depend on the suspect to tell the truth, and he could not even depend on the victim to tell the truth, but this bloody knife would tell the truth. The truth that the shots he fired saved the life of another.

"I wonder," thought Carpenter, who was a cop in his 30s with over half of his career ahead of him, "How many more times in my career will I hear those words... *shots fired?*"

CHAPTER EIGHTEEN

BURGLAR'S NIGHTMARE

When he walked into the lineup room, the place erupted. It was the first time in the history of the La Claire Police Department that a sergeant received a standing ovation at lineup. Compton was visibly moved. He set the lineup books down on the command table in the front of the room and the clapping seemed to go on forever, but if anyone would have timed it, the applause lasted for one minute and twenty-three seconds before Compton said, "Thanks ladies and gentlemen, it's good to be back." The applause subsided and the night shift took a seat.

Before Compton could start his lineup, Alice Compton walked through the door of the lineup room. She slid to the back of the room and pointed her video camera at her husband. Sergeant Compton looked at her and said nothing, stunned and confused. The look was out of place on Dave Compton's face.

Then a Barbershop Quartet in full regalia, decked out in their red and white striped traditional attire, walked in perfect step, singing to the tune of "Welcome Back Cotter," a personalized rip-off song welcoming Compton back. After they finished that tune, they sang another rip-off of the theme of *Cops*, "Bad Boys, Bad Boys, What you gonna do, What you gonna do when Dave comes for you…" When the song finished, Dave Compton got a second standing ovation from the shift, and this one Alice taped.

Sergeant Dave Compton walked over to his wife, took the video from her, and gave it to Maddy Brown. "Get this on tape, please, will you, Maddy?" Maddy backed up a few steps and lined up the shot, and Compton took his wife in his arms and kissed her for at least another minute and twenty three seconds.

After Compton finished his abbreviated lineup, he read the car and beat assignments. "Be careful out there tonight. Stay safe, stay strong, and stay positive," he said. All were beaming and some were smiling through tears. Sergeant David Compton was back!

Darnell was back in the Detective Bureau. The chief fulfilled his promise to Darnell. He was now Lt. Joe Darnell for serving so diligently on nights. Compton's Shift did not care if he was Admiral Darnell as long as he was floating through the world on any ocean but theirs.

Immediately the shuffling began as the officers kicked their chairs back and began packaging their gear to hit the streets and then Compton said, "Hold it!" They all stopped to listen. Compton stood up and began to scratch the scar on his left hand. "I did not want to tell you, but I feel I must. It itches tonight."

Compton was scratching a scar from a knife wound he had received at a domestic many years ago. He claimed when it itched they should pay attention. Something big was going to happen.

The entire group of officers looked back and forth, exchanging concerned looks. They would be busy tonight. Compton's scar never exaggerated nor misled. It was as reliable to this Midwest Police Department as the Farmer's Almanac was to the Midwest Farmer.

"Come on, Sarge. You're scaring the little ones," pleaded Brockman. "You know they believe that absolute bullshit."

"Stanley, vulgar prose," said Carpenter.

"Yeah, well Sandy isn't here, and how is she going to find out?" said Brockman courageously refusing to kowtow.

"Gee, Stanley, I don't know, however could she possibly find out?" asked Maddy, still running Alice Compton's camcorder. "Smile and wave, Stanley, smile and wave," said Maddy, aiming the camera at Stanley with one hand while waving with the other as she beamed.

Stanley turned to Maddy and stood with his mouth stationary but wide open as if someone had just walked across his grave, all courage drained from his face. "You wouldn't, would you, Maddy?"

"How much is it worth to you, Stanley Brockman? How about a day trade for next Thanksgiving?" said Maddy. "Quid Pro Quo."

"Is that Latin for blackmail?" asked Stanley.

"If that gets me Thanksgiving off, yes," answered Maddy.

Everyone laughed at the look on Brockman's face, which clearly showed the incorrigible Stanley Brockman would be working next Thanksgiving. The look said it all.

The shift shuffled out of the lineup room and hit the streets of La Claire secure in the knowledge that it was not "bullshit" at all. Compton's scar was itching. They would be busy.

It had been two weeks since Carpenter had shot the man wielding the Rambo knife. He had been on paid leave since then, waiting to be cleared fit for duty. If there is such a thing as a perfect police shooting, this was it. There were many witnesses who actually told the truth. The bullets hit the bad guy and no one else. The bad guy was indeed going to kill a defenseless victim. Carpenter had made the right decision and had saved a life.

When the perfect shooting description had been suggested a week earlier at one of the lineups, Stanley Brockman said, "Almost perfect, the little scum bag is going to recover." No one argued with Stanley's assessment.

McCarthy and Carpenter were scheduled to work tonight in a two-man trouble car. After the squad check, McCarthy winked at Carpenter and said, "Welcome back, Gary. You want to drive or ride?"

"Why don't you drive? I'd like to ease back into it. I still gots soul, but I gots to get my rhythm back. I feel a little rusty after two weeks off on 'administrative suspension.' I have never been suspended before," said Carpenter almost blandly.

"It's mandatory after a shooting. It does not reflect badly on you," said McCarthy.

"I know, but the whole thing could be handled better. You know, they take your weapon and don't replace it right away. Right after you have to shoot someone, the last thing you want to do is have someone take your weapon away and leave you sitting around with an empty holster," said Carpenter.

"You got that right," agreed McCarthy sliding into the squad and snapping his seatbelt on. As he began to back out he stepped on the brake to let Dooley out first. Dooley hit his lights and siren and headed out to an injury accident on the far south end. McCarthy then waved to Shep as he hit his lights and siren and tore out of the lot heading to the same accident. "Well, they're going to hit the ground running tonight." McCarthy then backed out and turned his squad north.

"All kinds of things are done to make you feel like a criminal," said Carpenter. "The news people and even investigators were calling the guy I shot 'the victim.' I had to keep correcting the investigators telling them I did not shoot any victim. I shot the suspect. The victim was the guy I saved. They kept looking at me like I was splitting hairs. It's not just semantics when you are the one who pulled the trigger. You want them to get it right."

"I hear you," said McCarthy.

"Then they interviewed me in the criminal investigation and again in the internal investigation. Then there is a use-of-force hearing. I was defending myself more in the last two weeks than I had to against Rambo-Ramon," said Carpenter.

"How are you doing with it all?" McCarthy asked.

"I'm fine. I just have to fix this so the next guy that has to do the right thing with his Glock doesn't get treated like a criminal," said Carpenter.

"If anyone can change the system, you can," said McCarthy. "Hello, what's this?"

McCarthy came to a stop at the intersection of Belmont and Juniper at a red light, and speeding toward the intersection side by side were two sets of headlights. The cars appeared to be racing except they were mutually ramming each other like a modern day version of the chariot race scene in the movie *Ben-Hur.*

"You're buckled, right, Gary?" asked McCarthy.

"Yeah, what are you going to do?" Carpenter asked as the cars careened off each other one more time.

"I am just going to stay put and hit our lights and see what shakes out." With that said McCarthy turned on his overhead lights and just moved across the cross-walk but avoided entering the intersection. "Come on and stop. Stop. Stop!" Dan pleaded.

Both drivers seemed to be listening because as they rapidly approached the intersection, their traffic light turned red and the drivers of both bumper cars hammered their brakes and slid to a stop at the crosswalk, side by side, about three feet apart.

"I'll contact the driver on the left; you contact the driver on the right," said Carpenter undoing his seat belt and hopping out of the car before the sentence was completed.

McCarthy slid out of the squad, and a small-framed blonde female jumped out of the driver's side so quickly, it appeared as if her car was equipped with an ejection seat. The blonde ignored McCarthy and the squad car and made a B-line toward the other driver screaming, "You fucker. I'll cut your nuts off, you fuck! You worthless piece of dog shit, I swear I'll cut your nuts off."

McCarthy reached her, but even though she appeared to pay no attention to him, she swung her elbow wildly at him, hitting him in the chest and yelled, "Get away from me you filthy fucking pig. I'm going to cut his nuts off." McCarthy caught her elbow and wrist and spun the female, leaning her over the hood of the car and waited for a moment for Carpenter, but he did not come. McCarthy applied pressure to the female's wrist and said, "Ma'am, relax. Stop resisting. You are under arrest." He handcuffed her and helped her off the hood of the car. He searched her and walked her to the squad, wondering where his partner was.

As McCarthy was tucking the female into the squad, he heard the strangely calm voice of Carpenter as if he was asking Dan to reach the salt at Thanksgiving dinner, "Hey, Dan. Do you want to give me a hand here?" McCarthy scanned the area around the smashed cars and then he snapped his head toward the center of the intersection.

Now Gary Carpenter was about the same height and weight as McCarthy. That would be 5'9" and 170 pounds. He was a former middle weight boxer and had boxed in the Army, and he was still built like one. He was in a boxer's stance circling the ring with his opponent. The ring was the intersection of Belmont and Juniper, and all traffic had stopped. The drivers at the intersection sat still as if they had acquired the best seats in the house for the main event.

By chance, Carpenter had chosen the driver in the car on the right. This was the husband in this violent mobile domestic who was an odd match for the smaller Carpenter and if one was to think it through, an even odder match for his diminutive wife. The man who was maneuvering to deliver a knock out punch to Gary Carpenter was 6'7" 230 pounds, and from McCarthy's point of view, none of the space on his body appeared to be wasted by carrying even an ounce of fat.

McCarthy slammed the door of the squad and ignored the female, who was screaming, "Leave him alone or I'll cut your nuts off, you fucking cock-sucking pigs!"

Clearly the tides of the battle she was waging had turned. The police were now her mortal enemy as she fell instantly back in love with her husband and fell back in line on his side of this potentially violent battlefield.

McCarthy attempted to maneuver to a position behind the incredible hulk, but the hulk merely shifted his stance quite adeptly, keeping McCarthy to his right and Carpenter his left. The man smiled and said, "Bring it on, oinkers," choosing one of the many acceptable variations of the 60's vernacular "pigs."

The widening circle of three shifted as they maneuvered cautiously. It is hard to describe what enables police partners to communicate without words and move as one, but after you have weathered one hundred fights together, it must be very much like having a longtime tango partner who senses the next move in the familiar music that is playing. As the hulk maneuvered himself back toward his vehicle, it appeared as if he was going to make a break for his car. He stepped, slid, shuffled, shuffled, stepped, but escape was not on the dance card.

At the same moment, McCarthy and Carpenter moved in and shot a single leg take down on the big man. McCarthy hit and lifted the right leg and Carpenter hit and lifted the left. The big man went straight up in the air with his arms swinging as if he was frantically trying to swim to the next cloud.

McCarthy and Carpenter now had the man in midair and were looking at each other. They smiled in recognition as if they were two acquaintances passing on the street and tipped him forward with all the momentum they had mustered, and the big man landed on the hood of his car and slid across it, over it, and off it. McCarthy and Carpenter held the Hulk with his broad chest on the edge of the fender, but his body was held suspended bolt upright but upside down by the two officers. If they dropped this behemoth, he would land on his head, focusing the small-brained mammal's 230 pound frame down onto about a 4" by 4" section of his cranium. The cement surface would crush the man's skull and quite possibly kill the man.

This had to be avoided at all costs, not just for McCarthy's and Carpenter's careers, but also for the safety of this prominent (in size only) citizen. Most importantly, if the hulk died it would deny his fragile but scrappy wife the unbridled joy of cutting his nuts off. Both McCarthy and Carpenter thought as one, "The man must be saved. We must hold him."

Then their eyes met again. They were firmly entrenched in a "What next" moment. This huge man was being held straight upside down with his feet locked skyward as if he was Greg Louganis attempting the perfect dive with no splash. Then McCarthy looked at Carpenter and said, "Carp, I don't know any moves from this particular position."

Then it happened. The hulk farted an "oh so teeny fart." Carpenter would later say it sounded like the kind of fart a princess would accidentally let loose on a first date with her prince. It was a "Squeeeeeeeeeeckerrrrrpp."

First came a snicker, then a chuckle, and ultimately an inappropriate gut busting guffaw. McCarthy laughed, Carpenter laughed, and the hulk puzzled about his predicament and finally he also gave in and started to laugh.

It is a scientific fact that a person who is sincerely laughing cannot maintain muscular tension. If it is not a scientific fact then should be. Now they were all laughing. It was the perfect laugh, coupled with the perfect, gradual tension release, in combination with the most perfect weight shift, ending with a perfect landing. The hulk was down without cracking his cranium.

The sudden lift followed by the prolonged suspension, adjacent to the unexpected fart, followed by the shared laughter preceding the gentle landing ended the resistance. The hulk seemed to realize these two cops could have hurt him and did not. McCarthy and Carpenter had the hulk's handcuffs on before he could say, "Gee that was fun let's do it again."

After the intersection was cleared, the loving couple was jailed in tandem, and the reports were written, McCarthy and Carpenter hit the streets again. "Do you think we will get grief about that one?" asked Carpenter.

"Do you mean a dual arrest on a domestic, or not enough hang time on the suspect?" asked McCarthy.

"Dual arrest. I think our hang time was to die for and will never be duplicated," answered Carpenter.

"I do not know how we could have avoided arresting both on this one, but I think we might hear about it. They both violated the rule though," said McCarthy.

"I don't know which rule, but I know that the husband violated the law of gravity for a little bit there," Carpenter laughed.

"So true, but not that rule, my rule, which is anyone who attacks me, my partner, or someone else in my presence gets arrested," explained Dan.

"I believe they both did all three," said Carpenter. "That guy must have been part Macy's parade balloon or something considering how long his ass stayed up," said Carpenter.

"I'd say you are right, because he didn't come down until he released some of the gasses holding him up," laughed McCarthy.

"Yeah, what kind of fart was that for a big guy? That was the wrong time to laugh, but how do you not laugh at a 6' 7" monster farting a hamster fart like that?" Carp laughed.

"Hold it. Did you see that?" asked McCarthy, as he turned out the lights of the squad and circled to the rear of Murphy's Farm Fresh Market.

"Yeah, the lights went out in the meat department — all of them not just one bulb," said Carpenter sitting straight up in his seat.

"Too early for employees and I have never seen that bank of lights off at night," said McCarthy, pulling to a spot on the northeast corner of the building.

The officers slid silently out of the squad car and pushed the doors to the latching point, paused, and slowly closed them, shutting them with only a quiet click breaking the silent night air.

As they padded silently around the building, they moved from door to door, finding each one intact until they reached a door hidden from view by a large air conditioning unit. The cylinder lock was pulled and lying on the ground next to the door. McCarthy peered through the opening in the door and clearly saw a man dressed in black moving about the inside of the store, piling and packing items as if he was going to steal enough food and drink to feed a small infantry brigade for a week.

McCarthy stepped back to the corner of the building as Carpenter ran to the opposite corner of the store, setting into place a secure perimeter. As they had done earlier, not a word was said between. McCarthy keyed his collar mic and as quietly as possible whispered, "255."

"Go ahead 255," answered the dispatcher.

"Send us some back up to Murphy's Farm Fresh Market. We have a burglary in progress. A white male dressed in black is currently in the northwest corner of the store and he is unaware of our presence. I am holding at the northwest corner and Officer Carpenter is at the southeast corner."

"10-4, 255," said the dispatcher, whose voice registered the mere .001 decibel rise in excitement that the call warranted. McCarthy was always amazed at police dispatchers and plane pilots in the way that they handled their emotions on the radio. Rarely can you find tapes of excited cockpit transmissions of airline pilots sounding emotionally out of control, whether they are reporting a change in the weather, a little turbulence, or that the right wing has just been sheered off. The transmission would be calmly made, "Our right engine has been sheered off. We'll be landing in the Hudson River. Thank you for flying United." Police dispatchers possess that same capability of remaining vocally calm under pressure, which is rare in humans.

"I need four officers to establish a tight perimeter, and when they are in place at each corner of the building, Officer Carpenter and I will attempt to establish contact."

"10-4, we'll have to break some officers out of the station," reported dispatch.

Before anything else could be said, McCarthy heard Maddy Brown, Mike Shepherd, Dooley, and Stanley Brockman all radio, "10-76 to Murphy's (en route)."

McCarthy crouched behind the corner of the air conditioning unit. He could see two doors on two sides of the building from his location. He scanned the lot and streets around the business and noticed a gold pickup on the far side of the lot with exhaust puffing out of the tail pipe. Then the truck started slowly moving through the lot with no lights on, but the taillights went on briefly as the driver tapped the brakes.

"255 to dispatch," said McCarthy.

"Go ahead."

"To the closest responding unit I would like them to stop a gold pickup which is exiting the Menard's lot adjacent to Murphy's. The driver has no lights on, and I believe it is probably involved," said McCarthy as the pickup pulled out of the lot and sped off.

"Got it," answered Maddy as if she was calling for a pop-up between center and left field. McCarthy pointed dramatically at the pickup, but the gesture was unnecessary since Maddy had already locked in on the truck.

The moment Maddy pulled in behind the truck, there was an incredible roar from the engine, turbo charged with the driver's fear of apprehension. The motor of Maddy's black and white Crown Victoria matched and surpassed the truck's ferocity and then came the unmistakable sound of the sirens tearing gaping holes in the night's shroud of silence.

"257, I have a 10-80 (high speed pursuit)," barked Maddy, her first transmission super-charged by the excitement of the chase.

"10-4, 257. Go to channel two with the 10-80. Officers at the scene of the burglary stay on channel one."

The excitement of the chase was lost to McCarthy now on channel one except for the muffled but frantic chattering that could be heard from the distant squad radio. McCarthy prepared himself like a runner in his blocks as the starter shouts, "ready." The man in black had to have heard the sirens from the pursuit.

He had, because at that moment the damaged door burst open and the man in black exited, stopped, and looked frantically about. McCarthy leveled his Glock at the suspect and blipped his sure-fire halogen flashlight into the eyes of the suspect in an attempt to rob him of his night vision, "Police, don't move. Get down on the ground! *Do it now!*" shouted McCarthy.

The late-night shopper turned and ran back into the store. "255. The suspect just exited and re-entered Murphy's. All officers hold your positions on the perimeter!" shouted McCarthy for the benefit of the suspect. He knew it was just he and Carpenter for a few minutes longer.

After a long ten seconds, the suspect cautiously pushed the second door on the rear side of Murphy's open and McCarthy hit him again with the halogen flashlight. The incredible new technology lit up his cornea with the candle power of a runway landing light, practically blinding the man in darkness. McCarthy shouted this time with his best phony Spanish accent, trying to leave the impression that there was more than one of him out there. "Poleez! Dun move. Put your hands eento the air. Do eet now!" shouted McCarthy. Then for good measure he added, "Manos arriba, señor (Hands in the air, sir)."

The door slammed shut and then after about ten seconds he could hear Carpenter shouting at the front, "Police! Don't move. Get down on the…" and the shouting stopped. This human turtle apparently popped his head out momentarily and then sucked it back into its shell.

First Dooley arrived, then Brockman, Hartley, and finally Shepherd. They were positioned to seal the perimeter. McCarthy and Carpenter met at the squad car and geared up for a building search for a known live suspect.

Carpenter by-passed the carbine in the squad and took out his shotgun of choice, the Remington 870.

"Aren't you going to charge it?" asked McCarthy, who noticed Carpenter had not racked a round into the chamber after taking it from the squad.

"Yeah, I will charge it when I decide to establish a meaningful dialog with the suspect. Hey, what was that 'manos arriba' shit and the cheesy accent?" asked Carpenter.

"I wanted him to think there was more than the two of us out here," reasoned McCarthy.

"McCarthy, you are a dichotomy, man," said Carpenter.

"Wow, there's a ten dollar word. How do you mean dichotomy?" asked McCarthy, attaching his flashlight to his Glock with his pocket mount.

"You have way too much fun while you are taking this job way too seriously," explained Carpenter as he and McCarthy padded toward the front door of the store, which the suspect had unlocked during his attept to escape and left open. "I think that's a dichotomy. Anyway, if it is, that's what you are. If it isn't, you're another word that means what I think dichotomy means."

"I'll have to take your word for it," said McCarthy.

As they reached the front door, they swung it open and moved quickly, lights out to a darkened friendly zone and paused. Carpenter then established meaningful dialog. He loudly, quickly, expertly, and deliberately racked a Federal Tactical double-ought buck round into the chamber of the Remington 870. That noise echoed ferociously through the darkened quiet store.

Shotguns have been in law enforcement for over 100 years in the United States. They do not shoot as far, as fast, or as accurately as many other weapons, but their bark is almost as intimidating as the thought of the promised devastatingly thunderous bite. No burglar hiding in a building can mistake the sound of the echoing promise of ugly painful death that an 870 pump action 12 gauge shotgun makes in a large quiet building at night. It is the kettle drum of the police orchestra.

The man in black had already spent the most frightening 30 minutes of his life. At every door he went to he was met by cop. At least one of them had apparently been summoned from Mexico or a B-grade Chuck Norris movie. His heart was pounding, the flood gates had opened from his sweat glands, his bladder had unintentionally voided, and he was seeing little bluish white balloons floating in front of his eyes from their blinding flashlights. If that was not enough, now came the echoing formal notification that the police were coming for him. "*Chick Chack*, Chack, chack, chack, chack." He had enough.

He stood up from behind the service meat counter, leaving the butcher knives that he had taken out lying on the floor. He would not be taking knives to a shotgun fight. His hands were high and his palms were forward with his fingers spread. He had done this before except not with so much fear. "I give up. Don't shoot," he screamed. He now thought, "Where are they?"

He ran out of the meat department through the metal swinging saloon-style doors, slipping on the freshly waxed floor and then tripping over the yellow "caution floors wet" sign. He slid into a display of Armor Chili Dog Sauce on sale and knocked the entire mountain of chili dog sauce cans to the floor but still no cops.

He then leaped back to his feet and threw his hands back into the air. He sprinted to the front of the store, up aisle number three containing breakfast cereals, and before he reached the end, he was shouted to the ground by McCarthy. "Get Down. Do it now!"

The man in black hit the floor on his belly and slid ten feet to a stop. He assumed a perfect ground cuffing position because this career criminal had been arrested by McCarthy before. McCarthy did not need to give any further commands because this suspect was already right where he should be, on the ground in a perfect position. McCarthy said to Carpenter as he applied the handcuffs to the suspect, "How ironic. This guy's luck ran out right next to the Lucky Charms."

"Like I said, McCarthy, you have way too much fun," observed Carpenter dryly.

"Fucking McCarthy, is that you? This is a fucking nightmare!" said the familiar voice behind the black mask.

"Zach, is that you?" said McCarthy.

"Yeah, it's me. This is a fucking nightmare," Zach repeated.

"If it is Zach, it's a recurring dream for you," said McCarthy.

Then what was said by Zach Mitchell, career criminal, would be the headlines of the La Claire news the next day. It was what every cop working the night shift would hope to be and Zach would declare it to be so. "Carpenter, McCarthy, I shit you not, you two fuckers aren't a recurring dream. You are a fucking *Burglar's Nightmare!*"

CHAPTER NINETEEN

WE DID IT FOR LOVE

After Maddy Brown had spotted the gold pickup truck that McCarthy had called in, she hit the lights of her patrol car. They brightly lit up the night with a brilliant display of spinning colorful confirmation that someone was having a bad day. If there was any doubt in her mind that the gold pickup was tied into the burglary in progress, those doubts were sizzled hot off her brain pan when the taillights of the truck abruptly began to get smaller and smaller.

"257, I have a 10-80 (pursuit)," radioed Brown.

"10-4," said Melissa in dispatch. She then said out loud to herself, "Jiminy Crickets!"

"Jiminy Crickets?" asked Jacob, who was dispatching for the La Claire Sheriff's Department. "What kind of exhortation is Jiminy Crickets?"

"It's an exhortation that you can say accidentally on a taped line without getting into trouble. I thought Carpenter and McCarthy would be half as much trouble working together instead of having them on opposite ends of the city kicking over shit cans to watch the maggots crawl out. Now that they are working together, they are just tipping over bigger shit cans! Every time they key the mic, the whole county suddenly goes on red alert," chattered Melissa, releasing her stress in the five seconds she would have to chat for the last time tonight.

"Taped line! Taped line!" warned Jacob.

Melissa then said defiantly before going back over the air, "Jiminy fucking Crickets." Then she was back into the chase.

"257, we are out bound on Highway 41 at 90 mph. The driver of the truck is swerving repeatedly across the center line."

"257, be advised that La Claire County sheriff's squad 190 says he can deploy spikes five miles out on 41 if you request his assistance," reported Melissa.

"10-4, if the driver stays on 41 have him do so please," answered Maddy.

"10-4." After a brief delay Melissa answered, "Be advised 190 is five miles out and set up for deployment."

"10-4," answered Madison Brown, calmly. She had settled into the chase. The speeds of 90-110 after a few minutes into a straight line pursuit seem only slightly faster than 70 mph. This driver had locked in on Highway 41 and was not going to let go.

The five miles at over 100 miles per hour passed very quickly. Brown backed off giving the fleeing felon space, and the pickup hit the spikes. The thump of the tires obviously startled the driver. Maddy saw the Sheriff's Deputy expertly, with a snap of the wrist, pull the spike strips off the roadway, allowing Maddy to continue in pursuit.

The driver of the pickup swayed back and forth and back and forth after going over the spikes. The spikes were hollow metal needles. The spikes stick in the tire and do not blow the tire but allow the tire to deflate gradually. All four tires had hit the strip and were carrying plenty of spikes to do the job.

After about three miles, it looked to Maddy that the driver was on the rims. "257. The truck is still outbound on 41 right now, nine miles out. The driver is doing 60 miles per hour on the rims."

"10-4. County 194 will be joining you shortly," reported dispatch.

"10-4, I have him behind me with 190 also," reported Maddy.

The truck's front right tire was the first to totally shred, and the rubber flew off and rolled and bounced to the side of the road like a blown up birthday balloon that was let go of by a child before it was tied off. Now the rim was spitting sparks, looking like a road flare warning all of the danger that was approaching.

Without warning, the brake lights lit up and Maddy responded by hitting her brakes, pumping them twice hoping the squad behind her would be more likely not to pile into her.

The truck shifted left and then swerved right coming to a stop sideways in the road. "257, I will be in foot pursuit. The driver bailed at the 13 mile marker on 41."

"Direction?" dispatched asked.

"Don't know," answered Maddy. She realized that she had not actually seen the driver run but knew that the driver was running. As Maddy rounded the truck, she saw that the driver was a blonde female, dressed in black. Maddy could see why she chose this spot to run. "257, she is running eastbound into a cornfield." Maddy was after and followed into the rows of corn.

The blonde was fast, but she ran through corn like she drove. She picked a row and just kept going straight. The corn was last year's field corn left up either for deer or feed or because the farmer was too sick to bring it in, but it was the only standing field of corn within twenty miles. Maddy was a member of the SWAT team, and her specialty was being one of the fastest runners on the team. Maddy could see this lady would not outrun her. She glanced back, and although she was only halfway through the field of corn that lay ahead of her, she had long lost her county back-up officers. They were hanging back on the chase to avoid a collision and had lost sight of Maddy and the fleeing driver after they both cut into the corn field. Darkness had folded over Maddy and the suspect because there are no street lights in corn fields.

Maddy stayed within sight of the driver. This was not just a driver fleeing. This was part of a burglary in progress. Burglars! She would not let a burglar escape. "God, she is even dressed like a cat burglar," Maddy said to herself out loud.

As Maddy burst out of the field of corn, she was only twenty-five yards back from the burglar in black. The burglar was having trouble making her way through the adjacent field which was planted for hay. The grass was thick, and her legs were starting to feel like logs; her lungs were pumping air about as efficiently as a leaky bellows.

Maddy was not fresh as a college sprinter on the first turn, but she could see she had more fuel left and higher rpms than her adversary. Maddy began planning the apprehension, "flying tackle or TASER?" She looked back in the darkness. There would be no help for her. All the flashlights of her backup were bobbing back and forth on the opposite side of the corn field. "They lost me in the darkness. I'm by myself," she thought.

Maddy had a habit of making up little songs in her head when she ran. It made the miles go faster. She made her decision and the decision took the form of a song, (sung to her favorite running tune "Ta-Ra-Ra Boom-De-Ay"). "Looks like a TASER Day, You shouldn't have run away, you should have stayed to play, Now it's a TASER Day." She thought she was singing it in her head, but the squad audio recorder picked up the tune. The recording would be played many times with much side-splitting laughter for her accompaniment at the next shift Christmas party.

Maddy checked the burglar's hands and saw there was nothing in them. She drew her TASER and held it in her right hand as she closed on the fleeing female who had lost much of her feline flair. She was now moving more like an old dairy cow running from the advances of the new bull. Maddy came up on the right side of the female and with her left hand directed her upper body forward and down, taking her balance way. The female skid into the tall grass; Maddy kept her feet and yelled, "Down! Stay Down! You are under arrest!"

The female was momentarily stunned and saw there was just a lone female officer. She thought she still had a chance. She started to her feet and Maddy shouted, "TASER, TASER, TASER!" as she fired, the two probes crackled out of the cartridge and both found their mark. One hit the female in the left shoulder blade and the second probe hit her, as Forrest Gump would say, "In the Butt-tocks!"

"Aieeeeeee," shouted the female for five straight seconds and then she lay back down. Like a charred steak, she was done on both sides, and aware she was truly "forked."

No one came to assist Maddy. She was winded and out of shouting distance. The pursuit had taken her out of walk unit range, and the two officers who ably assisted her in the vehicle pursuit were still trying to determine which corn row Maddy had disappeared into. Maddy held the TASER in one hand and handcuffed the suspect with the other. She then expertly removed the cartridge from the TASER, reloaded another, and holstered the TASER. Maddy then said, "This will sting a bit," as she pressed one hand down on either side of the each probe and quickly pulled each probe out. She then searched her suspect. "Are you OK?" Maddy asked.

"Now that those are out, yeah," answered the woman.

Maddy found nothing in the search of consequence, but she could see the forest through the trees. Before the night was over, Maddy would confiscate the female's black-as-night clothing as evidence, which was how the burglar inside Murphy's was dressed. In an act of love, they had purchased matching burglary outfits, using identical name brands and styles on the pants and pullover shirts. That's called circumstantial evidence in some circles.

Maddy advised the young lady of her rights and then explained, "We have a little bit of a walk to get back. It was your job to get away and mine to catch you. That being done, I want to let you know that there is no longer a reason for us to not get along. My name is Madison Brown; my friends call me Maddy."

"You're the cop who shot that guy who shot you, right?" asked the lady in black excitedly.

"Yes. I am." Maddy had achieved local fame when she shot a deranged man who had ambushed her. Maddy was seriously wounded but managed to draw and fire, killing the man. Madison Brown had fired two rounds into the suspect's head. Both rounds had gone into the suspect's head through the same hole.

"You were like my hero. I was sixteen when that happened and you were… a fucking girl, man. Wow. I got to be arrested by you. That is so awesome like… not that I got arrested, but that, like, I got to be arrested by Downtown Maddy Brown. You're my hero… like, I mean, as far as cops go, you know," chattered the female as Maddy began to retrace their steps to make certain nothing got tossed.

"What's up tonight?" asked Maddy feeling a rapport had set in or something very much like one.

"Me and my Zach are getting married. His parents are fucked up and my parents are fucked up, so we decided we had to do it ourselves if we were going to have a reception. Zach just got out of prison, and he was going to go straight except he decided to do this one burglary for me. He wanted me to have a real wedding, you know. Not in a fucking church or anything like that, but with a dress and a reception and all that. He was going to get brats, beer, soda, wine, and maybe enough money for a honeymoon, and then he was going to go straight. He was going to do it himself, but I said from now on we do everything together. We love each other. We are getting married, and I'm not even pregnant. That's a first for our family." She looked at Maddy and smiled and scrunched up her shoulders and cocked her head to the left and added, "The first to get married without having to let out the wedding dress if you know what I mean."

"Why did you take off?" asked Maddy.

"Because Zach said I should, so I did. He said if he got caught I was to take off. I could see the cops had him and there was nothing I could do about it. Then when I saw the squad car come after me, I thought maybe it was the same ones that were after Zach, so I thought I would lead them away, which would be a lot better for Zach because of his record, you know. I guess I didn't help him at all because it turned out to be you."

"How do you know I was not the one at the store?" asked Maddy.

"I saw the officers get out. One of them was that fucking McCarthy. Zach said McCarthy put him and his brother Billy in prison for their last burglary, and he said he had a bad dream. He told me that he dreamed that fucking McCarthy caught him again." She then looked at Maddy with sad doe eyes, "I'm sorry. I am not saying 'that fucking McCarthy;' that is what Zach was saying."

"I understand," said Maddy patting her reassuringly on the shoulder. "By the way, what is your name?"

"Pammy Mitchell. That is my name. I have the same last name as Zach's. I won't even have to change my driver's license. We have the same last name, but, like, we are not related. It's a real common name, you know."

Then what Pammy, the star struck lover, said would be the headline for the follow-up story on the burglary at Murphy's. "You know, like, Zach did this because he loved me, and, like, I did this because I loved him. I hope the judge understands, like, the reason we did this… anyone would. *We did it for love.*"

CHAPTER TWENTY

WILL THIS END

Ripp had worked his magic once again. Mother Nature has many types of predators in her arsenal: Those animals who prowl the Earth capturing prey with speed, strength, and a vicious relentless attack. The Venus Fly Trap attracts its victims by looking harmless and even pleasing to the eye. The spider which lies concealed and unseen until the hapless object of its hunt falls into its web, totally unprepared for the inevitable and violent end. The snake strikes quickly and suddenly, possessing poisonous venom that incapacitates its victim. After the use of such lightning speed on the attack it proceeds in a slow, methodical manner to devour its prize, savoring every moment of the kill.

Ripp had been all of these. There were times he received a rush during the sheer and utter violence of the kill. There were times he enjoyed the dance with victims who were wrapped in complacency and convinced of their indestructibility right up to the moment that they were faced with the recognition that they had arrived at the scene of their own sudden and brutal death.

Ripp sought variety because he bored easily. He had become bored with his life, his success, and the gift of his genius. That is what drew him toward the excitement of the kill. Each victim was a unique experience for William Ripp. He sought variety in victims, locations, and the manner of death. His motto was "variety is the spice of death." He also reasoned it would make it difficult for authorities to connect the dots, if the dots began to form an identifiable picture. His pattern of no pattern had worked for him thus far.

The one thing that linked his crimes was Ripp's perception that his victims were non-persons in society. They were people that the world could do without. They were so much his inferior that each one was a true "nobody." Ripp would say to himself,

"Nobody cares about them, nobody will miss them, nobody needs them, and each one of them is a non-person. Each selection was a perfect nobody."

Once again he had worked what he thought to be his magic. She was young and even attractive. He had become hungry and unfulfilled in La Claire. He longed for Darla but had decided it was too dangerous there. He had been incredibly lucky that Darla had a stalker or he would have been caught. He would satisfy himself with another.

He found her dancing in a club north of Bentonville, Arkansas. He had prepared a perfect spot for their "tryst." Ripp discovered her and she was an easy mark. Her name was Angela. She would go with him and do for him if the price was right. Ripp had never worked this area before but found the perfect spot. Even though the area north of Bentonville was bursting with development, it was still surrounded by vast stretches of wilderness.

After he had paid for a long, grinding, and delectable lap dance in the club Angela was working in, he arranged to meet for a private party in the parking lot of a hotel he said he was staying at. Ripp had not registered at the hotel, but he had picked it for the meeting because it was a hotel that had no security cameras. It was also a hotel that he had never stayed at.

As Angela got into his car, he said, "You are so beautiful," his eyes looking adoringly into hers.

She blushed, "Why thank you." She looked sheepishly away from him and returned the favor, "You're not so hard on the eyes either."

"I changed my mind," Ripp said nervously, "My first time I ever... you know, was in the back seat of a car in the boonies. You remind me of her. I will pay you extra if... do you mind... I mean if it is not too much trouble, could we?" asked Ripp.

She looked at him. He looked harmless and kind of cute, stammering like a school boy. He was too good looking to be a rapist and too bookish to be a killer. "I guess so, but it is $200 for every half hour, whether it's spent driving or fucking. Like I told you before, I do only straight sex, nothing weird."

"Her name was Darla. Can I call you Darla, or is that too weird?" He asked.

"Not at all, I can be Darla if you want me to be Darla, I can be anyone you want me to be. That's not weird. It's kind of nice," said Angela obligingly. "Hey are you a teacher? You look like a professor, or something," asked Angela.

"No. I am a freelance computer database consultant... Darla," said Ripp.

"Wow. That sounds really important," said Angela.

"I guess," said Ripp casually.

"Does it make you rich, if you don't mind my asking?" asked Angela.

"I do rather well," answered Ripp with an elite air about him.

"Rich men make me hot!" said Angela dropping her hand into his lap.

"Well, Darla, I made more money yesterday than you could possibly make the rest of your life," said Ripp entertained by the ironic truth of the statement.

"Can you drive when I do this," asked Angela, dropping her head down into his lap.

"It's hard to drive that way, but, Darla, you are making it so easy to be hard," he said as turned up the dirt road leading to the place he had prepared.

As the car came to a stop, Angela popped her head up and saw the clearing prepared in advance. There was a blanket and a bottle of wine a few feet away from the car. There was a basket with cheese, crackers, and a small meat tray on the blanket.

"Great! It's a picnic. I love picnics!" cried Angela clapping her hands together like a school girl.

Angela climbed out of the rental car and lay out sensually on the blanket. "I never fucked a computer database programmer before. What's it like?" she asked.

"We are known for our hard drive," said Ripp rounding the car.

"Hard drive, I love it. Take me now with your hard drive," she said rolling onto her back and slipping off her shorts and panties in one movement, revealing her soft rounded bottom.

She then rolled to her knees and pulled her top off over her head, then dropped her hands to the blanket. As she waited on her hands and knees she swayed her rounded bottom back and forth, beckoning him unconditionally. Her large breasts swung free and hung patiently waiting for what she thought would be a warm loving touch. She shook her head, expertly tossing her hair out of her eyes and she licked her lips. This was exciting to Angela. This felt more like a date than a John. "Take me now hard and fast."

Ripp entered her with a shared gasp. He began thrusting like the piston on a paddle wheeler. "Oh Darla, ARRRRGH," he cried out 30 seconds after he had begun.

Angela was as shocked by the immediacy of the intensity as she was disappointed in the brevity of the encounter. As a prostitute she was not in it for the pleasure, but even so this was an extremely long drive for such a short ride. Then she thought, "There is still hope for more," as she felt him slowly intertwine his fingers in her long brown hair as he continued to thrust in and out ever so slowly.

"Oh, Darla, you have such beautiful hair," moaned Ripp. Then suddenly, without warning, he yanked her head back, and for a fraction of a fleeting moment she saw the blade flash by her face. The pain was hot, sudden, and then she was... gone.

Ripp held her close to his body for a long while, bathing in the smell, the warmth, and the wetness of his completed act. "Oh Angela, you were good, but you are no Darla." He let her go and she slid to the blanket with her eyes wide open and sightless.

Ripp opened his eyes and was shocked to find his glasses covered in the blood of his fresh kill. He reached into his shirt pocket and found his handkerchief and frantically wiped the glasses as clean as he could.

He then dropped to the blanket and lay beside her for what seemed like a long time. When his energy returned, he popped up and said, "Well, Angela, time to get you home. I forgot you are on the clock," he chuckled.

Ripp then carefully cut a lock of her hair and took in its perfume. "Yes, that will do." He took out a Ziploc® baggie and dropped the hair into it. He searched her things and found an

Arkansas Driver's license and was surprised to see that her name was indeed Angela. He slipped the license into the baggie with the lock of hair and set it aside. He then stood up and wrapped Angela in the blanket. He carried her to the tree line and just beyond was the hole he had prepared. It was dug deep. He dropped her, letting her fall in a heap at the bottom of the deep, dark emptiness.

Ripp undressed and dropped his clothes onto Angela. He washed himself with a specially prepared soap and saline solution then dried with a towel lying on a blanket next to the hole. He dropped the towel into the hole and then Ripp stepped into the clean clothes lying on the blanket. After he was zipped and buttoned, he reached into the pocket of his freshly acquired pair of pants and found the comb he had placed there. He carefully combed each detestable hair on his head back into place, giving him the look of the harmless trusted professor once again. He looked about and threw all the remnants of this day's carnage into the hole. There was plenty of room.

Ripp picked up the brand new shovel leaning against a tree next to the hole and filled it in. He meticulously replaced the sod he had cut from the spot earlier and expertly camouflaged the grave where Angela had been sent to meet the angels. Finished with his day's work, he tossed the shovel into the woods and then stood silently over the spot and whispered gently, "Thank you, dear. Rest well." He turned and walked back to the car.

As he reached the car, Ripp popped the trunk and removed a worn black leather briefcase. He set the case on the hood of the rental car and deftly rolled the numbers into the right position and unlocked the case. He walked over a few paces and picked up the Ziploc® bag. He walked gingerly back to the open case and set the baggie down into it. He slipped a pen and a 3" x 5" index card out of one of the compartments of the briefcase and laid the card down on the fender of the rental vehicle. He held Angela's license and wrote the date, the time, and the location and details of his latest conquest onto the 3" x 5" card. Ripp took great care to write Angela's name and under the word "Comment" he wrote, "She was good, but she was not Darla (Knife)."

He slipped the card into the baggie and the baggie into the briefcase. "That's number twenty-three." He felt the breeze on his cheeks. He listened to an impatient tapping of a woodpecker and breathed the fresh country air into his lungs. "What a wonderful day to be alive." Then he shut the briefcase and snapped the latches into place. He shouted triumphantly, "That's number twenty-three!" He laid the briefcase in the bottom of the trunk and closed the trunk.

Ripp walked to the driver's door, opened it, and turned one more time to look at the matted down grass where he had taken young Angela, who had blushed when he said she was beautiful. He whispered sadly in another voice as if someone else occupied his soul, "That's number twenty-three. I wonder. *Will this end?*"

CHAPTER TWENTY-ONE

THE NIGHTMARE CONTINUES

"That was too much work, man," said Carpenter to McCarthy as he turned the squad on to the Causeway in La Claire three hours into the night shift the next night after the "fiancée felony." "If the burglary wasn't enough, look, we're three hours into the shift and have done nothing but reports," complained Carpenter.

"I'm not arguing with you. That was a lot of work. On TV the cops just shoot them and leave them DRT (Dead Right There). I never saw Dirty Harry write a report," agreed McCarthy. "If he did it would probably say, 'Saw suspect. Shot suspect. Finished hotdog,' End of report."

"Hell Dirty Harry? I never saw the camera man on *Cops* sit there in the report room with his camera running doing a complete half hour show on *Cops* watching a cop write a report," reasoned Carpenter.

"Yeah my theme song tonight would have been, 'Bad Boys Bad Boys, What you gonna do, what ya gonna do til my report is through?' Hey maybe they were out here waiting for us. Let's catch another one!" exclaimed McCarthy. "Should we find one more? Compton said at lineup his finger was still itching tonight. Come on, Carp. I found one last night, you find one tonight."

"OK, but it's going to be easier than that one last night. Just one guy stuck in a window with his big ass hanging out, OK?" said Carpenter.

"Sweet," agreed McCarthy. "Sniff that guy's ass out."

"What?"

"Sorry," said McCarthy. "Didn't mean it like it sounded."

As Carpenter drove, he rolled down the window of his cruiser and began sniffing into the air like a blue tick hound dog picking up the scent of an escapee from the road gang. He then cut the lights of the squad as it approached King's Ford on Causeway. He slowly turned into the lot letting the squad coast using only the idling engine for propulsion, quietly slipping through the lot like a shark fin through a tranquil lagoon. Carpenter continued sniffing all the way.

As they rounded the corner of the lot, there it was. The legs of a man were slipping through a window of the dealership. The window slammed closed loudly as the burglar hit the floor inside the dealership. "We're going to have to work for it. He didn't get stuck in the window," said Carpenter as he dropped McCarthy off.

"Even so this was well timed. Tell me later what a burglar smells like," McCarthy remarked as he quickly removed his seat belt, exiting the squad as if he had been ejected.

"Chicken. They smell like chicken," replied Carpenter matter-of-factly while he spun the squad to the opposite corner of the building.

As McCarthy reached the entry point, he could see that the night thief had seen the squad. He was at a dead run to the opposite side of the building. "255, we have a burglary in progress at King's Ford; suspect's running at you, Carp!" said McCarthy, carrying on two conversations at once.

"10-4 I see him. I'm in position. He is coming right at me," replied Carpenter.

At the same time at the opposite side of town, Maddy Brown was rounding the corner of Sonic Lanes Bowling Alley, and a tall drink of water dressed in black walked out of the kitchen door of the bowling alley. She immediately recognized that the business was closed and the guy coming out of the place carrying a black knapsack over his shoulder was not the night accountant, especially when she saw the door was so badly peeled back that it left a gap for the light in the kitchen to shine out when it slammed shut.

Maddy and the tall drink of water made eye contact momentarily, and then he was running. Maddy called in her foot pursuit at the same moment Carpenter called in that he had spotted his suspect and the suspect was coming right at him. All that anyone in the city could hear were buzzes, clicks, and hums with an occasional, "he's running," discernable in the perfect storm of impossible communication when multiple frantic cops try to talk at one time on one radio channel.

"255 go again, that's a 10-9 (I couldn't copy)," was the response of the dispatcher. The humming and clicking continued. Melissa's frustration rose while she hopelessly tried to untangle the mess. Maddy continued to attempt to call in her burglary in progress, while Carpenter and McCarthy continued in their updates as they ran back and forth cornering and losing the ping pong burglar. The frantic buzzing and clicking built to a frenzied crescendo, never to be surpassed as the back-up officers called in their locations, offering to assist Carpenter and McCarthy.

"255 we have hmmmmzzzzzticktick shump."

"256 I have the suspect zzzzzzznickznickznick hmmm click"

"257 I am heading toward a nickacnikacnikshummmp."

"All units I can't copy please zzzznickhummmmmmclick."

"259 be advised hmmmzzzznickhmmmclick."

And so it continued, Motorola Madness experiencing its finest hour. Melissa threw up her hands and said, "Jiminy fucking crickets," to Jacob.

"I hear you. I can't advise you on the communications mess, but I can tell you that the Jiminy Cricket's thing you have going to keep you from accidentally saying bad words over the air is truly a flawed plan. It's just not working for you," said Jacob.

McCarthy paralleled the window dropper the length of the building. The windows and the night lighting left on inside the business allowed him to follow the man's progress step for step. McCarthy reached the end of the building and saw Carpenter had the door that was about to be the exit of the window dropper. The door swung open and slammed shut just as quickly when window dropper saw Carpenter. Carpenter tried the door but it was locked.

Window dropper sprinted to the far end of the dealership again, this time paralleled by both Carpenter and McCarthy. He tried to exit a door at the opposite corner, and McCarthy shouted, "You are under arrest! Get down on the ground. Do it now!"

McCarthy tried to urge him to the ground with the muzzle of his gun pointed between his eyes, but the suspect slammed the door once again and then sprinted the width of the dealership to the nearest door on the opposite side of the building, and as he swung the door open, Carpenter shouted, "Police! Don't move! Get down, down, down!" and the door slammed again.

The sprint was on as window dropper cut angularly across the dealership to the opposite side and McCarthy took the straight line toward the exit that the man was running for. McCarthy then realized because the lights were lighted inside more brightly than outside, window dropper could not see the officers following his every footstep. As the corner door opened, McCarthy once again shouted, "Police! Get Down! Do It Now!" The door slamming was the only response. McCarthy thought, "This is like a pickle with a runner caught between second and third base."

McCarthy paralleled again the panicked window dropper, wondering how many rails this spinning billiard ball would hit before he rolled to a stop. His pace was still frantic. McCarthy tried to position cars by using the radio, but all he could get was a series of hums and clicks. "The first thing to go is communication," he thought which was the standard cliché during every after-action debrief of every tactical event in the history of law enforcement.

As window dropper crossed the large garage area of the dealership, he suddenly hit a large moving wall at a dead run and down he went. It was Dooley. McCarthy looked up and saw the original window that the suspect had slid into which had then dropped shut was now standing wide open. Dooley, a man of action who was the perennial perfect backup, had slammed into the frantic burglar and now they were on the floor of the garage and the battle was joined.

McCarthy tried every door and they were all locked, and he then concluded, "One way into this fight." He scrambled quickly through the open window and slid to the floor over a bench, tucked, rolled, and came to his feet.

Window dropper was swinging for all he was worth at Dooley, but Dooley rode him from behind using the riding techniques that catapulted him to a state championship in wrestling. Window dropper was beaten but not finished. McCarthy slid to the left side and pulled window dropper's left leg and left arm out, and window dropper hit the pavement hard. With both arms and a leg tied up, window dropper gave up the fight. He passively lay upon the oily pavement of the dealership garage floor and submitted to exhaustion, handcuffs, and arrest. McCarthy listened to the clicks and hums of the radio and waited for an opening. Finally one came. "255, we're 10-95 (suspect in custody) inside King's Ford."

"10-4, 255," came the clear response.

As the man with the black bag fled from the rear of the Sonic Lanes, Officer Madison Brown called in, "257, I am in foot pursuit from a burglary in progress at Sonic Lanes. We are southbound from the rear of the building." As she released the mic key, she heard the most ungodly clicking and humming on her radio as if a hysterical R2-D2 was trying to warn Luke of an incoming death ray from the death star.

The radios barked, hummed, and clicked without stopping. She realized for the second night in a row she was on her own. The bag man circled the building, and she followed staying within twenty-five feet of him. He had a good stride, but the bag was slowing him down. Whatever was in the bag was obviously heavy. She tried to assess what might be in it. "It could contain weapons possibly, but hopefully it was just a large amount of coins." She thought. "I will catch this guy for sure if he doesn't drop the bag."

As they reached the front of the building, the bag man cut through the parking lot and across the four lane highway in front of the Sonic Lanes. There was no traffic. It was 3:30 in the morning and the people that were going home from last night were home. The people who had to work in the morning were sleeping. The city of La Claire was once again sleeping through one of Madison Brown's most memorable moments.

As they reached the parking lot of the Gander Mountain, they ran through the lot and along the side of the business. As she passed the side door, she saw it had the same bowed and peeled configuration as did door on the Sonic Lanes. This man had broken into at least two businesses. Seeing this, she realized she had neglected one time-honored formality. Madison Brown shouted, "Stop! Police!" The tall man in black did not even turn around and if anything the command seemed to spur him on a bit.

His gait gradually turned from a sprint to a limp. The bag he would not give up was taking its toll. "Damn. This woman is going to catch me if I don't lose the loot or hurt her bad," thought the career criminal. This had been the best night of his life. He had emptied two well-filled safes and copped some handguns to boot. "Damn. I got a little greedy. Fuck! A lady cop is gaining on me."

Maddy could see he was sucking air and she had to decide, "Gun him, TASE him, or tackle him." She listened for an opening on the radio, but the frantic series of clicking, humming, and call numbers continued for what seemed like forever. In reality all this was happening in less than two minutes. Two minutes is a long time in a foot pursuit, a chase, or a fight in a dark alley for a cop without a backup. She did not want to engage a larger man in a physical contest when no one even knew where she was. She thought to herself as she ran, "I think it would be best if I...."

Before she could complete the thought, the man in black suddenly turned awkwardly as he swung the knapsack off his shoulder and as he spun he gained speed. He spun like a ball and hammer thrower in the Olympics, spinning the weighted bag at Maddy Brown.

Momentum is a funny thing. It can work for you or against you. The man in black missed Madison and lost his momentum because the bag was not a balanced ball and hammer. It was filled with cash, change, guns, and it was as awkward as it was heavy. As he swung the bag, the weight in the bag shifted mightily. The man in black appeared to be walking about on loose sections of ice floating on a thawing Wisconsin lake in April. He appeared to be on the verge of falling but still tried to muster enough energy to swing one more time at his pursuer. The man in black had misjudged his distance from his approaching rival, striking too early. Maddy showed the timing of Jerry Seinfeld. If Seinfeld saw what was about to occur he would say, "Did you hear about the sober burglar who tried to take on Downtown Madison Brown in La Claire Wisconsin. Well even though he did not have a thing to drink he still got *SMASHED!*" As the man in black swung his bag, Maddy swung wide, avoiding the impact and, on the run, leaped and expertly drove her right elbow into and through the man's jaw, breaking it in two places and knocking him out. He would remain moderately sedated by Maddy right up to the time the hospital staff would need to sedate him for surgery to wire his jaw.

"*Down!*" shouted Maddy at impact. She did not have to ask him twice.

As he hit the pavement, he landed face first. Maddy took his limp wrists, which had nothing to do with his sexuality because this man considered himself a manly man. This manly man would get grief from his cell-mates after they discovered he was thoroughly and instantaneously thrashed by a lady cop.

After Maddy safety locked the handcuffs, she could hear her breathing surrounded by the silence of the night except for the relentless clicking and humming of the radio. Then it stopped. After the briefest of moments, came the transmission from McCarthy, "255, we're 10-95 (suspect in custody) inside King Ford."

"10-4, 255," came the clear response.

"257. Puff puff puff," said Maddy cautiously hopeful someone would hear her.

"257, you can 10-22 (disregard). They do not need you. 255 is 10-95. You can remain south," answered the dispatcher, mistakenly thinking she was calling to offer her assistance to McCarthy and Carpenter.

"257 I am 10-95. I also have a burglary suspect in custody. He is unconscious from a blow to the jaw. He will need an ambulance. I will need some assistance. Sonic Lanes and Gander Mountain have been broken into. I believe I have the suspect involved in custody. I have not had the opportunity to check either business. I am in the lot adjacent to Gander Mountain. Please send units to both businesses to check for entries puff, puff, puff," and then Madison Brown paused to control her breathing. She began scanning the area for an accomplice. If the man in black had one, they were long gone. Maddy and the man in black were alone in the dimly lit empty parking lot.

"Jiminy Fucking Crickets," said Melissa turning to Jacob. "Tomorrow night I'm taking off."

After the second night of burglars entering the black hole for criminals which La Claire had become, the La Claire paper's headline read, *The Nightmare Continues.*

CHAPTER TWENTY-TWO

EVEREST

When William Ripp arrived home in Madison after his business trip to Bentonville, he could not sleep, he could not eat, and he could not concentrate on his work. Usually he experienced a honeymoon period after a successful "life-taking." He found no pleasure even after removing and admiring his souvenirs. Sometimes just opening the briefcase calmed him. Other times he would take each bag out and read the note card as he reminisced, handling each bag, opening it, and imagining. He would mentally commit the most heinous crime known to man, perfectly, over and over again. On most occasions in the past he could enjoy this simple pleasure of reliving each death.

William would usually find solace, comfort, and a respite from his own violent obsessions, which at times frightened even him. He struggled against his current obsession. He had ravaged Angela and killed her as a surrogate for Darla. He had experienced such an immediate and intense orgasm from just the thought of having Darla, he wondered, "Hell could have me if I could have the real Darla." The devil would not accept such a bargain for he already owned William Ripp's soul.

Having maniacal, homicidal fantasies was the absolute norm for William Ripp. What was incredibly unusual about his current fantasy, of enjoying the end of life experience with Darla, was that he suppressed it. Ripp had been acting out his fantasies for twenty years. He possessed very little impulse control. There were twenty-three victims lying buried all over the country as everlasting proof of this fact. Now he could not have the woman of his dreams. "It's not fair," he pouted.

Each day William Ripp was able to resist the urge to go to Darla and kill her. He tried to suppress these urges by going online daily to check the news from La Claire. Each posting on the police department startled him. "Shot's Fired in Downtown La Claire" told the story of Carpenter, Dooley, and McCarthy arriving on the scene of an impending homicide to shoot a knife-wielding maniac when certain death was imminent. All Ripp could think was, "That could be me."

Ripp read with great interest the article with the headline, "It Was a Burglar's Nightmare." He read how once again, Carpenter and McCarthy had arrived on the scene, spotting the burglary in progress and trapped the burglar like a cockroach in a corner. The newspaper reported, "The suspect, Zach Mitchell has been arrested before by Officer McCarthy and reported that he had foreseen last night's arrest in reoccurring nightmares. His brother Billy Mitchell is currently serving a sentence for burglary for taking part in the infamous Harley David Slade case. Mitchell was also arrested by McCarthy, and Slade's murderous rampage was ended by Sergeant Compton, Officer McCarthy, and the La Claire Emergency Response Team." Each story triggered more research until his neck ached and his eyes blurred from gazing into his computer screen.

Day after day, Ripp attempted to suppress his obsession to kill Darla by reading about the poor luck of criminals who came face to face with the names he came to know so well, McCarthy, Carpenter, Compton, Dooley, Brockman, and the female officer "Downtown Madison Brown," a local legend in her own right. His attempt to suppress an obsession became an obsession.

Ripp read about Compton's shot which ended the life of Harley David Slade as Slade counted down to the death of Judge Alice. Slade had taken the judge prisoner and condemned her to death in his personal war. He had taped a shotgun to her neck and intended on executing her in front of the police.

Ripp read with great interest how Judge Alice fell in love with her savior and married David Compton a year later in a storybook romance. He then queried Compton's name and found a more recent article on the courageous sergeant. Ripp sat, his mouth wide open while he drooled onto his laptop. He read how Bryce Packwood ambushed David Compton, shooting him until he was out of bullets and then slashing him with a knife, but Compton would not die. "Holy Satan!" shouted Ripp, spitting onto his computer screen.

He read how Compton calmly coached an explorer scout on how to remove the sergeant's weapon from its holster and had the scout place it in his wounded hand. Compton then shot and killed Packwood.

Ripp read about Gary Carpenter being shot in the chest and arm and then rising like a Phoenix from the ashes to return to continue his career, possibly better than new. He knew their names and their faces. His search engines were churning, digging, finding initial reports, follow up reports, and aftermath reports.

Ripp discovered that Carpenter's assailant later escaped custody and was hunted down by McCarthy and when challenged to give up, the man's last act on Earth was to fire one shot at McCarthy. McCarthy shot no more but missed less. McCarthy's "shot in the dark," according to one report, struck the man, "between the eyes."

Ripp moved on to devour the coverage of a gunfight with a bank robber called "Mad Mattix" who had set up an ambush of a team assigned to deliver a phone to establish communications. Mattix had hidden under a bed and duct taped his hand to a 45 caliber semi automatic handgun and after he fired on the delivery team of Brockman, Stammos, Dooley, Carpenter, and McCarthy, they returned fire. They were not hit even after Mattix's best effort, and Mattix died after being badly chewed up by over fifty rounds fired in a matter of seconds.

One local television news station did a five part series on all of these incidents and what citizens thought of such high profile events occurring in their city. One balding man with a pair of glasses balanced on the end of his nose looked as if he had been seated on a bench at a mall reading when the camera crew interrupted him. The man's observation said it all, "La Claire is a safe city to live in for everyone except criminals." He then picked up his book and looked away from the camera but turned back as if now he really had an important point to make. He looked directly into the camera and observed, "You know, I kind of like it that way."

The reporter concluded, "The La Claire Police Department periodically seems to be faced with crimes that blow in like a violent funnel cloud, but they continue to weather the storms. The citizens should not panic about the tide-like ebb and flow of violent acts that no community in today's world is immune to because in this reporter's view, thus far the lives that have been lost and the careers that have ended have belonged to criminals who have chosen to do their worst in La Claire, Wisconsin. While doing their worst they have met our best and found themselves wanting. In my five part series on crime in La Claire, I have concluded that there is crime in La Claire as there is in every community in this country. Our police department has met remarkable challenges and has performed remarkably. I believe, however, for the sake of truth in packaging, there should be small print added to the bottom of the Welcome to La Claire sign that says, 'Criminals beware. Criminal behavior within the city limits may be hazardous to your health.' This is Rachel Klein reporting."

After viewing this story, he closed it with a hard tap on the left click and pushed himself away from the desk angrily and said out loud, "Damn! Even the press loves the cops in La Claire! What's that all about?"

Ripp originally hoped to convince himself never to return to La Claire for business, recreation, and most certainly to pursue his obsession. Instead, as Ripp read and researched, he felt the surge of excitement mixed with fear as if he was on the ledge of a tall building twenty-five floors up, looking down. Every ounce of common sense told him everything that had happened was an omen. He told himself, "I have been lucky. I was forewarned. I now know that what I am dealing with is a small team of officers that are either very lucky or very good at what they do and what they do is capture criminals. Criminals who have done their best to escape or kill these officers have lost in each case and paid with either their freedom or even precious life. Don't do it!"

He leaned back in his chair and rotated it round and round with his eyes closed. He possessed an inner turmoil that paralleled his outward spinning. The more he learned about how dangerous it was for him to pursue the woman, the more he was drawn to do that very thing that could very well lead to his destruction.

Ripp thought to himself, "Some would say the plane is a perfectly good plane. It is thrilling to fly in a plane, but yet someone in history decided to be the first to jump from a plane." Ripp continued needing to justify to himself what he knew he must do. "Mountains are beautiful to look at in all their majesty, but some must climb them. They must climb even the highest, most treacherous of them, like Sir Edmund Hillary did when he conquered Mount Everest."

He stopped spinning in a direct line in front of his muted television and something immediately caught his eye. Ripp picked up his remote and hit the mute button, bringing the voice of Gretchen Carlson of Fox and Friends into the room. "Yes, Steve, this is incredibly dramatic video that we have just received which was taken from a security camera at the scene of a dynamic police arrest. What you'll see is a burglary suspect, dressed in black, who will... well, just watch the video."

The former Miss America's beautiful face was replaced by a bird's eye view of a parking lot and the side of a long building. A stumbling man in black appeared from the left of the screen, followed by a sprinting blonde female police officer, gaining on him. The man without warning swung a heavy black knapsack at the officer, and the cop without loosing momentum stepped wide and avoided the attempt to crush her skull with the obviously weighted contents. Then the attractive blonde officer launched herself like a cruise missile and with her entire body weight smashed her right elbow into the jaw of the man in black. He crumpled instantaneously to the ground, motionless.

Gretchen continued, "Wow. That gives me chills."

Steve Doocy with a cockney smile said, "Boy, he went down like Sunny Liston when he fought Mohammed Ali."

Brian Kilmeade then corrected, "Yeah, except he wasn't Mohammed Ali yet. He was still Cassius Clay, and," then Brian paused and became animated and nearly shouted, "this time you could actually see the knockout punch. Wow! Smash! Did you see that?"

"Yes we did, Brian. We all saw that," said Doocy a feigned annoyance after having his analogy challenged.

"Listen guys. This woman officer single-handedly apprehended this guy who had broken into two businesses. He tried to run, and it is interesting to note that the knapsack he was swinging about contained $12,000 in cash and three guns," reported Gretchen.

"He's a real smart guy, huh? He has three guns so what does he try to do? He tries to hit her with a knapsack. Brilliant!" Doocy exclaimed.

Gretchen then commented, "From what I have heard it might have been even worse for him if he would have pulled a gun on this officer. Her name, though, is Officer Madison Brown. She is as good with her guns as Wyatt Earp. Her friends call her Maddy, but she has become a role model for girls in Wisconsin where they call her, get this, Downtown Maddy Brown."

"Cool," said Brian, "but isn't that name already taken? Wasn't there a movie by that name? What was the name of the movie?" Brian began snapping his fingers again.

Doocy saw his opening and took it. He sarcastically reasoned, "If it was the name of a movie then the name would be..." he paused and put his pinky finger next to the corner of his mouth in his best Doctor Evil impression and said, "Could it be Downtown Maddy Brown, Brian?"

"All right guys. I think you are both wrong. I don't think there is a movie by that name," said Gretchen.

"Well there should be. Let's make one, but first let's Google it because I think there is one already," said Brian with a great deal of energetic righteousness his voice.

"Can you run that one more time for all the women out there?" asked Gretchen looking off camera.

The screen replayed the incident, and this time as Maddy's elbow impacted the suspect's face they all shouted "Bam!" and the graphics from the old *Batman* television series were recycled and a large red *"BAM!"* appeared on a yellow background on screen.

The entire cast and crew as well as the staff in the background could be heard to laugh.

William Ripp shook the remote once at the television, shutting it down. He set the remote down on his desk and covered his face with both hand. He growled with a rage, fear, anger, and excitement and proclaimed loudly, "Darla will be my *Everest!*"

CHAPTER TWENTY-THREE

I CAN DO THIS

Three days later in La Claire at the scene of a SWAT stand-off, Sergeant Randy Stammos, interim commander of the SWAT team, declared over the SWAT channel, "He says he's coming out." Compton, who was the officer in charge of the team, was back to work, but doctors had confined him to light duty. The team had been called to a violent domestic. An estranged husband had broken into his wife's home in the middle of the afternoon and grabbed their three-month-old baby. He had held a gun to his wife, to his baby, and then to his own head in the prolonged standoff which had been going on for four hours.

The negotiator, Gloria Dooley, Officer Dooley's wife, had convinced the man to come out. She told him, "Please, Robert, now set the gun down, give the baby to your wife, and come out. Let's end this thing. No one has been hurt yet."

An arrest team was set to take him into custody, but then Robert threw the team a curve. He walked out with the baby in his arms. He did not cradle the baby in his arms like a loving father; he carried his young off-spring like last season's football. The baby was crying. "Shut-up!" Robert shouted to the baby. "I want all of you fuckers out of here!" he shouted to the SWAT team. His left hand was empty and his right hand held the baby. The firearm was not on him, a small mercy.

Stammos saw an opportunity, "McCarthy, Carpenter, Brown, prepare for Baby Rescue," he said over the radio. After Brown, Carpenter, and McCarthy separated from the arrest team and moved into position, Stammos radioed, "His wife just called. She said he left the pistol inside. She thinks he is unarmed, but she is worried about the baby. He said he was going to snap the baby's neck. Baby Rescue!" he ordered.

With that, Maddy approached from the front with her hands empty and palms forward. "Robert. My name is Maddy Brown. I am here to help. Please, why don't I just take the baby and we can talk," she said in a soothing voice as she slowly moved closer and closer. His attention was drawn to this pretty blonde. She did not intimidate Robert in the slightest. She was alone. She was a woman. He was used to controlling his women. This was his third wife he had abused and the fifth woman with his violent breed of love which was a form of domestic terrorism. He did not see Carpenter and McCarthy coming in from the left and right of him. He found himself strangely aroused by the sexy blonde in the black SWAT uniform. He could control this woman easily. He knew how to do it. She was, after all, just another woman.

He then shifted the baby into two hands and held the baby by its fragile rib-cage in front of him "Fuck you! You know I could snap this baby's neck like a twig," shouted Robert. The baby screamed, crying loudly from the crushing pain. "Shut the fuck up!" screamed Robert, looking away from Maddy and at the baby, causing him to miss Maddy's signal to Carpenter and McCarthy.

As she signaled, much more subtly than a third base coach signaling a bunt, Carpenter, McCarthy, and Maddy moved as if one. Carpenter and McCarthy took control of his hands and arms locking him into a painful compliance hold called the "gooseneck" by military policemen because of the gooseneck configuration the arms and hands are placed in. As his arms were torn away from the crushing hold on the baby, Maddy rolled the baby gently and lovingly away from Robert, spun, and quickly moved away from the father. They had practiced this maneuver in SWAT training one hundred times before using a doll, and as the old adage goes, "practice makes perfect." The rescue and arrest went perfectly.

Stammos then radioed, "Suspect is 10-95. Baby secured. Entry team, clear the house. The only one that should be in the house is the wife."

Thirty seconds later Brockman radioed, "House secure. The wife is secured, but she will need an ambulance. She says he pistol whipped her. It appears her nose and jaw may be broken." He added, "A weapon has been secured."

"Awesome!" said Ripp as he watched from a rented vehicle at the end of the next block. He saw it all through his binoculars and heard it all on his newly purchased police scanner. "These guys are good, but I can do this," said Ripp to himself. He was a new man. There was a real perceived danger of apprehension that thrilled him. This would be his masterpiece of masterpieces.

He watched as the ambulance arrived and then sped away, wailing its way to the hospital. As traffic was opened up in front of the house, he set down his binoculars and boldly drove by the scene. He saw the suspect with his head dropped forward in anger and shame, planning his next act of terrorism against a wife who strangely still loved him.

Ripp slowed his car and stared at McCarthy who was standing outside the car containing the suspect. He was dressed in his SWAT gear. He wore a black helmet, outer vest, a Glock with a low ride holster, and he was writing intently in a small pocket notebook holding a short black pen in his tightly black-gloved hands. Seated in the squad was Carpenter, similarly dressed.

Ripp rolled by them unnoticed and undetected. There was power in seeing but being unseen. There was satisfaction in having watched the most observant group of officers, theoretically, on this department when they were at their highest alert, and yet they had not noticed him. A renewed rush of confidence emboldened Ripp. As he cleared the block, a police cadet who had just loaded a wooden traffic buck onto a marked police pickup truck looked at Ripp, smiled, and waved. Ripp smiled and waved back. This was not unusual to Ripp. To blend into the landscape in Wisconsin, William Ripp, a serial killer, had to perform countless acts of friendliness.

William Ripp kept smiling. The smile was not Ripp acting happy. This was Ripp being happy. He shouted loudly, pumping his fist, "Fuck McCarthy! Fuck Carpenter, Fuck Brockman, Fuck Compton, Fuck Dooley, Fuck Downtown Maddy Brown! Fuck them all! *I can do this!*"

CHAPTER TWENTY FOUR

BECKY'S ROSE

The Do Chang was a large empty room with a matted floor. The mat was a solid mat, hard enough to stand and fight on while soft enough for someone who was trained in the art of falling to land on. The flags of the United States and South Korea hung on the front wall. The flags paid homage to the birth place of Tae Kwon Do and the free republic of the United States of America, whose tolerance allowed this important piece of Korean culture to flourish in this country.

The opposite wall was completely covered by a mirror. It allowed students of Tae Kwon Do to either marvel at their acquired skills or identify and correct their mistakes, if such be the case. On the right wall was a long line of rails used for stretching and balance drills. Master Kane had kept them there when he purchased and renovated the building. The prior owner had operated a dance studio. The mirrored wall was also a holdover from the dance studio that had once occupied the premises. On the left wall was a beautiful hand-painted mural of a dragon surrounded by men and women students in various martial poses. One of the students, a graphic artist, paid for his lessons by painting the mural.

Possessing the hand of an artist was not an unusual talent for a dedicated martial artist. In each of the traditional styles of martial arts, there was an expectation that there must be a balance between fire and water, earth and sky, good and evil, physical and spiritual, the arts of war and the arts of peace.

The traditional martial artists were expected to not only practice with bow and sword, they were expected to plant a beautiful garden, paint a beautiful scene, write a beautiful poem, or play beautiful music. The warrior needed balance. The artist who painted the dragon progressed from brown to red, and the week he completed his masterpiece, he tested for his black belt.

Earning his black belt, next to his child being born, was the proudest achievement in his life to that point.

Darla loved working out at the studio. She wished she had done this sooner. She had been moved to take the classes after the stalker had pursued her and the two out-of-town strippers, Sugar and Spice. She had been training at the studio almost daily since that life altering event.

The investigation revealed that the man had been targeting Darla, so entranced was he by her beauty and her provocative dance. She thought herself lucky to have had police so close but knew they may not always be there for her. Survivors rarely come away from crimes the same people they were before they were targeted. Some survivors become more cautious, some become paranoid, and some become prepared. Darla had decided she would prepare herself if there was ever to be a next time. She would, as Larry Kane put it, "harden the target."

She had decided she would train in the studio of Larry Kane. Kane was a part time police officer and police trainer and a full time martial arts instructor. Kane had often been McCarthy's partner during the riotous Deutsch Days Celebration that occurred each year in late September. Kane was also his partner in teaching police officers in self defense. Both were certified instructors in the state system Defense and Arrest Tactics taught to all police officers.

The night McCarthy arrested Darla's stalker she asked if he had any recommendations for her to prepare to defend herself. McCarthy had told her, "Well I cannot recommend businesses, so I will tell you that there are many places where you can obtain the training you desire. As a police officer I cannot really endorse…"

Darla then interrupted, "I know what you can do, Officer McCarthy. I've seen what you can do. Tony at the RUMP says you are some sort of Karate expert. I just would like to know, where do you train? I'm afraid. I might not be so lucky the next time to have you there. I want to be able to do something for myself. Please tell me where I can go," she pleaded.

McCarthy saw the fear and determination in her eyes. She was serious. "I train personally in my studio at home, but I also train with Master Larry Kane. Kane offers a variety of martial arts in his studio. There is traditional Tae Kwon Do, Judo, Hap-Ki-Do, and also a women's program called W.I.S.E. that you might be interested in," confided McCarthy.

"Really? A women's program? That's what I am talking about, McCarthy. What does W.I.S.E. stand for?" asked Darla.

"It stands for Women Initiating Safer Environments. Kane offers it to women who are not sure if they want a long term commitment to the martial arts but have a desire to learn self defense. The system was started at a sister studio, Three Rivers Martial Arts in La Crosse, and Kane is a trained instructor in it. I know he allows attendees of the W.I.S.E. class to attend other classes at the studio with full membership while they are in the W.I.S.E. class. The class meets once a week for about nine weeks." McCarthy then pulled out his note pad and wrote down Kane's number and handed it to Darla. "Tell him Dyno sent you. He is a good friend and one of the best at what he does."

"I will call him. Would you please not tell him what I do? I'm not ashamed of it, but... well, you know," said Darla awkwardly.

"There is no reason for me to tell him what you do. I will not tell him," answered McCarthy. "It would make no difference if he did know. He would accept you as a student because you are a woman in need."

"Please don't tell him though," said Darla.

"I won't," promised McCarthy. "You're not a criminal; you're a dancer."

"Thanks, McCarthy, and when you see Carpenter tell him I said thanks again," said Darla squeezing McCarthy's arm.

Darla called the number McCarthy gave her the next morning.

"Hello, I'm Becky Glitz and I was referred to you by Dyno," said Darla, using her real name rather than her stage name of Darla Darling.

"Dyno Dan, yes he is my good friend. This is Master Kane; how can I help you, Becky?" asked Kane in his business voice.

"Do you have any W.I.S.E. classes that I can register for?" asked Becky.

"Why yes. We have one starting this evening, meeting at five o'clock. If you can make it you will be starting fresh with the rest of the students. Do you know where we are located?" asked Kane.

"Yes. Do I need to bring anything?"

"Just dress comfortably. When you arrive I will provide you with a do-bak, which is a traditional martial arts uniform. We can complete the paperwork before class if you get here by 4:30."

"I'll be there." She said enthusiastically.

Later that day, Darla sat in a circle on the matted floor of the do-chang (gymnasium) and listened, mesmerized by the words of Master Kane. He explained the W.I.S.E. concept that women can be powerful. She listened intently as Kane explained, "Some people judge a person's power by their size, but actually, size doesn't matter."

The women giggled and Kane's face showed confusion for a few moments before his face lit up as if he had unwittingly stumbled onto the joke.

He cleared his throat, "Continuing, ladies, the person who combines most effectively the components of power, balance, speed, focus, endurance, strength, flexibility, and simplicity of technique will win the confrontation."

Kane then said, "I am going to start by teaching you three techniques that are devastatingly powerful. To justify use of these techniques, you have to be in danger of death or great bodily harm to yourself or to someone else you are trying to protect. They will give you three options to three very vulnerable targets: the eyes, the throat, and the testicles. This will give you flexibility to strike when your hands are high," and Kane placed his hands in the air as if he was on either side of an invisible persons head, "medium," and Kane placed his hands as if the were at the throat level of an invisible person in front of him, "or low," and Kane then placed his hands at the groin area of an invisible person directly in front of him.

Kane continued, "We have decided not to teach you the names of the techniques given to them in the martial arts. We have let earlier classes call them something that made them easier to remember. The first technique is called, 'You only have eyes for me.' The second technique is called 'Y hit him,' and the last technique is simply called, 'The lawn mower.' If you forget everything else, remember these three techniques."

Darla was hooked after her first class. Her career and her most recent scrape with danger had convinced her she needed to learn to protect herself. She also thought Kane the most interesting single man she had become acquainted with since her disastrous relationship with her last love, a man she thought to have unlimited potential who was now serving time in prison. "I wonder..." she thought as her eyes followed Kane into his office.

The schedule was perfect for her. She would take Tae Kwon Do lessons during the 3:00 class, work out in the weight room, and then take the W.I.S.E. class at 5:00. Many of the movements came naturally since it was not much different than dance, and she had danced all her life.

Darla immediately canceled her membership at her health club and began a rigorous daily training regimen at "Kane's House of Pain," which the studio was affectionately called by the students. Darla was surprised to discover how much she enjoyed the social component of the studio. People were incredibly friendly, and she was amazed at how sharing the environment was. She felt that she was a part of a family.

Months after joining the studio, during a Tae Kwon Do class Darla was moving on command down the floor executing front punches. Kane slipped into his Korean Master persona and signaled out Darla saying, "Ah, Becky, you have beauty and grace of ballet dancer. Now must develop power of warrior since you already have the heart of warrior." Kane then moved within earshot and whispered, "mine."

Darla blushed and smiled a smile that had not lit her face since Bobby Bennett had asked her to homecoming in ninth grade English class.

Later Darla was in the weight room bench pressing 110 pounds for repetitions. She sat up and discovered Kane sitting on the floor stretching. When Darla looked toward him, he humbly said, "I must apologize to you. I hope I did not offend you. If you wish to leave I will give you a full refund. I would understand, but I must say I have been struck by your beauty and," then he reached around behind him and pulled a single rose out and handed it to her, "I would like to ask, may I buy you a coffee, a bagel, a steak, a pizza, a personal water craft, a puppy..." Just then an eight-year-old boy dressed in his do-bak with a green belt hanging around his neck burst out of the men's locker room and attempted to shoot by Kane who expertly scooped him up and spun him around, put him in a head lock and quickly scraped the boy's head with his knuckles. Kane then continued his offer to Darla, "...or possibly a small child?" He set the child down who resumed running the moment his feet touched the floor. Kane looked into Darla's eyes, cocked his head, and smiled.

Darla laughed like a school girl and blushed again, "Well..."

"I have to be honest with you before you answer," said Kane in a serious tone, standing slowly as he spoke.

Darla thought, "Oh no here it comes. He knows what I do or he's married." She said, "Yes?"

"Although most parents who bring their children to me would sell them cheap, I cannot buy you one because I am quite certain it is illegal to sell them. The rest of the offer stands."

Darla laughed again and continued to blush, "How about soup and salad at Panera, and it can be my treat," Darla suggested.

Kane, equally charmed, asked, "Tomorrow at 11:00 AM is OK for you?"

Darla paused, hesitant to begin what she hoped would be a lasting relationship without telling Kane who she was and what she did to financially make it through this world alone. "Master Kane..."

"Larry," interrupted Kane.

"Larry, before this goes any further there is something you should know," said Darla in a voice of determination.

"Don't tell me, you're married," guessed Kane.

"No."

"You are a Hari Krishna, and you want me to shave my head before we go on a date," said Kane.

"Of course not," Darla said losing the look of determination to a smile.

"You are actually a man trapped in a beautiful woman's body."

"Not even a little bit," Darla said with a giggle.

"OK. I give up. Tell me," said Kane dropping his hands to his side in defeat.

"I must tell you that I make my living as a professional dancer."

"I could have guessed this. You move like a dancer in class. Your techniques have the precision of a dancer. So why does this trouble you so?" Kane asked, his face contorted with puzzlement.

"I am an exotic dancer. I dance at the RUMPelstiltskin Night Club. I have been doing so for a number of years. I think before anything starts here you should know. My stage name is Darla Darling," said Becky with her eyes turning away from Kane, afraid that she had sealed the fate of a relationship that she longed for before it had even a chance to get started.

Kane closed the distance between them and slowly placed his hand on her chin and turned her face toward his. He then said softly so that she could hear him with her heart, "It does not surprise me that you would find a career that would underscore your grace and beauty for that is what I first noticed about you. I am thrilled that you would want to tell me about this before we even share a bowl of soup. That tells me you feel something between us also?"

"Yes?" Darla said feeling the unmistakable emotion of love welling up in her like a Hawaiian volcano, out of control, potentially destructive, and yet beautiful.

Kane leaned toward her and he looked into her eyes and saw love, innocence, warmth, and beauty—Becky's eyes. Their lips came together like a summer storm, warm, wet, quenching, and timeless.

As they parted Kane cocked his head and smiled as he said, "Next stop Panera?"

"Panera," said Becky, her cheeks blushing as red as her rose.

"I have to go," said Kane as he winked at her, "I have to teach the rug-rat's class."

Darla then tripped lazily through her workout. She enjoyed visiting this world where she could be Becky Glitz again. She had not been Becky for years. The beauty that drew Larry Kane to Becky was not the sensual naked beauty of Darla Darling the dancer. It was the simple and exquisite beauty of Becky Glitz.

She picked up her rose and smelled it. It tore her thoughts away from the caustically smoky and harshly lighted stage of the RUMP and to a gentler time on the recital stage in the Northrup Auditorium at The University of Minnesota where she had danced in a production of Swan Lake. It was a lifetime away before she chose the path she was now on.

Instead of being nude, glistening with baby oil, or wearing some shreds of sequined covered cloth, she was on stage in the college's theater dressed as a prima ballerina. Instead of dollar bills being tossed to the stage, roses had been thrown on the stage for the young dancers.

Becky took in the fragrance of the fresh-cut rose and mused, her whole being smiling, "This is not Darla's rose. This is *Becky's rose.*"

CHAPTER TWENTY-FIVE

THEY MAKE NO NOISE

It was another Saturday Night in La Claire, and Dan McCarthy had spent the first two hours of his shift on this call. He had begun the shift vainly attempting to revive an infant who succumbed to sudden infant death syndrome. As the emergency medical services took over and continued the effort to breathe life back into the infant child, McCarthy had decided to stay at the hospital with the single mother named Maria until her family could arrive from Rochester.

As he sat watching the beautiful young Madonna stare blankly at a painting of a doctor for whom the waiting room had been named, he noticed the steady stream of tears soundlessly slip from her eyes and down her cheeks. McCarthy had seen unbridled grief in his career, but he had never seen anyone so profoundly sad cry so continually without making a wail, whine, or even a whimper. McCarthy was now certain that when a heart breaks it makes no sound. He had witnessed it.

McCarthy thought of the old Sam Cook lyrics, "Another Saturday night and I ain't got nobody, I got some money cuz I just got paid. I just want someone I can talk to, I'm in an awful way." McCarthy thought, "I don't know why that song is in my head but the guy singing that song had the world by the ass compared to this poor soul."

Then she slowly turned away from the painting, and her glistening brown eyes looked into McCarthy's, "Officer Dan, could you please ask them if I may hold my baby one last time?"

"I will ask them for you." As he stood up, he was met by Father Tom, one of the La Claire Police Chaplains who had been summoned to the hospital by dispatch. McCarthy whispered, "Father, she had been profoundly saddened by this. Her baby is four months old. It had a sinus infection and was sleeping. She said she was awakened when she couldn't hear the baby's breathing. When she checked on the child, she saw the baby had stopped breathing. She has said little. Can you watch her, please?" Dan asked.

Father Tom answered, "Yes. I will pray with her. Do you know her faith?"

"She is a practicing Catholic," answered Dan.

McCarthy contacted Sergeant Stammos, the attending physician, and the medical examiner in the hallway outside the treatment room where baby lay in his eternal slumber. "Excuse me. I have a question from the mother, probably for all of you to ponder."

"Go ahead, Dan," said Sergeant Stammos, the investigator called in to investigate the death.

"The baby's mother would like to hold her son one more time. Is that possible?" asked Dan.

The three talked, and after a very brief conference agreed that this appeared to be an evident case of SIDS (Sudden Infant Death Syndrome). "There will have to be an autopsy, but in this case I would have no objection to having the mother hold the child one last time," said the medical examiner.

"We will be there, and I think not allowing it would do more lasting harm than allowing it. I don't see anything that indicates foul play here," said Sergeant Stammos.

"I am all for it," agreed the presiding physician.

The mother was brought into treatment room number fourteen by Josie. McCarthy was happy to see Josie on hand. She was the nurse who had attended Sergeant Compton less than a year ago and a longtime professional friend. Josie had arranged to have a rocking chair brought down from the pediatric ward. She stood holding the child wrapped in a white and blue blanket and lovingly rocked the infant so tenderly one did not have to ask if she had children of her own.

The grieving mother walked slowly to the rocking chair. Her slow measured steps were not caused by a dreading of these last few moments she would have with her child, but in an effort to prolong them. The young mother eased herself into the rocking chair. Josie gently laid the infant into her arms and said, "He's such a beautiful child."

The Madonna smiled at Josie and said, "Thank you." Then she brushed his cheek ever so softly and said, "It looks like he's sleeping."

The Madonna then began to rock the baby as if the child had just dozed off after having been awakened by a bad dream. She began to sing in a voice so sweetly resonant it could only belong to either an angel or a mother:

Hush little baby don't say a word.
Mama's gonna buy you a mockingbird

And if that mockingbird won't sing,
Mama's gonna buy you a diamond ring

And if that diamond ring turns brass
Mama's going to buy you a looking glass

And if that looking glass gets broke
Mama's gonna buy you a billy goat

And if that billy goat won't pull,
Mama's gonna buy you a cart and bull

And if that cart and bull turn over,
Mama's gonna buy you a dog named Rover.

And if that dog name Rover won't bark
Mama's going to buy you a horse and cart.

And if that horse and cart fall down
You'll still be the sweetest little baby in town.

When the song ended there was a long silence, except for the low continued humming of the tune by the mother and rhythmic creaking of the rocking chair as Maria gently rocked her baby into heaven.

Stammos and McCarthy made no effort to hide or dry their tears. They were cops, and all cops know there is a time to laugh together, a time to fight together, and a time to cry together. Nothing was said. Nothing needed to be said. They were silent. When cops' hearts break *they make no noise.*

CHAPTER TWENTY-SIX

SINGING IN THE RAIN

"255, I am 10-8 (clear) from the hospital," said McCarthy as he pulled out from the parking area at the emergency room entrance. Pausing, he checked his face in the rearview mirror. His eyes looked slightly reddened but no more than they ever did on third shift.

Red eyes were the rule of the day on this shift. Sometimes it was from the smoke-filled bars where cops plied their trade. Sometimes it was from a long day in court and a short day in bed. Sometimes it was from the sheer stark naked humanness of the job like tonight. McCarthy did not find the job moved him to tears often, but tonight he let them come and felt no shame in it.

When McCarthy was a rookie, Stammos had told him, "Cops are tough guys, generally speaking, but in this line of work at sometime or another it will bring you to tears. I guarantee it. When it happens don't feel bad. Someone once said, 'It's the tear unshed that scars the heart.'"

McCarthy then asked, "That's kind of cool, who said that," as the young rookie wrote the quote in his notebook.

"I did. What about it?" said Stammos almost embarrassed that he had to take credit for his wisdom.

After readjusting his mirror and taking a deep breath, he pulled out of the hospital lot and began to pilot the starship toward the downtown. It was 1:45 AM. He had been on this call since 10:30 PM, and now he had to somehow mentally shift into a mindset that could handle the drunken brawl that was bar time on Saturday night in downtown La Claire.

"255," said dispatch.

"255, go ahead," answered McCarthy.

"10-25 the station immediately and meet with Sergeant Compton," directed Melissa in dispatch with an urgency which suggested to McCarthy something substantial was on the horizon.

"10-4," said McCarthy.

"Be advised, bypass downtown on your return to the station," said Compton, breaking into the main radio channel.

"10-4," replied Dan. "Not good," Dan added to himself.

La Claire had a history of riots. Many times in the past, temporary alcohol-induced insanity had reigned causing drunken idiots to rush into the streets. The drunken Olympics featured events such as car tipping, window smashing, fire starting, and the final event of the competition was always the 100 yard dash after tear gas deployment. This civil unrest was not exercised to raise the public consciousness on a very pressing question that society needs to answer. It was not caused by a long, drawn-out military engagement, or to express frustration over poverty, or to protest or support abortion. La Claire's riots happened "for the fun of it." They were an odd sort of collegiate coming of age.

When Dan arrived at the station, Compton called him into the command room. "Dyno, I have called in the SWAT team. Keep on the uniform of the day, but go to long sleeves. Gear up with your straight baton, gas mask, carrier, and riot gear. It is a mess downtown. We are going to stand by and hope that everything goes well at bar time, which is about fifteen minutes from now, but there are more people down there than the streets can handle."

"What's going on?" asked McCarthy.

"The Boon Doggle. It's an event sponsored by the University of Wisconsin La Claire College 30 miles north of here in North Salem. It got really big last year. Too big, so some rocket scientist said, 'Hey let's avoid the confusion and get them all drunk and send them home early. Let's shut the beer tent down early this year.' So they shut the beer tent down this year at 7:00 to avoid the problems with the crowd and it worked. The entire crowd of drunken idiots moved en masse on La Claire, and we have as big a crowd as I have ever seen down there and they are getting frisky. It looks like they may be saving the last dance for us. There will be a briefing in five minutes in the lineup room. Gear up!" McCarthy wondered if Compton's doctors had taken him off light duty or if he signed the slip himself like a truant kid in high school who explained his absence in a note with a signature on the bottom, "My Mother."

When McCarthy entered the lineup room, he heard a familiar voice, "OY-Yah-Dah, my good friend!" He turned and saw Larry Kane in uniform.

"OY-Yah-Dah!" said McCarthy as he made his way over and shook his friend's hand.

"I am guessing Sergeant Compton made a request for mutual aid?" said McCarthy.

"Yes, he did and High Sheriff Dooley was good enough to call me at home sensing my desire to work with our mutual friend," said Kane. "Sit down. I saved you a seat."

Compton entered the room at a quick pace. The key section of the downtown had been drawn out on the white board in the front of the room. "Ladies and gentlemen, thanks for coming so quickly; I am going to make this fast. We have a three-block walk from here to where we will form up. Traffic is shut down here and here, and we have already set up a detour." Compton indicated the location of the detour with a LASER pointer. The red dot danced in deceptively happy circles at each intersection. "The crowd has the street, and our officers have pulled out. Chaos reigns down there, and we will need to bring peace back to River Street."

"We will form a line on the north end of River Street in full gear, helmets, and masks on because I am expecting a confrontation. We will advance at a slow walk south with batons at port arms and hold at River and Diamond Streets. I may have to stop us along the way if they advance to meet us. Whenever I make that call, I will declare the unlawful assembly and order them to clear out. If it becomes needed, I will dispense tear gas. We want to clear this crowd, not arrest it. We will take two transport vans following us in the event arrests are made. Make sure the suspects are properly identified as for charges and arresting officers, you know the procedures. Are there any questions?" Compton looked around the room and saw nothing but determined faces, "Let's go!"

The city and county teams trained regularly together for situations like this. They had been through "riots" many times before. The riot tradition had returned to La Claire about five years earlier at Deutsch Days, but now the college had found another way to facilitate their students' penchant for riots for fun twice a year instead of just once by unleashing the Boon Doggle on La Claire. This particular generation of college students preferred to have a legacy of drunken vandalism rather than academic achievement. "At least the little drunken pukes afford us job security," said Brockman. "If the university really cared all they would have to do is expel students who actively participate in the riot and they would stop, but that ain't going to happen."

After disembarking from the command room, the entire crew was formed by Compton in two columns on the sidewalk outside the station. He then reminded everyone, "The only way 40 officers can handle 3000 is as a team. No individual heroics tonight. No one goes into the crowd unless they are directed to do so. Hold the line and take the ones that challenge our line only. I want us all to stay to together. Forward, march!" barked Compton and the march toward the unknown began.

When the columns arrived on River Street, Compton gave the signal to form a line, and without a word the two columns came together at the center of the street and fanned out like a wedge of Southbound Canadian Geese that suddenly locked into a cohesive impenetrable line. The flanks were anchored solidly to the buildings on each side of the street. Compton shouted, "Forward at a walk... Move!" and move forward it did as a unit until it arrived at a distance of 75 feet from the main body of the crowd. The crowd became ecstatic and began to chant, "Nazis! Nazis! Nazis!" They shouted with a fervor and fanaticism which belied their former mundane identities. Those identities were lost to the identity they now shared. That was the single identity of a violent mob. Each person present was now an amoeba in a living breathing organism that this riotous mass of human beings had become, save one.

One member of the crowd had maintained his individuality. He was not about to succumb to the pressure of his peers. He had brought a distinctly formed personal identity to this city, and he would maintain it with dignity. He was William Ripp, a sociopath with psychotic tendencies, as yet undiagnosed. He entered the scene a maniacal opportunistic killer of many and he would remain a killer. As the crowd began to chant and the police moved instantaneously from two columns to a line with the bark of one command, he admired the pageantry of it all in the midst of such chaos. Ripp was moved to commentary by the events unfolding. He muttered, "Interesting. These guys are good."

Ripp watched with great interest as young man in his teens picked up a newspaper vending machine and tossed it through a large plate glass window of an antiques shop. He threw his hands up in the air and ran in circles as if he had just hit one over the center field wall with two outs in the bottom of the ninth and bases loaded in the seventh game of the World Series. The crowd roared in approval. As all members of the crowd let loose their roar, Ripp smelled the sickening odor of stale beer that oozed out from the crowd's collective breath. The police were now immune from this nauseating odor because they all had donned their gas masks.

"How delightful," Ripp said clapping his hands together. "I think that chap deserves some sort of recognition for his outstanding achievement." Ripp shadowed the young vandal who had smashed the antiques shop's window. The vandal did not notice Ripp. No one in the crowd noticed Ripp. In one instant Ripp had deemed the man to be a social outcast that nobody would miss.

McCarthy was scanning the crowd members, taking special notice of some for future reference. In riots he would always watch for the possibility of identification and arrest later since during the riots breaking up the crowd was the main goal with arrest being a secondary concern. He saw the young vandal throw the heavy newspaper vending machine into and through Bright's Antiques with the instant approval of the crowd. "There's one to remember. He will be easy to spot later with his UWL T-shirt and the woman's garter on his right biceps. I'll get him later. He's toast," thought McCarthy. Then McCarthy saw a man walking behind the young vandal so calmly his demeanor was as out of place in this crowd as a Buddhist Monk in a police lineup. "I know that guy," he thought to himself. "Maddy's serial killer, but I'll be damned if I can remember his name."

Ripp continued to follow the young vandal, staying within ten feet of him at all times and he thought, "When the opportunity presents itself, I shall announce my presence in La Claire, and this young nobody vandalizing the town will be my calling card. This will be a body that is found," thought Ripp lightly brushing the revolver through his coat that he had secured in a shoulder holster, making certain it was still concealed. "I will find an opportunity and just shoot him and leave him where he falls. I have never done that before," he observed once again to himself with a smile. "I'll try something new; after all, variety is the spice of death."

Sergeant Compton walked up to the line, turned the bullhorn on, and gave the commands, "I am Sergeant David Compton of the La Claire Police Department. This is an unlawful assembly and you are ordered to disperse immediately or face arrest!"

The crowd chanted, "Fuck you! Fuck You! Fuck You! Fuck You!" The young vandal popped out of the crowd, pulled a pool ball out of his pocket, and fired it at the police line. It hit Maddy Brown hard in the helmet and careened off harmlessly. Maddy took a step forward, tempted to go after the vandal, but readjusted her grip on her baton and stepped back in line. The vandal disappeared in the crowd that roared its approval, "Woooooooweeeeee."

Compton repeated his command and the response this time was the chant, "Eat Shit! Fuck you! Eat Shit! Fuck you! Eat Shit! Fuck you!" The massive wall of chanting derelicts suddenly opened up and coughed out the young vandal once again, and he ran in an arc and tossed a quarter-full bottle of Smirnoff Vodka at Mc-

Carthy who pivoted to the rear and left and the bottle smashed on the ground behind him. McCarthy immediately pivoted back to close up the line again.

Ripp, still following the young vandal, stepped to the front of the baying pack of wolves momentarily, trying to get his bearings on where the young vandal had been off to, and he saw his trophy toss the bottle at the police line. He saw the intended target immediately react, pivot out of the path of the bottle, and just as smoothly step back in line as if he was expertly performing a cha-cha with the crowd. Ripp was compelled to look more closely at the officer under the helmet and behind the mask, even squinting as if he was reading the fine print on a Tylenol bottle in the midst of this societal headache. He said out loud in recognition, "McCarthy. That's got to be McCarthy!"

McCarthy saw Ripp appear in front of the crowd at the spot that the bottle-tosser had come from and he immediately thought, "That's… what's his name again? Damn, what's his name?"

As Dan watched the professor, McCarthy read his lips as the man clearly could be seen to say, "McCarthy."

Then it came to McCarthy, "Ripp. That's the name, William Ripp." The moment was fleeting and passed in and out of his thoughts because the crowd began to chant and advance in response to Compton's last order to disperse, "No we won't! No we won't! No we won't!"

Suddenly, a tall man with a black mask over his face sprinted out of the crowd and tried to rip McCarthy's baton from his hands. He must have chosen McCarthy because he was physically one of the smaller men in the line. As the masked man clutched at the baton, McCarthy pivoted and swept him through the line. Then he pivoted back, causing the tall masked man to disappear into the horizon of cops as all mysterious masked men should. McCarthy shouted to Larry Kane who had the man secured in a truly artistic wrist lock. Then with a movement as smooth as a twelve year old boy's cheek after his first shave Kane had him in handcuffs. "That was McCarthy's arrest for disorderly conduct and unlawful assembly!"

Kane gave him a thumb up.

"And Attempted Robbery!" shouted McCarthy seriously.

Compton who had a canister of tear gas in his hand shook his head no to Kane and yelled to McCarthy, "Attempted Robbery?"

"He tried to steal my baton?" argued McCarthy.

"I don't think so," said Compton with a laugh, muffled by the canister. "Nice try."

In a muffled shout Kane said, "Got it ixnay on the obberyray," and although it was impossible to understand pig-Latin recited under a gas mask during a riot, Compton saw Kane had gotten the message.

Compton then shuttled down the line showing each person the tear gas canister in his hand so that there would be no surprises. When he reached the far left flank of the line, he stepped forward of the line and pulled the pin and held the spoon tight in his grip. He held the canister up high, displaying it to the crowd as if to say, "One last chance, go home now, folks." The roar of the crowd increased and its numbers did not diminish. Compton calmly dropped the canister, "POP! Shshshshshhhhhhh."

Compton then walked at a slow measured pace to the center of the line and dropped a second canister, "POP! Shshshshshh-hhhhh."

He then lazily walked to the far right of the line and pulled the pin on a third canister. "POP! Shshshshshhhhhhhh."

Compton completed his intended pattern by dropping a fourth canister between and slightly ahead of the third and second, "POP! Shshshshshhhhhhh." He then dropped a fifth canister between the second and first and slightly in front of them and as he pulled the pin the last pop was heard. "POP! Shshshshshhhhhhhh."

The wind was blowing south, and the wall of tear gas cocktail moved, swirled, and twirled whimsically and yet somehow determinedly toward the front line of the crowd, engulfing it. It was what the team called "Compton's last call" at bar time. That is when he served his cocktail "The Compatulli." He blended OC, CS, and CN with smoke as a chaser. The less determined rioters bolted and ran far, far away. The more determined rioters ran and slowed down about one and a half blocks away, and the truly courageous and determined rioters held their ground bravely for about fifteen seconds and then they fled coughing and hacking, drooling and sneezing like a nineteenth century nine year old who had just discovered grandpa's snuff box.

Compton then signaled the movement and barked the command, "Forward... Move!" In response the team took back the downtown one steady step slide at a time and the crowd slipped back like a lazy ocean tide on a warm summer day.

When the cloud of tear gas reached Ripp, he found himself needing to abandon his quest once again. "Fuck me blind!" He shouted out loud. He walked fast enough to stay ahead of the cloud, thinking he was safe. He realized almost immediately that he was still suffering. He smelled the pepper and began to cough, and his eyes began to water like a short order cook chopping onions. Ripp was smart enough to realize that he was getting doused by rioters running passed him. They were now carriers. He ran south, and when he reached the first cross street, he immediately cut west toward the river. After the killer ran one block, he cut through an alley and into a parking ramp. He climbed the stairs to the top level. The air had a twinge of pepper in it, but he could breathe again. He walked to the wall that bordered River Street to watch the action. "Damn!" Ripp was truly disappointed because four of his last five chosen victims had escaped him. There was Noah who was too prominent; Bill who decided to drive into a wall in front of McCarthy; Darla who was intercepted by a freak stalker; and finally the young vandal. "If not for the beautiful Angela, these failures would be unbearable," Ripp thought.

The La Claire Police Department line slowly advanced south on River Street with the crowd backing away, keeping their distance. No one wished to challenge the line. Occasionally someone would sprint at them and toss a chunk of rock or bottle at the line, but even if hit, the missile would bounce off the protective helmets, vests, and shin guards.

La Claire kept shields in reserve. They were hesitant to bring them forward because during the last Deutsch Days Riot the use of the shields seemed to invite more projectiles than when they did not have them readily displayed.

McCarthy gazed out at the smoky haze and watched as bottles smashed, Molotov cocktails crashed, and an occasional tear gas canister would get tossed back. He was enjoying those now. Initially, because of parked cars, Compton had to use non-burning tear gas canisters to prevent fires. Non-burning had less chemicals to be released and they were not hot to the touch, so they could be picked up and tossed. Now he was setting out burning canisters because there were no parked cars on this part of the street the line was on.

Crowd members would bravely run out in front of the line and pick up the burning canisters to toss and discover that 1600 degrees Fahrenheit is most awesomely hot. The burns on the hands would lead to arrests later. They were easy to find and the charges were easy to prove because along with the line, the La Claire Police Department had an experienced cameraman present. Each attorney would get one free 8 x 10 glossy of his client before trial. Usually in those cases the attorney never took it to trial.

McCarthy looked left and right as the group calmly took back the street. He listened to his breath, "click swooooosh, click swooooosh," and tasted the slight twinge of pepper sneaking into an obvious crack in the seal of his mask. The seal was probably compromised by the brief fracas with the baton-grabber.

McCarthy stayed in line moving and ringed his baton while he covered his breather and filter and blew hard. Then he held his breath while he quickly tightened the straps on his mask. McCarthy took a breath, "click swoosh, click swoosh, fresh air again," he thought. He then moved his baton back into En Garde position and continued down the street with the team.

"Left wheel... Move!" shouted Compton, and the team swept the intersection of River and Diamond, moving the line like a gate swinging shut. The crowd of seventeen, still tossing whatever they could find, coins, beer cans, and bottles, were dancing and laughing just out of reach and did not notice until it was too late that another police line had swung out of the alley and trapped them between the two lines.

Arrest teams stepped out of the lines and shouted the remainder, a truly manageable number of ne'er-do-wells, into a submissive pose and arrested them. One bolted and ran at McCarthy, who rung his baton and swept the rabbit to the ground. Kane was on the opposite arm immediately and they made the arrest. This man was one of the UWL Rugby Team who had been tossing beer cans at the line. "Disorderly conduct and unlawful assembly," shouted McCarthy. "It's me," shouted McCarthy through the mask at Kane.

"Oh-Yah-Dah, Dyno," shouted Kane back.

"Fuck both your Dahs," said the Rugby player in one last, fleeting act of defiance.

McCarthy looked up from the arrest and saw a figure standing on the top of the River Street ramp and said, "Ripp."

"What?" shouted Kane.

"Nothing. Rugby-man can be transported," said McCarthy.

"10-4," said Kane who was joined by another deputy as they walked Rugby-man away.

Dan then noticed a group of twenty crowd members who had circled around the police line attempting move up, undetected by the police, and rescue some of the POWs, 'Prisoners of Wantonness,' from the arrest vans. Just as they nearly reached the van, Compton stepped out and calmly asked, "Can I help you gentleman along?" He dropped a "Bouncing Betty," which was a round black tear gas canister that was not only effective but was fun to watch. It did just what its name suggested. It started bouncing and spitting tear gas, and the group decided that they "betty" get out of there fast. They sprinted away never to be seen again.

McCarthy laughed and looked at Ripp one more time and saw he was just watching as anyone might. McCarthy then returned to the mop up of the sweet sixteen left in the tournament of idiots.

Ripp stood motionless watching the line of officers sweep the street as they moved south. He watched them swing like a gate east on Diamond Street and then trap the hapless idiots between the two police lines. "These guys are formidable," said Ripp to himself.

"They do it all the time," came a voice from a man that suddenly appeared standing next to him.

Ripp was startled by the voice. He thought he was alone. He snapped his head and saw a tall gangly man with sandy hair dappled with gray in a red hooded sweatshirt.

"Yeah we have these things at least once a year. The police are not the only ones who prepare for it. Look," then the man pointed toward the sidewalk below.

Ripp looked down and saw a street vendor in a push cart wearing an army surplus tear gas mask. He was holding his ground on the sidewalk and selling slices of pizza to fleeing and coughing members of the riot that had worked up an appetite. They would buy a slice and run off. "Looks like business is brisk," Ripp observed.

"You're not from here are you?" asked the hooded man.

"No. This is my first… riot," Ripp confessed.

"This is my fourth," and then the man looked up as if the correct answer was written across the night sky, "no fifth," corrected the man. "It never gets old. I go to bed early and then set my alarm and get up when I think one is in the air. I saw on the news tonight that the Boon Doggle's beer tent was closing early tonight and I said that means," and then he broke into a song to the tune of "Respect," "R-I-O-T-T-T-T, find out what it means to me, R-I-O-T-T-T-T, find out what it means to me. Sock it to me sock it to me sock it to me…"

"That's funny," said Ripp, humoring the strange hooded man who seemed to be sent to him as a gift since he had lost the young vandal. Ripp was hungry for a kill in La Claire. He began glancing around the parking ramp for security cameras and witnesses. This city had thwarted him too often. As Ripp sized this tall man up as a possible calling card, he could not believe his eyes. There was the young vandal. He was third in a line of four that stood in the street facing the line of officers. They had moved up behind the sweeping line, and on command the four including the young vandal turned and dropped their pants, mooning the line of officers.

The young vandal then pulled his pants up and staggered south on River Street, turning east at the first cross street he blindly reached, apparently calling it a night. The vandal was staggering toward campus. The other three ran a short distance south and reformed their line, dropping their pants again, but this time they urinated toward the line of officers. As they began tucking their junk away, they were suddenly swept up by an arrest team that had been assigned by Compton to make them a project. All three were arrested and hauled away in a van.

Ripp, bid a quick farewell to the hooded man and quickstepped to the stairwell of the ramp. He ran down the steps taking two at a time and sprinted after the vandal. When he reached the street where he had last seen the vandal, he was gone. "What the hell?"

Ripp paused looking up toward the ramp and noticed the hooded man still there looking down. A decision had to be made. Ripp looked east one more time and there he was. The vandal staggered out of the alley, zipping up his trousers. "There he is. This is my lucky night," said Ripp falling nonchalantly behind his the vandal as he tripped up the sidewalk, still working on his zipper.

The young vandal had avoided arrest, lost in the mass of people drifting away from the chaos. He was just another face in the crowd. He had left his friends when they formed a line to urinate at the police. He possessed a shy bladder and even alcohol could not have induced even a trickle in front of witnesses.

The vandal, who had left a wet spot on the wall in the alley to mark his passing, struggled mightily with his zipper, but he had jammed the tail of his shirt into the teeth of the zipper. He finally gave up the good fight and left the proverbial barn door to hang open during his long trek home. The vandal was totally satisfied that he had done his worst during the riot, cloaked in the anonymity of the masses. He was not anonymous to William Ripp, who was following fifty feet back and waiting for the opportunity for trophy number twenty-four.

Ripp smiled and thought to himself, "This one I'll shoot, and then I am gone. This will be my easiest kill ever."

The young vandal reached a bench at a bus stop next to the post office. After his night of civil debauchery, he was plumb tuckered out. The poor baby had never worked a day in his life and was sent to school on his daddy's dime. He was not used to such rigors as these. He lay down on the bench, and using his hands for a pillow, he curled up into a fetal position and was sleeping the dreamless sleep of the drunk within moments.

"How opportune," thought Ripp. "Now I have time to do this right." Ripp circled, maneuvered, and scanned the area. There were no security cameras detectable. The passing crowd had dissipated because the young vandal was one of the last dogs hung. The gunshot would blend in with the noise of the night. There had been the popping canisters tossed by police and cherry bombs tossed by the rioters. Ripp would have to wait though. A few wandering packs of hooting, cheering drunks were scuffling along the sidewalk on their way home from the riot. Ripp concealed himself in the darkly shadowed recess of the post office building waiting for his own "all clear" signal. Then he would pounce.

The police line had gone to a knee and removed their masks. The cool air on Dan McCarthy's face felt great.

"McCarthy!" shouted Compton, a man with a mission.

"Yes, Sergeant Compton," answered McCarthy.

"Hop in with Sergeant Stammos and see what you can find. See if you can pick out any of the bad ones you recognize amongst the stragglers," said Compton.

"Let's go see who we can find," said Stammos.

"Yes, Sergeant," said McCarthy.

"You call me Sergeant again, McCarthy, and I will have to kill you," said Randy with the look of death in his eyes.

"Sorry, Randy. You know, you are a sergeant and I am…"

"I will have to kill you, Dyno," said Stammos. "Do you prefer small caliber or something in a larger size," as he reached toward the shotgun.

"Got it, Randy," said Dan.

Randy then began to cruise the area. There were singles, couples, trios, and clusters of former rioters walking, shuffling, and staggering back to their apartments, homes, and dorms. They did not see themselves as rioters now, however. Everyone else was a rioter and they were, in their minds, just present at a riot.

Stammos and McCarthy cruised in and out of alleys and streets. "See anyone you remember?" asked Stammos.

"I have some in mind who I would recognize if I saw them again. There was a group of four rugby team members dogging us all night long. We managed to arrest one, but the others drifted away. If we don't find them tonight I will get them next week at practice. They can wait, but it would be nice to get them tonight," said McCarthy with concern in his voice.

"Arresting them at practice would make an even bigger impact," assured Stammos.

As the last group passed out of sight, Ripp stepped from the shadow. He was well hidden in the recess of the building. It would be impossible to see him unless he either stepped out or someone lit him up with a spot light. Ripp knew how to use the darkness as his ally since he was a true creature of the night. Now he would make his move. The street was finally clear. "Shit!" he said as he ducked back into the darkness.

The gold Chevrolet rounded the corner slowly and seemed to be about to park in the no parking zone next to the young vandal. "Shit, why is it going so slowly?" whispered Ripp.

"Check it out, Randy. See that guy sleeping on the bench. He threw a newspaper machine through the window of Bright's Antiques, and if that wasn't bad enough, later on he threw a bottle of Vodka at me. To add insult to injury he mooned us. The last time I looked, those acts were all prohibited by Wisconsin State Statutes, and I would call them misdemeanors. Come on, Randy, stop. Stop! *STOP!*" yelled Dan. Stammos pretended he was about to drive by the subject just to jerk Dan's chain.

"Oh, did you want me to stop? I didn't hear you. I was calculating my overtime tonight, you know, doing the math in my head," said Stammos laughing at the features of Dan's face contorted by the momentary frustration. "I kill myself."

"Look at him, sleeping like a baby," said Dyno, savoring his good fortune. "I am now going to enter his dreams and apprehend him for his high crimes," said McCarthy.

"If you enter his dreams to make the apprehension, that technically becomes a nightmare and you need a warrant to enter a person's nightmare. The Supreme Court has ruled that a man's nightmare is his castle. You can't do it, Dyno. You need a warrant. That's an order. See these," said Stammos tapping his stripes.

"Really," said McCarthy, playing along.

"Yes, and I believe it is not a misdemeanor if he threw vodka at you as long as he also threw tomato sauce, Tabasco sauce, a stalk of celery, and a lemon wedge. It would be called a Bloody Mary and those are not prohibited by law," said Stammos with authority.

"How about mooning?" asked McCarthy.

"It's a little chilly tonight. That would make it a Blue Moon. We just can't do it. It's my favorite flavor of ice cream," said Stammos.

"Yeah? Well watch this. I am going to lock this guy's Blue Moon in jail. Dear God, please inspire him to resist," said McCarthy crossing himself.

"McCarthy, he's not worth going to hell for," said Stammos sounding almost serious.

"You're right, Randy," and McCarthy looked up to the heavens as he exited the squad and said, "Please disregard that last request."

Ripp watched the gold Chevrolet pull up to the curb and slowly approach the young vandal. It rolled and rolled and rolled and passed the vandal slightly and then stopped in the no parking zone. Ripp could not see who was in the car due to the street light's glare on the windows. No one got out. The car did not move for what seemed like a long time. "What are they doing? Are they going to pick him up or what?"

Then the door swung open and, "Fuck! Fuck, Fuck, Fuck, Fuck, Fuck!" whispered William Ripp to himself. "What is going on in this fucking town?"

McCarthy stepped out of the unmarked squad and walked over to the sleeping vandal. He talked, cajoled, and even pushed his finger into the pressure point, the "mandibular-angle," located in the pit at the bottom of the young vandal's ear, and he finally woke up. He sat up and rubbed his eyes and shifted in his seat. Then he put his hands behind his back. McCarthy handcuffed him and searched him. Ripp watched as McCarthy removed a scales, a wad of cash, and about five baggies of something from the pockets of the young vandal.

Ripp observed that McCarthy looked exceedingly pleased with this particular arrest. In fact, even from the distance between them, Ripp could see McCarthy look to the sky and mouth the words, "Thank you, Lord," after the fruitful search. Ripp watched McCarthy open the back door of the squad and cover the miscreant's head to protect it from hitting the side of the door when he was placed in the car. McCarthy then carefully seat belted the vandal into the backseat, got into the unmarked squad, and they were off.

"My, they treat people well who treat them like shit," Ripp said to himself as he walked out of the shadows and headed back to his hotel. "Well, fuck me all to hell. I guess I will not leave a calling card. Darla my love, you shall be my calling card. It's time. I hope my luck changes."

Just then the rain came down in buckets as if God had said, "Cue the rain."

"Shit!" He flipped up the hood on his jacket. "Boy, that little prick is a lucky bastard. He doesn't know how fucking lucky he is." Ripp had grown comfortable talking to himself. He had done it all his life. He had to be cautious at times when people were around or they might think him odd. He had talked to himself when he melted his toy soldiers. He had talked to himself when he burned ants, crickets, and grasshoppers with his magnifying glass and the sun as a child. He had even talked to himself when he drowned cats, gophers, and whatever other kind of animals he could capture. He felt he was talking to his best friend, his only friend. He was the only person he could ever confide in. The only person he knew that shared his unique tastes in entertainment.

"You know, things could have been worse," he said to himself as he walked in the rain. "I could have come out of my cubby hole thirty seconds earlier, and I would have been caught. I might just be the luckiest son of a bitch in the world. I am the only fucking criminal I know of that hasn't been caught in this fucking black hole." With that thought Ripp felt suddenly uplifted. "How's that song go again?" he asked himself out loud. "Oh yeah... like this," To anyone watching he would have looked like Gene Kelly, minus talent, as he danced, skipped, and hopped toward the hotel whistling the tune *"Singing in the Rain."*

CHAPTER TWENTY-SEVEN

MOCKINGBIRD

As McCarthy walked into the kitchen, his kids jumped up from their breakfast and shouted "Daddy!"

As they began their bolt toward their morning hug, Dan's wife Victoria caught them both and said in a motherly tone, "Both of you sit down and finish your breakfast. Daddy will give you a hug after he showers." She turned toward Dan with her nose scrunched, "I smell tear gas. What happened?"

"We had a riot last night," said McCarthy.

"Well I am glad you all had such a good time, but what happened?" Victoria asked with a wry smile.

"That joke is getting old," said McCarthy.

"Like a fine wine it gets better with time," countered Victoria and she pushed the chair back in for Christa after Dan's daughter climbed into it.

Then with a whining voice that felt like someone running their finger nails deep and continually across a chalkboard, McCarthy whined, "How about this for a fine whine... do you have to keep telling that joke every time we have a riot?"

"The whining joke is getting old too," said Victoria.

"That makes us even, in the bad and old joke contest so... does that make us stale mates?" asked McCarthy.

"Take a shower... please," said Victoria, rolling her eyes.

"What's with the rolling eyes; this is good stuff?" McCarthy asked.

"Daddy, my eyes are sore," said Christa.

"Sorry, hon. I'll take a shower. I forgot she is kind of sensitive to tear gas," said McCarthy heading to the basement shower room.

"I think everyone is, honey. That's why you guys use it. That's how it works," Victoria shouted after him.

McCarthy stood by the washing machine and undressed. As he took each article of clothing off, he dropped it directly into the machine. When every stitch was in the washer, he grabbed the big bottle of Tide and without measuring he poured some in and pushed the buttons on the machine to light load, warm wash and cold rinse, and the other dial to permanent press. "I have no idea if any of that is correct, but that should do."

He then walked in the half bathroom in the basement and stepped into the shower. The hiss of the showerhead carried his thoughts back to the hissing of the tear gas. He pictured Compton calmly walking in front of the line and dropping the canisters in the perfect pattern. "What a master," he thought. "That tear gas formed a solid wall, and the breeze carried that wall right into the crowd. From that moment on, the winner of that fight was already decided. God, I am glad he was back."

After all but the memory of the Compatulli was washed away, Dan let the water pour over his head, shoulders, and the rest of his body to wash any of the stupidity or maybe the insanity of the rioters. McCarthy felt the warmth flow over his body, washing away the cold harsh reality of his night.

As Dan stepped out of the shower and dried off, he realized Victoria had silently slipped into the bathroom and hung up his favorite, most comfortable "pajamas." Dan slipped on his soft gray sweatpants and his Bart Starr jersey, and then number 15 climbed the stairs with the echoes of the chanting crowd clashing with the beautiful tune Mockingbird in his cerebellum.

He rejoined the children at breakfast, a familial masterpiece and a work in progress which was being painted by Victoria every day of their lives. The children, for all intents and purposes, were finished eating their food but were still actively involved in playing with it, which has caused every parent in their career of parenthood to finally say, "Stop playing with your food!" Christa was making a mountain with her scrambled eggs and placing a bit of sausage at the top. It seemed that eating this food was not on her agenda today.

"What are you doing with your eggs, cutes?" asked McCarthy.

"I'm building a…" then she stopped and realized she was playing with her food, one of those things her parents did not like her to do even though it seemed such a natural thing to do. She just looked at him and smiled while she happily swung her feet. Dad was a sucker for that smile, small as she was she already knew, "when in doubt, smile." It was her nuclear option. She was 100 percent right today. McCarthy needed that smile more than he needed an explanation. The smile warmed him more then every drop of water in the water heater.

"Thanks, cutes," McCarthy acknowledged, leaving Christa still smiling and still swinging her feet wondering what she had done deserving of thanks.

Nate was "accidentally" repeatedly dropping pieces of egg and leftover sausage to their Dalmatian who never let one piece hit the floor. When the dog, Princess Jasmine or "Jazz" for short, noticed Dan enter the kitchen, it ran to the spot on the carpet it was regulated to during meals. It lay down as if it had no complicity in the disappearance of the sausages.

"Did you eat some of that, Nate?" asked McCarthy.

"Yes, Dad. I'm full. I took too much, cuz I really like sausage and eggs," answered Nate, quickly rolling up the small piece of sausage in the palm of his hand and putting his hand under his leg, hoping he had not been caught feeding the dog from the table.

Then Jazz got up as if she had just noticed Dan standing there. Wagging furiously, the dog slowly approached Dan. The distinctive smile of a Dalmatian, called by the experts a "smarl," spread across her face. Dan swept up Jazz and held her like a baby and scratched her stomach vigorously and then set Jazz down and growled, "WHO'S NEXT!" He did his best body builder pose.

Both kids took the bait and bolted from their seats and ran squealing in feigned fear and absolute joy. The three traversed back and forth throughout the house in a good five minute romp where both were ultimately caught on Dan and Victoria's queen-sized bed and tickled mercifully but generously.

"OK, you two, it's time to tuck Daddy in," announced Victoria. The rabble rousing gently subsided and the ritual began.

McCarthy crawled into bed. Nate approached and kissed his father on the cheek and said, "Night Dad."

Then Christa crawled up next to him on the bed and said, "Eskimo, butterfly, and princess, Daddy." She then rubbed his nose, fluttered her eyelashes against his cheek and then kissed the same spot on his cheek. Then both children crept quietly out of the bedroom after completing the truly splendid ritual.

Victoria plugged in the fan and turned it on, locking it in a stationery position and pointed it at the closet. The fan noise blocked out the noises of the day, simulating the quiet of the night the family slept in without Dan. She threw a blanket over the curtain rod, drawing a tea cup full more of soothing darkness into the room.

McCarthy thought how lucky he was to have them to come home to. He always appreciated them but never failed to realize it on days like today, following nights like this that could not even be described. He had witnessed in eight short hours a young mother bravely singing a beautiful lullaby to a gift from God, her infant baby, who had slipped quietly into an everlasting sleep. McCarthy would always connect that tune to the ultimate love, the love of a mother.

Dan had then been thrust into a riot with drunken, stupid, hateful people, who spent an entire night wasting the gifts and talents that they had been given by God trying to destroy the fruits of someone else's labor. He stood alongside his mates and brought peace back to the vomit and urine-soaked street and sanity back to the mad crowd of rioters.

"What are you thinking, sweetheart?" asked Victoria sitting on the bed and gently brushing his forehead.

He looked into her beautiful doe eyes. "Just… Just… Just… That I love you and I am glad you are my wife and maybe even gladder that you are the mother of my children, if that's possible."

"You're tired. You always talk like this when you are really tired. Good night, honey." She leaned down and gently kissed him on the lips. Her kiss was the embodiment of warmth and tenderness, wrapped in love.

McCarthy's eyes began to flutter and he said, "You know, sweetheart..."

She kissed him one more time softly, and as her lips parted she said to him one decibel above a whisper, "Shh, go to sleep now."

Victoria had worked her magic. She had brought tranquility to his mind and body. He fell asleep wondering if peaceful sleep and dreams would come. Without a shred of awareness, McCarthy found himself in a dream. He was looking out a large picture window and a crowd was chanting, "Pax Domini! Pax Domini! Pax Domini!" The chants were a Latin religious term meaning peace of the Lord. He had heard it often as a server when he was young. Victoria walked over to the window and closed the curtain, ending the loud chant. She picked up their baby wrapped in a blanket. He could not see which child it was, but he sensed somehow she had wrapped the whole family in her arms. She then rocked, creating a gentle rhythmical tune with each creak of the rocker, and Victoria began to sing, "Hush little babies, don't say a word, Mama's going to buy you a *mockingbird*..."

CHAPTER TWENTY-EIGHT
VERY SOON

Ripp, usually an early riser, woke up in his room at the Radisson at 1:00 PM. His research for this particular... mission had been so encompassing his body clock had seemingly been altered. To accomplish his continued goal of homicides without detection, he had decided he needed to be better than ever before. The La Claire officers seemed to possess an uncanny combination of luck, skill, and enthusiasm that presented a threat to Ripp. They seemed to possess a certain indomitable spirit unbeatable when faced with violence by individual criminals or thousands of rioters. "They are making it almost impossible for me to operate here."

It could not be pure luck that this department had been so close to him every single step of the way without being aware of his presence. Until now, he had been so certain about his own invincibility that he was almost glib in the way he carried out his missions of death. This time was different. Ripp had an intense feeling of high anxiety during his reconnaissance and preparation.

He had decided absolutely that his target would be Darla. He had raped many of his victims, but it had never been about the sex. It was always about his ultimate control of life and death. The sex had sometimes been experimental and sometimes a ruse to lure the victim. Ripp realized that an unsuspecting victim is in the most vulnerable pose during sex. This time he decided sex with Darla would be his reward for his efforts.

Ripp dressed quickly and jumped into his rental car. He was careful to pick a variety of rentals. They varied in color, but he avoided anything flashy. They had to be comfortable, inviting, and large enough to conceal and transport the victim. He avoided bright colors, too easy to spot. He avoided vans and convertibles, too memorable. He went after the brown loafers of automobiles. He wanted cars that were functional and not worthy of a second look.

Today's work would be simple, and he would have to work fast. He had slept away much of his sunlight. Today he would find and pick the spot. He would take a long drive in the country, which would not be unusual for a Sunday. "Sunday," he said out loud, slipping the parking token into the computerized parking attendant at the exit of the Radisson's security lot, "I missed church today. I hope I don't go to hell." He laughed as the coin dropped into the machine which voiced its approval with a "ding" and the arm lifted to allow him to pass.

"Every time a bell rings an angel gets his wings. Well, angel, you owe me, so you keep me out of hell if it exists." He laughed and drove out of the lot. Ripp did not believe in God. He thought he had the perfect argument against the existence of God. He reasoned, "If He exists, how can I? How is it possible for a loving God to have created me?"

Ripp headed out of town on 41 and felt lazy. He felt pressed for time and he did not feel inclined to drive far. Just after leaving town he came to an intersection and the sign leapt out at him, "Dyerson Road. Wow! This must be the place." He turned and followed the peaceful, lonely road until he found what appeared to be a one-lane trail large enough for a tractor, an ATV, a truck, or the car of a killer.

"Hello!" He said as he stopped just after he passed it. He backed up and then eased his car up the road through the woods to the top. At the top was a meadow, surrounded by woods except it was shaped like a large grass lagoon that opened up to a sea of farmers' fields. Below was an old farm house that looked abandoned. The slope of the land shielded the meadow from the view of anyone below. "Yes indeed, this certainly looks promising."

He walked to the tree line adjacent to the meadow. He hiked into the woods stepping through the light brush, and he assessed the soil. This soil was rich farmland and was meant to be worked. The soil invited the spade. That was why it was chosen 150 years ago by the settlers looking for a new life. It was perfect for his needs.

The sprawl of the farmland was protecting the woods, which in turn was protecting the sprawling farmland. Darla's body would lie undiscovered long after he was gone. She was a stripper. No one would aggressively look for a stripper, even the La Claire Police. Strippers come and go. To Ripp, a stripper was the ultimate "nobody," easily disposed of and easily replaced. If anyone did look for her they would most certainly not look here, and if they did she would be buried deep. "It will happen soon," he said to two squirrels chasing about on a fallen tree, *"very soon."*

CHAPTER TWENTY-NINE

COMPTON'S SHIFT

It had been ten days since the riot. It was hard for most to grasp, but the riots came and went in La Claire, much like seasons come and go in other parts of the country. There was a momentary moral outrage in the community, but that popped and fizzled out nearly as quickly as the canisters of non-burning tear gas.

Sergeant David Compton had come in on his day off and requested permission, through the chain of command, to speak with Chief Hale. Captain Jackson had approved the meeting. Hale made Compton wait in the outer office for 35 minutes and then rang his secretary and said, "Have Sergeant Compton step in."

As Compton walked through the door, Chief Hale was looking at budget figures and without looking up he said, "Sergeant Compton, I have been meaning to talk to you about your performance during the riot."

"Was there something I could have improved upon, sir?" asked the sergeant, standing in front of the chief's desk at attention.

Hale looked up and became immediately annoyed, "Sit down for Christ's sake; you're not in the marines anymore." Sergeant Compton nodded and took a seat, but it appeared as if he changed his position of attention to the seated position. "I wanted to ask you, what's the deal? You were approved to come back on light duty. Is a riot light duty?"

"Yes sir. I only gave a few commands, a few dispersal orders, and rolled some tear gas out into the street. The heavy load was carried by the teams." Sergeant Compton looked puzzled as if he was having a great deal of difficulty grasping how anyone could think what he did was anything but light duty.

"I am certain that your doctor would disagree with you, but we will forget about it. You were in your element once again. Good job!" said Hale begrudgingly.

"Thank you, sir," said Compton.

"So, to what do I owe the pleasure of this visit?" asked Chief Hale, getting to the point. "I need to move this along as I am preparing my budget presentation. The city council is talking about deep cuts for next year, and I have to convince them to look elsewhere for their cuts," said Hale looking at the clock on the wall and then his wrist watch impatiently.

"Chief Hale, I was told that Seth Johnson will be the next sergeant, and the letter will be cut sometime this week," said Sergeant Compton.

"The rumor mill is once again accurate, but that information is not for public release. As a matter of fact, the letter will be posted today. Why do you ask?" said Hale as if he did not already know.

"Well, Chief Hale, I have four good, no, great officers that finished higher on the test than Seth did, and they are much more qualified than he. They are the top street officers on the department," said Compton, pausing because he felt he should not have to say more in a fair and impartial venue.

"None of them have a master's degree. Seth has a master's degree and is the only candidate with one. He has eight years experience with the department. Granted the others have more, but other than Brockman, we are only talking about two to five years more," said Hale.

"Sir, Seth Johnson was barely out of field training when he was appointed to DARE. His street experience is minimal, and everyone knows that. Respectfully, sir, it will reflect badly on the department. There will be those who will say he was promoted because of who his father was and the four on my shift were passed over because of their involvement in the arrest of your daughter, sir. I am here to tell you what everyone outside your inner circle will be saying," said Compton. "Sir, these officers have worked hard. They deserve consideration. One of them deserves this promotion. If one of them does not get this promotion it will be seen as a slap in the face to the officers working on the street."

Hale's face became red and then redder as Compton spoke. It looked as if Hale was holding his breath until Compton finished and as he did Hale exploded, "Damn it all, Compton, you'll never learn will you? No wonder you're still a *God Damn Sergeant!* Hell, you've been here longer than I have. Do you know you're speaking to the Chief of Police?" Hale shouted.

"Yes, sir. Respectfully, sir, I am telling you what everyone will say to everyone except you after you make this promotion, sir," explained Compton.

Hale took a few breaths and calmed down. He realized he could be heard outside his office and probably down the hall. After composing himself he continued, "Sergeant, no matter what others say, I have to make decisions based on all factors. McCarthy, Carpenter, Brockman, and Dooley not only do not have the same educational credentials as Seth, but they also are too street oriented for this particular position. It is a sergeant's position in community services, and Seth has committed eight years of hard work to community services. They had an opportunity to do the same, and they chose to stay on the street rather than broaden their horizons," said Hale while trying to stick a smile on his face, but the glue wouldn't hold and the corners of his mouth kept slipping back down. "All four of those officers are too one dimensional to serve the community in community services."

"Seth has no substantive street time. Sir, these officers have been serving their community doing police work on the street on third shift in an exemplary manner for..."

Hale interrupted, his voice rising again, "What? Are you saying officers in community services are not serving the City of La Claire? I was in community services for twenty years, Sergeant Compton. Are you saying I did not serve the community? Are you saying only street cops do real police work?"

"No, sir, you served time on patrol. I know because we worked together. It was five years, I believe. Then you were a detective before you were promoted. That is vastly different than no substantive street experience," said Compton.

"Well, Sergeant Compton, in my perception Seth is the only one of the candidates that has specific qualifications for this promotion. He served in the community services, and he is my choice. This promotion has nothing to do with anything but qualifications. If any rumors to the contrary arise in your presence, Sergeant Compton, I expect you to quash them. That's an order. You're dismissed, Sergeant Compton!" said Hale looking at his watch and returning to his full attention to his budget.

"Yes sir. By the way, sir, I'm proud, sir."

"Proud of what?" said Hale, snapping his head back up disgusted by the statement without knowing why.

"I am proud to be, as you put it, a 'God Damn Sergeant,' of those four men, whether they are promoted or not. I have the best job on this department, and, sir, I will always be a Marine. Thank you for your time, sir." Compton stood up at attention, executed a left face and forward marched out of Hale's office. He thought, "Respect the position if you cannot respect the man."

Hale shook his head in disbelief. He would never understand the David Comptons of the world. Hale once said "The guy's always running around with his God, Country, Duty, Honor, Corps... Does he really believe all that bullshit?" Most people in the world since the beginning of time have scoffed at the David Comptons of the world and then run cowering to them whenever any part of the world needed saving.

Dave Compton had risked his life for his country and his department and had always done everything that was ever asked of him. Hale had an opportunity to return the favor and grant a reasonable request. That simple and reasonable request would not be granted for one simple reason. Chief Hale was not a reasonable man, and he had the authority to be unreasonable.

Later that night, Brockman was seated in lineup quietly fuming. He had been there for fifteen minutes just waiting for someone, anyone, to walk through the door so that he could release the tirade that boiled and bubbled inside him. He had just read a letter posted on the information board. McCarthy walked into the lineup room and Brockman fired his question off before McCarthy was two steps inside the door. "Did you see the posting?" asked Brockman before McCarthy could sit down.

"What posting?" Dan asked.

"Seth Johnson was promoted to sergeant. What the fuck is Chief Hale thinking? Johnson has no street experience. There are four more experienced people on the list in front of him and one of them is… this pisses me off," seethed Brockman.

McCarthy was immediately angry too. He had not seen the posting, and this was the first time he had to think about the unthinkable. Brockman, Carpenter, Dooley, and he had finished in front of Seth Johnson in the sergeant's examination, but the chief did not have to pick in order. He just had to pick one from the top five. "Kind of disappointing, I'll give you that," said McCarthy, letting his bag drop from his shoulder and slam to the table. He then slumped into his chair as if he was a dancing string puppet whose strings had just been cut.

"It's all bullshit. The whole damn system is fucked up. It's not what you know, it's who you blow, always has been, always will be." Brockman was building steam.

Dooley and Carpenter entered the room and sat down.

"Did you see it? Did you see the fucking posting?" Brockman asked. His words sounded more like an indictment than a question.

"What posting?" Carpenter asked.

"Seth Johnson was promoted to sergeant," said Brockman.

"Shit," said Dooley. "Don't they give you a spoon full of sugar to help the medicine go down?" asked Dooley. "Did they even know we were on the list? Did they know we all have more experience than him and were in front of him on the list? What were they thinking?" asked Dooley in shock.

"It is a little hard to handle," said McCarthy. "His only two qualifications are his master's degree and the fact that his father was the chief who recommended Hale for his position. This news hurts." McCarthy felt he was in uncharted waters. He felt like not only agreeing with Brockman but joining him this time on his rant. This was not a reasonable decision no matter how you analyzed it.

"Guys like Hale like it when it hurts," said Brockman. "The only warning they give you is when they say 'bend over' then they fuck you dry. It always hurts. They always enjoy it, and you always end up fucked. I should pull my old T-shirt out of the moth balls and start wearing it again. TJIF, this job is fucked," said Brockman. "We didn't have a chance. Everyone on that list had something to do with the chief's daughter getting arrested except Seth Johnson. That's the common denominator here. We all did better than him on the test. We all have more experience. Damn! If you are actually counting street time he doesn't even have a year on the street," complained Brockman.

"Well the position was for a sergeant in community services. Who would want that? Not me," said McCarthy looking desperately for the silver lining.

"There you go again, McCarthy, with that grapes are probably sour bullshit! Face it! We would all have liked to have had the opportunity to decide on our own if we wanted the position. On nights we are always treated like mushrooms. They feed us shit and keep us in the dark," said Brockman.

"Shit! Shit! Shit! This job is shit. It is like shoveling shit into a great big pile of shit. As if you don't get enough shit on the street, the administration has to make sure they serve you up some more shit. Then the public has to treat you like shit every night of the week when you are just trying to protect and serve their ungrateful asses. The media presents us as shit. It's all shit. You can only pile shit so high and then it slides down and gets all over your shoes. When that happens, the command gives us shit about our shoes and screams, 'Look at your shoes. They look like shit!' Then they make us shine our shoes and get all dressed up for work and we go home covered in the shit we have been wallowing around in all night." Stanley Brockman had slipped into one of his famous funks. When McCarthy first met him he was a full-blown ROD, retired on duty. He had struggled back and become a valuable member of the department, the SWAT team, and he even liked himself again. This promotion was not the first time he had been passed over but quite possibly had hit him the hardest because he was now worthy of a promotion, and he knew Seth had not earned it.

When McCarthy, Dooley, and Carpenter saw Brockman's disappointment, it made their own seem trivial. All four had agreed to remain friends no matter which of them were to be promoted, but this was a true blindside. No one thought Seth Johnson had even the most remote of chances. From most people's point of view, only an imbecile would promote him over McCarthy, Carpenter, Brockman, or Dooley. Since the chief was not an imbecile, it appeared he was someone with a score to settle. There would never be a way of knowing because the next sergeant was all powerful and all knowing. He had a master's degree. If it was a crime against fairness, it was the perfect crime committed by police administrations all over the country over and over, again and again.

Sergeant David Compton walked through the door of the lineup room and heard Stanley editorializing, and though Brockman acknowledged his presence, he did nothing to restrain himself.

"Why even do our jobs, I ask? We catch bad guys left and right, and some rookie with a master's degree and a chief for a daddy gets promoted without giving us so much as a fuck you very much."

When Brockman saw Compton walk into the room, he shifted his diatribe from complaining about the promotion to complaining about a specific incident which had happened the night before when Sergeant Compton was off. Brockman's capsule stopped orbiting the promotion and went spinning off tangentially into space. Compton had seen these rants by Stanley Brockman before, but it had been a while.

This particular rant Compton understood. In his heart he even agreed with Stanley, but Compton had to bring the shift, his shift, back up from the emotional depths they had immediately slipped into. This was a crucial moment for a shift. A great shared disappointment could impact them all negatively for the rest of their careers. Compton had seen the carpet pulled out from under officers before who had never recovered. He had to pick them back up but not yet. He let Brockman continue.

"We work our asses off to put these dirtbags away, and now with tax payer's money instead of putting them in jail, they attach little radio transmitters to their little fucking chicken legs. That is supposed to be some fucking kind of a punishment? Kiss my ass and call it foreplay, it not only does not keep them from leaving their homes, it doesn't even stop them from committing crimes," lectured Stanley.

"What's really got your goat tonight, Stanley?" asked Compton.

The rest of the shift officers waiting for lineup, McCarthy, Dooley, Carpenter, Brown, Hartley, and Shepherd, sat quietly to see what would happen next. Stanley had swerved off course, obliterating the cohesiveness of his rant. When Brockman went on one of his rants it was like a nearsighted bull humping a lonely mule. They had learned it was best to let him finish because if you interfered there was just going to be trouble and no one was going to be satisfied. Watching Stanley was in some way a soothing ointment on the sting.

Brockman thought about telling him about the promotion but instead continued on his tangent. Now he was pissed. You could see it in his face and hear it in his voice. "It's these ankle bracelets. Rather than putting these guys in jail, they put ankle bracelets on them. Last night when you were off we arrested Rich Rodman. He robbed the Motel Eight, and while we were out at the Motel Eight investigating that robbery, one block away he hit the Super America. Then some of us went over there and we are out at two places when he rips off the tip jar of the coat check lady at an event at the Best Western Hotel. Then McCarthy gets there after we are all tied up taking robbery complaints, and he goes to the Country Kitchen because tell him why, McCarthy."

McCarthy was surprised in the topical shift, but relieved, and he continued "Well, I got a hunch that if he hit that place it would be four corners of a perfect square. I didn't know what else to do since I was working the opposite side of town and I was late getting into the area, so I just drove up to the back door of the Country Kitchen to make sure everything was all right, and that's when Rodman bolted out the back door of the restaurant. I chased him and tackled him across the street. He didn't see me until I was on him. He had a gun on him, but after I found it on the search, I thought I found another one in an ankle holster, so I yanked at it but I could not get it off. It was not an ankle holster; it was an ankle monitor. The guy is on the bracelet. He was hitting places within his accepted range while he was on home monitoring," explained McCarthy.

"So you caught the bad guy; why are you so upset, Stanley?" asked Compton giving Stanley an opportunity to talk about the promotion. Compton had worked with Stanley Brockman a long time and knew he needed to vent in a safe environment.

"Don't you find that ridiculous? Rodman was on home monitoring for burglary, and so now he is limited to going out within an area before midnight. He can't break into anything good that is close enough because the places are all still open, so he moves up on the criminal food chain from being a burglar to being an armed robber. I can't believe this. You can't make this shit up, you know. The guy is technically in jail, so if we wouldn't have caught him, he would have had the perfect alibi," reasoned Stanley.

"I can see why you are upset, Stanley." Compton set the lineup books down on the command desk in the front of the room. He then sat on the front of the desk instead of on the chair behind the desk. McCarthy, Dooley, Shepherd, Brown, and Carpenter leaned forward instinctively in their chairs. They knew that when Compton sat on the front of the desk he had something important to say. When Dave Compton spoke, these officers listened. The man was a thirty-plus-year veteran of the La Claire Police Department. He was still a working third-shift sergeant. He not only helped run the shift, but he still answered calls and made arrests. He had been a highly decorated Marine for actions he had taken in Viet Nam. He was commander of the La Claire SWAT team. He had saved lives with his words and saved lives with his deeds, including his own. Dave Compton would be the best sergeant these officers would ever have the privilege of serving with. As a result, everyone listened whenever David Compton spoke. Everyone listened, no matter their rank or station... even Stanley Brockman.

"The system is flawed, but it is the best system going. All we can do is point out constructively the flaws when we see them. I will contact the people at home monitoring on this, but I am sure they are already trying to fix what is broken." Compton paused, looked back toward the lineup books and then turned toward his shift and says, "This isn't about home monitoring is it?"

Brockman was primed and he immediately snapped out, "Sergeant Seth Johnson? He hasn't worked even a year on the street and he makes sergeant while we are all asked to smile, drop our pants, and bend over and take it without so much as a reach around. It makes a street cop want to throw his hands up in the air and scream fuck it! Who gives a shit! I tell you..." lamented Stanley Brockman. Brockman was sliding toward cynical critical mass over-load. The corners of his mouth turned down and began to quiver and he stopped in mid sentence, surprised by the emotion welling up into his throat. He paused to regroup.

Compton began, "It's all right to be frustrated and disappointed, but it is never all right to give up. I'm telling you that you guys and ladies can and do make a difference, in spite of the system that we are saddled with. Policing in America is all about fighting the good fight. You can't give up in a good fight once you're in it."

"One cop working alone can make a difference, but you know what's even better than that? Two cops working as a team trying to make a difference, and do you know what? They will make a difference. Do you know what's even better than that?" Now Compton was up and moving. "What is even better than that is an entire shift that has decided to work together to make a difference. This shift is the best shift I have ever had the pleasure of working with, and if you let this promotion change that, it would be a tragedy. I am surrounded by the best cops I have ever known, and I have known some great cops. I am surrounded by heroes."

"We're nobody's heroes," said Brockman, who had triumphed in the struggle with his emotions.

Compton immediately rebutted, "You are exactly right, Stanley! You are nobody's heroes. Think about how many homeless people you have picked up and taken to the shelter in the winter, saving their butts because they are nobodies who nobody else wants to help. Think of all the battered wives who are nobodies to their husbands and who have nobody else to turn to that you guys have rushed to rescue because they are so important to you that you have made them your life's work. Think about how many men and women who are about to end their seemingly unbearable existences that each one of you have talked down from the ledge. All those people thought they were nobody until you came around and at least for a little while made those nobodies feel like somebody again. If any one of them was truly a card-carrying nobody, then all of you qualify as nobody's heroes."

"Stanley Brockman, you have brought babies into the world. Man, I stood by in awe while you took off your hat, rolled up your sleeves, and brought a little boy into this world. Remember that, Stanley. That night you were my hero."

Stanley could not help but smile, remembering. He had the little boy's picture hung in his locker. He then looked around the room and said proudly, "They named him Stanley. Nobody is named Stanley anymore. That little boy is, though."

"You know, you guys make a difference. The stats that people will look at for that deal last night will be four robberies and four clearances with one suspect arrested. There is a statistic that no one ever looks at. How many criminals decide to go elsewhere because they would rather mess with the rest than test the best? How many crimes do not get committed here because criminals know there is a high probability of being caught? How many people are alive in La Claire because this is a truly bad place to drive with a snoot-full? How many drivers every night toss their keys to someone else because you guys are going to be hounding them all the way home and they know it? There is no way to calculate the number of crimes you prevent or the number of criminals you scare the living beejesus out of just because you guys and ladies are incredible to watch in action."

"It seems reasonable sometimes to say 'fuck it,' but you can't give up. You say that and you're not there when someone needs you. Hell, your mind is not there when you need it. What goes hand in hand with 'fuck it' is you being out there and you missing something. Let's face it, ladies and gentlemen, we meet the good, the bad, and the ugly out there. We need to keep our heads in the game and never forget that this is not a game! If your head is up your ass or you are just having a 'fuck it' day, you might miss a bulge under the clothing, a hand disappearing out of sight, a gun in a search, a glance toward your weapon."

"You cannot afford to say 'fuck it' in our line of work. That is giving up. You can never give up. In our business when a cop gives up and says 'fuck it,' someone suffers. I can understand the sentiment, but I cannot stand by and let it happen. I know how good you are and what a difference you've made."

"Of all the people in the world, we are the ones who could be first in line to be able to eloquently debate the point 'Why no one should ever give a rat's ass,' but we can't. It is too important."

"I found out years ago staying positive is a discipline. At the start of every shift, I try to find a reason to stay excited. Since you folks have arrived, I no longer have to try to stay excited. Watching you ladies and gentleman not only excites me, but it inspires me. Don't give up and don't give in to the natural seduction of cynicism. Never give up. Giving up becomes easier and easier. If you learn how to give up when things really aren't so bad it will be easier to give up when your life is really on the line."

"Whether you are down because you didn't get a promotion or down in the middle of a fight on the street, you don't give up. Whenever you find yourself seduced by a feeling that anything would be better than the pain of this struggle to keep going, the discipline will pay off because you will not give up. You have prepared yourself every day of your life for the moment that you cannot give up. Don't ever give up. No matter how tough it gets sometimes, you never give up. *You never give up.* **Never while you're out there give up!**"

There was silence. Then Compton looked individually at each person in the lineup and said, "Promotions come and go. No one remembers them except the few that were thrilled or disappointed by them. Great cops like this shift, my shift, are remembered always by those whose lives they have saved and changed." His moving glance stopped at Brockman and he concluded by saying, "Cops like you, Stanley Brockman."

Compton walked to the seat behind the command desk. Just as he was about to sit down, Stanley quietly piped in, "Dave... I mean, Sergeant..."

"Yes, Stanley," said Compton slowly taking his seat.

Then Stanley, who was seated in the front row leaned forward in an attempt to speak only to Sergeant Compton, said one word quietly enough to barely reach Compton, but loud enough for all to hear and sincere enough for all to understand, "thanks." Dave Compton had said Stanley Brockman was the best of the best, his hero. Dave Compton had said that Stanley Brockman inspired him. It was the nicest thing anyone had ever said to Stanley Brockman. What more could any cop ask for?

Compton nodded in acknowledgement.

"What about the promotion?" thought everyone in the room. "Fuck it! Who needs it? We're the best. We're Compton's Shift!"

Compton's speech had served two purposes. It had been an emotional life jacket once again for Stanley Brockman, who seemed forever bobbing about in the sea of cynicism trying to keep his head above it. For everyone else in the room it did what Compton constantly did for them. It kept them energized on a nightly basis. As McCarthy left lineup he commented to Carpenter, "Isn't that an awesome thought, Carp?"

"What's that, Dyno? The bend over and fuck us dry without even a reach around thought?" asked Carpenter. "I didn't think you were into that sort of thing, Dyno."

"No," said McCarthy shaking his head with a pained expression on his face, "That criminals would be afraid to commit crimes when we are working," said McCarthy.

"Well, isn't that what you always say? We can't arrest everyone all the time but... What's that you always say?" asked Carpenter stumbling for the quote, "You're always saying something, and I can't keep them all straight."

"You mean we don't arrest them all the time; we just arrest them all," answered McCarthy.

"Yeah that's the one. We just arrest them all. I believe when we believe that, it becomes the truth. When the dirtbags realize it, we make a difference. When we make a difference, we do some good," said Carpenter.

"Pretty deep, Carp," said McCarthy.

"Fuckin' A."

"How do you feel about the promotion?" asked McCarthy.

"A little relieved," said Carpenter. "I mean, I would hate to think that it was because of the chief's daughter's arrest, but I don't think it would have been good for my future to turn it down, and I would have turned it down," said Carpenter.

"Same here. I am not ready to leave the streets and I do not believe I ever will be," said McCarthy. "Should we be mad?"

"Is it going to help?" asked Carpenter.

"No."

"Is it going to change anything?" Carpenter asked.

"No."

"Well if I could have had it, I didn't want it. If I wanted it, I couldn't have it. So I choose to say, Fuckin' A and be done with it. I am doing what I do best, with the people I like best, in the place I like best, on the shift I like best. I agree with Compton in that having a bad attitude and not giving a shit can get your ass fired and even killed, so what good is that? You know what my final words on this matter are?" Carpenter asked.

"Let me guess. Fuckin' A?" asked McCarthy.

Carpenter then answered "Your words not mine. But... I couldn't have said it better."

As the two separated, Compton came running out. He called to them, "Hey Carp, Dyno, right after you walked out the door it started itching." Compton was scratching his old scar. The men and ladies of the night shift refused to argue with the omen any longer. They lowered their heads and headed toward their squads as if they were walking into a stiff wind. They did not wonder if tonight's shift would bring a challenge. They wondered what that challenge would be and if, once again, they would be up to it.

The promotion was as forgotten as last Tuesday's breakfast menu. All anyone could think was, "Oh. Oh. The shit is going to hit the fan."

"Well nothing we can't handle, right, Dyno?" said Carpenter.

McCarthy answered, "You know it. Nothing a few good cops can't handle. The best sergeant I know just said we could. He said we're nobody's heroes. The devil be damned, we can handle anything he throws at us. We're *Compton's shift!*"

CHAPTER THIRTY

THE LAWN MOWER PULL

The time was now. Ripp had returned to Madison after the riot, and after much internal debate, he had come to the conclusion that the close calls had cleared the path for him. McCarthy and his ilk had a string of luck and that was that. It was purely an incredibly lucky coincidence. "What are the odds of us crossing paths during a fourth attempt?" He answered his own question, "Slim to none. The odds are in my favor. I was pushing it, planning an attempt during the riot. There had to be about fifty cops on that street.

Ripp had spent a restful night at the Radisson in La Claire. He woke at 11:14 AM and was proud to see that he had hung the Do Not Disturb sign on his door. It was a small detail, but he was convinced it was an omen for success.

Ripp left the hotel with a smile on his face. He took his locked briefcase along with him and laid it in the trunk. He slid it to the back and gave it a gentle pat. Looking at his precious black case, Ripp smiled and closed the trunk. "Now it's time to run my errands."

William Ripp's first stop of the day was at the nearest sandwich shop. As usual, he had trouble deciding; he liked them all, but today he ordered a cold cut combo with the works, a bag of chips, and chocolate milk. Ripp forced himself to have a hearty lunch because he knew he would be working through the afternoon.

William hopped into the car and headed over to the second stop on his list, the Home Depot. Ripp pulled one of the large orange carts and meandered through the store. He threw a shovel into the cart and then a large paint drop cloth. He chose a blue fabric drop cloth rather than see-through plastic. They served the purpose and had the feeling and appearance of a picnic blanket rather than a death shroud. Ripp purchased some coveralls, work gloves, and a pair of rubber boots. He whistled as he carted from department to department to collect what he needed. He savored the preparation.

As he passed through the checkout line, the young girl in her orange apron was especially cheerful. Her tag, which said "Hello I'm Cheryl," was bordered and heavily laden with customer service awards. "Looks like you have your work cut out for you today," chirped Cheryl with a smile that accentuated her dimples.

"Yes, I do," said Ripp.

"Project outside?" she asked. Making small talk last throughout each sale was Cheryl's specialty.

"Yes. My wife gets really upset with me when I dig holes in the living room carpet," laughed Ripp holding up the shovel. He had listened to a comedian once who said stupid people should have to wear a sign and smart people should be allowed to identify the dumb ones and hand out signs. He hesitated and said, "Which comedian is it that says, Hare's yer sign." He handed her an invisible sign and assumed a southern twang like the comedian.

Cheryl laughed, "That's a hoot. I guess that wins the stupid question of the year award. The guy's name is Bill Engvall. He came to La Claire once and my boyfriend took me to see him. You sound just like him. Hare's my sign!" Then she laughed with a snort and took the invisible sign from Ripp.

"I heard once that the only stupid questions are the ones not asked, but now I know that's not true because you asked one that truly was a stupid question," Ripp then handed Cheryl cash.

Cheryl shook her head, laughed, and snorted one last time as she made change for Ripp and then said, "You know what Gump says, 'Stupid is as stupid does.' You have a good day, sir. Ba-Bye now," Cheryl said as she waved and demonstrated her southern accent one more time, "Ya'll come back now, hear?"

"Ba-Bye now, Cheryl," mocked Ripp. "Someday I might have to come back for her," he thought to himself as he wheeled his purchases out the door, "I'd like to see how close she would come to the end before she stopped smiling. Not today, though. I reserved the whole day especially for Darla."

After loading the trunk of his rented Chevy Impala, Ripp headed out of the parking lot and down Highway 41. He caught himself daydreaming as he drove past the street sign he was looking for, Dyerson Road. He said it out loud and he liked the sound of it. "Dyerson Road. Dye-rson Road. How ironic Die-rson Road. I almost drove right by you."

Ripp pulled to the shoulder, checked traffic, and then spit gravel as he made a U-turn heading back to Dyerson. Ripp found the narrow road or cow path heading up the side of the hill. It was perfect with woods on either side all the way up to the top. There was barely enough room for one car, so Ripp steered the Chevy up into the woods. "This is why I love rentals. I certainly would never try this with my personal vehicle." When he reached the top, he found the small clearing surrounded by woods. The clearing emptied out across the tilled fields, but it was accessible and the perfect place for his needs.

After parking the Impala, he got out of the car and took a deep breath, "I love working outside," he said to himself, smiling and almost giddy. "Tonight I make it happen."

Ripp stepped into his coveralls and slid on the boots. He slipped on his gloves and then pulled the shovel out of the trunk. He started digging. He had dug twenty-three graves that had never been found because their locations were secluded. He picked his victims with perfection. None had been readily noticed missing nor sorely missed. He avoided witnesses observing the abductions, the assaults, and the killings. He was an expert in the disposal of their remains. This secluded spot fit the criteria perfectly and now all that was left was an afternoon of work before all fun could begin.

Ripp would try to schmooze, cajole, and finally threaten his victims to the place of execution, which would be at or close to the grave he would thoroughly prepare, in most cases, in advance. He spent three hours digging Darla's grave. It was in a pleasant spot. It was a perennially wooded area, next to multi-generational farm lands, with no encroaching urban sprawl and no new roads in the area. Ripp trusted that Darla's grave would never be found.

When he finished with her, all the evidence of the crime would go into the hole on top of Darla.

As Ripp dug Darla's grave, he thought about the perfection of his crimes. He would have to be caught or else he would be the only living witness to these horrific acts. He was so proud of his perfect crimes and would be satisfied except for one thing. He could tell no one. No one could marvel at his intelligence. No writers would pay homage to him either in life or after his death. That was for killers who were caught, and he could not be caught because he was too careful. He was too smart. He was too good. His ability to keep his secret from the world was central to his success. He would never be portrayed on the big screen by any actors with "Sir" in their names. No one would ever receive an Oscar for capturing his essence.

This should have made William Ripp joyful, but it did not. He possessed a gnawing desire to be added to the pantheon of serial killers: Henry Lee Lucas, Wayne Gacey, Jeffrey Dahmer, Ed Gein, and Ted Bundy, but they had all been caught. He sighed wistfully, "I'm never going to be caught."

It was like painting a masterpiece and having it hung on the wall of a school for the blind, or building a beautiful piece of architecture at the bottom of the ocean. It was so very frustrating.

When the hole was finished, Ripp took off his gloves, coveralls, and boots. He set them next to the hole and leaned the shovel up against the nearest tree. He hopped excitedly into the Chevy and drove back down the hill. He was careful to enter Dyerson Road when no one was coming. He whistled, unaware, "Singing in the Rain" once again as he drove back to his hotel. With the hard work done, all that was left was the fun. His spirits soared.

After returning from the dig, he showered and then lay down and slept. He wanted to be rested for his "date with Darla." When his alarm went off, the room was dark. He bounced excitedly out of bed and took another shower. He brushed his teeth and carefully combed his hair. He dressed in black slacks and black tennis shoes in the event he would have to run. He never had taken a precaution such as this before. He slipped on a black mock turtleneck shirt.

Ripp swung on his shoulder holster rig and secured it in place. He opened the cylinder of his revolver and saw each primer in the center of each bullet, waiting to be the one selected to be lucky enough to go "Bang!" So that each could have its chance, Ripp spun the cylinder of the revolver hard and fast and then slapped it shut on the randomly chosen lucky round.

Ripp then picked up his precious briefcase, spun the numbers into place, and clicked the latches open. Opening the case, his face lit up with pride. Lying within the case were the dreadful last re-mains of twenty-three souls Ripp had snuffed the life-light out of. "No one even knows I exist," Ripp said to himself with a recovered jubilance. "God, I'm good. McCarthy, Carpenter, Compton, all of you can eat shit and die! I can't believe I was afraid of you." He checked to make certain he was prepared to take his next souvenir. When he was ready, he shut and relocked the case.

He had purchased a new jacket just for the occasion. It was a black and gray reversible jacket. He would start the night with the gray turned out and end with the black turned out. After slipping on his jacket, he stepped in front of the full length mirror and combed his hair one last time. He sprayed some Drakkar Noir Cologne on to make himself pleasing to Darla. He then checked one last time to make absolutely certain his weapon and rig were well concealed.

As Ripp left the hotel, he held down the trunk release button on the key chain for his rental car. The security system let out a beep and the lights blinked their approval as well. The rental company had become, once again, the unwitting accomplice of William Ripp.

McCarthy was assigned to the downtown area, and Compton's scar had been absolutely wrong so far. The downtown area looked quiet. Everyone was strolling quietly from one night spot to another as if they had not received the memo on how to behave in the no-toriously rowdy bar district of downtown La Claire. McCarthy was not about to complain about a quiet night because that would most certainly bring on the event that was making Compton's scar itch.

As Dan drove by the Radisson Hotel, his attention was drawn to the lights of a car parked in the lot. The sudden beep and flash was announcing the arrival of the driver. He looked about the lot as he instinctively slowed down and saw a neatly dressed man in a gray jacket and black slacks. The man had sandy hair and glasses and looked like... a professor.

"I'll be damned. There he is again," said McCarthy out loud, "William Ripp." He saw Ripp walk to the back of the flashing car and open the trunk. He gingerly placed the black briefcase he was carrying into the trunk of his car as if it contained the queen's tiara. Ripp then carefully closed the trunk and left the car walking at a brisk pace toward the bar district.

"Well, at least he is smart enough not to drink and drive," thought McCarthy. For some reason McCarthy pulled his pen from his uniform shirt and wrote onto his large note pad as he drove, "11:30 PM: William Ripp, briefcase into vehicle parked at Radisson."

McCarthy was not sure why he wrote the note. He was not sure why he suspected Ripp of anything. All Ripp had done was witness one event, but something... something was not right and whatever that something was could not be explained by McCarthy until the reasons for his suspicions were clear. Right now it was a disturbance in the force, a funny feeling, a sixth sense, a 'what the fuck,' and it did not rise to the level of reasonable suspicion, probable cause, and most certainly not to proof beyond a reasonable doubt. It was definitely "something" though.

McCarthy watched Ripp in his peripheral vision until he passed, and then he watched him in his rear view mirror. McCarthy made a U-turn and headed back toward Ripp. "He was carrying a black briefcase; could it be drugs? Maybe I can spook him," thought McCarthy.

As Ripp left the parked car and headed toward the RUMP to check on Darla and take care of one loose end, he saw it. "Shit, a cop." He could not see who was in the squad, but he knew it was going slower than normal. "Be cool. Be calm. Be friendly," said Ripp, nervous as a feral cat at a NRA picnic. He forced himself to be calm and not reach for his gun. When the car passed it made a U-turn and headed right back at him.

As the squad approached, Ripp made every effort to not deviate one step from his course. He did not want to raise any suspicion. As the squad reached him, he waved and smiled at the officer. Then he saw him. It was McCarthy waving and smiling back. "Shit!" Ripp thought. "McCarthy!" He called out as he waved.

McCarthy continued on by while waving. He clearly saw Ripp mouth his name again. "He remembers me," thought McCarthy. "He sure is a friendly son of a bitch. Maybe I got him all wrong. It wouldn't be the first time." This was a little white lie McCarthy told to himself. McCarthy had never felt so strongly about someone being a criminal in the past as he felt about Ripp without being absolutely right. Regardless, McCarthy resumed his patrol.

Ripp said to himself, "What now? He saw me. He knows me, and he knows I am here. Cancel or continue?" He continued to close the distance between himself and the RUMP. "I'll decide when I reach the RUMP. I have done nothing yet. If there is no harm there is no foul."

Ripp arrived at the RUMP and paid the eight dollars cover charge, which included one drink and all the popcorn you could eat. He ordered a Club Soda and passed on the popcorn. He found a seat in the back of the room and sat down by himself. Looking about the room, he saw no one paying attention to him. He could just as easily have been invisible, which is what he preferred.

The bartender was a big man. He looked like one of the Goombahs from the *Sopranos* that had taken up a job tending bar after getting bumped off in the second season of the show. He was feverishly making drinks when something caught his attention backstage and he set the piña colada he was working on in front of a large fat balding man seated at the bar who had what looked like a bed roll of skin hanging out between his too-short shirt and too-tight pants. Santonio, known to all but Darla as "Tony the bartender," shook the sticky residue from the fruity drink off his hands. He picked up a bar towel, and as he wiped his hands clean, he walked to the end of the crowded bar and picked up a microphone. He tapped it causing three loud thumps with his sausage-like fingers, and after a brief squeal of feedback, he loudly announced, "Here she is, folks. The dancing darling of La Claire," he then paused and with a cigarette scarred voice reminiscent of Harry Carey, "your darling and my darling, I am proud to announce The RUMPelstiltskin exclusively brings you Darla Darling. Show them what you have, Darla, darling."

A lone spot light switched on, lighting up the previously darkened stage. Darla stood silent in the light at center stage. She had a long black wig on tonight. She was dressed like a gypsy. It was not the kind which paint your driveway with water color, collect, and leave town before the next rain gypsy. She was like the real gypsies who traversed Europe in the 1800s performing their magic, playing their lively music, and then riding off to the next town in their colorful circus wagons. The music started and she moved like the professional dancer she was. It was Cher's voice which told the story with her song. Darla told the story with her dance, "I was born in the wagon of a traveling show. My mama had to dance for the money they'd throw. Papa would do whatever he could... preach a little gospel... sell a couple bottles of Doctor Good. Gypsies, tramps, and thieves we'd hear it from the people of the town they'd call us..."

"God, she's perfect," thought Ripp. His heart leapt. He could love her except for one fact. He could not love anyone but himself. She drew him out of the shadows from the back of the room, and he elbowed himself into the last remaining empty seat available in the chairs around the stage. It was a large crowd tonight. It was Friday. There were at least three bachelor parties with three well-dressed blow-up dolls, complete with gaping, gaudily lip-stick-painted mouths. There was one raucous group of bridesmaids with the bride-to-be wearing a necklace made of condoms and a dildo as the centerpiece of the necklace. The bride was noticeably pregnant, and she and her unborn prodigy had decided to get drunk one more time before she was to say, "I do," seven months after she had already said, "do I!"

Even though he had moved front and center, Ripp would go unnoticed tonight. He was just another face in the crowd. If anyone would have taken the time to look, even in the low lighting, they would have noticed something about the face. There was an ominous longing in it. There was a dangerous lust that would have sent Darla screaming from the stage if she wasn't such a consummate performer. By the time Darla had finished the set, she was naked except for the brightly colored red and blue gypsy scarves in her long black wig. Her body glistened with the sparkles she had lightly placed on her skin and the sweat she had worked up throwing herself into her performance. She received a standing ovation from those in the front row even though none of them had left their seats.

She gathered the money scattered copiously about the stage that the patrons had held out and finally dropped trying to draw her to them for a closer look or perhaps a touch. Tonight was her night to dance. Weekends she danced to the crowd. She felt every bit the entertainer. She had started years ago intending to dance her way through college but suddenly realized that nude dancing paid well. She had learned that there was money to be made if you could entertain and avoid the pitfalls. The pitfalls were drugs, alcohol, and prostitution. She had managed to avoid them all and even found a home in La Claire with fans. She would get one serious proposal of marriage a month from a love-sick fan. Darla turned them all down since they were all pathetic. They were even more pathetic than the fact that she could make more money stripping then she could dancing with a major ballet troupe.

Darla would not date any customers. She had made that mistake once and she wasn't inclined to make any mistake in her life twice. She was in love again. She had told no one, but she knew it. She was certain that the days of her gypsy life as an exotic dancer were numbered and her future would be made alongside Larry Kane. He fell for Becky Glitz and she loved him for that. He accepted that at least for a while she would continue to be Darla Darling. She loved him even more for that. She would have to sort out the "What next?" in her life. She had to make a living and she had to dance. These things she knew. If she gave up exotic dancing, "What next?"

Darla did not dance solely to make money. She danced to entertain. She danced because she was a dancer. She had to dance. It was in her blood. The set tonight was a new set that meant a great deal to her. She was half first generation Armenian Gypsy. Her family had moved to the United States after Gypsies were targeted by Hitler's holocaust machine. Dancing and entertainment were in her blood. The story could have been written about her great grandmother. She thought about all of these things as she picked up the gypsy costume she had so erotically removed while she spun to the music. She reached down and smiled as one of her scarves was handed to her by a smiling gentleman in the front row. "Thank you," she said.

"You're welcome," answered William Ripp as he let the silky fabric of the scarf slip lightly from his grasp..

Ripp had done his research. He had found out almost everything he needed to know about Darla. He wanted nothing left to chance here. He was at great risk in this city. Targeting Darla in La Claire was against all his rules. She was somewhat of a local icon to a small contingent of fans in La Claire. The police department here posed what he could see as a tremendous threat. McCarthy had even seen him tonight. If Ripp was to have used simple logic, he should cancel, totally and irrevocably, this attack on Darla.

There was no turning back. Her soft voice, her goddess-like nude form twirling in front of him on the stage drew him to her. He could not let this opportunity slip away like the colorful silk scarf. If he had a normal libido, folks would have said, "William, you are smitten." If he were a young teenage boy he would have dialed her number and nervously listened to the phone ring, waiting for a young Darla to answer so that he could ask her out on their first date. His heart was pounding and his palms were sweating. The difference was Darla would not be asked to go on their first date together. Darla would not be allowed to decline his offer. Ripp's urges were nothing like a normal libido. Ripp had to have her. Ripp had to have her tonight.

William Ripp stood up, headed for the door, and left the RUMP. He had one last detail to take care of.

He noticed that the same people who had watched him arrive were watching him leave: no one. The bouncer at the cash register by the door had not looked up when Ripp came in and now did not bother looking up as he was leaving. Ripp circled the block and cut into the alley behind the RUMP. He passed the rickety, long-left-unpainted wooden staircases leading to porches on second story apartments above the sports bar at the corner. A Chinese restaurant was next to the sports bar and the army surplus store next to that. Ripp wondered, "Who lives in dumps like these? The noise and the smells must be unbearable." The question was rhetorical as nearly all of Ripp's questions were.

Ripp looked up and down the alley and saw no one. He stepped into the small parking area to the rear of the RUMP. He checked each car and saw no one. He walked to the back wall of the RUMP, reached behind some shrubs, and found a two by four that he had hidden earlier. It was placed there for its length and innocuous nature. It looked like a rotted piece of railing for one of the staircases to those awful second story downtown apartments. It would serve his purpose well.

He looked about one more time and then walked over to the exterior light outside the RUMP near Darla's car. He swung quickly and cleanly, hitting the light which made a quick "Pop!" Even if someone would have looked out to see what had made the noise, after Ripp broke the light no one would be able to see him in the darkness that existed. As usual, darkness was Ripp's partner in crime.

After Darla's admiring crowd had cleared the RUMP, Darla chose her costumes for the Saturday night performances. She had her own dressing room separate from the rest of the girls. The owner, Tony Formosa "sausage fingers," had nailed a star to her door, and then the enamored strip club owner had painted her name above the star.

After carefully laying out the costumes she would wear at the beginning of each of Saturday's sets, she thumbed through her CDs which she had burned. New technology allowed her to personalize the music for each set. With the help of make-up, a few wigs, and costumes, she could transform herself into the performers that sang the music—except in most cases, Darla was much more beautiful than the performers and her dancing made her far more sensuous.

After she was satisfied that she was ready for her sets on Saturday and also sure that the bar crowd had diminished, she left the protection of her dressing room and saw Tony counting the receipts from the night. "A good night," said Tony, referring to the money that Darla's dancing had brought in.

"That's great!" Darla replied. "A good night to you also, Santonio," and Darla walked directly out the back door of the RUMP.

Tony feigned tipping a pretend hat and said, "A good night to you, too, Darla, darling." He loved it when she called him by his given name Santonio.

Darla passed out of the low light of the RUMP and into the darkness of the empty parking lot on the alley side of the RUMP. The light over the door was out, which was unusual. She stepped on the small fragments of the smashed light which had been obliterated by Ripp. She did not distinguish them from the rest of the trash strewn about in the darkness. Tony was usually meticulous about maintenance, especially about security lights. She thought about returning to the RUMP and telling him but shook it off. She could tell him tomorrow. Tonight she was tired and wanted to get home.

She walked to her car, fumbling with the keys, and suddenly there he was.

"Hello, Darla," he said in a soothing tone that came on so suddenly she dropped her keys. "Oh, I'm sorry. Did I frighten you?" asked Ripp.

"You certainly did," answered Darla. "What are you doing lurking in the shadows?" She was calmed by his appearance and soothed by his gentle voice. He looked like a professor she had before she quit her studies to dance full time.

"One person's lurking is another person's waiting patiently I guess. I just wanted to tell you how wonderful you were. I was surprised to see a real professional in a place ah, well, you know, I don't mean any offense…"

"You mean a place like the RUMP," said Darla soothed further by the fact that the professor had picked up her keys and handed them back to her. As he returned the keys she remembered him. "You returned my scarf to me."

"Yes, I did. You have a very good eye for faces," answered Ripp. "I hate to offend you, but I find you so beautiful. Can I ask… uh… do you do private dances?" asked Ripp.

"Yes I do but by appointment only. Call Tony at the RUMP and he will arrange it," said Darla.

"I am only in town tonight. I had hoped we could work something out for now?" He reached into his jacket and pulled out what appeared to be a great deal of cash.

"I can't tonight. Special dances are by appointment only. The appointments are made through Tony only. I have a contract with him, and I will not violate it." Now her instincts were telling her something was terribly wrong. The first "no" had changed something in his face. There was a foreboding look in his dark eyes. "I'll just go in and talk to him. He is inside the bar right now. Maybe we can work something out yet tonight." She turned to try to get back into the bar.

The professor tucked the money back into his pocket, and when his hand came out it held a short-barreled Smith and Wesson 357 magnum revolver. It was stainless steel and seemed to shine even in the dark. "Take another step and you'll never talk to anyone again." He snatched the keys from her hands and continued, "Get in the car and slide over to the passenger side." His voice was cold and practiced, as if, Darla realized, he had done this before.

She took a moment to look at the weapon. It was real. She could even see the jacketed hollow point bullets patiently waiting their turn in each filled cylinder. She slid behind the wheel and then slid again slowly, cautiously, over to the passenger side.

"Now bend over and keep your head down. If you turn your head either way and look at anything but your knees, I will blow it off. Do you understand?" asked the professor.

"Yes. Just don't hurt me. I will dance for you. I will do whatever you want. Just don't hurt me," said Darla slowly, pausing between each word as if she was speaking to a foreign language student through an interpreter.

"Good. Then everybody stays happy and healthy," said Ripp with his soothing tone returning.

William drove out Highway 41 past Gibbon Park to the wooded area off Dyerson Road. He drove up the old trail to the meadow and wood line which he had prepared for her passing. He parked next to a blanket carefully laid out on the ground under the stars. There was a bottle of wine inside a bucket filled with ice, set on the blanket.

He opened the door, paused, and shoved the revolver into Darla's neck below her ear and cautioned, "Don't move or, to put it quite simply, you're dead." The steel on her neck was almost as cold as his words.

Darla somehow knew she was dead no matter what she did. She had played this scenario out in her W.I.S.E. class with Master Kane. Master Kane had said, "If it ever happens you will have to decide 'should I fight or should I submit?' If you choose to fight then the next decision is to decide when to fight. Two certain times to fight are when death is imminent or when victory is assured." Kane had told the class. "Someone and probably several of you will face sexual assault. Some of you already have been assaulted. If you are faced with this type of assault or even an attack on your life, you will either fight or submit, and that is your decision. If you submit, pay attention to details and survive. If you decide to fight, do not waste your life. Watch carefully and wait for the opportunity to fight and win. When you strike, hit hard and hit to a vulnerable area. Think and decide. Control the fear and survive."

His words were not a thought right now; they were booming in her head. It was as if he were speaking to her in a loud speaker placed somewhere in the darkness of this meadow. She calmed herself and decided she was too far away from help to fight and he had the gun. She would not risk her life to avoid rape. She would submit. That was her decision.

The professor came around and opened her door. He held his hand out and said, "My lady," as if he were a coach man helping Marie Antoinette out of a coach in front of an opera house in eighteenth century Paris, before the revolution. She stepped out of the car and noticed the clearing was brightly lit by the full moon. "To put your mind at ease I will put this away." He showed her the pistol and slipped it into a shoulder holster under his coat. He wanted her to know he still had the gun.

"I will bed you here, pay you very well, and then you can walk home from here. It will give me time to get far away. No one gets hurt. Is it a deal?"

"A deal," she answered, "I will do what you ask; just please don't hurt me."

He then slowly unbuttoned her blouse, slipped it off her shoulders, and let it drop to the ground. He unsnapped her bra expertly and let it fall onto the blouse. Her large breasts dropped out of the bra. Her nipples were taught with fear but still beautifully brown and large, matching her tanned breasts perfectly. His breathing was heavy, and his movements sped up, mimicking his breathing, which turned quickly into panting and gasping without rhythm as if he was literally drowning in her beauty. He unsnapped her wrap-around skirt and roughly ripped off her panties. Disregarding the blanket on the ground, he bent her over the front of her car and roughly penetrated her from behind without preparation or permission.

As he thrust and grunted, she kept her mind working. She tried to remember everything about him. She looked for a path, a light, any possible opening, and all she could see were trees. He continued to grunt and thrust and now called out foul words in a voice from hell.

She kept scanning. She looked closer at the picnic blanket on the ground next to her and saw that it was not a blanket but a drop cloth. She snapped her head around and gazed into the tree line at a metallic glint and she saw it. "Oh God! A shovel," she thought. She saw it clearly reflecting the moon light. It was a brand new shovel. She was going to die here. She would be buried here. No one would think to look for her here. She refused the thought. She refused the idea that she would die here in the darkness, alone with this mad man. She made her decision, "I must act before he does. I must look for the opening."

"Ahhhrrrg," Ripp growled as he spilled his venom into Darla. He did not worry about DNA. He had dug the hole deep. He was confident that no one would ever find her. He thought in the midst of his ecstasy, "That was so pleasurable, I must share some wine with her and do her one more time before I kill her."

Darla knew now was the time. His pants were down to his ankles. He was experiencing sensory overload and he was momentarily relishing his victory. Now was the time. She heard the words of Sun Tzu spoken by Kane, "When you strike, strike like thunderbolts from the nine layered heavens!"

Darla spun. She was a dancer and her movement was the essence of speed. There is power in speed. As she spun to face him, his expression was lit up by the moon and still contained the look of ecstasy, which melted into shock at the quickness of her attack. She formed her right hand into a Y as she had been taught by Master Kane in her women's class and struck him a hard blow directly into his trachea, which was widely exposed after he had snapped his head back in the throes of passion. She struck him a crushing blow making his next breath a long time in coming.

He stood there, stunned, with his manhood still engorged and his testicles hanging small and helpless below. She did not waste any effort trying to kick them or knee them, for they were there for the taking and she had practiced the technique often in her W.I.S.E. class. It was her favorite, called "the lawn mower pull." She thought in her line of work it might some day come in handy. She was correct. Darla took hold of both of "the boys," and after she had established a firm, crushing grip, she pulled like she was pulling the cord on a stubborn-starting Lawn Boy.

"AAAIIIEEEEEEARRRGH," was the noise the wretched man made as he crumpled to the ground cradling his bleeding, wounded scrotum.

He was down, and she paused just long enough to grab her blouse and skirt lying on the ground next to the scene of her defilement as well as the scene of her ultimate victory over this depraved monster with human features. After she swept up her clothes, she ran like a bounding deer spotted by the hunter as she crossed into the protection of the tree line. After she entered the dark veil of the woods, she heard the shots fired. They made a snapping noise as they pursued and passed her. She did not count them, but there were at least four, maybe six. They did not stop her. If anything, it urged her on for she ran, and ran, and ran. Her body had been conditioned by years of dancing and physical training to keep her female form pleasing to the eyes. She was solid muscle coupled with an indomitable determination. To some, her life was not a perfect life, but to Darla it was her life and no one was going to take it and discard her body in an unmarked grave like so much garbage. She was a human being worthy of life. It was a life worth fighting for.

Soon all she could hear was her own breathing and the crunching of the leaves as her feet found their way blindly but deftly through the darkened woods. The thought of being enveloped by the darkness of the woods in the dead of night would have frightened her in the past, but now the darkened stand of trees was her friend, her protector, her shield.

Darla stopped for one moment. Quiet! No one was following her. She could not believe it. She was free. She kept moving. As she ran she began to laugh, so pleased by her own victory. She laughed at the look on his face. She laughed at the noise he made, and finally she laughed at the sheer joy of knowing she would live to continue her dance through life. Most of all, she laughed at the thought, "It really worked, wow! I wonder what that must have felt like. Fuck him! I should climb back up that hill and give it to him one more time... the lawn mower pull. Fuck him. I hope he's up there looking for his nuts, and I hope some squirrels hide them on the fuck and eat them over the winter." She was no longer laughing. Now she felt the rage building in her. "The dirty bastard! I should have grabbed his gun." Her anger spurred her on. She was not home free yet. "You have to love it, though. I am going to have to kiss Larry Kane and tell him I owe my life to *the lawn mower pull!*"

CHAPTER THIRTY-ONE

A PROFESSOR

Maddy Brown swung through the lot of the Kwik Trip on Highway 41. The after-bar-time traffic had slipped its way home, and now all that was left maneuvering about the streets of La Claire were paper persons delivering their papers and bread men delivering their wares from store to store. Granted, there were a few bar flies who had found their 30 minutes of love after the bars closed and had quickly dressed and just as quickly escaped, chancing that the person lying warm, wet, and snoring contentedly next to them was not their life's soul-mate.

Maddy drove through the lot and then caught a movement among the trees across the highway. Then a figure appeared staggering out of the brush waving frantically to Maddy. Maddy spun out of the lot and crossed the highway, pulling as close to the exhausted woman as possible. The woman was in her late twenties or early thirties. She was wearing a blouse that was on inside out and only partially buttoned. Her wrap-around skirt was as covered with brambles and sand burs as her blouse, as if she had rolled through a patch of them deliberately. Her arms and legs were heavily scarred with a thousand scratches. She had been running in the bushes for some time. Only fear would drive a person into the woods at a run at night. "I was kidnapped and I've been raped. A man tried to kill me. I hurt him and got away." Maddy eased her into the squad car like a grocery bag filled with cartons of eggs.

"257," radioed Maddy.

"Go ahead," said dispatch.

"I have a female. She has been assaulted. I will be out with her on Highway 41 across from the Kwik Trip."

"What did the man look like?" asked Maddy.

"He was 6'1" with sandy hair, slim build, wearing a black jacket with a gray lining, black pants, black mock turtle neck, and he was armed with a shiny revolver he pulled from a shoulder holster. He was in his early forties. He had wire-rimmed glasses, and he looked like a professor," rapped Darla. She had been practicing the description in her mind as she worked her way through the woods. Darla had stayed in the tree line when she reached Highway 41 in the event that the mad man had followed her. She then paralleled 41, staying in the darkness of the tree line.

"Where did you last see him?" asked Maddy Brown.

"Take a left on Dyerson Road and go about one mile up, maybe less, you can see an old path leading up a hill to the right. It's not a road but a path. He took my car up to a clearing at the top. He had a gun. He raped me and tried to shoot me. There is a grave dug up there. He was going to kill me!" gasped Darla, who then began to sob uncontrollably. The image of her body rolled by the horrible man into that dark hole suddenly played like a movie in her mind and emotions swept over her like a Tsunami. "My God, I could be in that hole right now and forever!"

Maddy laid her hand gently on Darla's shoulder and assured her. "You're safe now." Her demeanor shifted from concern to determination as she picked up the mic and transmitted the information, which she hoped would drop the net on the animal that did this. "To dispatch and to all units, I am looking for a suspect in a kidnapping, rape, and attempted murder who was last seen near Dyerson Road. He is armed with a stainless steel revolver concealed in a shoulder holster. The suspect is a white male, 6'1" slim build with sandy hair in his early forties wearing dark clothes and wire-rimmed glasses. The victim says he looks like *a professor.*"

CHAPTER THIRTY-TWO

IN THE CLEAR

It was a full moon. In Wisconsin such a large round orange moon would be called a Harvest Moon. It was a bright orange ball that hung in the heavens, which made it appear as if the moon packed up and decided to move in next door to the Earth. Ripp lay in pain, cursing at the moon for what seemed like a lifetime. Time passes slowly when you are bathing in a pool of agony. The only good thing about the burning in his testicles was that he forgot about his inability to breathe. He had not even noticed through all the pain that he could breathe again.

As his faculties returned, he realized he needed to move and move fast. He had fired wildly and vainly into the darkness after her, but he was almost certain he did not hit her. He slowly pushed himself to his knees and crawled over to Darla's car. He pulled himself into a squat standing position and began to feel his way around the car. In his current wretched condition, racked, bent with his face twisted in agony, he could easily play the Hunchback of Notre Dame without a bit of make-up. The only difference between the two was that the hunchback's balls were operational. Ripp was not even sure if he still had possession of them. The area was too painful to examine by touch.

Ripp made it to the driver's door and fumbled with the latch as he opened the door. He slid cautiously onto the seat as if he thought it might be on fire. It may as well have been for the pain was nearly unbearable. He discovered being seated with his pants buttoned caused an incredibly tight constriction on his emasculated member, which he could feel swelling to a gargantuan size.

Ripp un-buttoned his pants and then unzipped them to relieve the pressure, but there was little relief. He shouted to the full moon "Bitch! You Fucking Bitch. I'll kill you if it's the last thing I do!" Ripp started the car, turned it around in the clearing, and then headed quickly toward the trail but immediately slowed his speed considerably. The unevenness of the terrain coupled by his impatience-inspired speed was dealing him a fair measure of "discomfort." He thought the pain could not be worse than it was, but when he hit a bump he realized that the pain could be considerably worse. He felt each bump and each divot in the depths of his groin.

When Ripp reached Dyerson Road, he stopped on the shoulder and cut the engine. He waited for Darla to come out of the woods. He had underestimated the strength and capacity of this dancer. She had passed this point long ago. He had lain helpless too long.

Ripp sat for about three minutes which seemed like an hour and then started the car and turned the lights on. He had lost his virtue of patience. He found it hard to sit patiently with his balls on fire. "I have to get out of this town now!" he said to himself after a sudden epiphany.

Ripp gunned the engine and spun the tires in the grass on the shoulder and the tires squealed as they continued to spin when they hit the pavement. Ripp headed back to his hotel. Ripp drove to the Radisson Hotel in Darla's car and then bypassed the driveway. "Got to ditch the car." He drove around the area and found a boat landing on the Mississippi just two blocks from his hotel. He left the keys in the ignition and wiped down the steering wheel of Darla's car haphazardly. He was in too much pain to be thorough.

He began his long walk to the hotel and noticed as he walked the pain was subsiding. He no longer walked like Quasimodo, but he still had a noticeable limp. "If I can make it back to my hotel and get out of this town, I'll be OK. There is nothing tying me to Darla." He was deceiving himself, but it was a pleasant deception.

Ripp limped his way back to the hotel. He paused at his car and thought, "No, I have to empty my room. It will look suspicious if I run off and leave my things. I need to get my things and just leave. No one will suspect me. If I can just get out of this fucking town, I'm *in the clear.*"

CHAPTER THIRTY-THREE

THE RECORD

Bar time had slipped by without much happening. It was shaping up to be a quiet night. "Maybe for once Compton's itchy finger was wrong," concluded Dan McCarthy. McCarthy had come to a point in his career where he liked the action but relished an occasional quiet night. He drove about his beat but decided to park the squad. He got out walking the alleys of the downtown. He loved the smells floating in the night air in the downtown bar area of La Claire. It was a smorgasbord of aromas that floated on the air. There was the stale beer, popcorn, and nachos, as well as the blended scents from the deep fryer grease that had cooked up every thing that could be batter fried from albacore to zucchini.

As McCarthy blipped the light at the lock plate of the back door on each business, he checked for fresh pry marks. They all had been worked on at one time or another, but he was looking for something new and exciting. He knew the doors, he knew their marks, and he knew the stories behind the marks. Some of the burglars he had caught, and some his shift partners had caught, and some slinked into the darkness with their loot.

McCarthy loved the night stalking of burglars. They were ever his arch enemy and a crafty prey, but the shift he worked with made the career of a burglar in La Claire short-lived and risky. Compton would say at lineup, "Burglar is working the flats. Go get-em ladies and gents. That was all Compton had to say and the shift would hit their beats like a bunch of bloodhounds on a trail. They would arrest them at alarm calls for certain, but Compton's shift would say, "Alarms? We don't need no stinking alarms."

McCarthy's silent stalking ended with an echoing "Ka-Wang!" Dan instinctively stepped farther into a shadow within the shadows and worked his way around to the corner of the building and came out low doing a quick peek. Then he smiled. He stood up and walked over to the dumpster at the rear of the Roundhouse restaurant. He sidled up to the little old lady standing on her tip toes fishing her cane about in the dumpster. "Anything good in there tonight, Annie?" asked McCarthy.

"There is something good in here every night, McCarthy. There are very few with the courage to reach in and grab it though. Just me! You know that. I can't believe what they throw away." Annie was five-foot-nothing and had white hair that still had its little girl natural curl that bushed out from under the scarf she had tied tightly under her chin. She wore wool gloves with the fingers cut off and sweaters. One brown pull-over and a second brown button-up left unbuttoned. She had a cane but did not need it for walking. She only used it for hooking "the good stuff" from the bottom of the dumpster.

Annie carted herself around town on a 50's vintage Schwinn girl's bicycle. It had three baskets on it. There was one on the back for cans, a second basket on the back carried food stuffs, such as outdated buns, lettuce, donuts, and wrapped hamburgers tossed out at the Burger King. The third basket in the front was for knick knacks that you might find at a rummage sale or flea market. "I see you have everything separated, Annie," said McCarthy with a legitimate interest.

"It's my filing system. That's what I used to do, create filing systems," Annie answered, turning toward McCarthy seemingly happy to take a break from her work. "I worked for forty years at the university finding new ways to retrieve old stuff. You can hardly throw out anything, you know; someone is always going to need it again some day," she added in a serious tone. "Look what we throw out here," she continued as she pulled out a head of lettuce, carefully brushing it off, then blowing on it, and tearing a few outer layers off it. "We could feed the whole city of Mumbai with what we throw away here each year."

When she retired, Annie discovered she had little to do so she decided it would be fun to "live off the land." She explained it made the life she had left "an adventure."

"McCarthy, check out my new filing system on my bike," she said as she tossed the lettuce head into a basket marked "re-chewsables." She told McCarthy, "My filing system is simple but essential. This basket is for re-chewsables," she said pointing at the basket on the bike. "This basket is for re-usables." Annie then said pointing at the front basket that carried a variety of what could only be described as knick-knacks and paddy-whacks. Then pointing at the basket containing the cans she offered, "This basket is for the re-newsables. Yes sir, McCarthy, that's my filing system. I have a basket each: for the chewsables, usables, and re-newsables. Now ain't that just fun!" she said with a smile that lit up the darkness, complete with a gold front tooth.

"Have a good night, Annie," smiled McCarthy as he continued on his quest for his next burglary arrest.

"Always do, McCarthy. You stay safe, my young friend," said Annie dipping her cane once again into the dumpster. The smile disappeared as the intense hunt for another chewsable continued. The Roundhouse after a Friday night was a treasure trove of chewsables. There was more there than she could ever use. She would have to be very selective.

McCarthy continued down the alley and circled the block pulling on the front doors thinking, "I bet that little old lady has a million bucks stashed under her mattress and she is digging in dumpsters. She looks like that Disney character, the lady singing on the church steps in the movie Mary Poppins, only skinny." The radio snapped McCarthy out his reverie. He heard Maddy Brown say something about a rape and needing an ambulance for someone at the Kwik Trip on Highway 41.

He jogged over to his squad and got in and started it.

Then Maddy continued, calm and clear like Maddy always was, "To dispatch and to all units, I am looking for a suspect in a kidnapping, rape, and attempted murder who was last seen near Dyerson Road. He is armed with a stainless steel revolver. The suspect is a white male, 6'1" slim build with sandy hair in his early forties wearing dark clothes and wire-rimmed glasses. The victim says he looks like a professor."

"Damn!" said McCarthy out loud to the cosmos. He then turned on his video camera as he keyed his mic, "255 to dispatch."

"255 go ahead," responded the dispatcher.

"Be advised I will be swinging by the Radisson Hotel to check for a subject I saw earlier tonight. I will send you his information via computer. He matched that description of the suspect," said McCarthy. He hung the mic back on the hook and paged his notebook open to the name, address, and date of birth of Ripp. He typed all of the information and then hit send as he swerved to miss a parked car. "Oops, sorry," he said for the benefit of anyone who might watch the tape later.

As McCarthy approached the parking lot of the Radisson, he slowed quietly to a crawl and cut the lights on the squad. He pulled to the curb in response to something that would have engendered that response even if he was not looking for a rape suspect. It was 4:00 AM and there was a dark figure limping through the parking lot.

McCarthy sat motionless, holding his breath. The figure was not going toward the hotel, but instead, he was heading for the parking area. The figure was not coming from the hotel either. It looked as if he had come in from the street. His right arm came up and the lights of a Chevy blinked twice. It was the same car Ripp had been to earlier. The dark limping man passed under a security light and McCarthy's heart rate increased instantly by 20 beats per minute. He took a deep breath in through his nose and breathed out slowly to calm himself down and reached for the mic.

He keyed the mic unconsciously and said in a near whisper, "I have William Ripp in the parking lot of the Radisson. He fits the description of the suspect down to the dark clothes. I would like to request a back-up to be sent to this location. I am going to be making contact. He is heading toward a vehicle and I want to contact him before he goes mobile." McCarthy then attempted to hang up the mic but missed the hook and it dropped to the floor. Instinctively, he pulled the mic back up by its coiled cord and hung the mic up more carefully.

As McCarthy pulled into the lot without the lights of the squad car, Ripp had reached the trunk which he had popped open with the remote. He pulled out the briefcase that he had placed there earlier. The last pre-McCarthy thought he had was, "Time to get rid of my souvenirs." Then he heard the sound of tires crossing from cement to blacktop and he turned toward the entrance.

The lights were out on the black and white car as it sleeked across the parking lot directly at him. If someone was watching the scene of the black and white closing ground, silently and unlit toward its prey, one could understand how they were once called "prowl cars" in a time long ago.

Ripp stood still for a moment, motionless. The prey had frozen in hopes that he would attain invisibility to the predator through lack of motion. This instinctive response of desperation rarely worked and did not work tonight.

McCarthy stopped the squad car, hit his lights, and swung the door open, but before he could exit the squad, Ripp was on a dead run. McCarthy had worked a miracle. He healed Ripp's bleeding and badly bruised scrotum. There was not a hint of a limp, other than the slightly off balance gait caused by the briefcase tucked under Ripp's arm like a big black square football.

McCarthy keyed his collar mic, "255, he's running. I am in foot pursuit westbound toward the river." McCarthy followed maintaining a speed to stay with the suspect rather than trying to catch him immediately. The suspect in the rape was reportedly armed. Ripp also had too much of a lead and McCarthy knew the area. The side of the Radisson he was heading toward had a wooden privacy fence. Ripp was heading for that fence. McCarthy thought, "He'll stop or I'll catch him going over the fence."

When the suspect went around the corner of the Radisson, he somehow picked up speed, and McCarthy, who tried to anticipate all possibilities, did not foresee what happened next. William Ripp put his arms up like an offensive guard leading interference for a running back and he hit the fence at a dead run. "Crack!" and the boards opened for him. Now he was through and still running.

McCarthy gained some ground on Ripp because all he had to do was navigate his way through the hole. "God that had to hurt," thought McCarthy. Then McCarthy realized he had not yet said anything. He shouted, "William Ripp! Police! Stop you are under arrest!" There was no reaction from Ripp other than to keep running. McCarthy thought, "Hell, if I don't have him on the rape, I sure have a good criminal damage to property on him for smashing that fence. The way he is running, though, this has got to be our boy."

McCarthy followed Ripp as he leaped a hedge on the river side of the hotel. McCarthy jumped the hedge, landing a little off balance, but his stride was still intact. McCarthy continued to run and keyed his shoulder mic, "We are still puff, puff, westbound heading toward the river. We are in front of the hotel on Mississippi Street, puff, puff. He is cutting through Riverside Park heading directly to the river."

Out of the corner of his eye, McCarthy saw Annie peddling for all she was worth. She was riding parallel with the foot pursuit just south of Ripp. Annie had a look of determination on her face as if she was digging in a dumpster at the Roundhouse reaching for the heel of a still cooling prime rib. She was peddling like she was vying for the lead on the first leg of the Tour de France.

Ripp was on the grass at Riverside Park, running with a stride like an Olympic miler heading for the finish line who had a Jamaican right behind him also going for the gold. McCarthy was maintaining his distance, but he was feeling the twenty pounds of cop stuff starting to wear on him. Ripp was inspired and that was making McCarthy tired. "255 he's in the park heading right for the river puff, puff, puff. Have the first responding officer, cut him off to the north and the second cut him off to the south puff, puff."

McCarthy hit the grass and was maintaining a distance of about 75 feet. Ripp was finally starting to slow down now as he adjusted the grip he had on his briefcase. He now was holding it down at his right side as if he was a business man running to catch a bus that was pulling away from the curb. It threw Ripp off his stride, and McCarthy started to make up ground. Once he realized he was making up ground, McCarthy picked up his pace to try to close on Ripp. Dan had acquired his second wind.

Ripp reached the sidewalk that ran along the river and turned and began to run northbound, with the river to his left. He swung the briefcase wide like it was a poorly designed discus with a handle and flung it toward the river. The briefcase cleared the distance between the sidewalk and the downward slope of the shoreline, which was covered with riprap, and the case hit the water with a splash. "Damn," said McCarthy. He then keyed the mic, "Ripp just threw a briefcase into the river. Have someone try to recover it before it sinks."

"255, your backup is still about two minutes out. Everyone was out on 41 looking for the suspect there. They are heading your way," answered Melissa, in her usual calm but "I wish I could be there to help" tone of voice.

McCarthy was gaining ground fast. Ripp was noticeably panting hard and his limp had returned. As McCarthy nearly reached him, Ripp spun and delivered a punch toward the head of McCarthy, but McCarthy was ready for it. McCarthy had spent his whole adult life making ready for this punch. He had practiced defending against this punch thousands of times. As the punch came around, Dan caught the punch with a hook block and harmlessly slipped it down and away from his body and instinctively countered with an inverted knife hand strike smashing the interior ridge of his right hand into Ripp's temple. The blow struck like a thunder clap, and Ripp saw a flash of light as if paparazzi had just taken a shot for The National Enquirer. Ripp went down hard and instantaneously. There would be no drawn-out battle between good and evil. Evil was going down after a one-punch fight.

As Ripp began his descent, McCarthy turned the hook block of Ripp's right hand into a wrist lock and laid Ripp out onto his back. As Ripp hit the ground, McCarthy held the wrist lock and placed his right hand into the interior biceps of Ripp, and Mc-Carthy merely walked quickly around Ripp's head causing him to flop over like a freshly caught crappie to his stomach. Dan immediately put Ripp into an especially painful rear compliance hold and added a heartfelt "don't you ever try to hit me again" pressure on the wrist. This caused Ripp to stop all movement except to arch his back in pain. "Give me your hand, puff puff, and stop resisting, puff puff, you are under arrest!" barked McCarthy.

Ripp could not resist any further. He had never really been in a fight until tonight. None of his victims prior to Darla had fought back. Each one of his victims had been fooled, ambushed, and blindsided with no opportunity to fight back. He had always, before tonight, been the predator, but tonight he was the prey. He did not like this at all. "This is not fun!" William Ripp blurted out.

McCarthy, puzzled by the comment, ordered, "Give me your other hand. Do it now!"

Tonight Ripp had already been thumped mercilessly by a stripper. He reasoned that if he could not beat the strippers in this town he was sure not going to beat a cop who had somehow found another part of Ripp's body to place into pain. He slapped his left hand up to join the right, and McCarthy slipped out his handcuffs and clicked them into place. "Fuck! I should have never come to this fucking town," whined Ripp, "I knew it. This place is a fucking black hole!"

McCarthy then keyed his mic and reported, "Puff, puff, the suspect is 10-95 (in custody)."

"10-4," replied the Melissa. Just two numbers, but McCarthy could tell by the tone that the dispatcher had been with him during the pursuit and was just as happy about the apprehension as he. He always wondered what it must be like to have to sit and listen to it all happening "out there" and not being able to help. He often wondered if they realized how much help they were. McCarthy literally could not, no, would not do what he did with out them… his life-line.

McCarthy keyed the mic one more time, "Thanks, dispatch."

"10-4," said Melissa in dispatch.

"Are you hurt?" asked McCarthy.

"I hurt all over," said Ripp.

"Do you need a doctor?" asked McCarthy.

"Fuck no," answered Ripp. "What am I under arrest for?"

"You are under arrest for criminal damage to property, resisting arrest, attempt to batter a police officer, kidnapping, and first degree sexual assault," answered McCarthy.

Then Ripp indignantly but inaudibly complained into the pavement, "I'm not a rapist. I'm a killer."

As Dan did a cursory search while Ripp lay on the ground, he immediately found the shoulder holster rig carrying the revolver, "Gun!" he shouted to no one in particular as he pulled the firearm out of its holster and slid it into his own side pocket.

As McCarthy conducted the search, Carpenter came running up, picking up his pace after hearing McCarthy's shout. "You OK?" asked Gary.

"Yeah, can you watch him, Carp? Leave him right here on the ground. I have to look for a briefcase he tossed into the river. I've searched him once and found a gun in a shoulder rig. Search him again to be sure," said McCarthy tapping the pocket weighted down with Ripp's revolver.

"Don't mind if I do, Dyno," answered Carpenter.

"Dyno? I thought his name was Dan McCarthy," asked Ripp as Carpenter conducted another thorough search of the suspect lying prone on the sidewalk.

"McCarthy is his name. We call him Dyno. I'm guessing you know why," said Gary laughing.

"It figures I would try to outrun a fucking Dyno. I think I met his wife earlier tonight or maybe his sister," said Ripp.

"When was that, Slim?" asked Carpenter.

Ripp just shook his head and became silent.

Gary Carpenter slipped his pocket notebook out along with a pen and wrote the quote down word for word. He wrote, "It figures I would try to outrun a fucking Dyno. I think I met his wife earlier tonight or maybe his sister."

Carpenter thought, "I do not know what it means, but that is what they call an 'excited utterance' that I believe is one for the report. It sounds significant."

McCarthy ran down along the sidewalk toward the spot where Ripp had tossed the briefcase. He had no trouble finding the location because parked there where Ripp had let loose of the case was Annie's bike leaning on its kickstand. McCarthy noticed it had been a good night for Annie. Her three baskets: re-usables, re-newsable and re-chewsable were full and were trying mightily to bring the bike down, but the customized, reinforced kickstand somehow held.

Down at the river's edge, Annie was fishing into the dark water with her cane. She had both of her feet on one large rock on the shore's edge. She was out over the water propping her body up with her left hand balancing on one large rock that was in river proper but partially protruding out of the water. With her right hand she was reaching out into the black water with her cane fishing about in the darkness. "Got it!" she cried joyfully as McCarthy managed to slip and slide over the rocks and down the embankment to the shoreline.

As Dan reached her he saw that she had hooked the briefcase with her cane, but now she was at an impasse. She had so extended herself out over the river that she could barely hold herself up, much less return to the shore without first falling into the cold black muddy murkiness that was the Mississippi River.

Dan reached her and took her around the waist and said, "I've got you."

"And I've got the case," said Annie securing the cane with two hands when Dan picked her up. "What is it, McCarthy? Drugs? Money?" asked Annie, as she handed the case to McCarthy.

"I don't know, Annie, but he was sure hot to get rid of it. Thanks a lot," said Dan.

"Glad to be of help. Like I always say, life is an adventure as long as you get out and live it," said Annie smiling and showing her gold tooth.

McCarthy truly relished the little old lady's smile. Whenever he ran into her as their work cleaning up the city of La Claire brought them together, he would try to make her smile just to see the little old rag lady's gold tooth. Sometimes he would elicit a toothy grin, but other times she would be so into her hunt for the treasures buried in the dumpster at hand that he could not illicit even a small smile. McCarthy could not help but smile himself as he looked at Annie's beaming grin containing the glistening chip of bullion lighting up the age-worn face and thought, "That's the second time in one night I've seen Raggedy Annie's gold tooth. This is a night to remember. By God, that's *the record.*"

CHAPTER THIRTY-FOUR
FUCKIN' A BINGO!

As Officer Maddy Brown drove toward the hospital, Darla heard the transmissions of McCarthy. "Is McCarthy chasing the guy that did this to me?" she asked.

"I do not know. He is after someone. That's all I know for sure. We may have you take a look at someone on the way in, but there are no guarantees that anyone we show you will be the man. You will have to tell us that. Are you sure you can identify him if you see him again?" asked Maddy.

"You can stick him in a crowd of 1000 and I will pick that monster out," said Darla confidently.

Maddy continued to listen to the pursuit while driving toward the hospital. Then she heard the magic words come over the radio when McCarthy panted into the mic that he was "10-95."

Darla asked, "What does that mean, 10-95?"

"That means the man he was chasing is in custody," answered Maddy.

"They have him. I want to see him. I can identify that bastard!" Darla insisted.

Maddy assured her, "There will be time for that." Maddy continued on her way toward the hospital. The direct route to the hospital took them by the Radisson. Maddy radioed, "255, is the party available for a show-up?"

"10-4. He's in my squad by the park," said Carpenter, who was going to transport Ripp for McCarthy.

Maddy drove toward Riverside Park. She turned to Darla and informed her, "Darla, we are going to drive by a squad car. Take a look at the man in the squad. We do not know whether he is the man that did this to you or not. We just want you to take a look."

"OK. By the way, my real name is not Darla. Darla is just my stage name," said the dancer.

"What is your real name?" asked Maddy.

"My name is Rebecca. Becky is what I was called. Rebecca Glitz," said Darla. "Not such a good name for an exotic dancer."

"Becky is a nice name. I had planned on naming my daughter that if I am ever so lucky to have one," said Maddy.

As Maddy approached the squad that contained Ripp, Carpenter turned on the interior lights of his patrol car. Maddy drove slowly by. They saw the sandy-haired man with the glasses perched on his nose, dressed in black. Darla jumped out of her seat and exploded in excitement, "That's him. That's that man who raped me! He shot at me. He was going to kill me." She then began yelling at Ripp, "I hope I ripped your nuts off!" as Maddy's squad was pulling away from the now hapless man in black. "Check his nuts. If they are still there I am sure there is a mark; what I did had to have left a mark," she added to Madison Brown.

As the squad passed, Maddy keyed the mic, "That's him, Carp."

Carpenter, who was standing outside the squad and had noticed the animated movements of the victim, answered, "I see that. It looks as if the identification was pretty certain."

"10-4," said Maddy, keying the mic as Darla yelled one more time even more enthusiastically for all those citizens still awake in scanner-land, "I hope I ripped your nuts off!"

Carpenter had turned the radio of his squad off for the duration of the identification so that Ripp could not hear the transmissions about the show-up so he was not privy to Darla's sentiments. Almost instinctively, his testicles began burning once again. He adjusted his legs and squirmed in his seat.

Carpenter noticed the movements and seconded Darla's emotion, "That would be so cool if she ripped your nuts off, dude," Carpenter said quietly to himself.

"I want to talk to McCarthy!" shouted Ripp. "Let's get this over with, God damn it. I want to talk to McCarthy!"

Gary Carpenter slipped back into his squad car and turned the radio on. "You do not need to see a doctor?" asked Carpenter.

"Fuck no. I want to talk to McCarthy," Ripp said with determination in his voice.

"You don't have to ask me twice, Slim," said Gary, even though he had asked three times already.

"Why do you call me Slim?" asked Ripp.

"I was just trying to be friendly. I don't know your name yet. I can call you sir if you like, or whatever you prefer," explained Carpenter.

"No. You can call me Slim. My name is William, but you can call me Slim. Hey. It's my first nickname," said Ripp with a smile. "That will make this a night to remember." Then the smile left his face and his face took on a look of brooding death.

"You got it! It's Slim then," Carpenter said with a wary smile, noticing the sudden change of mood of their captive.

At the station, Ripp was seated in an interview room with a white floor, white walls, a white table, and two black chairs. There was a mirror in the room behind which a camera was taping the interview.

When he arrived at the station, McCarthy obtained the key to a temporary evidence locker and secured the briefcase. He sensed it was important, but he did not open it immediately. He did not need a warrant because it was abandoned property the minute Ripp threw it. The problem was that the case had a combination lock and they would have to call someone in to open it. McCarthy did not want to spend any time with that since Ripp was asking to talk to him and not an attorney. He wanted to get a statement while the getting was good.

McCarthy entered the room and said, "Mr. Ripp, we are here tonight because you are under arrest for first degree sexual assault, while armed, attempted first degree murder, false imprisonment, criminal damage to property, attempt to batter a police officer, resisting arrest, and carrying a concealed weapon. I would like to read you your rights."

McCarthy then read the Miranda Warnings to William Ripp, and he instantly waived them. "I'll talk to you. I want to straighten this out."

Ripp signed the waiver and impatiently said, "Let's cut through all this legal bullshit and straighten this whole mess out."

"Go ahead, Mr. Ripp. I'm listening," answered McCarthy taking the signed waiver and slipping it inside his metal "easy writer" that held his notebook and important papers.

"I..." then there was a long pause that McCarthy was almost tempted to interrupt. He had learned from the best interviewer he knew, Sergeant Randy Stammos, that the suspect has a need to fill the silence. If you want him to talk give him lots of silence. He will talk. McCarthy said nothing. "...am not a rapist," declared Ripp. Then there was a long silent void.

Instead of answering, arguing, or pleading for an admission, McCarthy sat emotionless, looking at Ripp, waiting for the truth, a lie, anything, but he just waited. He sensed more was coming.

"I..." there was another long, tensioned-filled pause. McCarthy could see the sweat forming on Ripp's forehead and the tension in his face as if he was holding some terrible weight in that was pushing, pushing to get out.

"...am a killer. I've killed many people. They are buried all over the United States. I kill. I would've killed that bitch tonight, but she damned near tore my nuts off. Inside the briefcase you have everything anyway. You'll find out. You have my souvenirs. It's all there. I killed more than twenty, less than thirty. You have it all." It came out so matter-of-factly it was as if he was admitting tasting grapes in the produce section of a grocery store before purchasing any. "I would've tried to kill you with my gun except I didn't reload after I emptied it at that bitch."

McCarthy, who had been sitting up straight somehow sat up even straighter. "Damn Madison Brown. You're a genius. He is a serial killer," thought McCarthy.

"If you open the briefcase, I can explain it all to you. The combination to open the briefcase is 5455. 5455 is the code for kill on the phone. Catchy, don't you think?" said Ripp clicking his tongue and winking. "Open the briefcase and I'll talk to you more. It'll be much easier." Then Ripp sat back in his chair, crossed his arms and legs, and clammed up.

McCarthy stood up and tried to stay nonchalant and as he locked the door behind him. He shook the door to make sure it was secured, and, dumbfounded, he looked at Carpenter and said, "He says he's a serial killer."

"As my Granny says at St. Luke's Church every Thursday Night, *'Fuckin' A Bingo!'*"

CHAPTER THIRTY-FIVE

LOST IN BECKY'S EYES

Darla lay quietly on the gurney in the emergency room pulling the shapeless gown tight to her body trying to find some warmth in this white-bright but cold environment. She was freezing and shivering uncontrollably. Officer Maddy Brown had just finished a more in depth interview, and Darla was now waiting for the arrival of a "SANE" Nurse. This was a Sexual Assault Nurse Examiner who would gather the crucial evidence to link William Ripp inarguably and indefensibly to this terribly personal crime.

Josie, the night shift emergency room fixture, popped into the room and reported, "Rebecca, there is someone here who is wondering if they could see you. It is a La Claire County Sheriff's Deputy."

"Larry Kane?" asked Darla hopefully.

"Yes. He said he didn't want to disturb you but was wondering if you would like to see a good friend right now?" said Josie.

"Absolutely. Please send him in," said Darla, sitting up and straightening her hair.

As Kane entered, he did so leaning his head into the room first with a look of concern.

"Come on in," said Darla motioning with her hand. "How did you know?"

Kane entered the room and answered, "I was covering a beat for the county tonight and I heard about the… assault. I started listening to the city channel pretty intensely because I was looking for the guy and listening to updates. Then when Maddy Brown said the victim had identified the suspect I heard the voice of a warrior, my lovely warrior, come over the radio and I started heading in this direction."

"I heard your voice tonight too," said Darla motioning Kane to come closer.

"On the radio?" asked Kane.

"No. When I was… when he was… when it counted, your voice was telling me what to do. You saved my life," Darla said holding her arms out like a lost child who had just been found.

Kane came to her and they embraced. "You're shivering," said Kane.

"I can't get warm. I'm so cold."

Kane looked around the room and opened a cabinet and took out two white folded blankets. He brought them to Darla and put his hands on her shoulders and lowered her back down on the gurney. He unfolded one blanket and spread it over her, carefully tucking in the sides and then unfolded the second with a snap and laid it over Darla. This time he carefully tucked in the blanket below her chin, leaned down and lightly kissed her cheek. "Now rest. Heal."

"Don't leave me," begged Darla.

He took her hand and held it to his heart as he gently brushed her forehead and said. "I will stay with you as long as you want me, Becky. That's what people do when they are hopefully in love with someone."

She smiled and asked, "Don't you mean hopelessly in love?"

"Now that I have found you I will never be hopeless again," said Kane, *lost in Becky's eyes.*

CHAPTER THIRTY-SIX

SLAM DUNK

Compton was finishing his conversation with Maddy Brown as McCarthy walked into the command room, "Thanks, Maddy, McCarthy is here." Hanging up, he turned to McCarthy and asked "What do you have, Dyno? Did he lawyer up?"

"No, quite the opposite, Sergeant Compton," said McCarthy. "This guy, William Ripp, clearly kidnapped and raped Darla Darling, but he says he's not a rapist. Apparently it's a case of semantics. He does not want to go to prison as a rapist. He says he is a serial killer. He claims he has killed more than twenty and less than thirty, and they are buried all over the United States. He offers to tell us all after we open the briefcase. He explained it will be easier to make a statement when he has the souvenirs that are in the case. He gave me the combination to the briefcase."

"Ripp says he doesn't want to be known as a rapist so he is copping to a couple dozen homicides. That's the worst case of plea bargaining I have ever heard of, but I think we should accept the deal," said Compton looking a little bit startled. "I have some detectives coming in. Stammos will be coming in to help with the statement. I called them in as soon as Maddy radioed in what she had. Randy should be here any time now."

As if that was his cue, Sergeant Randy Stammos entered the room and said, "I was all warm and toasty dreaming I had hooked "Old Buck," that trophy Musky I have been after my whole life. I have never in my life hooked one that big, not even in my dreams. I had just gotten it next to the boat and was watching it thrash about and realized it was too big for my net and almost too big for my boat and you know what happened, Dyno?" asked Stammos.

"The phone rang?" guessed McCarthy.

"No, phones don't ring anymore. The phone played 'My Baby's Got Back,' and poof just like that "Old Buck," my trophy Musky, got away in my dreams. That is not a good omen," complained Randy Stammos. Randy Stammos was the cop who taught Dan McCarthy how to be a cop. He had been his main Field Training Officer and the two had become like brothers on the street and off.

Stammos had been promoted to sergeant and after a brief stint on night shift as a sergeant, he was assigned to the Detective Bureau as a Detective Sergeant. His talents were recognized and put to use. He was considered one of the best interviewers on the department. He was as good as they get, a master. McCarthy was thrilled to see that he would be handling the case. "Randy, that dream might have been an omen all right, but the Musky might just be a metaphor for the biggest case of our lives."

"No shit. What do you have?" asked Stammos

"This guy, William Ripp is his name. He has admitted to raping Darla Darling, but he says he is not a rapist," explained McCarthy.

"Yeah that's common. What does he claim; she gave him consent?" assumed Stammos.

"Not exactly; he claims he is not a rapist because he is actually a killer. He said he has killed between twenty and thirty and they are buried all over the United States," answered McCarthy.

"Hello! Now we're talking. If this is true, fuck the Musky. Are you shitting me? Do you think he is telling the truth?" asked Stammos flabbergasted.

"I believe him. This guy says after we look in his briefcase where he keeps his souvenirs he will talk to us. He says it will be easier that way," said Dan.

"Why is he telling us this?" asked Stammos.

"I think he knows he is going to prison for what he did tonight. He knows we have the briefcase and suspects that we are going to find out any way. I think his main reason for telling us is that he doesn't want to go to prison as a rapist. I sense he thinks there'll be prestige attached to the world knowing what he has done. He says he will talk after we look in his briefcase," explained McCarthy.

"What's the story? Do we need a warrant for this briefcase?" asked Stammos.

"That's what I'm here for," said Bob Waters as he blew through the door with an energy which belied the fact that he had been sleeping twenty-five minutes earlier. Bob Waters was an Assistant District Attorney and career prosecutor. He was as good in court as anyone gets and he had an enthusiasm that matched McCarthy's and a passion for doing the right thing correctly. Compton, McCarthy, Stammos, and Waters had forged a professional friendship that had put hundreds of criminals behind bars. "Tell me what you have, Dyno."

"I just spoke with Maddy Brown. She is at the hospital with the victim, Darla Darling. She is a well known exotic dancer at the RUMP," explained McCarthy.

"Before you get any further," interrupted Waters, "Is she a prostitute also?"

"No. She is just a dancer. I have answered trouble calls in the past when people think she is something more, and they get bounced," explained McCarthy. "She also has been taking classes at Kane's studio of late, and she actually seems very nice."

"Well, anyway, I am sure she is not a prostitute. She was taken at gunpoint by this guy from the rear of the RUMP after the place closed. The suspect we have in custody is a guy named William Ripp. He is a freelance computer database consultant, and he does a lot of traveling. He has a clear record. No criminal history at all, nada, zilch."

"He takes her at gun point and drives her to a field off Dyerson Road in her own car. He already has a grave dug and a drop cloth for the body, but before he kills her he rapes her. Darla, ah, I mean Rebecca sees that it is just about all over for her and decides to do something. While he is in the midst of ecstasy she takes the opportunity to spin, hit him in the trachea," McCarthy then demonstrated the trachea strike, "and then follows-up with a technique," McCarthy demonstrates the lawn mower technique, "that must have felt like he just got his nuts ripped off. While he is doubled over in pain, she runs and disappears into the woods. He shoots at her six times but misses."

"No shit. Just about rips his nuts off?" says Stammos laughing.

"Yeah, he hasn't showed them to anyone yet. He has denied treatment, and I am guessing we may have to take them as evidence if they are still there in the interest of being thorough," said McCarthy.

"Take them as evidence?" asked Waters. "There may be some justice to that, but I believe except in the Middle East there is no legal precedent."

"Maybe we can make it a test case, Bob," said Randy with an evil smile.

"I think not, Randy, my Machiavellian friend," said Bob.

"Machiavellian?" asked McCarthy. "Nevermind, what I meant is we can take pictures of them as evidence," said McCarthy correcting himself.

McCarthy continued, "Becky runs through the woods until she sees a squad car at the Kwik Trip on 41. She is afraid of every set of headlights because she thinks it might be Ripp. She finally sees a squad and she flags down Maddy Brown and tells her the whole story. Well, I'm in the downtown area and a description goes out: white male, forties, a guy dressed in black with glasses and looks, according to the victim, like a professor. Well I have met this guy in the past. He seemed a little strange to me."

"Tonight early on I saw him again in the lot at the Radisson. He was dressed at that time in dark clothes. He was carrying the black briefcase, and he threw it into the trunk of a car and walked downtown. I drove by him a second time, and he waves at me and he says, 'Hi, McCarthy.' When Maddy called in the description of a guy dressed in black looking like a professor I thought of him right away and headed over to the Radisson. I get there and he is limping through the lot."

"I am guessing having your nuts ripped off will make a guy limp," observed Stammos.

"At least," agreed Waters with a wince.

"Continuing, he limps over to his car and he pops the trunk and grabs the briefcase. Ripp sees me, and bolts like Carl Lewis."

"Who's Carl Lewis? The name sounds familiar. Did I handle that case?" asked Waters.

"He was an Olympic sprinter," said McCarthy. "Sorry, I didn't mean to confuse you."

"That happens this time of day. When I get woke up in the middle of the night, I should bring a court recorder to have them read it all back to me in the morning," said Waters. "Continue."

"Well I chase him and he is carrying this briefcase. He runs through a fence straight to the river and heaves the briefcase into the Muddy Mississippi. Then he keeps running."

"Did you get the briefcase?" said Waters with concern.

"Yes we did. I'll get to that," answered Dyno.

"Sorry. Go on."

"Well I chase him and he suddenly spins and takes a swing at me. I hook blocked the punch and hit him in the temple once with an inverted knife hand strike, take him down, and handcuff him. He really tried to knock my block off with a hard right."

"Dyno, I love it when you do that chop-sockey shit on them. I'd pay to see that. You have to take me on a ride along some time. I'll pay you. Is it allowed?" asked Waters opening a fresh pack of cigarettes, tapping one out, and lighting it in one smooth motion as if he did it fifty times a day.

"I don't think I can take money for a ride along, and I am sure I cannot guarantee any, as you would call it, 'chop-sockey shit.' There's more. Do you want to hear?"

"Yeah go ahead. Is it all right if I smoke, you guys? It really helps me think this time of night."

"Go ahead," said Compton. "There is a ban on smoking, but all the people who give a shit are home in bed sleeping. On third shift the inevitability of lung cancer contracted from the second hand smoke of one of Bob Waters' cigarettes registers pretty low on our concern-o-meter."

"Thanks, Sergeant Compton," said Bob as he blew his first cloud of smoke straight into the air with such force that it looked as if he had just come up from under water and taken his first breath of fresh air.

Dan continued, "After I handcuffed him, I searched him and found a revolver in a shoulder holster rig. He did not shoot it out with me because he said he had fired all six rounds at Darla already. I am guessing the six rounds are buried in trees out where he raped Darla. We will be lucky to find them, but it is possible. I am guessing after he emptied his gun he didn't think to reload before he ran into me," said McCarthy.

"I still would have loved to see that Hi-Yah, chop-sockey shit," said Waters making a Karate chopping motion, causing sparks to spit off his cigarette and float gently toward the carpet below cooling to a gray ash as the hit the floor. Waters stepped on them and continued talking without a pause, "Tell me about the briefcase."

"After I handcuffed Ripp, Carp was there and he stood by Ripp while I ran back to see if I could recover the briefcase before it sunk and we'd have to call out the dive team. I got down to where Ripp tossed it and I found Annie fishing it out with her cane."

"Raggedy Annie?" asked Stammos,

"Yeah, Raggedy Annie," answered McCarthy.

"Who's this Raggedy Annie?" asked Waters.

"She's a night person. She's a dumpster diver that goes out every night, and I mean every night, scrounging dumpsters," said McCarthy. "She's a nice old lady, and I think she'll be a good witness. Anyway, she hooked the briefcase with her cane and dragged it in, and then I dragged Annie in and now we have the case. I got Ripp in here and Mirandized him, and he does not want an attorney. He wants to talk to us. He says he has killed over twenty people and is not a rapist, but a killer. Those are his exact words. He wants us to get the case and he will be able to tell us more. The case is in my temporary evidence locker," said McCarthy. "Oh yeah I almost forgot. He gives us permission to open it and he says the combination is 5455. He said the number stands for 'kill' and I checked the phone code and it does. Well, Bob, should we open it or get a warrant? I know it's a no-brainer, but since you're here, you might as well make the call," Dan asked Waters.

"Thank you, Dyno. You are correct. It is a no-brainer. He tossed the case making it abandoned property which would allow us to open it. He also has given us consent to search it. Therefore if you are satisfied that it is not something dangerous, I would say open it, by all means open it!"

Fifteen minutes later, McCarthy, Waters, Stammos, and two additional detectives, Brickson and Jefferson, were gathered in the lab. Brickson and Jefferson were the primary drug investigators, but they were called in to assist on this case by the head of the Detective Bureau, Captain Severson.

Stammos' gloved hand slowly and cautiously turned the numbers on the briefcase, and as he rolled one number at a time he said, "Five, four, five, five," while every person in the room lip-synced the numbers. Stammos then looked up and made eye contact with each person in the room. "Here we go." He clicked open the tabs and slowly opened the briefcase as he tipped his head horizontally to peak in.

As the briefcase opened wide, so did every eye in the room. Inside were Ziploc® freezer bags. Each bag contained a picture identification. There were men, women, blondes, brunettes, and redheads. There was one clear pattern. If these were his victims, the pattern was that there was absolutely no discernable pattern. Each bag contained a three by five index card with a brief hand-written description of the circumstances of the abduction and death of each victim. The documentation was brief but telling. Ripp had identified the location of the murder as well as the "death date" and time of each extraordinary end of life experience. Each bag represented the death of an innocent victim who was just trying to get a little happiness in life and had the misfortune of meeting a predator of the lowest order.

Every Ziploc® baggie contained a shock of hair held together by a tightly wrapped rubber band. The hair did not look real to them. It looked like a doll's hair or possibly snippets that a loving mother would clip and slip tenderly into the pages of a baby book.

The bags also contained one unique item which Ripp had taken as a memento of each victim. One bag contained a high school class ring whose fighting name was the "hurricanes." The ring contained a beautiful ruby red stone setting. Another bag had a pocket watch, the type that is passed from father to son in a family as a ritual of manhood. The face was cracked and the watch had been stopped at 12:03 as was the life of its last recipient.

One baggie bulged, containing a pair of pale blue panties. The bag appeared more worn than the others indicating Ripp had a particular preference for this memento. As Stammos picked up the bag, a grim pallor shrouded his face and he proclaimed, "Sick bastard."

Ironically, one bag contained a lucky rabbit's foot key chain, containing a key from a GM car. "That foot was about as lucky for the owner as it was for the rabbit," said Stammos glumly.

Brickson held a camera and digitally recorded the opening and each movement Stammos made. Jefferson snapped still shots of each step of the procedure. Stammos careful laid out each bag on a long table covered with a long, wide strip of paper.

Stammos wrote down the name of each victim from the identifications he found inside the bags. As he wrote he turned to McCarthy and said, "Get Carpenter up here ASAP. I have a job for him."

McCarthy hustled to the report room where Gary was completing his report and said, "Carp are you finished with your report?"

"Yeah, I didn't have much to do with any of it. Why?" he asked.

"Stammos wants you in the lab ASAP. He has a job for you. It looks like we have caught ourselves a real bad dude. This is big."

Carpenter and McCarthy came into the lab, and Stammos looked up from the carefully laid out Ziploc® bags and said, "Twenty-three souls lost if this is what I think it is, and I believe it is. Gary, I want you to just work on one name. We are going to be tied up for some time, but I would like you to get confirmation if you can that this one person is actually reported missing. If there is a hit, then contact the originating agency and get as much information on the missing person report as possible," he then handed Carpenter a notebook page with the name Lindsey Brinkman from Stillwater, Minnesota.

"Right away," said Carpenter snatching the paper and leaving the room.

Then Stammos said, "I have the names. I could read through the bags. I am going to lock down and seal this room until we have time to get back to it. We're going to have to document and process everything in this case. That will be a massive undertaking in itself. I want to talk to this guy first while he still wants to talk," said Stammos.

Stammos gobbled up as much background as he could. He called Maddy who was still with Darla at the hospital. Darla was having evidence gathered by the Sexual Assault Nurse Examiner. They were specially trained nurses who treated victims and aided police with the insane crime too often committed, rape. These nurses were not only medical nurses, they were also specially trained evidence technicians, interviewers, and counselors wrapped in one neat and invaluable package. This victim survived, and with her cooperation the physical evidence collected would put Ripp away for a very long time.

Maddy detailed once again the information she had received from Darla. There was no doubt on the case against Ripp in the kidnapping, rape, and attempted murder of "Rebecca Glitz."

Armed with so much information, Stammos could take a comfortable approach on this interview. He was not pressed to even get a confession because of the mountain of physical and testimonial evidence against Ripp. Stammos desperately wanted to get a confession. Darla Darling's daring escape had delivered to the police a rock-solid case from the time she stumbled out of the tree-line. Having no pressure to get a confession always worked to Randy's advantage. In this instance if Waupon State Penitentiary was the hoop and Ripp was the basketball, this was shaping up to be a *"Slam Dunk!"*

CHAPTER THIRTY-SEVEN
THE DEMON

When Stammos entered the room, Ripp sat waiting with his arms folded on the white table and his legs crossed at the ankles, looking strangely resigned. As Stammos positioned his own chair and sat down on the same side of the table as Ripp, William Ripp combed his hair with his fingers and sat straight back in his own chair, then leaned one elbow on the table for support as he turned to face Stammos.

"Mr. Ripp, I am Sergeant Randy Stammos of the La Claire Police Department. I have been assigned to this case and Officer McCarthy has indicated that you understand your rights and you wish to make a statement at this time," began Stammos.

"Yes. I do. I do not wish to be labeled as a rapist. I am a killer and a rather good one at that," answered Ripp with a cocky air in his tone. "Are you going to bring the briefcase in here? I can give you the specifics. The proof is all there."

"There will be time for the specifics. I would like to get some general information from you first, and then we can work our way toward the specifics," said Stammos looking more like a political candidate with his blue suit and red tie as he dominated the room with his presence. He had changed his clothes before beginning the interview. He saved his blue suit for his most important interviews. He called it his "power suit." He was certain that there was a time to dominate an interview room and the way to do it beyond your personal skills and attributes was by clothing. Stammos would say, "The blue suit and red tie will get you as many confessions as a good line of bullshit."

Stammos continued, "Normally, I ease into these things, but, Mr. Ripp, you look like you're anxious to tell us your story." Stammos laid out the copied sheets containing the victim's information down in front of Ripp. Randy asked no question, he just ended the sentence with the statement in the air. The ball was in Ripp's court and Stammos was positive Ripp would return it.

"I see you have been in my briefcase. That briefcase has been with me since Isaac. He was my first. I saved a clipping of his hair and his class ring, and then it got to be a habit... not just the killing, but the collecting. I documented each killing with its own bag... so they would be remembered."

"There were twenty-three bags. Is that all of them?" asked Stammos.

"Yes. That was all of them," answered Ripp shrugging his shoulders. "There would have been more if I would never have come to this, pardon my French, fucking town and met that fucking wench Darla."

"Tell me about Darla," said Stammos getting comfortable in his chair seeing that even though this might be the most important interview of his life, this would also be the easiest interview he had ever done. "I sure didn't need the suit for this one," Randy thought.

"What can I say? I was strongly attracted to her. I would have left town and never returned if not for that woman. She held me in some sort of trance. You have to admit she is beautiful," Ripp paused, waiting for acknowledgement.

Stammos nodded almost imperceptibly and said nothing, knowing his silence was golden in this interview.

"You know, I had intended on killing a man, two men actually, in this town, but I was interrupted."

"How's that?" asked Stammos, interested.

"I came to town and spotted a drunken nobody, and when I approached him, just for the satisfaction of the kill, McCarthy showed up from out of nowhere and scared the piss out of the drunk who proceeded to drive right into a wall. Then I was about to hit another victim the night of the riot. He was asleep or passed out on a bench and McCarthy showed up and arrested the guy," explained Ripp.

Stammos jotted down, "victims foiled: drove into wall, passed out on bench. I was with McCarthy."

"I became obsessed with taking a victim in this town. That was my first big mistake. When I saw Darla dance, I became obsessed with her being my next victim. That was my second mistake. Tonight I picked her up behind the RUMP and convinced her to come with me to the place I had chosen as her final resting place. I try to pick a nice place for them all, you know. It was a beautiful spot to be laid to rest. I took her there and tried to show her it was all happening because... you know... it was kind of like love at first sight with me. It has been an act of love with some of my victims. I don't do it because I hate them. I have this uncontrollable passion inside me that has to come out. I intended to love her and then extinguish her life-light so to speak."

"What was the hole for?" asked Stammos. "I am not and idiot, but I have to hear it from you."

"Of course, I understand. I was going to shoot her and drop her into the grave that I dug earlier in the day in preparation. I believe in being prepared. Isn't that the motto of the Boy Scouts or the Marines? I think it is somebody's motto. Well it's mine too. Be prepared," said Ripp proudly. "I thought I was prepared for Darla, but the girl caught me off guard," he said unconsciously wriggling in his seat. "I emptie7d my gun at her when she left, but I don't know, well I'll ask you, did I hit her, Sergeant Stammos?" asked Ripp.

"No, she wasn't hit. She is going to be OK," answered Stammos.

"That brings me no solace, Sgt Stammos. Damn!" replied Ripp, registering anger more than disappointment in his face. "This was definitely not my best night. Well that's it. She got away and now I'm here."

"The others, tell me about them. I want to know," was all Stammos had to say and the homicidal odyssey of William Ripp unfolded like some Greek tragedy without any heroes. In William Ripp's epic journey there was neither Achilles nor Hector to meet in an honorable struggle, only unsuspecting victim after unsuspecting victim. There was no glory, honor, or meaning in any of the deaths. It was simply death.

As Ripp related the story of his quest for the death of others, he smiled, winked, and at times seemed almost orgasmic in the excitement he found in the telling of it. "I liked to have a variety of experiences. The young lady from Stillwater, for example, was a rare beauty. She was a runaway, and I paid her for sex. I always paid if they would take the money. I did not like to force myself upon them for the sex and mostly did not have to. I was kind, even generous, and they usually never saw the end coming until it was upon them. I was very merciful in that way."

Stammos had to suppress a response to that comment. Randy felt that his suppression actually physically hurt.

Ripp continued without noticing the inner turmoil he was creating in Stammos. "We sat in a wooded area and drank beer. Then we had what I would call, and I think she would agree with me on this point, glorious sex. Afterwards we drank some more beer. She talked about how her parents treated her like a child and all that crap. I put some GHB in her beer, and she got really drunk really fast. Then I had sex with her again. She passed out and I rolled her into the hole just like that. I didn't even have to kill her; I just covered her up," said Ripp without a care as if he was talking about tossing out a half eaten chili dog.

"So what you are saying is you buried her alive?" asked Stammos writing the words, "Lindsay, beer, GHB, sex for money, passed out, buried alive, woods," in his notes.

"Yes. I wanted to try something new. She was the only one I did that to. I felt I cheated myself out of my," Ripp hesitated, struggling to find the right word, "just due... my reward. I would never do it that way again. It was like having sex and stopping before the climax. She got off easy though. She could not have known the difference. She was out. She very well may have been dead already. I gave her enough GHB to knock down a hippo for a week."

"You said Isaac was your first. How did you kill him?" asked Stammos.

"I gave Isaac LSD. While he was tripping, I let him listen to the Grateful Dead, and then I used a knife on him. I cut him too much though. Messy! I really made a mess. I decided I did not like the mess of it. I was living with my parents at the time, and they were out of town. There were too many close calls. I had to hide him in… well, you know, pieces. I finally bagged him up because he began to smell so bad. Then, you'll love this, when I was traveling up to northern Wisconsin to place him to rest, I got stopped for speeding and the cop just gave me a speeding ticket. He asked me what smelled so bad, but I told him it was just garbage and I was taking it to my parents cottage to dump it because I missed garbage day," chuckled Ripp.

"He bought it?" asked Stammos.

"He bought it," answered the killer, obviously proud.

"That's thinking under pressure. You possess undeniable panache," said Stammos seeing the killer liked the word panache. It stroked this man's ego. The man was evil incarnate. Stammos wanted to knock this smiling troll out of his chair, but he would have to play the game to bring these victims home.

"Not bad for a newbie. I learned a lot. Never even came close to getting caught again, until La Claire," said Ripp.

For the next three hours Ripp related a litany of facts and details about the deaths of twenty-one more men and women. He would say, "Shot him with a shotgun," and "Cut her throat and sprayed blood all over my glasses; I always carry a handkerchief since." Ripp then looked traumatized as if he had been unjustly victimized by this event and whimpered, "Since then I can never seem to get my glasses clean enough. When they get the least bit smudged, I swear it is her blood. I have stabbed but never dismembered another. It's just too messy."

Ripp then reached the long, belabored, terrifying conclusion through the synopsis of who he killed, when, how, why, and where. "I strangled her with a piano wire, you know, like they do in the gangster movies. That was too much work for me," said Ripp. He related the stories of each senseless death like an architect describing how he blended four grains of wood into the flooring of one of his creations to form an intricate eagle design. He was proud of his life's work.

Then Stammos asked a question whose answer would insure the harshest sentence possible from every judge in every state where he would face sentencing. "It seemed that some methods of killing were such that you found too messy and too much work. Did you find a method you preferred?"

"The Nazi's had it figured out. I tried to achieve their efficiency, but they could kill one hundred times as many in twenty minutes as I did in twenty years. You have to admire their efficiency. I found the method they used in their early years on the Eastern Front the most efficient for my purposes. I would select them just like the Nazis. I would choose people who were ready-made victims. They were all nobodies who society could do without. I would lie, bribe, and as a last resort threaten them right up to a pre-dug hole. It's really quite easy, you know. No one wants to think they are about to die. Then what glory it was to see the looks on their faces when they knew it was all over for them. They suddenly faced a realization that it was their death moment and then, Bam!" As Ripp shouted the word he slammed both hands down on the table in an obvious attempt to startle Sergeant Stammos.

Instead, Stammos merely tightened the squint in his eye. Ripp saw Stammos would never be a fitting subject to be chosen as a victim. This man had the look of a predator and could never be the prey. Ripp sat back in his seat and thought, "Darla, Stammos, and McCarthy were obviously not the stock that victims were made of. They were the top of the food chain. I wonder what's in the fucking water in La Claire?"

Ripp showed his disappointment in his inability to even startle Stammos, and he slumped back into his chair, realizing he would never be free to kill again. "Damn how did I come to this?" Then Ripp brought his story to an end, "Plop into the hole they go. I was efficient."

"I'd like to say one more thing. I cannot believe I came here to do this. I had been so careful. When I almost snatched the guy that drove into the wall at the Kwik Trip, I figured it was a fluke. Then when I tried to get Darla the first time..."

"The first time?" asked Stammos, immediately disappointed in himself for interrupting Ripp when he was on a roll.

"Yeah, I went after her once before, and some guy who was stalking her tried to snatch her. It was incredible. He got sucked into this whirlpool. McCarthy and Carpenter just stood there and kept catching criminals who just kept coming to them, one after another after another like they were some sort of black hole in the universe for criminals. I stopped and watched. I should have taken a hint, but then I got kind of seduced by the idea of doing a crime here and getting totally away with it. It would be my ultimate triumph. I researched all of you. I know you, Stammos." Ripp curiously raised one eyebrow.

"What do you know about me?" asked Stammos.

"I know that you and your friends shot a bank robber over fifty times, and the folks at home bought your explanation hook, line, and sinker."

Stammos said nothing. Ripp could read no reaction in his face.

"I researched this town. It is somewhat of a statistical phenomenon. It is one of the nicest places to live in the country as long as you do not commit crimes. You have an incredibly high arrest rate, an incredibly high clearance rate, and an incredibly low crime rate. I know. I did some comparisons of comparable agencies."

"How do you find all this out?" asked Stammos.

"I am a computer database programmer. It is what I do. I actually created a program for gathering the data I needed. All of the statistical data told me not to come to this town and attempt this. I tell you it is a vortex and fucking black hole, the end of the line and I knew it. What the fuck was I thinking?" said Ripp covering his face in shame at his stupidity.

Stammos wrote a note to himself, "Warrant to seize all of Ripp's computers."

"Why did I come to this place? I read about Maddy Brown shooting a guy twice in the same hole. She shot the guy twice in the *same fucking hole*. Did that really happen?" asked Ripp in disbelief.

Stammos once again gave a slight nod in confirmation.

Ripp continued, "Then there was Compton! Incredible! He was shot, stabbed, beaten, and he still kills the devil himself. The guy had horns tattooed on his head. I love that Brockman guy. He was with you when you shot that bank robber right?" Ripp looked for acknowledgement.

Stammos gave him none. Stammos had moved around the opposite side of the table and now just sat blankly with his chin propped on his hand, listening to the prattling on of a true psychopath. He no longer was interviewing. He was just watching in amazement as if he was an astronomer who had just discovered a new galaxy and could not decide what to name it.

Undeterred, Ripp continued, "Stanley Brockman gave the news helicopter the finger, flipped them the bird, signed them a personal fuck you on national TV. I asked myself, who does that sort of thing? Then I researched it and discovered it is actually more common than you think. It happens all the time. Brockman's was one of the only ones that made it out of the bloopers reel to the news coverage. If I would have read the writing on the wall, I would never have come here. I could have continued and maybe reached fifty dead nobodies, no one hundred!" Ripp said.

All Stammos could think of as he listened and jotted notes, was "Damn. No death penalty in Wisconsin. It would be a wonderful thing to witness this man's execution. I would happily pull the switch myself on this sorry, soggy bag of shit!"

As McCarthy watched from behind the mirror with Bob Waters, he shared Stammos' sentiments. "Too bad there is no death penalty in Wisconsin." Stammos and McCarthy had been partners a long time and sometimes could finish each other's sentences , but this was not about partners thinking alike. Anyone would love to flip the switch, inject the needle, drop the trap, or fire the round to kill this man if their son or daughter was lying alone in one of those distant unmarked grave.

It was difficult to watch how Ripp relished reliving each horrible end. He thrilled in the re-telling and the re-living of these brutal murders. Then Ripp said, "In general that is all of them. I can get more specific, and it would help if I could use my notes, but there you have it. What can I say? I was good. Like I said before, I would still be working if it wasn't for this fucking black hole," Ripp concluded.

Stammos then stood-up and walked to the door. He looked at his watch and then looked up at the camera and read off the time and date and said, "At this time I will be concluding my initial interview with Mr. William Ripp." He exited and carefully locked the door and double checked it after shutting it. He took a few steps away from the door and returned, giving the doorknob a tug to make certain he had actually locked in *the demon*.

CHAPTER THIRTY-EIGHT

GOD BLESS TEXAS

When Stammos was satisfied the demon was secured in its cage, he walked slowly toward the command room. He looked like a soldier walking off the front line in a hot war, shell shocked. His humanity was overwhelmed by Ripp's inhumanity. He had spent three hours looking into the human face of evil incarnate. He had seen neither a single body nor a single grave, but he knew Ripp was real. Randy Stammos had met the boogey man. Just before Randy turned the corner to cover the last few feet to reach the command room he stopped and pinched himself. Then he shook his head in disappointment, "Damn, I was hoping this was a bad dream."

Carpenter saw Stammos outside the interview room, and he quickly approached, anxious to share the information he had learned. He had received an answer earlier for Stammos but had not wanted to interrupt the interview. He knew the interview was an important one since Gary had discovered some crucial information on the first follow-up investigation after the discovery of the souvenirs. "Sergeant Stammos, I contacted the Stillwater Police Department. They were able to confirm that Lindsay Brinkman has been missing since 1998. They faxed me a copy of the Missing Person's Report. She disappeared from the face of the earth without a trace," said Gary.

"Thanks. Do a report on who you talked to and everything you learned from that conversation and the missing person's report," said Stammos. "Nice work."

"Yes sir. Thank you, sir," said Gary and then he was gone.

"Randy, what's your take on this," asked Compton, who was on the phone as Stammos finally reached the command room. "I have Chief Hale on the line. He wants to know if this is legitimate?" asked Compton, covering the speaker on the hard line desk phone.

"No, it's not legitimate. The killing of twenty-three innocent human beings and burying them in unmarked graves all over creation is not legitimate. It is very much illegitimate and absolutely against the law, and I believe this man has done that very thing." Stammos made the statement with such conviction Compton knew it to be true. McCarthy came up behind him and could see Stammos was certain.

Compton took a moment. He was slightly overwhelmed and then spoke into the phone, "Yes, Chief Hale, the suspect indicates that he has killed and buried twenty-three victims around the country. Sergeant Stammos believes a case recovered at the scene of the arrest contains identification of those victims and what looks like hair from them. Apparently, this guy kept some souvenirs along with a synopsis of each crime. Stammos interviewed the suspect who has been talking for the last three hours, and he believes the man is a killer. Carpenter has verified that one name in the case corresponds with an open missing person case in Stillwater, Minnesota."

Compton then paused to listen and then turned to ask Stammos, "The chief wants to know if any of the victims were from La Claire?"

"They were all killed elsewhere. Darla Darling was the only victim in La Claire," answered Stammos.

"Chief, Stammos says that the dancer was his only victim in La Claire. We have no bodies to dig up here," Compton reported to the chief. "What's that? I'll tell them. Thanks, Chief. Good night." Compton hung up and said to all present, "The chief says great job."

Compton turned immediately to his notebook in front of him and circled another phone number. "Stammos, we're calling the FBI since all of these killings happened elsewhere."

"You'd have to since they all were murdered out of our jurisdiction. Ripp was bemoaning his poor luck and stupidity to have ever come to this town. He felt it was his great misfortune to have chosen Rebecca Glitz as a victim and the city of La Claire as a location," said Stammos.

"Hindsight is 20-20," said Compton, proud of his officers after receiving the back-handed compliment Ripp had paid to his shift. "He is not the first bad guy to made that mistake,"

"Ripp apparently took a beating from Glitz, which if it had been recorded would have made millions on pay per view. Then he was humiliated once again by McCarthy, but my life's number one disappointment will always be that after what I know now, I didn't get a legitimate opportunity, no privilege, to thump the scumbag myself," declared Stammos.

"Who is Rebecca Glitz?" asked Compton.

"Darla Darling. That's her real name, Rebecca Glitz," said Randy.

"Really? Darla Darling the stripper is Rebecca Glitz." Compton scribbled the name on his note pad in front of him. "Darla Darling is Rebecca Glitz. Interesting," Compton repeated to no one in particular.

"We are going to have to package his clothes, photograph his injuries, scrape his fingernails, get a sample of his pubic hair, etc. and then run down some of his stories and these victims. We need to take his glasses from him also. He told me blood of one of his victims splattered on them once. There should be some trace evidence left on them."

"I believe there is enough work here to establish a multi-agency task force. This will keep someone busy for at least a year," declared Stammos, "probably longer. We're talking about forensic recovery teams finding, recovering, and identifying bodies and evidence from twenty-three unmarked burial sites located all over the country."

"We also will be bringing an answer to twenty-three families who have had no answer to the disappearance of their lost loved one for years. That must be torture, not knowing what happened to a son or a daughter," observed Dan.

"I think you're right, Dan," said Bob Waters entering the command room. "It will bring a lot of people closure. I hate that word. It is over-used, but I think that now is the time to use it. You are also right, Randy. This case will keep many busy for at least a year, probably longer." Bob had watched the interview incredulously behind the mirror with McCarthy.

"If someone would have picked up on this guy's spree earlier, there would have been a task force put together long ago. These killings stretch back twenty years. His first was someone named Isaac who is buried in northern Wisconsin. I think it should be a joint task force using the La Claire Police, FBI, and the Department of Justice's Bureau of Criminal Investigation for starters. Someone is going to have to supervise it and make sure the information is properly documented. It looks massive, but there is one advantage," said Stammos, pausing as he looked over his many pages of notes.

"What's that?" asked Dave Compton.

"The pressure is off. He's in the coffin, and we are just nailing on the lid," said Stammos. "No one else will die, except him, hopefully."

"Not even him. There is no death penalty in Wisconsin," complained Waters.

Randy Stammos answered, "Two bodies in Texas. Texas has the death penalty, and they are not afraid to use it on special occasions. I would say William Ripp is a special occasion if he has killed as many as he has claimed to have killed. I, for one, have no doubt that he has killed twenty-three people." Randy digested it all for a moment and with a smile, predicted, "Some day, many years from now, but some day, Texas is going to smoke this guy."

Stammos then added, "There's a country western song whose name describes my view of the death penalty in Texas right now." He paused and noticed the smiles of acknowledgement and with one voice everyone in the room chimed in, *"God Bless Texas!"*

EPILOGUE

It is 6:00 AM on a Monday morning. It has been twenty-two years since Dan McCarthy collared William Ripp and Ripp revealed his homicidal obsession. Lt. Dan McCarthy combed his thinning and graying hair and straightened his tie in the living-room mirror. He looked disparagingly at the white uniform shirt of a lieutenant. He still prefers his black street uniform designating him as commander of the SWAT team, but today there are a number of news interviews scheduled with the local and national media.

When they spoke two days earlier, Chief Randy Stammos asked Dan to wear white for the interviews.

"Yes, sir, Chief," answered Dan.

"You call me Chief one more time and I'll have to kill you," said Stammos, reaching his hand menacingly toward his Glock.

"OK, Randy," answered Lieutenant McCarthy.

After Dan straightened his tie to his satisfaction, he opened the front door and bent down to pick up the La Claire newspaper. The headlines heralded the most important local news of the day. "WILLIAM RIPP TO BE EXECUTED AT NOON, LOCAL TIME." Dan shut the door and walked slowly back to the kitchen table. Victoria was seated at the table spreading strawberry jam on warm toast and she looked up and smiled.

"William Ripp is going to be executed today in Texas," said Dan.

"Really? What's their rush? It's only been twenty-two years," said Victoria taking a bite out of the toast.

"First, there was the lengthy investigation. Then, there was the fight over who got to prosecute him, and when Texas got dibs he was convicted and sentenced to death. Since then, he has tried every maneuver possible to avoid this execution and now he is out of appeals. I believe it will happen today. Randy is down there. He is going to witness it as our department representative. Becky Kane is down there also."

"Is Larry with her?" asked Victoria.

"Yes, he is. Becky felt strongly she should represent all of the victims since she was the only one to survive," said McCarthy.

"You know, following this case over the years has amazed me. Women have wanted to marry this guy and carry his baby. He has written a best selling memoir, *The Redemption of a Serial Killer*, in which he explains how he has found the Lord. There are people camped outside the prison singing 'Amazing Grace.' They are demanding the governor commute his sentence or the president pardon him."

"This guy has played the media and the public like he played his victims. I am convinced that none of them saw it coming. He was just too nice. I will breathe a sigh of relief when he is gone," said McCarthy.

"At his age, do you think he is still dangerous?" asked Victoria.

"Absolutely, the man wished he could be as efficient as Hitler was. He was almost orgasmic when he was describing each of the killings. He was the most dangerous man I have ever seen in my life, and what made him so dangerous was that he looked so innocuous. No one could see it in him," said McCarthy.

"You saw it in him," said Victoria.

"I did not believe my own gut when it told me something was wrong," said McCarthy.

"No one who knew Ripp saw the evil in him. The main thing is he will never hurt anyone again and now he is going to pay for his crimes," reasoned Victoria.

"I wonder about the redemption thing," said McCarthy.

"What do you mean?" asked Victoria.

"In his book he says anyone can be redeemed and that he found the Lord. I wonder if there is truly a place in heaven for this man?" asked McCarthy.

"God knows," said Victoria.

William Ripp's mind was racing. He had always been obsessed by death, but it had always been the death of others. He was now facing his own. There were no more lies to tell. He had lied to each one of his victims to facilitate their deaths. He had lied to judges, prosecutors, priests, reverends, and even defense attorneys in an effort to secure a release and then a commutation of his sentence followed by delay after delay after delay.

Ripp knew there would be no more delays. He would lie no longer. "Get the fuck out of here!"

The chaplain cringed and said, "My son. Don't you want to ready your soul to meet your personal savior?" They had prayed often in the past, but it was only for Ripp to show some evidence of remorse for crimes he had no remorse for.

"Get the fuck out of here with your phony magic tricks. I don't believe it. I never have. In fact, it took all the control I had not to strangle the life out of you every time you were in here praying with me. Get the fuck out of here now!" Then his eyes transformed to a demonic piercing glare and his words were spoken in a throaty growl, "No! Come back in here. I have an idea how you can grant me one final wish." He rushed toward the priest and the truth was in his eyes. William Ripp was a killer twenty-two years ago and he was still a killer now. Prison had not removed the desire; it had just separated him from the victims and removed the opportunity.

The corrections officers caught Ripp and spun him down to his small bed in his isolated cell. The chaplain backpedaled out of the doorway tripped and fell to the floor hard, lacerating the back of his head. He was taken quickly to the infirmary for stitches. He put his hand to the wound on his head and gazed in disbelief at his own blood.

Two hours later Ripp found himself lying strapped to a stainless steel gurney. He looked at the bag filled with transparent fluid hanging menacingly above him as his death warrant was being read. He tried to move his arms, but he was tightly secured. The words echoed and bounced off the white walls and were all lost on him. His brain was racing. This was the end. He thought about his life and his thoughts were drawn to his victims. They all came to him on this morning. As their faces floated in and out of his consciousness, he could not help but notice they were smiling. They seemed to know it was his turn.

Then he thought, "I gave none of them a chance to prepare for the end. None of them saw it coming." Out of nowhere came an unsolicited thought that he did not own. It did not belong to him, but it came booming into his brain. "Now and at the hour of your death you will be judged." Ripp panicked. He began to scream at the nearest attendant, "Who thought that thought? Did you? Is that your thought?"

Someone from the other side of the room asked Ripp, "Do you have any final words, Mr. Ripp?"

"No! You can't do this. Not now! I'm not ready! I need more time!" There was a tingling in his arms, and a warm wave traveling through his body. His last words were, "You can't do this," and it was done.

William Ripp thought, "How strange," as he hovered above himself, looking down at the cluster of people in gowns and masks, checking his vital signs. He felt good. He was free of his bindings. He was free.

It was a fleeting thought for William Ripp as he found himself walking down a long hall, but it wasn't a hall. He could not describe what it was, but he knew what it wasn't.

When he reached the end, he saw a door. It was a door, but it wasn't door. He would have called it a door for lack of another word. On the door was written a script he had never seen before, but he could read it though he did not understand why. Written on the "door" were the words, "William Ripp's Eternity."

In life William Ripp would have asked for an explanation and then he would have used his free will to decide should I enter or should I leave. Now William Ripp could do nothing but push the "door" open. There were no more choices for William Ripp. He had made his choices and they had brought him here.

William Ripp looked upon his eternity and was immediately enlightened. Twenty-two years after he had claimed his last victim on earth, William Ripp discovered there was indeed a life after death. He discovered that there was a God and it was not William Ripp. He also found at the hour of his death there was a judgment. Ripp looked at his eternity revealed before him and said to himself at that moment of amazing discovery, "Well, I'll be damned..."

THE END

ABOUT THE AUTHOR

Lt. Dan Marcou retired as a highly decorated police officer in 2006 after 33 years. He experienced most of what a police officer can experience in a career. Dan is an internationally recognized police trainer, speaker, and writer. His first novel, *The Calling, The Making of a Veteran Cop,* shot up the Barnes and Noble Bestseller list and was deemed so real that it is being used in police academies as a primer for recruits.

Marcou's readers immediately asked for more and so he penned *SWAT: Blue Knights in Black Armor,* the second in the McCarthy series.

Now "Lt. Dan," offers up *Nobody's Heroes,* bringing to you once again the indomitable Sgt. David Compton, Dan McCarthy, Randy Stammos, Gary Carpenter, Maddy Brown, Dooley, Larry Kane and the irascible Stanley Brockman.

Although Marcou's novels are fiction, they have the feeling of reality due to his personal experiences as a police officer. He has been in dark, urine-soaked alleys fighting for his life at three o'clock in the morning. He has pursued felons at over 100 miles per hour with his heart beating louder than his screaming siren. He has gone through countless doors into the unknown and worked side by side with real-life heroes. He has shared the fear, frustration, sadness, joy, and camaraderie that police officers experience 24 hours a day, seven days a week all over the world. Now he weaves those feelings and experiences into his novels.

Not since Joseph Wambaugh has a police writer been able to share so realistically with readers the gritty and dangerous world of American policing.